Her Demonic Angel

Felicity Heaton

HER ANGEL SERIES

Her Dark Angel
Her Fallen Angel
Her Warrior Angel
Her Guardian Angel
Her Demonic Angel

Find out more at: www.felicityheaton.co.uk

CHAPTER 1

It was the Devil who took her.

Erin was sure of it.

It was the Devil who had come in the dead of night, entering the bedroom of her loft apartment like black mist to take her as she slept.

And he wasn't red all over or had hooves and horns like in movies or fables.

He was immense, with skin as black as coal, eyes that shone red like car brake lights and the wings of a dragon curling from his back.

He had brought her here to a fiery, broken and inhospitable land where perpetual tormented screams chased every shred of calm and peace from her soul and the air was so thick with the stomach-turning stench of sulphur that she couldn't breathe.

It was Hell.

At first, Erin had thought the whole event was a vivid and disturbing nightmare, worse than any she had experienced before, but she had hurt herself on one of the shards of black rock that formed the floor and the three walls of her cell and she hadn't woken.

And then they had hurt her too.

The Devil had come alone at first, entering her cell to glare at her in silence and ignore her pleas to tell him what he wanted with her. Not a word had left his wide black lips. The only time she had gained a response from him was the one instance she had felt brave enough to stand up to him and had tried to force him to speak. Then, he had bared sharp crimson teeth at her and hissed. She had fallen on her backside trying to escape him, afraid that he would attack her, and had cut her palms and scraped the soles of her bare feet as she had crab-crawled away from him.

Now, he no longer came alone.

Now, she no longer feared him.

She couldn't muster that emotion whenever he visited her. Fear had given way to anger, leaving her brave enough to face death in order to get some answers.

Two other smaller but similar creatures accompanied him. None of them spoke. They didn't even flinch when she hit them in an attempt to make them talk and tell her what they wanted with her, bashing her fists against their thick limbs and the granite band of stomach exposed between their red-edged black chest armour and the strips that protected their hips. She wanted to punch them in the face but they towered over her, at least three feet taller than she was. Several times, she had struck them hard in the groin but each had only gained her pain rather than satisfaction. They were quick to retaliate, slamming meaty arms into her stomach and sending her crashing into the rough black walls of her prison.

Each visit lasted only fifteen minutes or was it longer? She had lost track of time in this hellish place. Minutes seemed like hours.

5

Erin was too tired to hit them now. Hunger had set in she didn't know how many days or weeks ago and now she was so weak that her head swam and she spent most of her waking hours hallucinating about food. Petrified pained screams rang in her ears as she sat near the open wall of her black cell, staring wearily into the hazy fiery distance. The black jaw-length jags of her hair hung across one side of her face, stinking of boiled eggs. The smell had invaded everything. Her small black sleep shorts and tank top, every inch of exposed dirty skin, and her mind too. She closed her eyes and leaned her head back against the jagged wall behind her, too tired and hungry to sleep, using all of her strength to keep breathing.

They would come soon.

She hadn't seen them in what might have been a day.

There was no sky in the view from her cell. Just an endless black vault above her, and fields of lava and brimstone as far as the eye could see several hundred feet below.

Erin inhaled slowly and smelled steak.

She frowned. Steak. She swore she could smell it.

Someone had invented a new form of torture. The scent of juicy frying meat wafted through the huge open wall and before she could consider what she was doing, she was standing at the edge of the floor and staring down into the glowing abyss. Hot air battered her as it rose from the inferno below. Her vision swam from the heat and her hunger, causing the sheer cliff face to wobble and distort.

Her mouth watered.

Her stomach growled.

The door at her back opened and she turned sharply. Her foot slipped on the loose stones at the edge.

Before her gasp could escape her lips, a man was holding her with one arm snaked around her back, bending over her. She stared down, wild eyes watching the rocks bouncing off the endless black cragged cliff and disappearing into the fiery river below. Her heart hammered erratically against her chest and she instinctively grabbed the man's arms, desperate to save herself from following the rocks and afraid that he might drop her over the edge.

"Careful," the man whispered close to her ear, his voice deep and exotic, sending a strange hot shiver through her. He righted her, kept one hand on her arm and led her away from the edge.

Erin stared at her handsome saviour, mind racing to catch up with everything that had happened in the past few seconds. He still held her arm, his smile perfect though lacking emotion and golden eyes bright and alluring. She couldn't take her eyes away from them and the longer she stared into them, the more relaxed she felt.

His sensual smile widened and he released her arm, preened the longer tendrils of his black hair back from his face, and then frowned at his hand. Touching her had dirtied it. His expression curled into one of disgust and he turned his back on her.

The heavy compliant feeling that had been building inside her disappeared in an instant and the delicious scent of food assaulted her.

Her gaze snapped to the door and the source of the tempting smell.

The Devil.

He stood there flanked by the two smaller creatures like him, his glowing red eyes fixed straight at her over the head of the elegant man now strolling towards him. The two of them couldn't have looked more different to each other. The Devil was a beast, black-skinned and huge, his massive dragon-like wings furled against his back, and his body barely covered by crimson-edged obsidian armour. The man was all dark beauty and refinement, dressed sharply in a black suit that highlighted his pale, flawless skin and glossy black hair.

The man waved his hand and the Devil held something out to him.

A tray with a very elegant domed silver plate cover on it.

Erin realised her mistake.

Not the Devil, but a servant.

Erin stared at the man as he took the tray from the beast she had thought was the Devil, removed the cover with a flourish, revealing the most amazing and mouth-watering food she had ever seen, and turned to hold it out to her.

Tempting her.

He was the Devil.

Erin backed away on instinct, aware that before her stood a man who had made her feel compliant by only looking into her eyes and behind her was a sheer drop to a very painful death. She swallowed, heart hammering, and clenched her fists, determined to stand her ground. She had feared the three demonic creatures that had regularly visited her cell but she hadn't let them get the better of her, and she hadn't let her captivity break her. She wasn't going to let this man sweep in and do in seconds what they had failed to do in days.

She straightened and glared at him, lifting her chin in defiance. She was strong. Brave. Her limbs trembled but she refused to let her fear show. The Devil surely thrived on the fear of his victims and making them suffer. He would get no satisfaction from her.

"I apologise for the way you have been treated, Erin," he said, his deep voice sending another burst of heat over her skin. The sickening feel of it distracted her from what he had said but the moment it had passed, she frowned.

He knew her name.

Erin supposed that shouldn't surprise her. He was the Prince of Darkness after all. It answered one of the questions that had plagued her during her captivity. He had come specifically for her.

"What do you want with me?" She stood her ground as he moved a step closer, still holding the tray out to her.

"Why don't you have a seat and enjoy this meal, and we will discuss why I desired your company."

Erin frowned. "There is nothing to sit on besides the floor."

He smiled and a large dark carved wooden table appeared behind him, followed by two matching tall-backed chairs with black padded seats. He bowed his head and swept an arm towards them.

"Is this better?" he said and set the tray of food down on the table. "Whatever comforts you desire are yours to have."

For a price, no doubt. Erin didn't move. She didn't trust this man. If she sat on the chair, it would probably wrap itself around her to trap her or something bizarre like it. Her head reasoned that if he wanted to hurt her, he could probably do so without tying her up first. He was the Devil, and he had already shown her that all he had to do was stare into her eyes and she started thinking about doing whatever he asked of her.

"Come, Erin." He held his hand out to her, the sleeve of his crisp black jacket pulling back to reveal the cuff of his equally dark shirt and glittering jet-black cufflinks. "I have apologised for your treatment, have I not? Can we not talk like civilised people?"

"No, thank you. Your goons took me in the middle of the night and you've been holding me in this cell for God knows how long."

The Devil hissed, his straight white teeth sharpening to points and his eyes burning red.

Erin backed away another step.

He smoothed his hand over his black hair and cleared his throat. The crimson drained from his golden eyes. "I apologise. That word does not sit well with me."

"What word... oh... God?"

He snarled and was before her in an instant, his fingers closed around her throat and choking her, sharp black claws digging into her skin. He released her as quickly as he had grabbed her and distanced himself.

Erin couldn't move. She had gone rigid, frozen to her core, the moment he had launched himself at her. Her heart felt as though it wasn't beating.

Note to self. Never speak about God in the presence of the Devil.

"Self-righteous bastard," the Devil spat and snarled again, pacing away from her, his body shifting with the sensual and lethal grace of a predator. He turned red eyes on her and frowned. "You would do well not to believe in such a malevolent conceited creature. Now, sit!"

Erin didn't get a choice. One moment she stood near the edge of her black cell, the heat buffeting her as it rose from the abyss, and the next she sat at the dark wooden table with the tray of food in front of her.

"Eat." That word was little more than a growl.

She didn't trust the delicious-looking steak, potatoes and vegetables in front of her but she wasn't about to tell the Devil where to stick them when she had already managed to royally piss him off. She took the fork in one hand and the steak knife in the other, and paused to stare at it.

"Do not even think about it." The Devil casually slid into the chair opposite her. He crossed his legs at the knee and leaned back into his chair, his eyes amber again and a false sense of calm about him. She glanced at the three huge black-skinned demons protecting the door.

Erin cut into her steak. Eating the food was probably the wisest move she could make. Not only would it give the Devil a chance to get what looked to be a temper that surpassed everything she had heard about it under control but it would give her much-needed strength. If she was going to survive whatever ordeal lay ahead of her and get the heck out of Hell and this mess, she was going to need her strength.

She devoured the food, uncaring of the way she looked to the three creatures and man, if you could call the Devil a man, watching her.

It was delicious and strangely revitalising. Every mouthful she swallowed filled her stomach and sent heat flowing through her veins, urging her into taking another bite. Was there something in it?

That thought made her pause and she looked up from her plate to the Devil, meeting his gaze. "What sort of steak is this?"

He smiled. "I believe it was the last unicorn."

Erin retched and covered her mouth, barely managing to keep the food down. "You're kidding. Right? There's no such thing as unicorns."

"Not anymore, there isn't." His smile held and she could see the truth in his eyes. God. She was eating a horse. Not just a horse, but a mythical creature. Didn't unicorns have amazing powers of healing or some rubbish like that? No wonder she felt so revitalised.

And sick.

Erin pushed her plate away.

"You are not finished." The Devil frowned at the remains on her plate, leaned across the dark wooden table and pushed it back towards her.

Erin shoved it back at him and then smiled politely. "I really couldn't eat another bite."

His look darkened. "Sentimentality will be your failing. I find it disappointing to discover such feelings in you."

She didn't care if it turned out he was right or what he thought about her. She didn't want to eat horse, let alone the last unicorn. The sick feeling in her stomach worsened, the food she had consumed sitting like lead in it now.

"Please tell me you didn't kill it just for this meal?"

The Devil smiled. He had. She felt lousy. She was personally responsible for the extinction of a creature.

"I had to find a way to restore your strength. See, these idiots were not supposed to take you from your home until yesterday and it was supposed to be done during the day... and they were supposed to have brought you directly to me."

That sounded like three strikes to Erin. The Devil's golden gaze remained on her but her attention leapt to the three creatures standing in front of the cell door. The one who had taken her shifted foot to foot, a nervous edge about him now.

He looked down at his feet. The ground there burned bright orange and began to bubble. The creature took a leaping step forwards, straight into the path of the Devil. She hadn't seen him move. He grabbed the large demon by the throat, swung himself up onto his back and took hold of his wings. The creature shrieked and snarled, and frantically tried to shake the Devil off his back. The two other creatures remained at the door, eyes forward, not watching the horror as it played out in front of them.

Erin didn't want to watch either but she couldn't take her eyes off the fight. The huge demon struggled but it was no use. The Devil planted his shiny leather shoes between the creature's shoulder blades, held his leathery dark wings at their base where they attached to his immense body, and leaned back. The demon arched forwards and roared in pain as his wings tore from his back. Blood splattered onto the black floor of her cell, drenching and then soaking into the basalt.

The Devil landed on his feet and casually discarded the pair of wings.

The demon stumbled forwards, face contorted in pain, and tried to get away. It was no use. There was nowhere for him to run. The Devil stalked towards the creature, his expression a mask of darkness and his eyes glowing bright crimson, and grabbed him by one thick arm. He spun on the heel of his polished shoes, swung the demon towards the open wall of her cell and released him.

He screamed the whole way down. Erin covered her ears, closed her eyes, and curled up in her chair.

She had presumed the Devil would be a sadistic and vicious bastard, but he exceeded her expectations. The table knocked against her elbows and she peered up, afraid of what she might see. The Devil sat opposite her, blood splattered across his handsome face and coating his hands. He huffed, produced a deep red handkerchief from his breast pocket, and set about cleaning the blood off his face.

"Now, where were we?" he said and discarded the bloodied handkerchief.

He had missed a spot, a single red streak that cut across his sculpted left cheek, but she didn't have the courage to mention it. All of her bravery had drained from her and she trembled in her seat, afraid that she would be the next one he pitched over the edge and into the abyss.

"You have lost your fire." He frowned, black eyebrows pinching tightly, and then sighed and relaxed into his chair. "I apologise. I should have meted out his punishment in private. It was not my intention to startle you."

Startle? She wasn't startled. She was petrified.

Erin shook her head, unable to do anything else or speak.

The Devil smiled at her. "Now, I believe you asked why you are here?"

She nodded, heart pounding, fearing what he would say.

"The answer is very simple. It regards a game and your role in it."

"A game?" She swallowed. What sort of sinister game was he talking about? He nodded and she found her courage. "What's my role?"

His smile widened, turning cruel and evil.

"You are bait."

She frowned. "Bait for who?"

Who did she know that the Devil was interested in luring down to Hell?

He waved a hand and a shimmering image appeared behind him. A tropical island. The image zoomed in to the white shore and a woman there.

A shiver cascaded over Erin's skin and icy fingers squeezed her heart.

Her silver hair reflected the bright sunlight and that part of her didn't make sense to Erin, but she knew her without a doubt. She would recognise this woman anywhere, had spent the past few months worried about her because she hadn't been in touch since then, and her calls had been infrequent since a year before that.

Her sister.

Erin's throat closed and her eyes filled with tears of relief that her sister was safe even while the claws seizing her heart tightened their grip.

"Amelia."

CHAPTER 2

Veiron stalked through the dense humid jungle, cutting a path through the bracken with his broadsword. Marcus had better have a damn good reason for dragging him out to such a hellish place just to speak to him. Veiron growled when another insect stuck him with its pointy end and slapped his hand down hard on it, killing it and leaving a small red spot on his tanned skin. What had happened to the good old days of meeting on a nice sunny and remote island? He didn't like it in the jungle as it was and this one was high on his list of areas to avoid.

There was a gate to Hell here.

He had spent the past year and a half avoiding the gates to Hell, unwilling to get himself caught by making such a rookie mistake. The Devil wasn't happy about Veiron's rebellion and wanted him to pay in blood for disobeying him by assisting Amelia and Marcus in their fight against the eternal game that Heaven and Hell was playing with her, and them all.

Amelia was the current reincarnation of the original angel. The only female angel in existence. God had given her too much power and the Devil had tampered with her creation so her soul had been born in Hell. She had led men to sin and to war with each other. God had killed her but angels were immortal. Her death had only triggered her reincarnation.

That reincarnation saw her born in the mortal realm as a human. Under normal circumstances, Heaven and Hell allowed her to live her life as a mortal and die as one. Things changed when the planets came into alignment. Then, the two realms proved just how sick and vicious they could be.

Heaven sent Apollyon, the great destroyer and one of the angels of the Apocalypse, to kill her and awaken her in her angel form. Then, it was all hands on deck in a race to be the first to get their mitts on her. Heaven won most of the time, using Marcus to capture the errant female angel and bring her to the altar in Heaven where she would be sacrificed, her blood used to seal Hell for centuries.

Veiron had won a few times.

For him and Marcus, it didn't matter who the victor was. They both died whenever she did because her death reset the game. Veiron was reborn as a guardian angel along with Marcus, only he was destined to fall into dispute with Heaven and to fall into Hell shortly following that.

He never had a choice.

Neither did Marcus.

Both of them were pawns in the game. Heaven and Hell forced them, and other angels like Apollyon, to do their bidding against their will.

At least Marcus and the others forgot everything that happened to them when they were reborn. Veiron generally had a few centuries of peace as an angel, oblivious of everything he had done in his past lives, before he fell and pledged himself in service of the Devil.

When that happened, he remembered everything. He remembered killing the female angel and spilling her blood, and dying himself, or the countless times Marcus had been the victor and Veiron had dropped dead somewhere. He didn't want to remember the terrible things he had done and how he'd had no choice other than to do them. He didn't want to remember that it was going to happen all over again because Heaven had agreed with Hell that the terms of their eternal game would include him being the Devil's pawn.

He hated Heaven for that, but not as much as he despised Hell.

Veiron hacked at the undergrowth, tempted to blast it out of his way with his power to unleash some of his rage. He couldn't risk it though. It was dangerous at the best of times to use his power. The Devil could use it to pinpoint his location and send his army of angels after him. At the worst of times, like the one he was currently experiencing, it would be a grand mistake. This close to the gate, the Devil would easily sense him if he used even the barest slither of his power. Fuck, he couldn't even use his wings or his spear to get him to his destination. He was reduced to wading through a hot, sweaty, disgusting jungle using a mortal weapon.

Veiron snarled.

Marcus had better have a damn good reason for dragging him out here into the middle of nowhere.

The sun began to sink lower, the dense jungle around him darkening. He checked the GPS device Marcus had mailed to his hotel in Rio de Janeiro. Still miles to go. Veiron huffed and tucked the small dark grey device back into the pocket of his black jeans. His feet ached.

He grunted.

Flying would be sweet right about now.

Another insect bit him and Veiron barely stopped himself from taking his sword to it. So what if he lost an arm? It would be worth it to stop the little fuckers from feasting on his blood. They were getting worse with each minute.

He paused and raised his arm, glaring at the mosquito. It flew away before he could flick it off him. He hoped the fucker got sick from drinking his demonic blood.

Veiron growled and stalked on, trying to rein in his temper. Even that would get him noticed if he wasn't careful. All it took was his eyes to change, revealing his demonic side, and he would pop up on the Devil's radar.

He wasn't sure how much more of this lying low crap he could take. The past eighteen or so months had been torture and he was close to hauling arse down into the bottomless pit in Hell and having it out with the Devil face to face.

What a bloody way to go.

The Devil would take him down before he could even step within forty metres of him. His master didn't tolerate insubordination and helping the enemy was probably punishable by an eternity of torture.

Veiron's death would be endless.

The light faded. Veiron stopped, sheathed his broadsword in the case strapped to his back, and rifled around in his small black backpack. He shoved past his folded up leather jacket and grabbed the flashlight. He clicked the button. It didn't come on.

Just great. Stuck in the middle of Hell on Earth, being eaten alive by bugs, in the dark. He shook the Maglite and looked down at it as he clicked the button again. It came on, blinding him, and he swung it away. White spots winked over his vision.

Veiron sighed and leaned back against a tree, resting there with the torch pointed at the floor. He tipped his chin up and looked through the canopy to the inky sky beyond. It was alive with stars. The only times he had seen this many were when he had visited the island where Marcus and Amelia had remained hidden until recently.

Heaven didn't have night. It was perpetual daylight there. Hell had a roof over it.

This was the one reason that he envied the mortals. They were able to see such beauty on a grand scale if they only looked up.

Well, this and alcohol. Heaven forbade such substances in its environs. Hell made a wicked form of liquor that could burn the roof off the top of a man's mouth and leave them unable to taste anything for a week. It wasn't quite the same as mortal-made alcohol. Mortals knew how to live it up. A million different flavours and none of them designed to knock you dead after one shot.

He could use a shot of something right about now.

Veiron untied his long flame-red hair, raked his fingers through the sweat-soaked strands, and then tied it back into a ponytail, the bells on the end of his leather thong jingling as he did so. His black t-shirt and jeans were equally damp and uncomfortable, and his army boots felt as though someone had poured a bucket of water into each one.

Why the Devil had Marcus chosen such a horrible fucking place as a meeting point?

He was going to wring the angel's scrawny bloody neck when he eventually found him.

Veiron drew his sword from his back, clutching it in his right hand and the torch in his left, and trudged on. Nocturnal creatures of all sizes crossed his path during the trek, took one look at him and scattered into the jungle. Wise animals. His stomach grumbled, as though he needed the reminder that he hadn't eaten in too long. He doubled his pace, crashing through the undergrowth, uncaring that the sound of his movements carried for miles through the night.

Anyone around here looking for trouble was welcome to come and try him on for size. The mood he was in right now, he would slaughter them.

The GPS device bleeped, signalling that he was close. He checked it again, juggling it and his flashlight. Very close. A few hundred metres now. He shoved it away and trekked onwards, and clicked his torch off when an orange glow cut through the trees ahead.

The undergrowth thinned and a small clearing came into view. Marcus sat on a log, the fire in front of him and his bare back to Veiron, exposing the elaborate blue-grey wings engraved on his shoulder blades. Veiron grinned.

He crept forwards, his sword ready to strike. This would teach the former angel for making him come out here into this godforsaken jungle. Marcus would probably jump higher than Heaven when Veiron tapped him on the shoulder with the sword. His grin widened.

Something cold pressed against his throat and he froze.

His dark eyes slid to his left.

Amelia stood there, dressed head to toe in black combat gear, her small dagger held to his Adam's apple. She smiled and her grey eyes brightened, but the fatigue and worry he could see in them didn't lift. The past year and a half had been difficult for her. It had been difficult for them all. He had never seen her so on edge before though. Had someone found them and tried to kill her?

Both Heaven and Hell had been quiet since Marcus had fallen and joined with Amelia, allowing her to become his new master, endowing him with the same silvery unusual wings that she had, a mixture of feathers on top and leathery dragon-like membrane on the bottom half, and the same incredible powers.

"Been training?" He pushed her arm away, removing the blade from his throat.

Marcus didn't look back at him. He prodded the fire with a charred stick. "We heard you coming from miles away. Subtlety is not your forte, is it?"

Veiron shrugged and slid his broadsword into the sheath on his back.

He walked into the clearing, dumped his backpack on the leafy ground and undid the leather straps that ran under his arms and held the sword case against his back. He let it drop to the ground next to his backpack and sat on a tree stump near the fire. Small insects drifted too close to the flames and fizzled out of existence. He faced that sort of end if the Devil ever got his hands on him.

"So... what the fuck am I doing in the middle of the Amazon, close to a gate that spells certain doom for me?" Veiron looked from Marcus, with his silver-blue eyes and stoic expression, to Amelia, deciding she was the easier target and the reason Marcus had requested his presence judging by the feelings she wasn't bothering to mask.

She sat down on the log opposite him, her black clothes blending into the darkness beyond her but her silver hair making her stand out. It was up tonight, tied back in a tight ponytail like his. She looked as though she was enjoying the humidity of the rainforest as much as he was, so why had she chosen this as the location for their latest meeting?

Marcus wore similar black fatigues on his lower half, his own black shirt laying over the log to his left. His bare muscular chest bore the scars of a recent battle and there was a thin dark line cutting across his jaw.

"Why do I get the feeling we're in a whole heap of shit?" Veiron said and Amelia stared at her feet. "Is someone going to tell me why I'm here, or do I have to beat it out of Marcus?"

He grinned at Marcus when the black-haired man glared at him, his pale eyes dark and daring him to try.

Marcus cleared his throat but it was Amelia who spoke.

"I need your help." Her soft voice drifted across the crackling fire, conveying every ounce of worry that he had seen in her eyes. "I want to go myself but Marcus won't let me."

"Go where?" He didn't really need to ask that question. Cold realisation sank deep into his gut. They were close to one of the gates to Hell for a reason, and it was one he really didn't want to contemplate. Amelia had to have a damn good reason for wanting to go into Hell and Marcus had to have an even better reason for making her call in a favour from him.

"I can't leave her there."

Her? He looked at Marcus. The ex-angel sighed, lifted his gaze away from the fire, and looked across at him.

"The Devil has her sister," he said, voice laden with a mixture of anger, concern and fear.

"I can't leave her there, Veiron," Amelia whispered and tears lined her grey eyes. Not the waterworks. He could handle anything but a crying woman. "Marcus won't let me go and I'm afraid that if he goes alone, he won't come back... or he won't be able to find Erin. Please... I know I'm asking a lot of you but I need someone strong who knows Hell and won't rouse suspicion. I need her back."

Fuck, what was he supposed to say to her? Sorry, Love, I'm not interested in saving your dear little sister from the Devil and getting myself killed in the process? He was only alive because Amelia was. If she went down into Hell, she would get herself killed by the Devil or any of the other million vicious creatures that had orders to separate her head from her body by any means. If that happened, it was game over and he would wake up a guardian angel again, unaware of everything that had happened in his past lives and destined to fall and remember it all.

Still, he really didn't feel like venturing down into the bowels of Hell on a suicide mission to save a woman when he was high on the Devil's shit list himself. Everyone was looking for him, both up here and down there. The slightest mistake on his part and his former colleagues, the army of Hell's angels belonging to the Devil, would be coming after him to haul his arse in for the crime of assisting Amelia and Marcus in their battle against the game.

"Please, Veiron?" Amelia whispered again and he couldn't stand seeing the tears in her eyes. She had already been through hell because of this vicious game and had almost died by the hand of her lover, Marcus. She deserved to live, and so did he.

They all deserved some peace.

Veiron closed his eyes and huffed.

"Fine. I'll take a trip to Hell," he said and he could almost hear Amelia smile, could sense a glimmer of her relief and hear her heartbeat pick up.

"Thank you," she said and he looked across the fire at her and shook his head. There was no reason to thank him.

He hadn't promised that he would find her sister and bring her back in one piece.

He had only said that he would make the journey to Hell.

Whether it would be a one-way trip or not was yet to be seen.

It felt like a suicide mission to him.

CHAPTER 3

Erin sat with her back against the wall opposite the open side of her black rocky cell and stared into the hazy fiery distance, watching volcanic vents spewing lava high into the air and listening to the constant screams. She couldn't remember if it was five days or twenty since the Devil had visited her, but it had been a long time since she had seen anyone.

The other two who had been with the Devil during his visit hadn't come back to check on her. Someone slid a meal through a grate in the bottom of her door from time to time. She ate only the vegetables, unable to stomach the thought of eating more of the final unicorn in existence let alone the meat itself.

She could have been somewhere more comfortable if she had complied with the Devil's desires.

He had told her that before storming out of the cell and slamming the door behind him, leaving her alone with the dismembered wings of the last creature who had dared to defy him.

She had felt sick, reliving the Devil ripping them from the demon's back, whenever she saw them so she had gingerly dragged them to the open side of her cell and tossed them down into the fiery river far below.

She could have escaped this place if she had gone with him. Not the Devil, but the other one who had visited her. At first, she had thought it was the Devil. The man had flown up from the abyss on huge black feathered wings, his wild hair as dark as midnight and his eyes as golden as a hawk's. The only items of clothing he had worn were a black loincloth covered by tattered age-worn strips of armour and boots that reached his knees and had gold-edged black moulded plates that completely covered his shins.

His sudden appearance had startled her and he had looked so much like the Devil that she had fled to the back of her cell and had done a double take. Only on closer inspection had she realised that this man was different. If it hadn't been for the black wings, she would have thought him an angel. He had been handsome, but darkness had clung to him, a sense of evil in the twist of his lips as he smiled at her and told her that she could have her freedom if she came with him.

It had tempted her more than the Devil's offer and she had almost considered placing her hand into the man's and letting him take her away. Only that lingering sense that he was evil beyond words, as likely to murder her as he was save her, had kept her at the back of her cell. He had hovered near the open wall of her prison, beating his wings and using the rising heat to keep him close to stationary. When she had refused, Erin had expected him to enter her cell and force her to leave with him, but he had snorted, a feral sound that had made her jump, and then swooped out of sight.

She had been too scared to race forwards and see if he really was gone. She had sunk to her backside close to the door of her cell and stared out at the world beyond her prison, wondering what would have happened if she had gone with the stranger. Would he have freed her or would he have taken her to the Devil, or would he have killed her?

His reluctance to enter her cell and the wary glances he had given it had left her with the impression that he hadn't been willing to breach it for some reason. He had wanted her to extend her hand to him, beyond the boundaries of her prison. That had led her to settle on the idea that if he had entered the cell, something would have happened. What, she didn't know, and she didn't care.

She would have her freedom somehow, but it wouldn't be with the help of a man who had looked like some sort of demonic angel.

Erin rubbed her knees, idly trying to get rid of some of the layers of dirt from her bare skin. At least it was warm in Hell so her scant clothing wasn't a problem. She laughed at herself, the sound loud and echoing around her cell, jarring with the endless screams that rose up from the abyss.

Was that where the Devil was right now? Too busy tormenting his victims to come and visit her and try to convince her to do as he had asked.

He had told her that she could have her freedom if she would cast aside her sentimentality and kill her sister. Her stomach rolled in response to that memory and she slammed her mind shut against it, unwilling to contemplate such a thing.

Erin buried her face in her knees and hugged them, tired right down to her bones and starving. The few morsels she ate whenever food came through the door weren't enough to keep her going. Without eating the unicorn meat, she was slowly growing weaker, the effects of the few mouthfuls she'd had wearing off a little more each day. Her throat felt like sandpaper too. The Devil clearly didn't understand that the constant heat of his hellish realm was dehydrating her.

Then again, did he really care if she died?

She was bait. Whether she was alive or not didn't matter. Or did it? He had been genuinely angry that she had been held captive for days on end without him knowing and without food or comfort. She could have had that comfort and all the food she could eat if she had only complied with him one way or the other. Play bait or do his work and kill her sister for him.

Erin wanted to do neither. She didn't understand why the Devil wanted her sister but she didn't want Amelia to come to Hell and try to save her. She would rather die here and rot in this cell than see her sister come to harm.

She shifted onto her knees, the rough basalt floor cutting into her dirty flesh, and pushed herself onto her feet. Her steps were unstable but she made it to the side wall of her prison and held onto it as she moved forwards, towards the edge.

Hot air blasted upwards from the inferno hundreds of feet below and almost knocked her backwards. It curled around her, blowing the fringe of her straight black hair upwards and stinging her eyes. She squinted and stared out at the unforgiving bleak landscape that stretched around her, all black rocky crags and flaming rivers. Huge black-skinned beasts roamed the land, their dragon-like wings furled against their backs and weapons in their hands. They tormented any smaller creature they passed, bullying it until it either escaped or gave up and cowered at their feet.

She had grown strangely used to the existence of this place and the creatures that dwelled within it, as though she had always known it was real and not the stuff of legend and myths.

Her gaze tracked the demons far below. Erin had watched the comings and goings of the creatures who guarded the prison, trying to figure them out and see if they had any weak spots. They didn't. Nothing could stand up to them.

Nothing except the Devil at least.

She couldn't see him amongst the creatures below her.

Erin leaned further forwards and assessed the ragged cliff face. She might have been able to make it down that way if she had been a champion rock-climber. She wasn't. She was a weak, exhausted and sometimes scared woman who had never climbed anything bigger than a hill, let alone scaled a sheer rock face several hundred feet high.

The door opened behind her and Erin didn't make the mistake of whirling to face the visitor this time.

She turned slowly, expecting to find either the Devil or one of his cronies come to torment her.

It was neither.

A bloodstained and beaten man wearing tight black jeans that emphasised the thickness of his thighs and a black t-shirt that stretched across the impressive hard cut breadth of his chest stood in the doorway.

He was holding a very big sword.

Erin swallowed.

Had he come to kill her?

She glanced back at the abyss below her feet. What would be a better and less painful death? Falling to this scarlet-haired man's sword or plummeting into the volcanic river?

"Erin, I presume?" His deep voice wrapped around her and Erin couldn't miss the concern that laced the weariness and irritation in it.

Erin looked back at him.

He slid the broadsword down his back and scrubbed his hand across several days' worth of dark growth on his handsome face.

One good-looking man had fooled her already and it wasn't going to happen again. This man was every bit as lethal, brutal and vicious as the Devil. It was there in his eyes and the way he held himself, legs spread in a warrior's stance, ready for a fight.

He looked as though he had already been through several battles recently. Now that she looked closer, she spotted tears in his t-shirt that revealed startlingly enticing glimpses of hard packed muscles.

Erin dragged her gaze down to her own feet.

She must have lost it in the past few days. She had finally plunged into crazy, her mind frazzled by her captivity and being in Hell. She had to be insane to be ogling the man who had clearly come to kill her.

"Why don't you just do it and get this over with?" she said, feeling a spark of defiance ignite in her chest. If she was going to die, she might as well go down fighting.

"Excuse me?" He frowned at her, a quizzical look filling his dark eyes. "Get what over with?"

"Killing me."

His dark red eyebrows pinched together. "If you're not Erin, I might."

It was her turn to frown. "You don't want to kill me?"

"Are you Erin?"

She nodded.

"Then I don't want to kill you." He stepped into her cell and she noted that he didn't bother to stay close to the door. If she were entering a cell on a mission to save someone, she would certainly keep one foot in the door in case a bad guy came along and shut them both in. Did he have another means of escape if that happened? He raked dark eyes over her and she shivered under the heat of his gaze. "You are not what I was expecting."

"Ditto," she said and shrugged when he looked into her eyes, confusion lighting his again. "I was expecting the Devil to come back."

"The snide little fucker actually paid you a visit in person?"

Erin frowned at how casually he badmouthed the Devil, as though he wasn't afraid of him. She stared at the man, taking in his impressive height and build. He was taller than the Devil and much broader too, thick sinewy muscles visible beneath his tight clothing. His biceps were huge, so large she would struggle to wrap both of her hands around one arm. Her fingertips and thumbs wouldn't touch if she tried. Matching black and red tribal tattoos curled around those biceps, a tantalising peek of a larger design that disappeared under the sleeves of his t-shirt.

Erin found herself wanting to strip his top off to see the rest of it.

She really had lost her mind.

"Are you alright?" He frowned again.

"Just a little brain damage," she said, trying to make light of everything.

He crossed the black floor and stopped before her, towering close to a foot over her, his immense body overshadowing hers and making her feel tiny. He slid one large hand along the line of her jaw, tilted her head back, and stared down into her eyes.

Erin swallowed. It should be illegal for a man to be so handsome yet so lethal-looking. He screamed danger but she wasn't quaking under his touch because of it. It was a whole other feeling that had her trembling.

"You don't look crazy," he whispered and she added his sultry low voice to the list of reasons someone should stamp him with the words 'dangerous' and 'forbidden'. "Now... all opposed to being rescued, raise your hands, otherwise, I'd like to get the fuck out of here."

Erin didn't argue, not even when he clamped one strong large hand around her slender wrist and drew the broadsword strapped to his back with the other. She stared at the open door, battling a flood of emotions that threatened to sweep her under. Freedom. This man was here to save her. It was too sweet and glorious to believe. It had to be a cruel trick, another form of torture to break her.

She didn't have much time to take in what was really happening when he pulled her over the threshold and into a long black corridor that ran between the cells. Before she could even glance back at the cell that had been her home for God only knew how many days, he was dragging her along the hallway.

"Can you run?" He glanced over his broad shoulders at her and didn't give her a chance to respond before he started at a pace.

Erin tried to keep up. The prospect of actually surviving and escaping Hell flooded her with adrenaline that had her bare feet moving but she couldn't match his long strides. A bright flash blinded her but it didn't slow her companion. He kept running. They passed a large open room and she turned her head in time to see several dead bodies strewn across a floor slick with blood. More flashes lit the darkness and with each one, a body disappeared.

They looked like humans. Had the man killed them to reach her? What was that light and why were they disappearing?

She started to ask but her gaze settled on the hard angles of his profile and the stern set of his jaw and she thought better of it. This man was her ticket out of Hell and she wasn't about to piss him off, not when she had the impression that he was quite content with killing.

Erin pounded along the black-walled corridor beside him, her legs beginning to tire and each step jarring her bones and sending pain shooting across the soles of her feet. She lost her footing on one of the sets of steps that led downwards and almost fell. The man's hand on her wrist stopped her. He pulled her up by her arm as though she was nothing but a ragdoll in his hands, suspending her off the ground for a second before setting her down again.

"You are weak," he said and she bristled at the double meaning in his words. He wasn't just saying she was weak from her captivity, but that he thought she was weak period.

Erin snatched her wrist free of his grasp and rubbed it. She turned her nose up and stormed ahead of him, feeling crazy for taking the lead when she didn't know where she was going and she didn't have a weapon, or the knowledge of how to wield one. She couldn't let him think she was weak though.

He followed behind her, a dark shadow barely a few feet from her, his footsteps almost silent.

They reached a split in the corridor and Erin paused. Neither of the avenues she could take looked inviting. Both were pitch-black and voices came from one. Or was it the other? Everything echoed in the corridors and it was hard to distinguish which would lead her to a grisly death and which would lead her to freedom.

She chose the right.

The man grabbed her around the waist from behind, twisted her in his arm, and slung her over his shoulder.

Erin struggled and his arm tightened against her back, causing his thick shoulder to press into her stomach. Her organs protested, sharp pain lancing each one.

"You'll fall off. I need to move fast and you're slowing me down."

Well, that was just rude. Erin punched his backside. God, it was like a rock. She almost purred. Could this man get any smexier?

"You can't carry me and fight your way out of here."

He laughed, the warm timbre of it echoing around the dark walls. "Believe me, Sweetheart, I can fight with both hands tied behind my back. You're no hindrance at all."

He jogged down the left corridor with her, each step jolting her on his shoulder until she felt close to losing what little remained of the last thing she ate. Erin grabbed his leather belt, hooked her thumbs into the waist of his jeans and pushed herself up enough that it didn't hurt as much as he ran.

This was just embarrassing now.

It was bad enough having her rescuer belittle her.

Having him carry her fireman-style to freedom was making her wish he had left her in her cell.

Warm fresh air assaulted her, as fresh as Hell got anyway, and she looked up to see the huge black walls of the prison fortress bouncing away from her.

"You can put me down now," she said but he didn't hear her. Either that or he was ignoring her. She was tempted to punch him on the backside again but gave up and let him have his way.

The jagged towers of the prison slowly wobbled into the distance and were lost from view behind the spires of black rock that lined the path her hero had chosen. Vents in their sides and tops belched hot acrid smoke that stole her breath. She pulled his black t-shirt up, exposing a lean delicious back, and covered her mouth with it. How the hell could he run in this?

Erin wanted to be sick.

She counted the bounces in his step to keep her focus off the horrendous smell of rotten eggs invading her lungs and the increasing number of bleached bones that lined the path as though someone had kicked the bodies out of the way and just let them rot there. Or perhaps some smaller creature had picked the bones clean. There were grooves in some of them, as though sharp teeth and claws had scraped them. Erin hoped it had happened after death and that the screams still ringing in her ears weren't the death cries of people being eaten alive.

The man managed over three hundred steps before he finally stopped and set her down with surprising care in a wide clearing.

"Are you alright?" He held her at arm's length, looking her over.

Her blood heated when his dark eyes lingered on her breasts and then the tiny shorts she wore.

"Do you always dress like this?" He raised an eyebrow.

Erin folded her arms across her chest, covering her breasts. The black pebbles of the path cut into the bare soles of her feet. "I was in bed when they took me."

He ran his gaze over her again and a touch of crimson ringed his dark irises.

Erin took a step backwards.

That had to be a reflection of their fiery surroundings. It had to be.

Mr Tall, Dark and Deadly couldn't be something straight out of Hell.

He frowned at her feet. Erin gasped as his large hands settled on her waist and he lifted her onto a relatively smoother rock on the side of the path.

"I didn't anticipate this." He rubbed his stubbly jaw and crouched before her. His hands were gentle as he lifted one of her feet and inspected the sole, his thumbs pressing in and sending a warm jolt up to the apex of her thighs.

She placed one hand on top of his head to steady herself and tried to resist the sudden desire to comb her fingers through the long crimson lengths of his hair.

She had dated a few men with long hair in the past but none of them had dyed it the colour this man had chosen. It was like blood.

"I like your do," she said with a smile. "It's pretty cool."

He frowned up at her. "Do?"

"Your hair."

His frown intensified. "We are trapped in Hell and you are discussing my hair?"

"I have to do something to take my mind off the fact that I'm trapped in Hell. What dye do you use?"

The man straightened and even when she was standing on a rock, she was still shorter than he was. "It is not dyed."

"That's natural?"

"If you would like, I can prove it to you." His smile was nothing short of salacious and he reached for his belt. "The carpet matches the curtains."

Erin blushed and grabbed his hands to stop him from going ahead and flashing her. He looked as though he really would go through with it and while the thought of seeing every inch of this man nude was appealing, it couldn't stand up to her greater desire to escape.

The man shrugged and then did something that really challenged her ability to think straight and focus on escaping.

He removed the leather contraption that held his sword to his back, reached over his head and tugged his black t-shirt off, revealing a body so perfect that it would make angels weep. Every inch of lightly bronzed skin stretched taut over granite hard muscles. They shifted in a sensual symphony as he easily tore his t-shirt into two pieces. Her gaze ambled over him, ignoring her commands to focus on anything other than his godly form, then he upped the stakes and it was game over.

He crouched again and bent over her feet, giving her a glorious view of his strong back and the detailed red and black tribal tattoos that swept up his thick arms and down his shoulder blades. They curled there, skirting identical ridges of scar tissue.

Erin leaned forwards as he finished wrapping one of her feet in half of his ruined t-shirt and started on her other. She swept her fingers along the wide dark scar that slashed up his left shoulder in line with his spine.

The man was gone in a flash, standing several feet away from her and breathing hard.

"What the fuck?" he snarled and Erin flinched, her hand still poised where his back had been. "Don't touch me. Understand?"

"I'm sorry... I just saw the scars and wondered what had happened to you." She hated that she couldn't get her voice above a whisper and that she couldn't look at him. Shame burned her cheeks. So much for her insane thoughts about paying back her glowering saviour with some naughty time when they made it out of Hell.

Erin stared at her feet. He had done a nice job of covering them with his t-shirt. She supposed she should thank him for coming to save her and for not doing the whole thing with her slung over his shoulder, leaving her feeling weak and pathetic. Maybe she should just ask him to point her in the right direction and she would find the way out on her own. Her gaze shifted to his sword where it lay on the ground. On second thought, he was armed and if she ran across some of those demons, he might be able to fend them off or even kill them.

"Thank you for coming for me. I owe you my life," she said and finally managed to find the courage to look him in the eye again.

He casually shrugged his wide bare shoulders. "You own me nothing. I'm only here because Amelia would have come if I hadn't, and if she dies then that's my life over."

"Oh." Erin's gaze ate basalt again and her cheeks scalded, her burning heart heating them. He was with Amelia. That made sense in a strange way, although it only left her with more questions about why Amelia knew about Hell, what the Devil wanted with her and how she had met this man.

A man who had taken her place, risking his life to save Erin so she didn't have to.

Erin stepped down from the rock, feeling as though someone had just popped her favourite balloon. She knew she should feel happy that her sister finally had a man in her life that had a noble and good bone in his body but she couldn't muster the emotion when jealousy was riding her.

Her amber eyes met his dark ones but she couldn't hold his gaze. It fell to the ground again. She didn't want to look at him anymore. The blood staining his face and the harsh cuts across his bearded jaw and neck did nothing to dampen his feral handsome looks.

Erin envied Amelia for having him in her life.

"I want to keep moving." She started off without him, following the winding path that was surrounded by black jagged rocks and bleached bones and stretched into an equally dark and bleak distance.

Erin was beginning to hate black.

The man easily caught up with her in a few long-legged strides and fell into step beside her, his broadsword strapped to his back again. He cut an imposing figure as he strolled along beside her, his air casual yet throwing off a lethal don't-even-try-it vibe.

She wanted to give him the silent treatment but it had been days since she had spoken to someone and he was currently her mind and heart's favourite subject. She wanted the goods on this man, every juicy bit of them.

"So... were you a captive here once too and that's why you know your way around?" That question hung in the air between them.

His lip curled, revealing a flash of straight white teeth, and he frowned.

Clearly, he was still pissed at her for touching him. Well, sorry. She couldn't have stopped herself if she had tried. She still wouldn't be able to if she so much as glanced at the scars that he had evidently tattooed around, as though they were central to the design.

He was silent a few seconds longer and then looked down at her out of the corner of his eye and smiled.

Erin walked on a few paces, towards a long sloping drop into a valley below. She glanced down, seeing that the path she was on turned a corner ahead and continued close to a hundred feet below her.

He finally spoke. "You could say that I'm local."

That unnerved her, especially when coupled with the bright crimson that flared in his dark irises, a corona surrounding his narrowed pupils.

Erin stepped away from him, backing towards the edge where it was rocky and the stones were loose underfoot. Her gaze darted down to the path far below her. Her footing was poor where she was but she didn't want to be near him until she was sure it was safe. She would sooner risk falling than being within his reach.

He frowned at her and then at her feet, and held his hand out to her. "Come away from the edge."

Erin shook her head.

If he was something terrible, then she was going to hit the slope, slide down to the path below and make a break for it. She would probably cut her bare legs up but it was better than being tortured by a demon. Had he only rescued her so he could toy with her and hurt her? Was this just another trick after all?

Her sister would never associate with something demonic and evil.

"Do you work for the Devil?" Erin shuffled backwards. His dark eyes flicked to her feet and then back to her eyes, and he stretched his hand closer to her, an impatient and concerned expression on his face. The Devil could change his appearance. This man had a voice that could melt her and so had the Devil. They were one and the same. "Are you the Devil?"

He laughed. "Hell, no. I'm not that evil. Do I look like I go around getting manicures between torture sessions?" He sighed and smiled at her. "I swear to you, Erin. I'm not here to hurt you... and I will keep you safe. Trust me?"

"No, I don't trust you. I don't even know you... you say you're local but you don't work for the bastard who held me captive, and you expect me to believe that shit?" She edged further away from him and he frowned, his eyes narrowing and expression switching to one of irritation. Anger flared in his eyes.

He growled, low and vicious, and the flecks of red in his eyes brightened. "I expect you to believe it because it's the truth. I hate the bastard who kidnapped you, and would like nothing more than a chance at separating his head from his body. I'm risking my neck to save you and you dare accuse me of being the one loathsome creature I despise above all others?"

Erin backed off another step as he advanced one, until the balls of her feet hit the slope. Her heart thumped out a hard rhythm against her breastbone and blood rushed through her ears. His gaze locked on hers, challenging her to accuse him again, to voice any belief she still had that he was unworthy of her trust. She trembled and stared up into his eyes, searching them for a sign that he was lying to her.

His anger seemed genuine, born of hatred for a man that she too despised and disgust at being compared with him. He couldn't blame her for being cautious though, surely? After everything she had been through, it was only natural for her to think everyone in this horrible place was out to get her, and he had admitted that he was a local.

The man backed off at last, the anger in his eyes melting away together with the red, leaving his irises dark. He sighed, his shoulders heaving with it, grimaced and rubbed a hand over his face.

"What am I supposed to say to make you believe me?" he whispered and met her gaze again. "Tell me that, Erin. I've trekked through Hell to find you, have fought and killed to reach you, have carried you and tended to you. I've risked my life to save you. Doesn't that make me worthy of a little trust? You think I want to be here?"

No, she didn't. He had mentioned more than once that he was risking everything by being in Hell, by saving her, and she felt terrible for doubting him.

He held his hand out to her again. "I swear to you, Erin, that I mean you no harm and I am here purely to rescue you and reunite you with your sister. Will you trust me to do that? Can you trust me?"

Erin's better judgement said not to but she slipped her trembling right hand into his and stepped away from the edge. She looked up into his eyes. They glowed red around the edges again and in the centre too, highlighting his wide pupils. His gaze locked with hers and rocked her with a jolt that reached her soul.

"What's your name?" she whispered, captivated by his eyes and lost in them. They had more power over her than the Devil's had. She wanted to stare into their flaming depths for all eternity.

"Veiron," he husked, his warm breath caressing her face, and Erin's senses came alive, lighting up like an electrical storm. His masculine scent of dirt, aftershave and fresh sweat filled her nostrils. The warmth of his hand clasping hers heated her right down to her bones. The sound of his voice made her blood burn to hear him speak again. Her gaze delighted in discovering every tiny fleck of fire in his dark irises. The only sense left was one that cried out for a taste of him.

She might be losing her mind, but she knew without a doubt that she wanted this man regardless of what he was.

He was the most dangerous man she had ever met and he belonged to her sister, but there was something about him, something sensual and powerful, deadly and alluring, that she couldn't resist. He had the smile of a demon, the body of a god, and the tenderness of an angel when he let his guard down.

Her captivity had been a nightmare.

But travelling through Hell with this man at her side was going to be a worse form of torture.

CHAPTER 4

The last time Erin had spoken to him, it had been to point out that he jingled with each step and that, because he was apparently a guy who could move with stealth, it didn't suit him. She had fallen quiet after he had touched the leather thong he tied his scarlet hair up with and told her that it was a gift from a lover, and that the two small bells attached to each end were there to ward off evil. A protection charm.

A short time after that, she had trodden on a sharp rock and had sworn at him and swatted his hand away when he had tried to help her and offered to carry her again. She had turned her nose up and hobbled on defiantly.

That had been hours ago.

Veiron wasn't sure what he had done to deserve her wrath, but she was dishing it out like there was no tomorrow.

He walked a few paces behind her, close enough that he could easily intervene should anyone dare attack her and could touch her shoulder to direct her whenever she took a wrong turn, which happened often when she was in the lead.

Erin was nothing like he had expected her to be. He had pictured her looking like her sister, with silver-grey eyes and full breasts, and the sort of attitude that said she was in command and everyone had better fall in line or suffer the consequences.

The willowy woman storming ahead of him looked little like the one he had left in the jungle just a few days ago. She had the most incredible amber eyes, an impish nose and sensual soft full lips, curves in all the best places, and small firm breasts that promised to fill his hands quite nicely. Not a trace of make-up touched her face and she didn't need it to enhance her natural beauty. Even with the smudges of dirt and the faint bruises, she was breathtaking and he was finding it hard to keep his eyes off her.

The lilac streak down the right side of her sleek black bob said that when she got out of Hell and got herself dressed, it would be in clothes similar to those he preferred.

No pretty colourful summer dresses and cute pumps for this woman.

She would go for all black and utter rebellion to match her hair and that sassy attitude of hers. When he had finally found her cell, having almost freed the wrong woman, something he would be having words with Amelia about later since she had failed to adequately describe her sister, and had opened the door, she had faced him with defiance in her eyes that had almost masked the underlying fear. She had asked whether he was there to kill her and the set of her jaw and tilt of her chin proclaimed that if he was, she was damn well going to fight him. Layers of filth, some bruises, and dark circles beneath her eyes spoke of what she had been through during her captivity but he still couldn't believe that she had survived the one thing that would have had most people on their knees.

He had almost choked when she had told him the Devil himself had come to see her.

The bastard normally stayed closer to the centre of the pit, safe in his fortress, only venturing out when bored to torture any poor soul that happened to pass by.

Erin had fire in her all right. Not the uptight and I'm-the-boss sort that Amelia had. No, Erin's attitude was all defiance and fight, strength and determination to survive.

When Veiron had called her weak, she had looked as though she had come close to slapping him. He couldn't imagine the hell she had given the Devil. The man had a tendency to try to bargain and Erin didn't look like the sort his bargaining would work on. He hoped the bastard had come away smarting and with his pride thoroughly dented.

Veiron smiled and checked himself when his gaze slid down Erin's spine to her backside, the black tank and shorts combo almost doing him in. He wished he had been the one who had taken her from her bed. He had heard the rumours while travelling through Hell to free her. The Devil had sent one of Veiron's kind to retrieve her in the dead of night. Mercy, he would have had a hard time carrying out that command. Take her from her bed and bring her down to the Devil? Hell, he would have just taken her.

He looked off to his right, using his senses to track her instead and shoving aside thoughts of bedding her. The area they were passing through was quiet enough but they were coming up on a rough one inhabited by countless lower forms of demon that had a taste for human flesh. He would have to keep Erin close to mask her mortal scent with his own immortal and demonic one.

Erin grumbled and hopped a few paces. She raised her right foot, catching it in her hands and bending forwards so she could see the sole. Veiron cocked his head to one side, appreciating her graceful form, and then told himself that as soon as Erin was safe, he was leaving. He had only agreed to come for her because Amelia had gone all weepy on him and Marcus had given him a black look that promised pain if he refused her request to save her little sister. Once Erin was back in her arms, he would resume his pursuit of the one thing that had kept his cold heart warm these past few centuries in Hell.

Revenge.

As an angel, he had lived by the same creed as the rest. The mission was what mattered. He had never felt any allegiance to those words until recent years. Now the mission was all he could think about. It was all he dreamed about. Hunger for vengeance lived in his veins, keeping his heart pumping and his feet moving forwards.

It wouldn't be satisfied until he had the Devil's head on a spike and had shaken Heaven to its foundations.

Until that moment of victory was his, Veiron wouldn't rest.

And he certainly wouldn't get involved with a mortal female. As tempting as she was, he wasn't what she needed in her life. He could never give her what she needed and she would be a complication that he couldn't afford. A weakness. A need to protect her had been steadily building inside him since he had opened her cell door and set eyes on her. That need included protecting her from himself. She had been through enough in the past few weeks. As soon as she was with Amelia, he was gone, out of there. Danger followed him everywhere, constant and unrelenting, and he wasn't about to drag a mortal female into his life and into the path of that.

Erin might think she was strong, but in his world, she was weak. A kitten. A baby. She wouldn't last five seconds against the lowest form of demon in this realm, let alone the beasts that hunted him on a nightly basis.

She would become a pawn, something they could use to distract and weaken him, and that was something he didn't wish on anyone.

No. The sooner Erin was out of his life, the better it was for everyone involved.

His back shivered, the scars where his wings hid tingling with the memory of that soft sweep of her fingers.

She had just had to touch him, hadn't she? He had noticed from the moment he had stormed into her cell that Erin was as forward about being forward as he had ever seen. Hell, she was so far ahead of forward that forward looked chaste and innocent. The heat of her gaze on him had been hard enough to handle but when she had dared to run her hand down his bare back, he had felt her touch as a fifty thousand volt shock.

His wings had pushed for freedom and it had taken every ounce of his considerable willpower to convince them it would be a bad idea. Very bad. One tiny crimson feather emerging from his back would be enough to send a warning straight through Hell to his former boss, alerting him to Veiron's exact location in his domain.

But damn, it had felt good.

He couldn't remember the last time a woman had caressed those lines. He wasn't sure there was a time. Not the way she had done it, gently following the scar tissue with her fingertips, curiosity and a dash of desire in her touch.

Veiron blew out his breath.

Just thinking about it had his wings pushing and his head spinning off to imagine her running those fingers over his feathers.

Veiron stared at her. She bandaged her foot back up with the black material and then looked over her shoulder at him. Her bright amber eyes met his, sending a hot shiver through his blood that only increased in temperature as her gaze slowly fell to his bare torso and her pupils dilated. She glanced away a split second later and started walking again.

That wasn't the first time she had given him the wicked once over and then darted her attention away from him. She had done it countless times in the past few miles alone and he had the distinct impression that he had done or said something that had made her feel as though he was not for her.

Which he wasn't, but he wasn't averse to her thinking that he was throughout the duration of their journey because she had been a lot more talkative and better company during his first hour of knowing her. They had days of walking before they reached the gate where Amelia waited on the other side. He really didn't want to spend it with Erin blowing hot and cold on him. He had never been a fan of the silent treatment. He didn't have the patience for it and trying to figure out how to get the woman to speak to him again twisted his head in painful knots.

What had he done or said that had altered her so dramatically from the woman who had given him heated looks that openly declared she was interested in all things Veiron?

A few things came to mind, most notably the moment where he had revealed that he was a local.

If the demon thing didn't sit well with her, what the hell was she going to make of her sister and Marcus? They were technically part-demon now.

Veiron drew his sword and stalked forwards to catch up with her.

She jumped when she saw the sword and edged away, placing some distance between them on the narrow black path.

"Stay close," Veiron barked, his patience wearing thin and the fragile tethers holding his considerable anger over the whole situation, and Erin's behaviour since his revelation, at bay close to snapping.

She didn't argue this time. Sweet mercy. The woman might just live to see the mortal realm again after all.

At least, he might not kill her.

Her gaze burned into his profile. He slid his dark eyes to meet hers out of their corners and she blinked, her own eyes going wider. Startled. She didn't look away though.

"I'm tired, I'm hungry and I'm thirsty."

This was just what he needed. Complaining female was right up there with weepy on the list of things that lit the touch paper of irritation that could easily detonate the fifty-kiloton bomb that was his anger.

"Tough luck. We can't rest here."

"My feet hurt."

Veiron frowned, what little pride he had telling him he wasn't going to let this one slip. "I offered to carry you. You refused. Again, tough luck."

"You're not very nice. I really can't see what Amelia sees in you," she snapped and her cheeks blazed. Her gaze zipped to the path, so her black hair fell forwards and obscured her face.

"What Amelia sees in me?" He stopped, aware that he was contravening his own rules about not resting. It wasn't a rest. It was a pause. A brief punctuation in their trek so he could figure out what the fuck she was babbling about.

Erin kept her gaze downcast and wrapped her arms around her slender frame. "As a lover."

Veiron spluttered. Not the manliest thing he could have done given the situation but what she had said, and what she clearly thought, had him reeling so hard he was surprised he didn't fall on his arse.

"Lover?" he said with so much disbelief that she finally looked up at him.

Her amber eyes were huge against her dirty face. "You're not lovers?"

He shook his head. "No way. No. Marcus would break my balls if I so much as looked at her sideways and she's not my type."

Veiron's eyes disobeyed his direct command not to take Erin in from head to toe. They roamed over her, liking what they saw. Forbidden. Off the menu. He was not looking for a romantic entanglement. He was looking for revenge.

Besides, Marcus would probably kill him for looking at Erin too, even though she was definitely his type. Smart-mouthed, sassy, and bewitching.

"Who's Marcus?"

Amelia really needed to keep her little sister in the loop. "Amelia's lover... boyfriend... hell, he could be her husband for all I know."

Erin's eyes managed to go a little wider. "She would have told me if she had married. But you said that if Amelia died, you would too..."

Hell, Veiron could see where she had gotten the impression that he and Amelia were lovers now. So was this why she had gone from giving him 'come hither and let's party despite my hellish surroundings' looks to withering glares?

"I was speaking literally," he said and her frown didn't lift. "It's a long story and not one for here. We have to keep moving."

She didn't look as though she was going to heed that command. There was no way in this realm that he was going to stand around in the open and attempt to explain, without making him sound more terrifying than she already thought he was by just knowing he was a demon, the whole situation with himself, Amelia and Marcus.

Veiron grabbed her arm and started marching.

Mercifully, she didn't protest. She kept pace beside him, her gaze boring into the side of his face, burning with questions that he really didn't want to answer.

If she didn't like the idea of him being a demon, how was she going to react when she discovered that he was like the one who had taken her from her home and dragged her down into Hell?

Veiron vowed that it would never happen. He couldn't use his powers in Hell without alerting the authorities so there was no reason for her to find out exactly what sort of man was playing her bodyguard. As soon as he got her safely topside, he would say a few choice words to Amelia, tell Marcus that he could go to Hell on the rescue mission next time, and would get as far away from Erin as possible and as quickly as he could without his wings.

Heck, he would sprint through the jungle and not stop until he reached the nearest airport.

And he would never set eyes on Erin again.

It was how it had to be.

Because a woman like her could never love a demon like him.

CHAPTER 5

Erin stuck to Veiron like glue, so close that she had bumped into his back several times in the past few minutes alone. She had almost tripped him once, accidentally treading on the back of his boot. That had earned her a glare that could have scared the Devil himself. He had told her to keep close to her when they had entered an open area that could have passed as a village. Small black square huts with holes for windows and doors dotted the undulating basalt landscape, upwards of twenty of them. A path wound through the ramshackle buildings. She followed Veiron along it, her gaze darting around, fixing on each black hole in the huts, trying to see if there were things inside watching her from the shadows.

Veiron had said that if she strayed too far from him, they would smell she was mortal and she was high on the list of food preferred by the creatures who dwelled here. Were they the sort of demons that had left those sharp grooves in all the bones she had seen? She didn't want to meet anything that could do that. Surely, they could see she was mortal?

She glanced up at the back of Veiron's head, watching the bells on the end of the thong that held his long red hair in a ponytail as they swayed with his heavy steps. He was a demon and he looked human. Most of the time. There had been moments when he had looked at her and she had seen the darkness in his eyes, the crimson that edged them and served as a reminder that he wasn't like her.

How evil was he on a scale of just a bit wicked to the Devil?

And how did he know her sister?

Erin had tried to ask him about the relationship he had with Amelia but each time he had shot her down, telling her to keep quiet and keep moving. She was beginning to think he was using their current location as an excuse to shut her up. If he said that demons could tell she was a tasty snack by the sound of her voice, she would probably believe him.

Did he eat people too?

She couldn't hold that one in.

"What sort of things are your favourite foods?"

He looked over one wide shoulder, his eyebrows knitted together and his eyes dark. They brightened a second later, as though he had figured out what she was really asking.

"Babies," he said.

Erin stopped dead.

He huffed, turned to face her, and the muscles in his jaw ticked beneath his stubble. "I was joking. God, what sort of monster do you think I am?"

Before she could respond, he had turned away and was stalking ahead. Erin shot a nervous glance at the two small black huts either side of her and raced to catch up with him. A little too fast. She almost ran into the back of him and had to use her hands as a buffer. He tensed and snarled when they settled against his lower back.

Erin leapt backwards. No touching. She had got the message loud and clear the first time. He didn't have to growl at her. Would he have preferred she ploughed into his back?

"You're not a monster," she whispered but it didn't even sound convincing to her. Right now, she wasn't sure what he was, but she knew she didn't appreciate jokes about eating babies. "So what do you eat?"

"Down here, I don't need to eat anything, so you're safe, okay?" Could he sound any more offended? He had practically growled the words at her.

"What about when you're not down here?" She moved to walk beside him so she could see whether he really was angry with her. He had expressive eyes that hid nothing, as though he didn't feel the need to guard his emotions from anyone. If he was angry, the world knew it. If he was happy, they knew that too. She was beginning to think that happy was a rare emotion for Veiron.

"Food... just like you."

"Why don't you eat anything down here?" She had expected him to tell her that he never ate, not that he ate part time. She rubbed her stomach as it rumbled, thoughts of food filling her mind. How long had it been since she had eaten? The landscape of Hell all looked the same to her and there was no night or day, so she had lost track of time again. Only her aching feet told her how far she had walked. Too far. She needed to rest before she collapsed from pain or hunger but now wasn't the best place for stopping so she didn't mention it. Talking kept her mind off it though, and since Veiron seemed to be in the mood to answer basic questions, she would do her best to learn a little more about her guardian. "Do you pig out when you're up there?"

"No. It's the same for all... never mind. Forget it."

"For all what?" Like hell she was going to not mind it and forget it. The hard set of his jaw said he wasn't going to answer. Erin reached out to him and his gaze followed her hand. She laid it on his forearm. "Veiron?"

He closed his eyes and inhaled sharply. At least he didn't tell her to get her hands off him this time. Score one for her. If he anticipated her touch, he didn't shove her away.

"Angels."

Erin stopped dead again, her fingers tightening around Veiron's arm. He halted and shifted to face her.

"You're an angel?" she said and frowned. "But you said you were local..."

He nodded.

"Local and an angel?" Was that even possible? There was so much suffering down here. If he were an angel, why would he tolerate it? Wouldn't he want to do something to end it?

"Of sorts," he said, turned on his heel, and kept walking.

Erin stared at his back. An angel without wings. Her gaze looked beyond the black leather scabbard that held his sword against his back and settled on the two long vertical scars highlighted by the matching red and black tribal tattoos on his shoulder blades.

"Has someone cut off your wings?" She hobbled to catch up with him.

He shot her a look that plainly told her to shut up and drop the subject. Like hell. She had gone from wanting to know why her sister knew a demon to why her sister knew an angel, and she wanted answers.

"Oh my God... you're fallen!"

He turned on her with a snarl.

Something told Erin that it wasn't the G-word that had upset him, not as it had the Devil. Veiron had used the G-word himself without any obvious anger. The rage that burned in his eyes was because she had struck the nail firmly on the head and driven it hard into some place it hurt.

"Sorry," she whispered but he wasn't listening. He was already striding away from her, leaving her exposed to any watching eyes in the huts around them.

Questions burned on the tip of her tongue but the black look on Veiron's face warned that putting voice to them might make them the last thing she ever said so she quietly walked beside him.

They left the bleak village behind and entered a wide open area where the black cragged land belched flames and fiery orange cracks spewed lava. Erin couldn't imagine how horrible it would be to live down here if she had lived in Heaven. She had no doubt that the other realm existed. She was walking through Hell with a fallen angel as her guardian. Why had Veiron fallen?

She glanced up at his face. Pain edged his dark eyes as he stared ahead into the endless black. Voicing that question would only hurt him and she had done enough damage already. He had gone through Hell to free her and was leading her out, taking her to her sister. She should have been thanking him, showing her gratitude, rather than playing the painful version of twenty questions.

Erin averted her gaze, no longer sure how to speak to him or what to say if she could find her voice. Shards of black rock edged the right side of the winding path through the fiery broken black fields, obscuring the way ahead. She frowned as they turned a corner and she saw a group of rickety rusty cages ahead. They weren't empty.

Three women dressed in rags, filthy and emaciated, huddled inside them. They reached through the bars of their cramped cages and looked up at her, dark eyes wide and laced with tears.

As she approached, they pleaded her to help them. Veiron strolled right past them without even sparing them a glance. How could he be so unfeeling? He didn't even break his stride.

She couldn't ignore their cries.

Erin reached for one of them.

Veiron's hand snapped around her wrist and yanked it back.

"Don't," he growled.

"But they're scared and starving! I can't let them just die here." She wrenched her arm free of his grip and stood up to him. It was hard to intimidate a man who stood over a foot taller and around two feet wider than she was, but she wouldn't let that stop her from trying.

"You damn well can because they're starving all right, and if you open those cages, it will be you on the menu." Veiron grabbed her upper arm and pulled her against his hard body, so her back pressed against his front.

Erin looked down into their dull eyes. "They're demons?"

"One of the nastier kinds," he murmured close to her ear, sending a shiver through her limbs. She barely resisted the temptation to lean back into his torso so she could feel his skin on hers.

Veiron launched a heavy boot at one of the cages, rattling it with a hard kick. The woman in it changed, brown-orange scales erupting across her flesh and her eyes burning blue as she hissed at him.

The creature spoke, lisping a language Erin didn't understand through sharp teeth and with a forked tongue.

Veiron seemed to know it. He grunted, shrugged and levelled another swift kick at the cage.

"Tell him that if he listens to you," he snarled and tugged on Erin's hand, dragging her along behind him. "We have to keep moving. It isn't safe here."

Erin wasn't about to argue but she didn't understand Veiron's sudden haste. The bruising grip he retained on her arm and the pace of his strides had her almost falling with each painful step she managed.

"I need to rest," she said and he turned dark eyes on her.

"We can't. Not now. Not here."

"Because of that thing?" She hadn't been born yesterday. "She's going to tell the Devil, isn't she?"

"The bastard won't listen to her. She would need to escape that cage and reach the bottomless pit first. The Devil's men would rip her apart before she even laid eyes on the old git."

"Those horrible black demons with the red fangs and eyes?" She shuddered from the memory of them. "I never want to see another one of those bastards again in my life."

Veiron suddenly released her arm and prowled on at a faster pace, heading up an incline. Erin tried to keep up but he was moving too quickly and her feet were killing her. Each step sent fire burning across her soles and she wasn't sure how much longer she could keep going without a rest.

"Veiron?" she said but he didn't stop. He kept going, the gap between them gradually growing, until he was more than one hundred feet ahead of her and she began to feel exposed and scared again.

Erin held herself and kept hobbling on, tears stinging her eyes. Her gaze darted around and she swore she could feel eyes on her, following her. She shivered, cold to the bone with fear, and her heart rushed in her ears.

"Veiron?" She tried again and he still didn't acknowledge her.

He disappeared over the brow of the hill. Erin panicked.

She ran despite the fire that licked her feet and the pain that jolted her bones with each step. The land beyond the hill came into view as she neared the brow and she slowed when she saw Veiron standing there, his back to her and his hands clenched into fists at his sides.

The hill ended abruptly, as though someone had carved away the other half of it. It dropped off into a valley over a hundred feet below her. Bright, boiling fire filled the world as far as her eyes could see.

"We will have to go around," Veiron said, voice deceptively calm and emotionless.

She could easily fool herself into believing that he had just gone on ahead to scout what waited on the other side of the incline but she wasn't that sort of woman. He had intended to leave her. She had put her foot in it again. Was it because she had placed them in danger by trying to free those creatures?

"I wish there was an easier way." Veiron looked down at her but she kept her gaze on the brutal landscape. There wasn't even a path. It was endless fire. "Hell is ever-changing. A few days ago, we could have passed through this way. There is nothing I can do to make this journey easier on you... if I use my powers, they will know that I am here. With that demon wailing about you, it won't take the Devil long to figure out that you're missing and that you're with me."

"What sort of powers?" She glanced at him.

He grunted and turned away. "We can follow the ridge and rest up ahead. Can you manage it, or are you going to swallow that pride of yours and let me help you?"

She would rather he answered her questions and stopped evading them.

"I'm fine," Erin said instead and began walking again, trying not to wince with each step so he had no reason to call her stubborn and force her to let him carry her. As much as she wanted to be in his arms, she didn't enjoy the prospect of being slung over his shoulder again, and his current mood said he would be carrying her that way or no way at all.

Two hundred yards down the rocky path, Veiron shocked her by speaking.

"I could teleport you out of this place," he said without looking at her. "I could materialise you boots so you didn't have to hurt your feet and clothes so you felt more comfortable. I could even produce some viable source of nourishment or perhaps even water if I focused enough... although I am not sure how good it would taste. I could do a lot of things, but the moment I use a fraction of my power, everyone will know where we are."

That wasn't so hard now, was it? Erin sighed and wished that he could do all that for her too, but it wasn't worth the risk. If Veiron not using his powers kept them off the radar of the locals and allowed them to get out of Hell unscathed, then she wasn't going to complain. She touched his left wrist and he looked at her. He had told her a little about himself and she was grateful, because she knew that he had a good heart underneath his hard lethal exterior. He had used her to illustrate his powers and that told her that he cared about her condition and he wanted to alleviate her pain. She couldn't let him use his powers, but she could let him use his strength.

"Can you carry me now?" she said and his look softened and he nodded.

Sparks of nerves danced in her stomach when he opened his thickly muscled arms to her, bent at the knee and wrapped them around her. He didn't sling her over his shoulder.

He lifted her in one arm and slid the other beneath the crook of her knees, carrying her like a princess in a fairytale.

Erin leaned her head against his bare shoulder. "Thank you."

He shrugged. "We'll be somewhere safe soon. Get some shut eye and I'll wake you when we reach it."

Erin thought she was too wired to sleep, too alert to the dangers around her, but the moment she closed her eyes and drew in a deep breath of Veiron's smell of aftershave, dirt and heat, a wave of fatigue crashed over her and the world faded away. She felt so safe in his strong arms.

CHAPTER 6

Carrying Erin like this was a mistake. A grand fucking one.

Veiron stared down at her where she lay with her head nestled so sweetly against his shoulder, face soft with sleep and beautiful despite the smudges of dirt.

He should have tossed her over his shoulder. Like this, she was a temptation, so innocent and fragile in appearance, calling to his dark need to protect her. God pity anything that crossed his path while he was holding her like a sleeping babe in his arms. He would tear them asunder with his powers regardless of the fact it would light up his position like a beacon in the Devil's mind.

He would kill without mercy to protect this delicate impish beauty.

They reached the place where he intended to rest with her and he was relieved to see that the area was intact, unaffected by the recent changes in the landscape of Hell.

He wasn't pleased about something though.

He didn't want to put Erin down or have to wake her. She had fallen asleep in under a second and clearly needed the rest. He had felt the change in her heartbeat and heard the switch in her breathing the moment her head had hit his chest.

How long had it been since she had last slept?

When was the last time she had felt safe enough to let down her guard like this?

It touched him that she trusted him, even after what she had said. Her words had cut him to the bone and he should heed them as the warning they were, that things wouldn't end well for him if he didn't start reining in the dangerous desires she stirred in him and forgot about her. She hated his breed.

Despised him without knowing it.

She never wanted to see another of his bastard kind. He could easily imagine the horror that would show in her eyes if she ever saw him in his true demonic form, and it was something he never wanted to witness.

It didn't matter that he was the one holding her now, protecting her from the cruelty around her, guiding her safely back to her sister. She would forget all that in a heartbeat, in the time it took for her to realise that he was the same as those bastards that had taken her from her home and cast her into this nightmare.

His heart ached.

If he had ever needed a reason for keeping his distance from her, this was it. Scratch his need for revenge and his mission. It was the thought of her looking upon him with hatred blazing in her beautiful amber eyes that had him emotionally taking a step back and closing himself off to her.

Veiron set her none too gently down on her feet, the action jolting her awake. She murmured and looked up at him with sleepy eyes.

"We're here," he said gruffly and didn't wait for her to fully wake before he hit the severe slope that ran into the fiery valley below.

He skidded down and dug his heels in to stop himself from going too far and passing the small outcrop of rocks that hid a small cave.

"Come on." He held his hand out to her but she looked wary, eyeing the slope with fear.

Veiron started to lose patience as she shifted at the edge of the path above him, uncertainty written in her eyes. She nibbled her lip and edged her right foot forward.

It slipped.

Erin screamed and skidded down the slope towards him, arms flailing wildly. His heart pounded, adrenaline flooding his veins, released by the thought of missing her and seeing her tumble into the flames far below. He would never let that happen. He launched both hands at her as she came close, missing her with one and snagging her wrist with the other.

She kept screaming even when her backside hit the rocky slope and she stopped moving.

Veiron hauled her up to him and she quieted. "I've got you. You're safe."

She trembled against him, hands clutching his shoulders, her breathing fast and shaky. He wrapped one arm around her and held her until her shaking subsided and her grip loosened. When she was close to calm again, he lifted her onto the small ledge beside him and followed her onto it. He motioned towards the cave.

It wasn't large, barely big enough for two people to crawl into and sit up without banging their heads, but it was safe. No creature would cross the fields of lava below them, unless they wanted their wings singed, and the rocks shielded them from view from the path above.

Erin crawled into the dark cramped cave and settled near the back. Veiron caught her fearful glance at the edge of the small ledge that separated her from a long drop to a fiery death and settled himself at the mouth of the cave, his back against one curved wall and his legs stretched across to the other. The sight of him there, blocking her fall, seemed to calm her.

He could understand her nerves. She had spent the past few weeks in a cell with only three walls and a very long fall to one of the primary rivers of Hell. The poor woman would probably spend the rest of her life afraid of high places where she felt she could fall.

"You can sleep," he said.

"What about you?" Her voice was soft in the low-lit cave.

Veiron shook his head. "I'll keep an eye on things here, and on you. You'll be safe here, Erin, and you need your rest. Once I feel you've rested enough, we'll continue. It's only another day's march from here to the gate."

Her eyes didn't brighten at that bit of news.

Erin pulled her knees up to her chest and wrapped her arms around them. "I have nightmares when I sleep."

He found that both difficult and easy to believe. She had been through a lot and seen things that would haunt her forever, but she hadn't shown any sign that she had been having a nightmare when sleeping in his arms.

"I'll keep the demons out of them too."

She smiled. "I'm not five. I doubt you can keep my nightmares away. If you can, and it's another power of yours, I wish you had been around my whole life."

"Why?"

She lowered her chin and rested it on her knees, and looked up at him through her fringe. He had thought she had looked small and fragile when sleeping in his arms. He had been wrong. The way she had curled up and was holding herself, the tone of her voice, and the trace of fear in her eyes all combined to leave her looking vulnerable, and it made him want to pull her onto his lap and wrap his arms around her. Not just because he wanted to protect her, but because he knew she was letting him see this side of her, that she wasn't this unguarded with her fears and her feelings around others, and it touched him. A kindred spirit. He hadn't realised how strongly she felt things and that she guarded her heart as fiercely as he guarded his.

Her eyes met his, open and honest, speaking to his tainted soul. "I've always had horrible dreams... the things I see... my parents even had me tested once to put all our minds at rest."

Veiron leaned towards her in the cramped cave, reached over with his right hand and brushed the black lengths of her hair from her face, hoping to comfort her. "What sort of things do you see?"

"Places like this sometimes... only worse. Horrible things that I don't want to speak about." She looked away and then closed her eyes.

"You didn't have a nightmare when you were in my arms." He wasn't sure why he put that one out there. Tormenting himself? He was the big bad hero who chased away Erin's nightmares and made everything right. Her knight in tarnished armour. Yeah, right. It didn't matter what he did, or how alike they were beneath the surface. As soon as she realised he was one of those bastards she hated so much, it would be game over and goodbye Veiron. Kill it before it started. It was the only way to save himself.

"I didn't. Can I sleep next to you?"

"Sure." Way to resist and keep that all necessary distance between them. What was it about this woman that had him going against his better judgement? It was more than her beauty and how similar they were to each other. It ran deeper than that.

Erin moved closer, flashed him a tired but grateful smile, and settled on her side with her head on his thigh. Hell. He warned the part of his anatomy that she had chosen to snuggle up right next to not to get ideas. Those dirty thoughts spinning out of control in his mind were not going to happen.

Do not touch her. Do not lay a hand on that smooth but dirty slender arm of hers and stroke it to see if her skin feels as soft as it looks. Do not.

Veiron ran his fingers along the length of her arm.

"Veiron," she whispered, his name like ambrosia to his aching soul as it fell softly from her lips. "I can't sleep. Talk to me."

"What about?" Any subject but himself. Keep it professional. Keep some distance. Any subject but himself.

"About you."

"Sure." Fuck. Why didn't he just smash his fist through his ribcage and tear out his heart right now to save himself the inevitable pain in his future?

"Are you fallen?"

He grimaced.

"You don't have to answer that if you don't want to." She tipped her head up, rolling slightly onto her back so she was looking at him. "Tell me if I'm being too nosy."

He didn't want to answer it, and she damn well was being too nosy.

"I am," he said rather than refusing her and wished she would go to sleep. He shouldn't have woken her. He should have tried to carry her down the slope. He might have made it to the ledge even with her extra weight rather than tumbling into a volcanic abyss.

Veiron looked down at the bubbling flame-filled plain below. Fiery painful death was beginning to look good but dying was off the menu. Not going to happen. Death meant rebirth, and rebirth meant a return to Heaven and forgetting everything until he fell again.

"Did they cut off your wings?" She glanced away when his gaze darted to meet hers. "You don't have to answer that."

If he didn't have to answer any of these questions, then she should stop asking them and just go to sleep.

"How do you know my sister?"

Evidently, she had taken his silence to mean he wasn't answering any questions about wings. If she knew he still had wings, she would ask what they looked like, and then it was a small leap to realising just what sort of creature's thigh she was using as a pillow.

"We had a problem in common. I helped her and Marcus deal with it."

"Is Marcus an angel too?"

"Of sorts."

She smiled. "Are all angels of sorts? You say that every time. You don't like to talk about angels, do you?"

He shook his head. It wasn't his favourite topic. Just the word had his hatred bubbling to the surface and awakened his desire to unleash every drop of his rage on Heaven and Hell.

"Do angels wear robes and fly around Heaven playing harps and singing?"

Veiron laughed. "Fuck, no. We wear armour and fly around carrying out our master's wishes with angelic weapons... and those missions often entail spilling blood in copious quantities."

"Like warriors?" She was starting to sound sleepy.

"To the core." He stroked her arm and then her black hair from her face, curling it behind her ear so he could see her face while she slept. She closed her eyes and sighed out her breath, resting her cheek against his thigh. Her right hand settled further up his leg, her heat burning through his black jeans and making him painfully aware of her proximity and touch, and how good she felt against him.

"I think you're my guardian angel," she murmured and his fingers froze against her face.

She didn't notice. A soft snore broke the heavy silence.

A guardian angel. He hadn't been one of those in centuries and he had no desire to ever become one again. Not a guardian angel. He was her demonic angel, a man driven by cold fury to pursue something that might end in his death and inevitable rebirth.

Veiron stared into the hazy heat filled distance.

When that rebirth came, he would make sure it was into a different world, one devoid of the Devil and God. They would both pay for the vicious game they played with his life against his will.

Veiron growled under his breath and then inhaled slowly, trying to calm the anger surging through his veins and threatening to seize control. It didn't matter that he was in Hell right now, under the Devil's nose, close enough to reach the bastard's fortress and have the fight he had been itching for these past centuries.

He slid his gaze to Erin where she slept softly with one hand and her head on his thigh.

He had wanted to leave her earlier when she had voiced her hatred of his kind but he hadn't been able to convince himself to go beyond the reach of his senses. He had needed to know that she was safe.

The Devil would have to wait.

His mission would have to wait.

Erin was what mattered.

Until he got her safely to her sister, she was his primary concern.

His anger subsided as he watched her, calm settling over him that only increased when he set his hand on her bare arm and felt her heat against his palm.

He watched over her, his fingers lightly running up and down her arm, waiting for a sign that her nightmares had come to rob her of sleep and torment her. She slept soundly, as still as she had been when he had carried her, as though his touch really could keep her bad dreams at bay. The only disturbances were a few deep sighs that could have been moans in the right situation and the odd flush that heated her cheeks.

Veiron grinned.

Looked like good dreams to him.

He inhaled slowly. Centuries of service in Hell had rendered him immune to the stench, letting him smell beyond it to the remnants of Erin's soft warm perfume and the undeniable hint of desire.

Very good dreams indeed. The best sort.

Her lips parted and she sighed again.

He wished that he could join her but angels didn't need to sleep when they were in their natural environment. He could close his eyes and hope that sleep would come. It wouldn't.

Veiron watched her instead, putting every pale freckle visible on her dirty skin to memory and listening to her soft steady breathing. Minutes ticked by and slowly turned into hours. Time moved as strangely in Hell as it did in Heaven. A few minutes here was hours topside. He would have to wake her soon.

A sense that they weren't alone prickled down his spine.

He stilled right down to his breathing.

Someone was close. He leaned further into the cave, hoping to conceal himself and Erin. Three Hell's angels flew by, barely two hundred feet from him and staying over the basalt slope to protect their wings from the intense heat of the boiling lake beyond. They didn't look his way but it was only a matter of time before they came back. The demon in the black plains would get their attention and tell them what she saw.

"Erin," he whispered and nudged her arm, feeling guilty for waking her. "We have to go."

"Just a few minutes more, Mum."

"Mum?" He pushed her arm again and her eyes opened.

She lay there for a few seconds and then groggily looked up at him. "I was having a really good dream."

"Tell me about it later. We have to move."

A frown creased her dirty brow and she yawned. Veiron moved his thigh out from beneath her and her head hit the dirt.

"Ow." She rubbed the side of her head and pushed herself up onto her knees, looking more alert now. "Did the bad guys find us?"

Veiron nodded. "They will soon. I'll carry you. We can head for the nearest gate."

"I thought that was a day away?" She crawled forwards and Veiron turned away so he wasn't tempted to look down her black tank top at her breasts.

He reached the ledge, stood and offered his hand to her. "The gate we should have exited through is... but this is an emergency."

She slipped her hand into his and he pulled her onto her feet and then straight up into his arms. He set her down again.

"You're not carrying me?" she said with a sleepy frown.

"I am but I can't run with you like this." He unbuckled the straps of his scabbard and let the sword fall into the cave. Erin rubbed her eyes.

"Don't you need that?" She nudged the discarded sword with her bandaged foot. "How are you meant to fight without it?"

"I'll think of a way but I'm not planning on this coming down to a fight." Because that would be a very bad idea. He didn't want Erin anywhere near a fight with one of his kind, let alone three of them. Even if he had his sword, he would still lose control if anyone went after her and then she would see him for what he was.

Erin picked up the scabbard and struggled with it, trying to get the straps on over her arms.

"What are you doing?"

"Arming myself. I don't have fancy powers." She managed to get one strap around her shoulder and started on the other.

Veiron didn't have time for this, but arguing with her would probably take longer than strapping the damn sword to her back. He tugged the straps until they were tight and the sword lay flat against her back, and buckled them. The sword was almost as tall as she was. She didn't have a snowball's chance in Hell of wielding a blade this size but the steely glint in her amber eyes said that if it came to a fight, she was damn well going to try. He had to admire her tenacity.

He crouched with his back to her. The moment she lifted her right leg, he grabbed her under her thigh and swung her up onto his back. She slipped her arms around his neck, her supple body pressing into his back, and sighed right into his ear.

This was fast becoming a day full of grand mistakes. He had thought that she would wreak less havoc if he carried her on his back, not more. The way she pressed into him and the feel of her inner thighs against his hips and her arms around his neck had him thinking about her in a reversed position, against his front, and naked. He growled at the thought of sliding his cock in and out of her hot sheath, her breathy moans in his ear and body trembling with pleasure.

"Veiron?" she murmured.

Veiron struggled to clear the image of making love to her from his head.

Something shrieked in the distance.

That did it.

He bolted up the slope to the path, clutching Erin's hot soft thighs as she clung to him for dear life. The moment he hit the flat, he broke into a sprint.

Erin moved against his back, twisting away from him.

"Veiron?" she said, a note of panic in her voice. "Can you run any faster?"

"Three of them?"

She buried her face against his back.

"No... it's more like twenty."

Veiron growled. Fuck it. Desperate times and all that shit. They already knew where he was. Maybe he could lose them or at least slow them down.

He released one of Erin's thighs and held his hand out in front of him, focusing a short distance ahead. The landscape there shimmered and distorted, and then disintegrated into curling black smoke. Erin's arms tightened to a death grip on his throat that choked him.

"What the hell is that?" she shrieked close to his ear.

Veiron grinned as the portal erupted into fierce white flames.

"Our ticket out of here."

CHAPTER 7

Erin had screamed at the top of her lungs from the moment Veiron had leapt headlong into a flaming vortex until they had exited it in another area of Hell. He hadn't stopped there. He had produced another wall that had the look of a painful death if you made even the slightest mistake and leapt straight into that one. They had done the sickening jump several times and had eventually ended up next to another of the small groups of buildings that were scattered around the black and fiery landscape of Hell.

Veiron didn't make another vortex this time. He ran with her through the village, heading up a winding wide road that led towards a plateau that had a sheer drop into the buildings on the left and a huge wall on the right.

Erin felt sick.

With all the jumping from one place to another and the fear that churned her stomach to acid, she was close to throwing up all over Veiron. She didn't think he would appreciate it.

He set her down on the wide ledge that overlooked the village and walked towards a huge stone arch cut into the sheer black wall that rose up into the endless darkness above her.

"Is this a gate?" she said, unwilling to let herself believe that she was this close to freedom until Veiron confirmed it.

He nodded. Erin's knees weakened. Veiron was there before they gave out, his arm around her waist, holding her steady. She cursed herself for looking so weak in front of him and clutched his biceps, breathing slowly to calm her feelings. A gate. She couldn't believe it. She had thought her nightmare would never end and now she was on the verge of escaping Hell.

Erin slowly raised her eyes to meet Veiron's dark ones, waiting for him to call her weak again. He didn't. His expression remained soft but intense, edged with warmth that sent her temperature rising and tempted her to drop her gaze to his mouth, lift her lips to his and kiss him.

"It isn't the gate we were supposed to use. Your sister isn't on the other side." His deep voice sent her insides trembling and increased the temptation to look at his mouth.

"Why can't you zap us to that gate?"

He shook his head, released her waist, and a solemn look entered his eyes. "Amelia and Marcus are waiting there. If I teleport to that gate, then I'll be leading the Devil's army straight to her location. I came here to save you so the Devil wouldn't find her, so he couldn't kill her."

"I get it." Erin took his hand, marvelling at how small it made hers look, and squeezed it to let him know he didn't need to explain. She understood. If they went to that gate, the demons would follow them and find Amelia. She would have to wait to see her sister again.

She stroked her thumb along the length of his. Maybe waiting wouldn't be such a bad thing, if Veiron stayed with her until he reunited her with Amelia. Erin could certainly think of some delicious ways to pass the time. Would he stay with her? His mission had been to free her from Hell. When they reached her world, that mission would be over. Wouldn't it?

"What happens when we go through the gate?" she said, struggling to get her voice above a whisper when fear of his answer squeezed her heart.

He glanced down at their joined hands, and then back into her eyes.

"When we reach the other side, we can't stop running. Hopping around might have thrown them off my scent for now, but it won't take them long to discover which gate we used. They will come after us." Veiron led her towards the huge stone arch. Liquid darkness filled it, inky and rippling, reflecting the fires of Hell that glowed behind her. "I will find a way to get you safely to Amelia."

Erin nodded and took comfort from his words. He was going to stay with her and help her and she was glad because she wasn't ready to say goodbye to him yet. The more time she spent with Veiron, the more she wanted to get to know him and unlock his secrets. He had risked everything to help her escape, had revealed himself by using his powers and placed himself in danger. She was grateful to him for that, but it wasn't the reason she wanted to kiss him as she looked up at him, lost in his dark eyes.

He had tasted so good in her dream, had felt so good as he moved above her, his eyes locked on hers, body gliding in and out, taking her to Heaven.

He scared her but he fascinated her too, and spoke to everything that was woman inside her. He was lethal beauty and deadly grace, vicious yet tender, a world of contradictions wrapped in a body that was all honed muscle and masculine strength. A body she wanted to touch and a soul she wanted to taste in a passionate kiss that she knew would ruin her to all other men.

Veiron's hand shifted. "Take a deep breath."

Erin did, but purely because it hitched when his long fingers entwined with hers, locking their hands tightly together.

He stepped into the wobbling wall of black and slowly disappeared, swallowed by it. Erin followed him, their linked hands disappearing first and her arm following it. The inky liquid was hot against her skin. She sucked in another sharp breath, closed her eyes and stepped into the gate.

Cool air froze her bare skin.

"You can open your eyes now." Veiron's deep voice curled around her, chasing the chill away.

Erin slowly opened her eyes and couldn't believe what she was seeing.

London.

She would recognise this city anywhere.

Home.

She stared out from the mouth of a narrow alley at the mixture of building styles that lined Oxford Street, the wintry cold night lost on her as the sight of her city warmed her. White lights twinkled in the leafless trees dotted along the pavements and decorations hung from lampposts that stood on small islands in the centre of the road. Shop windows declared fantastic savings in the Boxing Day sales.

When she had been taken to Hell, it had been early November. How long had she been gone?

Erin stepped out onto the wide path that lined the street and then looked back at Veiron.

"Time moves strangely in Hell," he said as though he had read her thoughts.

A passing group of men raked confused but hungry eyes over her and then raised their eyebrows at Veiron. The chill came back, numbing her bare legs and arms. Veiron didn't seem to notice the cold.

Erin looked over her shoulder at the men just as they looked back at her. Their eyes widened when they saw the sword strapped to her back.

"We should keep moving," Veiron said and before she could agree, he scooped her up into his arms.

Erin couldn't stop herself from snuggling into him, as close to his chest as she could get. He was warm, radiating heat that kept the chill off her exposed skin and she liked it. He held her close to him and strode down a side street, heading away from the main road and into the heart of the Soho district.

"Where are we going?" she said and looked up at him, studying his focused expression. He had looked stern enough when they had been in Hell. He looked even more alert now and something told her that it wasn't because he was waiting for the demons to find them again. Didn't he like it on Earth? "We could go to my place and I could get some clothes."

That got his attention. He looked down at her, eyes black in the low light from the streetlamps. She didn't need to see them clearly to feel the heat of his gaze and she didn't hide her desire from him. Getting clothes wasn't the only reason she wanted to convince him to come back to her loft apartment. In fact, they were last on the list of things she wanted to do when she got there. Number one was getting naked. Number two was getting Veiron naked. Three would take them to the shower under the pretence of getting the ash of Hell off their skin. Four would lead that passion party into the bedroom. Five was getting fresh clothes on her body, preferably the morning after a marathon lovemaking session with the sexy hunk of fallen angel who had his arms wrapped tightly around her.

"No way," he grumbled and strode on as though she had never mentioned hitting her place or suggested with a wicked smile that she would make it worth his while.

Erin blew out a sigh. How could someone so good-looking be so damn stubborn? He was fallen so he couldn't pull the virtuous thing. Surely all those morals and things people associated with angels had burned to ashes during his time in Hell?

"So where are we going?" she said and he turned down another side street, a darker one this time that had her edging closer to him. His legs hit the sword strapped to her back whenever he took a step. He wanted to avoid the bad guys but it would be the police they would have to avoid if many more people saw her walking around with a huge sword. Or being carried around anyway.

By a bare-chested dark beauty.

Her toes curled and warmth purred through her. Damn, there had to be a way to convince Veiron that hitting her place would be a really great thing.

"Veiron?" she said.

"No. Remember what happened the last time you were there? They will be monitoring your apartment."

When he put it like that.

"Will I at least be able to get some clothes where we're going? And some food and water? Basic necessities?" she snapped and his dark gaze fell to her bare legs, slid slowly over their lengths until they reached her bandaged feet, and then raked back up, lingering on her sleep shorts and top.

"I will do all I can." He didn't sound very inclined to make a sincere effort.

Erin supposed that should please her. Veiron liked her scantily clad, and freezing. It was one thing dressing like this in Hell, where it was warm and dry, but completely another when wandering around the streets of London in the middle of a cold damp winter.

"Thank you... and again, where are you taking me?"

He grinned down at her, pure sex and sin. "Cloud Nine."

Now that was a look she liked on him and a place she would gladly let him take her.

He picked up the pace, passing several clubs and bars where patrons spilled out onto the streets despite the frigid weather. They gained a few curious looks from men and women. Erin ignored them. It wasn't every day that a sword-wielding barely-dressed woman was carried past you by a topless man with the body of a god. She would have stared too.

They rounded a few more corners and ended up on a very dank narrow street. Music pounded ahead and the chatter of people rose above it. Lots of people.

Veiron didn't slow when he turned the next corner. A queue lined one side of the street, flowing towards her from the bright neon sign on the featureless brick wall of Cloud Nine. Half-dressed men and women cast dirty looks her way. Judging by their appearances, she and Veiron were going to fit right in if they made it into the club. A three hundred plus pound bouncer blocked the door, a mountainous man who almost made Veiron look small in comparison. That was until Veiron strode right up to him, towering a good six inches taller and a few inches wider.

The man didn't give Veiron a dirty look. The black look in his dull pale eyes was positively friendly compared with the one he cast at her.

"Sinking low, my man." His voice was so deep it rumbled through her.

Erin glared at him.

"Mind your tongue," Veiron snarled and the man shrugged thick hewn shoulders and grunted as he shifted aside enough for Veiron to pass.

Veiron kicked the black doors open and music assaulted her, ear-splitting in volume and with bass so heavy it pounded in her chest and made her feel sick. She covered one ear with her hand and pressed the other against Veiron's bare chest. His heart thumped steadily against it.

He manoeuvred through the dense crowd with her, his height giving her a clear view over the heads of most of the patrons to the dance floor. Dear God. What sort of pervert club was this? There was a little more than the usual groping and snogging going on. The men and women on the dance floor were close to taking things deep into the indecent exposure list of crimes.

Veiron covered her eyes.

It was too late. The sight of the near-orgy happening on the dance floor was seared on her eyeballs.

She grabbed his arm and pulled his hand away from her eyes. He scowled down at her. A threat? Was she supposed to interpret that look as a warning not to gawp at the perversion playing out all around her?

Score two for Erin. She had the man jealous. Why couldn't she get the man naked? That was what she wanted to know.

He strolled through the crowd and Erin watched how they parted, fascinated by their reactions to Veiron. As he approached, everyone turned to stare at him, fear in their eyes, and moved aside, giving him a wide berth. She looked up at his face. He was scowling and his eyes looked crimson in the flashing lights of the club. Not just the usual touch of red that edged them at times, but complete saturation.

Veiron's gaze remained firmly fixed ahead. They walked in line with the long curved black bar to his right. Bright colourful bottles lined the mirrored wall behind it and spotlights switched from white to blue to purple to red, washing the bartenders in those colours. Erin caught sight of her reflection, and frowned. She looked around and stared at a beautiful dark-haired woman as she passed. This one didn't look afraid of Veiron.

The woman tossed a flirty smile in his direction. Veiron didn't seem to notice.

Another one further in tried her luck but Veiron turned away and set Erin down beside the bar, his back to the blonde beauty. Erin positively seethed. What had the world come to when a man carrying a woman was still a target for whores?

Bitches.

Veiron leaned across Erin, his body shielding her from the brunt of the crowd, and flagged one of the bartenders, a young handsome brunet. "Water."

Erin closed her eyes and melted at the thought. Water. She had never been one for her eight glasses a day but she had found a new love for plain boring water.

The man slid a tall cold glass across the black bar top to her. Erin stared at the clear liquid, mesmerised and deeply in love. She wasn't sure whether to drink it in one gulp or savour it slowly like a fine wine.

She grabbed the glass and gulped it down. The cold hurt her teeth but she didn't care. Veiron chuckled and she stopped, and slid her gaze across to him. He smiled at her, devastating, too sexy for words, and reached out. His hand was warm against her face and tender as he brushed his thumb across her cheek.

"Do you want to clean up?"

Did she ever. Even what was likely to be a grotty club bathroom seemed like a luxury spa to her right now.

"I'll take that dreamy smile as a yes," he said with a smile of his own and motioned to the bartender again. The man returned with a whole pitcher of icy water this time.

"On the house, Vay." He grinned across the bar top at her. "You look as though you need it."

Veiron grabbed him before he could leave. "You seen V around here tonight?"
The man nodded and pointed further along the bar.
"My gratitude, my man." Veiron patted him on the back.
"So, Vay, who's V?" Erin grinned when he scowled at her. "I take it I'm not allowed to call you Vay?"
He shrugged. "I would rather you called me Veiron."
Erin frowned and poured herself another glass of water. "Be like that."
Veiron huffed. "God Almighty, you are infuriating. It isn't like that." He rested an elbow on the black bar top, bringing him down to close to her height. "I don't really like the nickname. Satisfied?"
"Not really. Why let people call you it if you don't like it?" People had tried to pin her with nicknames and she had shot them all down, even the pet names her parents had used for her. Erin was a perfectly good name. Amelia didn't seem to mind when people shortened her name. Each to their own.
"It pays to be friendly sometimes." He sighed and scratched the thick stubble coating his straight jaw. What would he look like without those whiskers? He was handsome enough with them. Without them, he could probably lay waste to women with just a wink and a smile. "I'm not exactly welcome here."
"Now I'm satisfied. So who is V?" She swigged her water, the cool liquid like bliss on her tongue and parched throat. She never wanted to drink anything other than fresh cold water for the rest of her life.
"Someone I don't want you to meet but I think it wise that we stick together, at least until I know it's safe here." He straightened, his dark expression conveying the equally black feelings behind his words. Not jealousy this time. Not fear. A strange mixture of those two emotions, plus wariness and other ones that made him look as though keeping her with him was a struggle and all he wanted to do was keep her out of sight while he spoke to this V character.
He took a deep breath, his broad honed chest expanding deliciously with it and shattering her serious thoughts, and then waved a hand over his head. The action was more like a command, the sort of click of fingers you gave to a dog to get its attention.
Erin turned to see who he was signalling and found herself only a few inches from a pale, sharply dressed dark-haired man. His crisp black suit didn't quite fit with the club, at odds with the scantily clad men and women. The man's pale eyes slid down to her and his dusky lips curved into a sensual smile.
Veiron's arm closed over her chest and he dragged her back against him.
"V," he growled and the man's icy gaze shifted up to him.
The man called V offered him a toothy smile that revealed canines that were either fakes or real and she was about to add vampire to the list of supernatural creatures that existed. After everything she had witnessed in Hell, nothing surprised her anymore. Vampires were probably just another type of demon after all, and she had catalogued plenty of different breeds of that particular species while waiting in her cell for visitors. The man in front of her was a vampire and the man at her back was a fallen angel, and who knew what else lurked in the club?

"Veiron. To what do I owe the pleasure? If the boss sees you here, she will not be pleased. You know her policy. No angels allowed, even if they are serving the right master."

"Choose your words more wisely, Villandry, or we shall come to blows." Veiron's arm tightened across her chest and the vampire looked down at her, all charm as he smiled.

"I never thought mortal females would be your style. She's pretty, I'll grant you that, but last I recalled your tastes were a little more wicked... like mine." Villandry raked his pale eyes over her and then curled his lip in disgust. "You know, I still haven't forgiven you for storming into my home and nearly exposing me to sunlight."

"I apologised, didn't I? It's the most you're going to get out of me, so get over it. It isn't why I'm here. I have a business proposition. I need you to keep your ear to the ground and let me know if you hear about anything major leaving Hell in the next few days."

Erin frowned. Had they come to blows over a past lover? Erin didn't like the thought of Veiron fighting for another woman. She tried to break free of his embrace but he tightened his grasp and held her firm, pinning her back against the solid heat of his front.

"Sounds dangerous, and expensive." Villandry signalled the bartender. A pretty thirty-something blonde woman came straight to him and set a martini glass filled with dark liquid down on the bar. He smiled at Erin, lifted the glass to his lips and drained it in one go. He set the empty glass back down on the bar. "I want her."

Veiron snarled and his grip on her shoulder tightened. "No fucking way."

"I admit, I had said that I wouldn't date your cast offs again, but this one is mortal and I would make our few short hours together pleasurable."

"Please." Erin resisted the temptation to hold onto Veiron's arm across her chest for comfort and courage, glad now that she hadn't managed to escape his hold. "I wouldn't screw you if you were the last... thing... on Earth or in Hell. Sleazeball."

"Erin." Her name was a low warning curling from Veiron's lips and she leaned back against him, afraid that she had pushed the man opposite her too far. His eyes began to darken, the paleness swirling together with what looked like pure black under the flashing coloured lights. "She is tired. You could say she has been through Hell."

That was a poor joke. She rolled her eyes at it.

The vampire still didn't look pleased.

"I am sure we can come to some agreement. I will keep my ears and eyes open and will have my men do the same. If anything comes here looking for a tasty little human and her escort, I will let you know." Villandry waved to the woman serving behind the bar again.

"Thank you." Veiron managed to growl those words in a voice that said quite the opposite. He wasn't grateful at all to the vampire and his death grip on her shoulder conveyed a deep desire to make the man pay in a very painful way for requesting her as his remuneration for services rendered. "Does Taylor still live in London with Wingless?"

Who was Taylor and who was Wingless?

Erin turned to look up at Veiron to ask him that question but her gaze caught on someone who chilled her more than the Devil.

She shrank back into Veiron's embrace, trying to avoid the man laughing and talking to two women across the room. People streamed between them but he would only have to glance her way at the right time and he would spot her just as she had spotted him. She had already gone through Hell. Couldn't someone up there cut her a break? She hadn't seen her ex in close to three years, since he had got drunk at her twenty-seventh birthday party and made a pass at Amelia, and four of her friends. Her sister had lousy luck with men but it looked stellar compared with Erin's own run of worthless boyfriends.

Her gaze shot over the heads of the crowd and found the pink neon sign for the women's bathroom. Safety. She could hide there and clean up while Veiron finished his conversation with the vampire. He could come and get her when he was done and they could hightail it out of the club together.

A larger group of people entered the club and began drifting through it towards her. It was her chance.

"I'm going to use the bathroom," she said it loud enough for Veiron to hear.

He nodded and Erin made a break for it, merging with the group.

She was halfway to the bathroom when someone grabbed her arm. Tightly. She thought it was Veiron changed his mind about her being alone in the club but the hand on her arm was too small. Erin slowly turned to find her ex, Adam, staring in horror at her clothes. His look only worsened when his dark eyes reached her face. She probably looked as though she had been caught in a volcanic blast and had starved while escaping.

The roughly chopped lengths of his dark hair hung over one side of his face as he gave her another once over and his grip on her arm tightened when he reached her bandaged feet.

"What on Earth happened to you?"

Erin wasn't sure how to explain everything she had just been through without sounding as though she was crazy and she didn't feel the need to explain herself to him anyway. She had called Villandry a sleazeball but he wasn't a patch on this man.

"Get your hand off me." Erin tried to twist free of his grasp.

He dug his fingers in even harder. "No, Erin. I want to know what happened. Christ, your face... your legs... where did you pick up all those bruises and cuts?"

"Seriously, Adam, get your damn hand off me!" It came out louder than she had intended and several people nearby stopped to look at them.

Adam pulled on her arm when she struggled and she clawed at his hand, trying to prise it off her. He was hurting her.

A deep growl curled out over the music.

The entire room froze.

CHAPTER 8

Veiron needed to work on his impulse control.

He knew it, and so did the hundred people who had stopped dead and turned to stare at him when he had unleashed an ungodly snarl in Erin's direction.

Villandry made a grab for his arm to stop him but Veiron easily shook the vampire off and stalked across the rapidly draining club to the man who had dared lay his filthy hands on Erin and upset her.

Erin paled as he approached, her amber eyes going impossibly wide. The human male with his hand on her seemed frozen in time, his fingers locked around Erin's slender wrist and his back to Veiron.

Big mistake.

The man should have remained cognitive enough to get his fucking hands off Erin and get the hell out of Dodge with the rest of the mortals in the club crowd.

Veiron came up behind him and politely tapped him on the shoulder.

The mortal male turned slowly and looked up at him.

"I think it would be best if you did as she asked and removed your hand from her arm before I remove it for you... and I mean that literally. I'll give you one second to take your hand off her or I'll chop the damn thing off." Veiron grinned down at the little man, showing him that he was serious. He might have reined in his temper enough to speak to the flea without going nuclear on his arse but the tethers holding his rage at bay were beginning to twist and snap.

He didn't want to lose it, not when it would reveal himself to Erin and place her in danger by alerting any of his kind nearby to his location.

The man released Erin's arm but didn't back down. He did the one thing in the situation that was guaranteed to push the button on the detonator of Veiron's anger.

He squared up to Veiron.

"Did you do this to her?" the man positively growled the words and Veiron frowned down at him. One of the tethers on his rage pinged and snapped. Three more and this man was dead. "What sort of sick fuck beats a woman?"

Veiron's blood boiled. He might be a Hell's angel but he would never hurt Erin. He would never lay a finger on her in that way. He snarled. Erin looked as though she wanted to say something to defuse the situation but it was too late.

Ping. Ping. Ping. And his rage was free.

Veiron growled, locked his hand around the mortal's throat, turned with him, and drove him across the room until his back slammed into the curved black bar.

He bent over the man, tightening his hold on his puny neck, and lowered his face so all the man could see was the fury blazing in his now red eyes. Veiron growled low in his throat again, the feral sound rumbling through him, and felt his teeth shift to sharp crimson points and the skin around his eyes begin to blacken. The voice of reason at the back of his head screamed on repeat that he needed to calm the fuck down. The voice of pure primal rage obliterated it.

This man would pay.

The mortal panted beneath him, skin blanched and eyes staring in wild terror into Veiron's red ones. His heart hammered, a jittery beat that made Veiron's smile widen. He should fear. By the time Veiron finished with him, he would be pissing his pants.

Veiron shoved the man down into the tacky bar top, forcing him to bend backwards at a harsh angle. The mortal rallied and swung a punch at Veiron's shoulder. Veiron felt nothing. He grasped the man's wrist, twisted it until he screamed, and snarled in satisfaction.

"You ever... touch her again... it will be the last... thing you do. Do you... understand?" It was hard to form sentences when his head was pounding, blood rushing like a torrent through his ears, and he was trying to fight his desire to change completely and rip the man to shreds with his bare hands and trying to retain a little sanity so Erin didn't see him for what he was.

She couldn't see his face from where she stood, couldn't see what this man did when he stared into Veiron's fiery red eyes and saw the darkness around them and his sharp red teeth.

The lights above the bar dimmed, the area around him darkening as his rage began to slip beyond his control. Veiron sneered, flashing his fangs at the petrified mortal, relishing the gasp he released and the way his heart skipped several beats.

"Please don't kill me." Those words were jittery, quiet, a plea that spoke to his sane side and said that he should be satisfied now. He had the mortal quaking. Let him go.

No.

Veiron squeezed his throat harder, feeling bones creak and muscle bruise. The mortal choked and gasped, wheezed as he tried to breathe.

"Veiron?" Erin's soft voice reached out to him.

No.

He shook away the part of him that felt soothed by her voice and growled in the man's face.

"Veiron!" The sharper female voice and the cool hand that firmly grabbed his shoulder had him shutting down his anger in an instant because he knew what was coming next and he couldn't allow Erin to see his face as it was now.

The woman hauled him to face her and his gaze flicked to Erin where she stood a few feet behind her. She looked horrified. Veiron cast his eyes down at the floor, not wanting to see in hers that she already thought he was a monster.

A demon.

"Do I need to remind you of my club's rules?" the blonde in front of him snapped and swept the short strands of hair from her face with a defiant flick.

Her dark gaze locked with his.

Veiron shook his head and released his stranglehold on the piece of shit human male. The last thing he wanted to do was piss off the boss. She was fine when she was in a good mood, but when she lost her temper, her true appearance shifted over her skin, all scales and ugliness, and she could tear even the strongest angel a new one.

The man spluttered and coughed, and wheezed.

Veiron strode across the club, grabbed Erin's hand, turned towards the doors and growled at the man on his way past. The human's knees gave out and he crashed to the floor. Erin stumbled along behind Veiron. He knew his pace was too quick for her when her feet were sore from trekking through Hell but he needed fresh cold night air in his lungs to quell the heat of his rage.

"We have to leave." Veiron shoved the double doors open. A few mortals and demons in their human forms milled around in the alley outside the club. They all backed away when they set eyes on him, giving him space. Probably the wisest thing they had done in their short or long lives.

He didn't slow until he was three streets away from Cloud Nine. Each breath of cool fresh air soothed a little more of his anger and brought with it painful awareness of what he had done.

He had lost it.

He had exposed them both because of his inability to keep a lid on his temper where this woman was concerned.

His focus shifted to Erin. She felt shocked on his senses and he could hear her heart racing, and feel her hand trembling in his.

"I'm sorry." Those were the words he had always found hardest to say but they came so easily tonight. "I didn't mean to scare you."

"It's okay," she whispered and then her voice grew stronger. "He deserved it."

"Who was he?" Part of Veiron feared the answer to that question. He had a feeling he knew what that man had once been to Erin and the thought that he had been allowed to touch her, to taste her and do everything with her that Veiron denied himself, had his chest burning and blood heating to a rolling boil.

Erin was his.

Erin was not his.

She was just a mission. As soon as he got her safely to her sister, he was gone. Goodbye. Sayonara. Have a great life. Erin was a complication that he didn't need. She made him weak when he needed to be strong and keep a level head. He hadn't spent the past few centuries plotting his revenge only to throw it away now that he was so close to seeing all his plans come to fruition.

"I went out with him a few years ago. It wasn't my greatest hour. I dumped him after he hit on my sister and friends at my twenty-seventh birthday night out."

He felt her shrug, as though it was nothing, but he heard the truth in her heart and the glimmer of her emotions that he could sense. The man had hurt her. He had betrayed her trust and her love.

Veiron wanted to kill him.

He kept his face turned away from Erin so she couldn't see the change as it came over him, turning his eyes red and teeth crimson and sharp.

"We need to get off the street," he said but it came out as more of a snarl and Erin's hand tensed in his. He cleared his throat, reined his anger in, and tried to sound more normal. "I know a place where we might find sanctuary."

Veiron stopped and looked down at Erin's feet and her bare legs. She was shivering again and it wasn't out of fear this time. The night was cold against his chest and back too. Sharing body heat sounded like a reasonable way of keeping warm.

"Come on," he said and crouched with his back to her.

Erin climbed up onto him, her soft body pressing into his back and her thighs against his hips. Devil, she did feel good right there, snuggled close to him. She settled her arms on his shoulders as he straightened, his hands under her thighs, supporting her.

Veiron blew out his breath at the feel of her fingers sweeping across his shoulders and then down them. They paused and he kept walking, concentrating on the action to purge his desire to absorb the warmth and softness of her caress. If he didn't focus, his wings were likely to erupt from his back and knock her flying.

Not the way he wanted her to see them for the first time.

Her fingers drifted over his biceps and then followed the sweeping curves of his tattoos to his back. She held onto him with her left hand and traced the tattoo on his right shoulder blade with her other one.

"They're very beautiful," she whispered, voice soft but not from her concentrating on his tattoos and being absorbed in following the design with her fingers.

There was desire in that voice, hunger in her tone that made him wonder if she was thinking about running something other than her fingers over his back.

Just the thought of her sweeping her tongue over his tattoos had him hardening painfully in his tight black jeans.

"Thank you," he uttered, distracted by his thoughts and how good she felt against him.

He fought the urge to turn down the next dark alley, drag her around to his front, pin her to the wall and scratch the itch he had for her.

If he could just scratch that itch, that dark hunger to know her taste and her body, he was sure that he could get her out of his mind and get it back on his real mission.

Wasn't going to happen.

Veiron plodded on, hands burning where they touched her bare legs so close to her bottom, mind racing as she continued to swirl her fingers around every curl and along every spike of his tattooed right shoulder.

A shiver raced across his back and it had nothing to do with Erin's touch this time.

"Hold on," he said.

Time to run again.

He pounded the pavement with Erin clutching his shoulders, her rapid pulse thumping in his mind, whispering her fear to him.

"How many?" He felt her twist, knew she was looking back.

"Just three."

He liked the way she said that. Just three. Like three Hell's angels were nothing for them. They could handle such a paltry number.

He could, but with Erin around, he would be distracted, concerned that she might end up dragged into the fight somehow and injured.

"Veiron... they're flying."

That was just cheating.

Two could play at that game.

Veiron stopped, pulled Erin around so she was against his front, and started running again.

His wings burst from his back, he ran up the back of a parked car, boots denting the trunk and roof, and launched himself into the air.

Erin gasped.

Cold night air swept through his crimson feathers as he beat his wings, carrying them higher into the alley.

"You have wings. How do you have wings? You said you didn't have wings!"

"No, you thought I didn't have wings." Veiron flapped them harder. Stay red. Please stay red. When his mood was degenerating as rapidly into anger and violence as it was now, it was normally impossible to keep the feathers on his wings. "This really isn't the time for this argument."

Erin mercifully remained quiet.

Veiron's red gaze darted around, searching for the right direction. If he could get Erin to Taylor's, he might be able to set her down and tell her to ring the bell and ask Wingless for help while he drew the Hell's angels away.

He spotted the small square near Taylor and Wingless's home and shot towards it. The enemy were gaining on him.

"How close?" he said over the noise of the wind.

Erin shivered against him, her body freezing under his hands. "Too close. They're practically on us."

"Fuck." Veiron dived, heading back to street level, and beat his wings, desperate to put some distance between them and their pursuers. Erin tensed in his arms and buried her face against his throat. He levelled off but didn't slow down. "Listen. I'm going to put you down and draw them away."

"No." She threw her arms around his neck and locked her legs around his hips. "No. I don't want you to ditch me."

"Stubborn," he growled and tried to prise her off him but she did the most marvellous impression of a limpet he had ever seen. He couldn't shift her without using more of his strength and he wouldn't risk hurting her by doing so. "Fine. Change of plans. I'll set us both down. You hide behind one of the parked cars on the street and I'll fight the bad guys."

"Liar." She snarled the word at him. "You're going to ditch me."

He was. He didn't have time to argue about it either.

Veiron hit the ground running, furled his crimson wings against his back, and peeled her off him. She tried to hold on but relented when she looked over his shoulder. They were closer now. He could feel them.

Her feet hit the pavement next to a parked black four-wheel-drive vehicle. It was tall enough to conceal her while he fought their three enemies. Erin reached over behind her with both hands and tried to pull the sword out of the scabbard.

"What are you doing?" he said and she grunted, her face screwing up in frustration. She managed to get the sword up several inches but then a flaw in her plan showed itself. Her arms weren't long enough to draw the sword.

"You need this so you can fight."

Veiron smiled, drew the sword for her, and handed it to her. She frowned at it and then up into his eyes.

"A mortal sword will be of no use to me in this fight... and I have already revealed myself to them. I might as well use a weapon I favour." He held his right hand out beside him and a black staff materialised in his hand.

Red patterns decorated the short black rod and red curved blades appeared at each end. The staff itself was only the length of his forearm as it was now, the blades equally as long, but he could increase the length of the rod if he needed more room in the fight.

"Stay here." Veiron touched her dirty cheek. She didn't look at him. She was staring at his hand and the spear he grasped as though he had just performed the most amazing magic trick.

Hey presto.

She should see some of the other things he could do.

Veiron beat his wings and flew over the square.

The Hell's angels appeared and split up as soon as they spotted him, one diving off to his left, the second to his right, and the third heading straight for him.

All three of them were in their true form, making them larger than he was, huge black-skinned beasts with dragon-like wings. The yellow streetlamps reflected off their obsidian armour, draining the colour from the scarlet edging on their breastplates, greaves and the vambraces that protected their forearms.

He wished he could call his own armour but Erin was watching him from the shadow of the Range Rover and if she saw his armour, she would realise that he was like these creatures.

Veiron held the short staff of his double-ended spear in both hands and slashed at the first demonic angel as he lunged at Veiron with his black sword. Veiron knocked the blade aside and snarled as he sliced across the angel's thick black arm. The angel roared at him and attacked again, quicker this time, and Veiron struggled to counter each strike that drove him backwards through the air. His senses blared a second before a blade cut down his back, narrowly missing his wings.

He cried out and Erin shouted his name.

Foolish woman.

One of the angels turned her way and zipped towards her.

Like hell Veiron was letting him near her.

Veiron beat his wings and shot after the demonic angel, the cold air buffeting him. He extended the staff of his weapon and swung with it, catching the man hard in the waist and sending him careening through the air. The angel crashed into a parked car up the street, the sound of the impact echoing around the Georgian townhouses lining the square and the shockwave sending the alarm of every vehicle in the area shrieking.

Veiron hit the pavement, took two strides, and grabbed Erin around her waist. She gasped and he kicked off, shooting into the air again with a single strong flap of his crimson wings.

The sword fell from her hands and hit the pavement with a clang.

Veiron scoured the area for a safe place for her. The two conscious angels chased him, their leathery wings creating eerie noises amongst the wailing car alarms. There was another square up ahead. The one he had hoped to reach without incident. He couldn't fight there. It was too close to where he wanted to take Erin once they had lost their tail.

They needed somewhere else.

Veiron held his hand out in front of him and a bright fiery portal appeared. He shot through it, holding Erin close to his chest, and came out near the broad black swath of the River Thames.

He set Erin down on the pavement under a pedestrian bridge next to the river.

"Stay in the shadows." Veiron went to leave and then came back to her. He laid his hand on her cheek, feeling her shaking, and looked deep into her eyes. "Don't hate me."

Before she could ask why, he ran a few paces and took off again, using his wings to carry himself high into the air where she hopefully wouldn't see what he was about to become.

He couldn't fight the demonic angels off as he was. His true appearance unleashed his full strength and power. He needed that if he was going to protect Erin.

The first demonic angel appeared through a vicious orange streak in the sky, scanned the darkness, and spotted him. The second tore a rip in the world a few hundred yards further away. Just the two of them.

Maybe he wouldn't need to go nuclear after all.

Veiron beat his scarlet wings and caught the second angel unawares, cutting him across the neck and then following through by twisting his double-ended blade and slicing down his back. The blade caught the male's left wing, tearing through the leathery membrane, and he shrieked and plummeted into the river. A bright orange glow lit the water as it boiled, telling Veiron that the angel had returned to Hell to heal.

That left him with one.

Veiron grinned and turned to face the remaining demonic angel.

Erin screamed.

CHAPTER 9

Veiron's gaze snapped down and his heart stilled, sharp claws squeezing it tightly. The angel he had tossed into the car was back and had Erin in a chokehold from behind. She yanked on his thick arm with both of her hands, gasping for air, her amber eyes wild with panic and fear that Veiron could feel in his blood. The large black demonic man clawed across her arm and chest, cutting deep into her flesh.

Veiron saw red.

He flung his arms back and roared. His skin darkened to black and his form changed, limbs growing and muscles expanding. The red dripped from his wings, revealing black feathers beneath that fell away in clumps, exposing the leathery membrane of his real wings.

Obsidian armour appeared on his huge body, encasing his chest and back at first. His black loincloth followed next, replacing his ruined jeans. His boots disappeared and black and red ones took their place. His greaves appeared, the crimson-edged jet plates protecting his shins. Finally, his vambraces melted into existence on his forearms.

The blades of his spear glowed red.

Veiron launched forwards, grasped his blade with both hands, and attacked the angel nearest to him. He dodged the strike of the man's black sword, shoved one blade into his stomach, and flipped himself over his back. The red-hot blade of Veiron's spear sliced out of the angel's gut and Veiron landed on his wings. The Hell's angel dropped from the sky with Veiron on his back. Veiron snarled and plunged the other blade of his spear through the man's back, and then kicked off, leaving him to hit the pavement with such force that it formed a crater and a plume of dust rose into the air.

He snarled and shot towards the angel still attacking Erin. The smell of her blood assaulted his senses and he lost control.

Veiron landed hard, shaking the ground, sprinted at the angel and punched straight through the back plate of his obsidian armour. The man shrieked and released Erin. She dropped to the floor in a heap.

Veiron lifted the man, his hand closing around his spine, and slammed him hard into the wall of the bridge. He smashed him against it again, causing shards of brick and dust to rain down on the pavement, and then again. The angel struggled and writhed, clawing at him and trying to beat him away with his wings.

One of them struck Veiron in the face, cutting across his cheek. He growled, grabbed the leathery wing, and snapped it.

The demonic angel's shrieks annoyed him so Veiron closed his hand over the man's mouth, suffocating him at the same time. His struggling slowed and Veiron grinned as the man began to change back into his human form.

Veiron snarled. "Give God my regards."

He snapped the man's neck.

His red gaze fell to Erin.

Her eyes were on him.

Veiron dropped the body and shook the blood from his hands. White light burst against the darkness and disappeared just as quickly, leaving no trace of the man behind. He would be back in Heaven by now, being reborn as an angel.

Veiron's skin paled again, muscles shrinking and body returning to his normal appearance. His armour disappeared and he called his jeans to him and his boots. He called his leather jacket too. Erin would need it to keep her warm.

"Erin?" he whispered and her eyelids drooped.

She struggled to open them again.

He crouched beside her where she lay on the pavement. A torrent of crimson flowed from the deep wounds across her chest. His stomach turned and he used his powers to produce crepe bandages out of the air. He bent over her, carefully raised her off the ground and set one end of the roll of bandage against her back. She moaned and twitched as he tightly wrapped the bandage over her shoulder and across her chest. It turned red each time it passed over the wound, blood instantly soaking through the pale cream material. She was losing too much but it was all he could do and he could only hope it would stem the bleeding enough to buy her and himself enough time.

She groaned and grimaced, her blood-streaked face contorting in pain he could feel flowing through him.

"I'm sorry. I need to make sure it's tight." He kept his voice low and soothing. Her brow crinkled and her whole body tensed in spasm. He paused and stroked her cheek with one trembling hand, trying to relax her so he could finish tending to her wound. She slumped again and her breathing slowed. Veiron growled. "You stay with me... you hear me, Erin?"

She didn't respond. He quickly finished bandaging her wound, laid her down and pressed one hand against the wad of material over her chest, applying as much pressure as he could without breaking her ribs.

"Erin?" He patted her bloodstained cheek. "Wake up. Don't go to sleep. Don't leave me."

She murmured something and relief beat through his blood. He had to get her to Wingless and fast. Taylor's angel lover was fallen but he still had the power to heal.

Veiron carefully slipped his beaten up leather on Erin's small frame and picked her up. He focused so his leathery wings shrank into his back and called a portal. He couldn't use it to go to Taylor's house but he could exit somewhere close to it. He stepped through it and out into the square where he had tossed the angel into a car. The alarms were silent now but there were people out on the street. Not the sort of audience he needed when he was carrying a bleeding woman.

"Stay with me, Erin," he whispered to her and her head lolled backwards. He jostled her carefully so she was more comfortable. "You hear me? You fight. Don't you dare give up."

She mumbled again, a welcome sign that she was still with him. He called another portal and then let it disappear. Hopefully the angels the Devil sent to track him would think he had gone through it.

He crossed the street and stuck to the shadows as he walked swiftly towards the next street. He couldn't run when Erin was injured. He stared down at her, gaze constantly on her ashen bloodied face. His heart pounded in his ears. His own injuries stung but he ignored them, focusing everything on her. He wasn't important. She was.

She had to be all right.

He carried on at a brisk pace through the next square and then along another elegant street full of Georgian townhouses. They towered over him, three storeys above ground and one below. Expensive cars lined the streets outside them, marking the affluence of the neighbourhood his ex-lover had chosen as her new home.

Veiron shoved the black wrought iron gate on one of the townhouses open and carried Erin along the path to the porch. He took the stone steps up to the wide black door and knocked with his foot. Loudly.

His eyes darted back down to Erin, monitoring her for a sign that he was losing her.

"Keep fighting, Sweetheart," he whispered and held her closer.

She was tougher than his spinning mind gave her credit for. She had to be. The smell of her blood choked him. He could feel it on his hands and hear it dripping down her back. He had probably left a trail to Taylor's house but he didn't care anymore.

He kicked the door again and growled.

They had to be in.

He clutched Erin to him, hating how fragile and pale she looked in his arms.

A light finally appeared through the stained glass on either side of the large black door. It swung open.

Taylor stood before him, dressed in her favourite black jeans, heeled boots and t-shirt combo, her sleek black hair tied in a ponytail and her blue eyes conveying her annoyance.

"What the hell are you doing here?" she snapped, shoved one hand against her hip and cocked her head to one side.

"I don't have time for this. Tear me a new one some other time." He tried to get past her and she stepped into his path, blocking his attempt. His eyes blazed red. "She's going to die."

Taylor looked down and her blue eyes widened.

Wingless, known to everyone other than Veiron and Villandry as Einar, appeared behind her, his broad frame almost filling the doorway and obscuring the foyer behind him. The tawny-haired male's rich brown eyes locked with Veiron's briefly before falling to Erin and narrowing. He touched Taylor's shoulder and she moved aside but not enough that Veiron could enter with Erin. Veiron growled at her.

"We need to get her upstairs." Einar herded Taylor out of the way so Veiron could pass her. He was grateful to the fallen angel and ignored Taylor's glare. If she had tried to turn him away, he wasn't sure what he would have done, but it would have been ugly. Erin's life depended on Einar now. Veiron didn't know anyone else who had the power to heal such savage wounds.

Veiron followed Einar across the marble foyer and up the elegant wooden rectangular staircase, taking care as he turned each corner so he didn't bang Erin's head. Einar looked over his broad black-clad shoulders at Erin, his brown eyes awash with concern.

"She is mortal," he said and Veiron nodded, knowing all too well what that meant now. Such an injury wouldn't be a problem for his kind but it was deadly to her.

They reached a floor with a large living room. Oil paintings hung on the deep red walls and dark antique furniture cluttered it despite the expansive size. Masses of weaponry occupied a large oak table and one of the sofas.

"Set her down here." Einar arranged some pillows at the end of an empty couch, close to the roaring fire. Veiron carefully carried Erin across the room and gently laid her down. He cleared the black hair from her face and frowned at how pale she looked despite the warm glow from the fire.

She had to be all right. She couldn't die. He wouldn't let her.

"Just you keep fighting, you hear me?" he whispered, gaze darting around her face for a sign that she had. Her brow puckered and then relaxed. Veiron stroked her cheek, unable to deny his need to touch her and feel she was solid, alive, still with him.

Einar squeezed his shoulder. "I will need room to work."

Veiron nodded and reluctantly left her side.

He stepped back, giving Wingless the room he needed to perform what would be a miracle. Erin had to live.

He felt Taylor enter the living room but didn't turn to acknowledge her. His gaze remained rooted on Erin.

Einar removed the leather jacket and handed it to Veiron. He couldn't hold it. It was bad enough seeing the blood on her, let alone feeling how much of the precious life giving liquid drenched his leather.

He set it down on the small wooden coffee table between the two sofas.

Einar picked up one of the knives off the table and cut away the bloodstained bandages around Erin's chest. He hissed a ripe curse and Veiron joined him. The wounds looked worse in the light, deep gouges that were still seeping rivulets.

Taylor rounded the back of the couch where Erin lay and frowned down at her.

"Who is she? Someone you picked up at a bar and got a little too rough with?" Taylor shot him an accusatory glare.

Veiron growled a warning. He was getting sick of people accusing him of hurting Erin when all he had done since meeting her was try to protect her.

"It was Hell's angels. I had it under control but one of them survived and went after her." Veiron's hands shook as Einar crouched next to Erin, closed his eyes and held his hands out above her injury. Pale golden light filtered down from the fallen angel's palms.

Veiron held his breath.

This had to work.

"How do you know her?"

Veiron ignored the question.

Einar huffed. "Can we save the interrogation for later, Taylor? I need to concentrate."

She pouted, went to the oak table, and began cleaning one of the guns.

Veiron's gaze followed every move that Einar made. He had never liked the former angel before but he loved the man now. He vowed never to call him Wingless again. At least not to his face. If he could pull this off, Veiron might just kiss him.

Einar grunted and frowned. His hands wavered. Veiron's nerves got the better of him. He moved around the sofa to the back and started pacing, taking agitated strides across the rugs on the wooden floor, trying to expel the sense of uselessness and tension from his tight body before he exploded.

Taylor's eyes followed him, burning with curiosity.

Einar was right. Questions could come later and he would answer any they had. Right now, everyone needed to focus on Erin. Her life was on the line and it wasn't the thought of facing Amelia and telling her that her sister was dead that had him silently praying that she would pull through. He couldn't lose her.

Veiron dug his fingers into his long red hair, tugging it loose from his ponytail.

Erin looked so small and weak on Einar's sofa, blood coating half of her torso and face. She had been so strong in Hell, soldiering on, bravely taking it all in her stride as he guided her to freedom. She had even stood up to him a few times and had looked close to taking Villandry on at the club. It had fooled him into believing that she really was strong, not the weak mortal she truly was.

The slashes on her chest were slow to close. He watched them shrinking, willing each one shut and willing Erin to keep fighting and not give up, projecting that thought towards her in the hope she would sense how desperately he needed her to live.

Eventually, the last wound closed, leaving only drying blood on her as evidence of what had happened. Einar sat back on his heels, pale and drained, his dark eyes full of fatigue but relief too.

"Will she be alright?" Veiron couldn't contain that question. Erin was still pale, her lips almost as white as her cheeks.

"It will be a while before she comes around and then we shall know." Einar clutched the arm of the sofa and pushed himself up onto his feet.

"I need to keep her hidden," Veiron said and felt Taylor's gaze shift back to him. "I need her off the radar until she's strong again."

"The entire house is protected by my power. The strongest enchantments I know. This place is a fortress against anything demonic or angelic. Whatever trouble you've stirred up, it won't find you here." Taylor set the gun down and came to stand next to the fireplace, close to Erin's head. She looked down at her, a frown marring her face. "So who is she?"

Veiron walked the length of the back of the antique sofa, leaned over and softly stroked Erin's cheek. "She's Amelia's little sister."

"Her sister?" Einar's eyes shot to him.

Veiron nodded.

"Did something come after her?" Einar sounded concerned now.

"The Devil had her. The little fucker was using her as bait for Amelia. I went to Hell to get her back." Veiron leaned one arm on the back of the couch, his strength leaving him now that he knew Erin would be safe. He had never felt so bone-deep tired before. "We had to exit in London rather than where we were meant to meet Amelia and Marcus. I need to hide Erin until I can get a message to them to tell them she's safe and arrange a new meeting place."

"I can send Marcus a message. We've tested the distances and we can still communicate telepathically even when he's thousands of miles away."

That was a relief. Veiron nodded his thanks.

"We have a man who can arrange passports for you to travel on so you remain below the radar," Taylor said and he was grateful that she had changed her mind and was willing to help him now.

He nodded again, unable to find his voice as he stared down at Erin. His throat felt too tight. It was difficult to breathe past the knot in it let alone speak. He clung to what Einar had told him. She just needed some sleep now and then she would wake and he would see that she was fine.

His back burned.

Veiron gritted his teeth against the pain.

"Are you all right?" Einar shot him a concerned look and Veiron swallowed and then shook his head. He collapsed against the back of the sofa, chin hitting the wooden frame and sending sharp knives stabbing across his skull.

Einar was behind him in an instant, his hand hovering above Veiron's back, above the long gash that cut down from his right shoulder to his left hip. "You should let me take a look at this for you."

Veiron shook his head again. "You've already used up so much strength healing Erin. You don't have to worry about me. I'm fine."

"No, you're not. You're still as stubborn as a mule." Taylor grabbed his right arm and dragged him up onto his feet. She slung his arm around her shoulders and guided him to the other couch.

Einar cleared the weapons off it and Veiron flopped down onto his front. He turned his head to his right, staring across the coffee table to Erin where she lay on her back on the other sofa, her bloodstained face soft with sleep.

Veiron stretched his arm out towards her, resting it on the wooden table, wishing he could hold her hand and feel she was solid and whole, and would be all right. He focused on her as Einar set to work on his back.

He wished Erin would wake. He needed to see those amber eyes of hers and see that she didn't hate him. She had witnessed him in his true form. She knew what he was now.

When she woke, would she still look at him with passion swamping her beautiful eyes or would they show him only pain and fear?

CHAPTER 10

Incredible warmth suffused every inch of Erin's body, heating her right down to her marrow and leaving her feeling so relaxed that she didn't want to move. She lay in silence, still and content, drifting between sleeping and waking. She wasn't sure what she had expected to feel but this bone-melting heat certainly didn't seem right to her.

"Erin?" A deep voice laced with warmth and concern floated around her. She murmured her appreciation of that beautiful baritone and snuggled into the soft blanket covering her. The voice came again. "Erin?"

Erin sighed and frowned. She didn't want to wake but she didn't know why. Something deep within her told her to remain asleep. Why didn't she want to wake and see the handsome face that went with that delicious toe-curling voice?

Images stuttered and flashed across her mind, a broken replay of a fight that she didn't quite remember happening but felt that she had been involved in.

She burrowed deeper into the blanket.

A warm palm cupped her cheek, fingers sliding along her jaw, teasing her awake.

No. She didn't want to go back. She wanted to hide here where everything still made sense and nothing could hurt her.

It was too late though.

The touch lured her up to wakefulness and she fluttered her eyes open. A fuzzy mess of colours greeted her and slowly came into focus, revealing an unfamiliar room and a man who could melt her with just a wicked smile.

Veiron leaned over her, tangled threads of his scarlet hair caressing his cheeks and concern in his dark eyes.

"Are you all right?" he said and she closed her eyes at the sound of his voice, savouring the effect it had on her.

Erin nodded and heard other voices. She rolled her eyes back open and sought the owners of them. A man and a woman. They stood near her feet. She looked down the length of the black fleece blanket to them and then followed the line of her legs to her chest. Something burned there. Erin pushed the covers back, still groggy from sleep and finding it hard to move when she felt so relaxed.

Her black top lay in tatters on one side. A flash of long dark valleys cutting through her flesh and blood spilling over her breast replaced the smooth clean skin she could see.

What had happened?

Erin looked up to ask Veiron and it all came sweeping back to her, crashing into her mind like an icy tidal wave. The demons had come for her and Veiron had fought them. One had got past him.

She stared up at his face and it flickered, violently switching between how he looked now and how he had appeared the last time she had set eyes on him.

Red eyes.

Black skin.

Dragon wings.

He was one of them.

Erin shook her head, her eyebrows furrowing as her heart set off at a pace. She scooted away from him on the sofa and fell over the arm of it, hitting the wooden floor hard. The heat of a fire blazed against her back. Veiron took a step towards her.

She evaded his hand as it swung at her and dived to her left, tripped on the rug, and hit the floor again.

"Get away from me." She pushed up on her hands and made a break for it when Veiron rounded the end of the sofa nearest the fireplace. Her eyes shot wide when she spotted the woman with long black hair standing right in front of her and she tried to veer left. The tawny-haired man stood there blocking her path.

"Erin," he said, hands raised in a calming gesture.

Erin backtracked like a startled animal and fell over the back of the sofa, bounced off the seat and hit the coffee table at a painful angle.

She clutched her aching hip and looked up. A door. Freedom.

"Erin, wait," Veiron said and she threw a wild look over her shoulder at him. He was coming for her. She shoved the wooden table with all of her strength and he grunted when it slammed into his shins. Erin launched herself forwards.

She had made it halfway to the door when Veiron grabbed her from behind and lifted her feet off the floor.

Erin screamed at the top of her lungs and lashed out with her legs, aiming for anything. She managed to get one arm free and smashed her elbow into his stomach with as much force as she could manage. He grunted again but didn't drop her.

"She's going to wake the neighbours," the woman drawled.

"Shut up," Veiron snapped and Erin wasn't sure if he was speaking to her or the woman, and didn't care.

She kept screaming until her throat burned.

Veiron clamped a hand down over her mouth.

Erin bit into his palm, brought her foot down hard on his knee, and slammed her elbow into his cheek.

He dropped her.

She hit the floor knees first, sending a painful jolt through her bones that didn't slow her down. She ran for the door, bare feet burning with each step, bringing back the horrors of Hell and what Veiron's kind had done to her there.

Veiron reached the door before her and she ran straight into his arms.

"Erin, calm down!" He grabbed her waist but she refused to give up.

She rained blows down on his chest, pounding it as hard as she could, struggling the whole time. It had no effect, just as her punches hadn't bothered the demons guarding her cell in Hell. Her throat closed, skin prickled, and heart raced. Images of burning rivers, black cragged spires, and endless darkness flashed across her eyes. The stench of sulphur choked her lungs. Tormented screams echoed in her ears.

"I don't want to go back to Hell! I won't go back." She punched him across the jaw, snapping his head to one side. He closed his eyes, the muscle in his cheek popped, and he frowned.

Pissing him off was probably a bad move. She went back to smashing her fists against his hard chest, reddening his bare skin.

Her punches grew weaker and her head spun, her stomach rebelling in time with it. Oh, she really didn't feel too good. Her hands settled against his chest, his strong heart pounding against her palms. She trembled, limbs weak and muscles twitching, heart a timid thing behind her breastbone.

Veiron gently cradled her, strong arms easily supporting her weight, and his chest heaved as he sighed.

"When have I ever given you the impression that I was going to take you back to Hell?" There was hurt in his voice and in his eyes when she bravely met them and it tore at her. "I have done nothing but help you."

She couldn't deny that. He huffed, carried her back across the room, and shoved her down onto the sofa.

His hands didn't leave her shoulders.

He sat on the coffee table and stared at her.

"I know what you are," she said with a glare aimed at intimidating him but failing dismally judging by how irritated he looked.

"No shit." He rubbed his bare chest with one hand, keeping the other firmly on her shoulder.

Her thoughts raced and collided and she had half a mind to tell him to get his hands off her. She couldn't think straight while he was touching her, or looking at her, or even near her. She needed some space or her head was going to explode. Her mind and her heart were pulling her in two different directions and she felt close to snapping.

"You're one of them," she whispered, unable to look him in the eye and see the pain her violent reaction to that had caused. Flipping out hadn't been the smoothest move on her part but she hadn't been able to stop herself. Everything she had been through had come flooding back and it had been too much for her to handle. Veiron probably thought she hated him now.

Don't hate me.

He had told her those words just before he had gone off to fight the demonic angels.

He had known she would see what he really was and he hadn't wanted her to flip out, and she had done just that. She had gone all psycho on him and tried to run away from him, from Veiron, the man who had walked through Hell to save her from the Devil and his own kind. The man who had taken care of her as best he could and had exposed himself to his enemies by using his powers for her sake.

Erin buried her head in her bare knees, clasped her hands over the back of her head, and cringed.

"Are you at least a good one?" she murmured into her knees.

Veiron's grip on her shoulder loosened and she closed her eyes when he settled his hand over hers on the back of her head, his thumb stroking her interlinked fingers.

"You already know the answer to that question in your heart, Erin." The woman. She had a British accent, London born and bred, just like Erin. Her tone carried no warmth though. Erin's reaction hadn't only annoyed Veiron. It had irked this woman too.

"Leave her alone, Taylor," Veiron snapped and Erin felt a thousand times worse. He still defended her even after she had hurt him.

The beautiful Taylor was right. She did know the answer to her question. Veiron was one of the good guys and she felt sick to her stomach that she had accused him of being anything else.

"I'm sorry," she whispered and long seconds ticked by in silence. She couldn't blame him for not speaking to her, but perhaps she could make amends and explain her actions. "I panicked... just... everything hit me again and got muddled in my head... and it doesn't matter. I shouldn't have freaked out. I shouldn't have doubted you."

His hand stilled against hers and he squeezed them and sighed. "You don't need to apologise, Erin. You've been through a lot. Freak out all you want. I won't mind."

She didn't believe that for a second. She had hurt his feelings and he deserved an apology from her, and if she couldn't get him to accept it, he would always believe that she feared him.

"Just take it easy when you do, you're still healing." The softness of his voice failed to cover the strained note in it. Erin slipped her hands off the back of her head and sat up. Veiron's hand shifted to her cheek, his thumb sweeping across it as his dark eyes held hers. "You had me worried there for a moment."

His gaze dropped to her chest and his hand followed. Erin inhaled sharply when he stroked the top of her breast and looked down, seeing her flesh cut to ribbons and blood pouring from the wounds. Her heart missed a beat and then another, and then thumped hard against her ribs.

"I thought I was going to die." She blinked slowly to clear the tears rising in her eyes and the blood and wounds disappeared, leaving behind the reality of Veiron's fingers gently caressing perfect skin. She raised her head again and looked into his eyes. "How?"

"Einar healed you for me. There are some tricks I can't perform," he said, voice low and filled with regret. He frowned and then the darkness in his eyes lifted again and he settled his palm back against her cheek. "I should've done a better job of protecting you."

The heat in his eyes couldn't mask the pain and Erin knew it wasn't his fear of her dying or anger over his failure to protect her showing. He could pretend all he wanted, but his eyes betrayed his heart and told her that her reaction to discovering he was a demonic angel had deeply hurt him.

She leaned into his palm, wishing she knew what to say to make it all better, and frowned as the room whirled again, spinning violently.

"Are you feeling ill?" The other man this time. His concern surprised her and she slowly looked across at him, causing Veiron's hand to fall from her face.

Rich brown eyes met hers, golden flakes in them shining in the firelight. He was as large as Veiron, thickly muscled and handsome too, wearing a black t-shirt and dark blue jeans. The man crouched beside her and touched her forehead.

There was strange heat in his touch that sent a hazy warm feeling flowing into her mind.

Erin closed her eyes and sighed, feeling infinitely better. This man's touch was like a drug, a painkiller that pharmaceutical companies would kill to have.

"The healing is holding but you are tired. You need more rest," he said and she nodded absently.

No, not rest. What she really needed was Veiron to accept her apology and then some answers rapidly followed by a shower.

"That's enough, Wingless," Veiron snarled and the man's hand disappeared from her forehead.

Erin opened her eyes to see Veiron's fingers locked tightly around the man's wrist and his face a mask of darkness, a red glow around his irises.

The man he had called Wingless snapped his hand free of Veiron's grip and held his glare. The gold in his eyes brightened and swirled. "If you want our protection, you had best start reining in that mouth of yours, Demon."

"Boys," Taylor said and shoved Veiron to one side. She sat where he had been on the coffee table, directly in front of Erin, and her red lips curved into a smile that would have had most men's hearts thumping.

Erin glanced at Veiron.

He was watching Taylor.

What made the tight hot feeling in the centre of Erin's chest worse was that when she looked back at Taylor, the woman was giving Veiron a look that left Erin feeling horribly like the two of them were or had been more than friends.

Veiron moved off to stand with his back to the fireplace. The flames cast his shadow over Taylor and Erin's legs.

"I'm Taylor, and this is Einar." Taylor intimated the man now sitting next to Erin on the fancy sofa, the one Veiron had called Wingless. "And this is our home."

"And what are you?"

Taylor frowned at her. Erin didn't apologise for the bluntness of her tone. Veiron jingled and Erin glanced at him out the corner of her eye, not missing the look he was giving Taylor as he toyed with the thong in his hair.

So this was the lover that had cared about him enough to give him a protection charm?

But the woman was clearly with the man beside her.

As if reading her thoughts, Taylor reached over and touched Einar's hand where it rested on his knee, and looked into his eyes with blue ones that conveyed the depth of her love.

Veiron moved away, circling around the back of the empty couch behind Taylor, and picked up a short sword. He stared at it, murder in his eyes.

Erin felt sick.

"I'm part demon," the woman said with a soft smile and then glanced back at Einar. "He's an angel."

"Like Veiron?"

Veiron snarled, flashing sharp red teeth in Einar's direction.

Taylor continued as though the interruption had never happened. "No, Einar was a hunter angel until he fell in love with me, and I in love with him."

Those words had the dark look on Veiron's face turning blacker. He stabbed the tip of the sword into the table and left it standing there.

"Do be careful of the furniture." Taylor didn't look at him. "Honestly, the man is little more than a beast when his temper gets the better of him. Where was I? Einar chose to be with me, so Heaven chose to remove his wings."

"That's terrible. I thought Veiron had no wings." Erin risked a glance at him.

He prowled around the shadowy far corner of the red room, toying with the weapons as he passed, a lethal yet graceful predator. He spun a dagger against his palm, caught it by the hilt and dug it point first into the small lamp table it had been on.

"All angels can hide their wings. It takes effort to hide them in the way Veiron is doing," Einar said. "There are easier methods open to them, such as using a type of glamour, a spell if you like, that will change their appearance to mortal eyes. Demons and some gifted humans can see through the spell… and some angels choose to hide their wings in the way Veiron is, by putting them away. The angel needs to maintain constant control over them then though, and there is the danger that their concentration will slip and their wings will come out."

"What about his armour?" Erin ran her gaze over Veiron. He wore just his black jeans and his boots but when he had turned into something demonic, he had been wearing black and red armour.

"I am in the room," Veiron snarled. "No need to speak of me as though I'm not."

"The mood you're in, it would be best if you weren't in the room." Taylor stood and scowled at him, her hands on her hips. "You stick a knife, dagger or anything into another piece of my furniture and I will stick one in your gut, so help me God."

Veiron just exposed his red sharp teeth at her.

"That is childish." She huffed. "I swear, you haven't matured at all since I had the disappointment of dating you all those years ago."

He spun another dagger in his palm and then launched it at Taylor. Erin ducked. Taylor dipped her body to one side, neatly avoiding the whizzing blade, and it thudded into the far wall.

"That's it. Bad dog. Out!" Taylor stormed across the room, grabbed Veiron by his left arm and slung him through the open door onto the landing on the other side. She slammed the door in his face and held onto the handle, bracing one foot against the wall, when he tried to open it. "No. Not until you can form sentences like a good boy and grow up."

An unholy roar shook the room.

Taylor cringed, gingerly released the door handle and turned back to face Erin. "I would give him five minutes. He's probably stomping around in his beasty form now. I'm guessing you would rather not see him like that again?"

Erin shook her head but couldn't stop her gaze from drifting to the door.

Veiron had looked truly frightening when he had been in what Taylor called his 'beasty form', standing three feet taller than usual and twice as broad, with black skin, glowing red eyes and sharp red teeth.

But she had known in her heart that he wouldn't hurt her.

He had lost control because that other demonic angel had cut her and tried to kill her. He had fought to protect her.

Low growls sounded from the hall and she could hear him pacing, frantic heavy steps that echoed through the wooden floor to where she sat.

"He's a good bloke really." Taylor resumed her position on the coffee table. She flicked a glance at Einar, clearly met a disapproving look, and rolled her blue eyes. "He is. He helped out when he didn't have to and for all his noise and swagger, he does have some good bones in his body."

Erin picked up the black fleece blanket and wrapped it around herself, feeling cold and uncertain now that Veiron wasn't around to protect her. He had brought her here to these people and knew them, so he must feel that they would protect her, but she didn't know them from Adam and she wasn't about to trust anyone without them earning it first.

"Where were we? Armour. Angels can materialise things," Einar said.

"Like weapons? I saw Veiron make a weapon out of thin air."

He nodded and a strand of tawny hair fell down from his short ponytail at the nape of his neck. He curled it behind his ear. "We can do the same with clothes, and our armour."

"Veiron mentioned that when we were in Hell. He wanted to make me boots and clothes, and wanted to try to make me some food and water." Erin glanced at the door again. The pacing had stopped and so had the growls. She wanted to go to the door and open it so she could see that Veiron was all right and that his anger wasn't solely because of her reaction. "Is he going to be okay?"

Taylor smiled. "He'll be fine in a jiffy. His feelings just got a little dented."

It was her fault then. "I didn't mean to react like that. I wasn't lying earlier when I apologised to him."

"Tell him again later. I swear it takes three different instances of apologising to get the message through that thick skull of his sometimes. Just say it twice more with a few minutes between them, and I'm sure he'll finally be glad to hear it." Taylor touched her knee and looked deep into her eyes. "I don't know what has happened between you two, but Veiron looked like a man not on the edge but firmly over it when he came here carrying you in his arms. I think you scared him pretty good. He was even nice to Romeo here so he would heal you. Not that Einar wouldn't have healed you if Veiron had been his usual self around him."

For a moment, Erin had felt lost but then she had realised that Romeo was Taylor's pet name for Einar. Like Veiron called him Wingless. Erin thought Taylor's name was far kinder, and cuter.

"He growls and snarls but that's only because he has a warm heart beneath that vicious exterior and he's protecting it," Taylor said.

Erin wanted to mention that it was a heart that clearly still belonged to Taylor but held her tongue. She couldn't believe that Taylor wasn't aware that Veiron harboured feelings for her. It was as clear as day to Erin, and she was no competition for the beautiful, part-demon woman sitting in front of her.

Suddenly Erin wanted to be alone too.

"I think I'll feel better when I'm cleaned up. Do you have a shower I can use?" she said and Taylor's expression softened.

"Sure. There's a room free upstairs. I'll take you to it and I'll find you some clothes while you shower." Taylor's red lips curved into a playful smile. "I have to say, you both stink."

Erin was sure that she did, and that it would take more than just one hot shower to get the rank stench of Hell off her skin and out of her hair.

She thanked Taylor with a smile and stood. Einar held her arm to steady her. She smiled at him too but she couldn't hold it.

"I'll contact Marcus and tell Amelia you're safe. Anything you want me to pass on to your sister?" he said and rose to his feet.

"Just that I'm fine and I'll see her soon." She wanted to speak to Amelia herself, wanted to tell her all the crazy stuff that had happened and hear her sister tell her that it was all going to work out in the end. She had never needed her sister so much.

Taylor opened the door. Veiron stormed in looking one hundred percent human and one thousand percent mad but Erin kept her head down, passing him in silence.

She followed Taylor up the rectangular wooden staircase to the next floor, and into a large pale green bedroom with a double bed and a single table beside it. The lamp there was on, casting warm light around the room.

"There's a shower through there." Taylor pointed to the door on Erin's left. "Should be towels and things. Einar likes to keep it stocked up for visitors. We never know when one of his friends might drop in."

Erin presumed friends of Einar's would be angels. Did all angels have red wings like Veiron, or did they have white wings as they did in stories? Or black wings like the man she had met in Hell?

"Thanks," Erin said and sighed when Taylor flashed a smile and left the room, closing the door behind her.

Erin couldn't remember the last time she'd had a shower or taken care of things that were high on a woman's list of priorities. Like shaving. She entered the pale green and white bathroom. It was nothing fancy but it looked like the finest hotel suite bathroom to her. She opened the doors of the white cupboard that supported the sink in front of her and a smile spread across her face when she spotted the razors.

She stepped over to the large double-width shower cubicle, slid the glass door open and turned on the water. Erin slipped out of her skanky black shorts and ruined tank. She grabbed the razor, walked into the shower cubicle and slid the door closed. Hot water beat down on her body. Bliss. She took her time showering, scrubbing every inch of skin three times over with the strongest smelling gel she could find. When she had done that, she took care of her legs and armpits with the razor. Three shampoos later and her hair felt somewhere close to normal. She sighed.

Water was the sweetest ambrosia now and a shower was a gift from the gods. All the things she had taken for granted before her captivity in Hell were now the things she craved most.

Erin shut the water off and stepped out of the cubicle, dripping water all over the white floor tiles. She grabbed one of the large white towels and wrapped it around her body, tucking it closed under her arm, and took one of the smaller towels for her hair. She scrubbed it against the wet black lengths and moved in front of the mirror.

The room in the reflection had a new addition.

Veiron.

He sat on the bed, hands splayed out behind him and bare torso on view. Tempting. Terribly tempting. Water dripped from his scarlet hair onto his chest and he had shaved, revealing a strong jaw that only made him even sexier. The thought of him naked and wet, showering at the same time as she had been, put thoughts into her head about water conservation and doing her part for the environment by sharing the shower with him. Erin pushed them away, not in the mood for such thoughts right that moment, not when so many things were playing on her mind and ninety percent of them involved the gorgeous man reclining on her bed.

When she turned, he picked up a tray of food and offered it to her. Her stomach turned at the gesture, mind flashing back to the food the Devil had offered with a similar flourish, and she took a step back, her bottom hitting the vanity unit.

"Are you all right?" Veiron said and a frown pinched his red eyebrows together. "I just thought you might want to eat something. There's water too."

Erin wasn't a fool. She knew a peace offering when she saw it and she appreciated the gesture and hoped it meant he had accepted her apology. She nodded.

"The last thing someone offered me like that turned out to be the final unicorn," she said as way of an explanation for her reaction and Veiron grimaced.

"You didn't eat it did you?"

She nodded, still feeling a little sick from the knowledge that the Devil had made an entire species extinct just to feed her.

"Bet that was nasty." Veiron smiled, causing subtle dimples in his cheeks, and she was glad to see his teeth were white and blunt. "Taylor only had fruit and healthy rubbish. I don't know how Einar eats this crap."

He picked at the grapes in the platter.

Erin's palms sweated and her heartbeat picked up. "So, how long have you been nursing that broken heart of yours?"

His head shot up, eyebrows raised high on his forehead. "Excuse me?"

"I saw the way you looked at her... how you couldn't bear to see her with him... how you played with that charm you love so much." Her voice hitched on the last sentence. Damn. She had almost got a perfect score from herself for sounding so calm about it all.

She took the plate of fruit from the tray and nibbled on a slice of apple, trying to look unaffected and fine with the fact that Veiron had brought her to his ex-lover's home and was clearly still crushing on her.

"I was the one who left her." He rose to his feet.

She didn't like it when he towered over her so she moved away, taking the fruit with her. Her heart leapt around all over the place in her chest. Her fingers shook.

"And?" She turned to face him, keeping the bed between them so she didn't feel as small. From this distance, he didn't look as tall or imposing. "I've been there and done that too, and it still hurts to see the bloke with another woman."

He frowned, crossed the room in three long strides and took the plate from her. He set it down on the bed and settled his hand against her cheek. His dark eyes met hers, flitting between them, soft with understanding.

"You want me to take care of it for you? If it was the guy at the club, just say the word and he's dead."

It was a poor joke considering the things she had seen him do but she laughed anyway. "No, I'm over it."

"Just like I'm over Taylor." He sighed and ran his fingers down the curve of her jaw, and then combed them through her wet hair. "I am, Erin."

"I'd like to put that to the test."

He frowned. "How?"

Erin tiptoed, placed her palms against the granite slabs of his bare chest and slid them up to his neck. His gaze darted between hers, watchful now, a touch of wariness battling the hunger that she could see rising within him. She felt that hunger stirring deep within her too, and she wanted the taste of Veiron that she had been waiting for. She caught his nape with one hand and lured him down to her. The moment he was within reach, she meshed her lips with his, closed her eyes and kissed him.

His hands captured her waist and dragged her against him, bending her into the hard steel of his body. He growled, slanted his head and pushed his tongue past her teeth. Erin moaned and melted into him, surrendering to the dominant force of his passion.

Veiron pulled away, hands clasping her waist, elbows locked tightly and holding her at a distance.

"We shouldn't," he said, shooting her down from her passion high. "You don't really know me."

"I know you enough to know that I'm attracted to you." She smoothed her palms over his bare shoulders and he groaned, his eyes squeezing shut.

He released her waist, grabbed her wrists, and brought them down between them, holding them captive there.

"You screamed bloody murder at me less than an hour ago, Erin."

"It was shock and I apologised, didn't I?" Erin wrenched out of his grip and sat on the bed. "You might have warned me that you were a demonic angel. Maybe I would have taken it a little better!"

He sighed. "Maybe... but it doesn't change the fact that it scared you."

"It did not." She glared up at him, meeting his hard look and not wavering. "I swear... and I'll prove it to you."

"How, by kissing me again?"

That sounded appealing but it wouldn't prove anything other than she still felt attracted to him, unless he wanted her to kiss him when he was nine feet tall and black all over.

"Change," Erin commanded and got comfortable on the bed, sitting with her legs crossed and her hands in her lap so she didn't flash Veiron.

He looked uncertain.

"It's the only way. Show me the other side of you, the one you think I fear, and I'll show you that it doesn't scare me." Well, it didn't scare her as much as he thought it did anyway.

"Very well." Veiron stepped back, coming to stand in an open space in the large pale room.

He looked up and stretched one arm above his head. Erin realised he was checking the ceiling height. He seemed pleased that he couldn't touch it. Was that his measure for how much he grew?

He took a few deep breaths, looked as though he was going to go through with it, and then stopped and glanced at her. "You're sure about this?"

She nodded. "I want to see you as you are, Veiron. You don't have to hide around me."

He drew a slow breath, his chest expanding with it, and blew it out.

"Wait," she said and he blinked. "Will bad guys come if you change?"

They hadn't so far when he had been showing his wicked side but she didn't want to risk being found.

Veiron shook his head. "No. There are protection spells on the house. No one will sense me."

Erin nodded again, satisfied that he wasn't about to alert his own kind to his location by using his powers.

His eyes began to change. Were they always the first thing to alter? Was the occasional hint of red around his irises a warning that he was on the verge of turning demonic?

Pale golden flecks swirled amongst the scarlet, entrancing her. They gave his eyes an otherworldly look and she couldn't drag hers away. The skin around them darkened, slowly turning black. The change swept outwards from there and other things began to happen. When the black reached his shoulders, his jaw tensed and he began to grow, muscles expanding at the same rate as his height. His jeans disappeared, replaced by a black swath of material that covered his hips, and darkness continued to sweep down his legs. By the time it reached his feet, Veiron stood three feet taller, the top of his head close to the ceiling, and at least twice as broad as he had been.

He wasn't finished.

He growled, exposing rows of red sharp teeth, twisted his head to one side and wings grew from his back. He stretched them as wide as they could go, so the longest feathers touched the walls either side of him. They were beautiful, crimson feathers shining in the lamplight, stealing her breath. She stared at them now, drawn to watching the way the scarlet slowly drained downwards and dripped from there to the floor like blood, revealing black feathers beneath. When the red was gone, the feathers fell away in clumps, falling into the blood and exposing black leathery membrane beneath. Finally, a large claw grew from the joint in the top of each wing. Veiron flapped them and then furled them against his back.

Erin had expected to feel some residual fear but all she felt was compassion. He stood before her, demonic, vicious-looking, but there was no trace of pride or any threat of danger. His eyes were downcast, body held in a way that made her want to stand and cross the room to him, and wrap her arms around his thick waist to let him know that whatever he was feeling, she was there for him.

He was nine feet tall, black all over, and his eyes glowed like the fires of Hell, but he was still Veiron. His features hadn't changed. They had only grown larger. He was like a slightly scarier and black Hulk.

Erin hated to see him staring at the floor, braced for a reaction he was convinced would be negative. She wanted to prove to him that he couldn't be more wrong about her. She wasn't afraid of him.

He was still Veiron.

She would prove that.

Erin got to her feet on the bed, wobbled a bit on the soft mattress, and then straightened, facing him. His gaze slid to her and he frowned, turning his expression evil and vicious.

"Come to me." She held her hand out to him.

He didn't move.

Erin held both hands out to him and tried again. "Please, Veiron."

He huffed, sounding every bit the beast, and slowly approached her. She still wasn't quite eye level with him even when she was standing on the bed. Erin flexed her fingers to stop them from shaking. She didn't want Veiron to think that she feared him, even when she did a little. He was so big up close, his eyes blazing red and gold, reminding her of the fiery rivers of Hell.

Erin lifted her hand and lightly ran her fingers down his cheek. His black skin was rough beneath their tips. He sneered and took a step back. She caught his thick arm in both hands so he couldn't distance himself again. He might want to believe that she was scared of him but she wasn't going to let him.

The tattoos that curled around his biceps and up to his shoulders were still visible, the red showing on his black skin. She traced them upwards and he closed his eyes, exhaling through his nose. Erin swallowed and continued, stroking the muscled incline of his shoulders to his neck.

From there, she swept both of her palms up to catch his cheeks. They were huge against her hands, making them look tiny. When she bravely ran her right thumb across his lower lip, his mouth opened and he hissed through his sharp red teeth.

"Look at me, Veiron," Erin whispered and he obeyed, his black lashes lifting to reveal those incredible eyes. She stared into them, studying the way the flecks of gold shifted amongst crimson. He blinked slowly, eyes never leaving hers, calm and quiet. She felt as though he was a feral beast, a lethal predator, and somehow she held him under her control.

Erin leaned in and gently kissed his lips.

He instantly changed back, his mouth moving against hers the whole time and his hands coming to claim her waist. Erin slid her arms around his neck when he was short enough that she now towered above him, and sighed into his mouth, enjoying the soft sweep of his lips across hers.

Veiron drew back again. "Why did you do that?"

Erin brushed her palm across his cheek and felt sorry for him when she saw hope and anger battling in his eyes. What sort of life had this man led to make him believe that a woman could never like his other side?

"Because I wanted to, Veiron."

He closed his eyes and lowered his head. Erin stopped him, lifting his chin, not wanting him to hide away from her. She wanted him to see in her eyes that she was telling the truth and she had wanted to kiss him when he had been demonic. She hadn't done it to prove anything. She had done it because it had felt natural and she had still desired him. Demonic or not, he was still the most gorgeous man she had ever met. He was still Veiron.

"No one has ever kissed me when I'm like that." Those low-spoken words stirred pity in her soul and she wrapped her arms around his neck and held him.

"Do you believe me now?" she whispered into his ear and kissed the lobe.

Veiron nodded, pushed her back, and kissed her again, his lips searing hers, dominant and hungry, everything she had wanted their first kiss to be. She leaned into the kiss, a burning need for more igniting inside her, and tangled her tongue with his. His fingers tightened against her back, pulling her flush against his body, and Erin moaned.

The door opened.

"God, Veiron, put it away... you'll scare the poor girl!" Taylor's voice was a high-pitched squeak of horror.

Veiron growled and pulled away, and Erin looked down in time to catch a glimpse of his hard length. Impressive didn't cover it.

Unfortunately, Veiron did. He waved a hand and his black jeans snapped back into place on his legs, spoiling her fun.

"I brought you some clothes, Erin," Taylor said, her gaze fixed on the floor. "And Einar needs to speak to you, Veiron."

Veiron sighed. He looked back into Erin's eyes and she smiled, showing him that it was fine and he should go and speak to Einar. It was probably more important. Her heart screamed that nothing was more important than where that kiss might have been heading. She told it to shut up. Veiron would come back soon enough and she would be waiting for him when he did, and they would continue where they had left off.

He smoothed his palm over her cheek.

"Are you sure you'll be alright alone?" he said, deep baritone making her insides flip and heart warm.

Erin nodded. "I'll be right here, stuffing my face like a pig."

"You need to sleep. Get some rest and I'll come check on you later."

She didn't nod this time. She didn't want to sleep. If she closed her eyes, she would relive everything she had been through, or worse, she would start seeing the terrible things that often haunted her dreams.

The only times she hadn't had nightmares recently were the two instances where she had fallen asleep on Veiron.

He kissed her cheek. "I won't be long."

Erin managed a smile. He padded barefoot from the room, leaving her alone with Taylor. Erin sat on the bed and picked at the fruit again. Taylor set the clothes down on a chair in the corner of the room. Erin appreciated the offer but the thought of dressing like Taylor didn't appeal. She didn't want to give Veiron a reason to see Taylor whenever he looked at her, not when she had just started believing that he might be telling her the truth and might be over the part-demon beauty.

Taylor sat on the bed beside her.

And grinned.

"So, you want the dirt on Hell boy or not?"

Erin smiled and nodded.

CHAPTER 11

Burning.

Everything was burning.

Not Hell this time. London. Erin's city blazed below her. Sirens wailed, drowning out the screams of dying people and the murderous shrieks of the creatures responsible for their demise. Buildings crumbled and spewed flames so hot they reached her even though she was high above the horrific scene.

Flying.

The sound of wings beating air surrounded her.

Her wings.

She looked down at her waist. Strong male hands held it. Not her wings.

"Veiron?" she said, sure that he was the one behind her, holding her close to his body, carrying her away from the terror of her city burning to the ground.

They reached an area beyond the fiery inferno and destruction and he set her down on an untouched rooftop. The black tar was sticky beneath her feet, melting from the heat of the fire only a few hundred yards away.

He walked around her and Erin frowned and backed away a step.

Not Veiron.

The angel before her had snow-white hair and eyes as pale as frosted grass. He wore rich blue armour edged with silver and his silver-blue wings stretched and then furled against his back. Twin curved silver blades hung at his hips, knocking against the rectangles of metal that protected his backside and groin.

"Who are you?" Erin said, her voice wavering. The world distorted, trembled beneath her feet, and a building in the distance collapsed, sending a huge plume of ash into the air.

"Your guardian angel." Those words were calm and cold, as void of emotion as his jade eyes. He drew his blades and held them down at his sides and Erin moved another step backwards, eyeing them and then the flat rooftop.

She didn't know this man and instinct said to keep some distance between them. "Where are you taking me?"

"Somewhere you will be safe."

Why didn't she believe those words? He spoke them with warmth, with a flicker of concern across his handsome face, but they felt cold to her, unfeeling and dark. Wherever this man intended to take her, she would be far from safe.

"Come, Erin." He sheathed one blade and held his left hand out to her. "We must go now before it is too late."

The ground shook again.

Erin threw a glance around her at the flames now licking up the sides of the building. The heat of them scorched her skin, driving her away from the edge, closer to the angel stood in the centre of the roof. She had no choice. It was go with him or die here.

Erin swallowed and held her hand out to him.

Their fingers almost touched.

Veiron came up out of nowhere behind the angel, launching high into the air, his double-ended spear held above his head in both hands with one of the curved blades pointed directly downwards at the man's back.

Only he didn't look like the Veiron she knew. No black armour or long scarlet hair. His armour was blue and silver, the same as the angel's, and his pale wings shone in the light of the fires blazing around them. His hair was short now, wild on top, and no tattoos adorned his powerful arms.

He yelled and came down hard at the man in front of her, one knee tucked up to his stomach and the other leg stretched out long behind him.

The angel turned with his blade in a blur and knocked Veiron's spear aside.

"I should have put you down when I had the chance," the angel snarled and attacked.

"Veiron!" Erin screamed and ran for him.

Everything slowed and then fell apart. The world unravelled around her and a new nightmare constructed itself in its place. Endless black caverns lit by an inferno that shattered the basalt around her. Tall black rock spires towered over her in a semi-circle, closing her in. Before her, a huge obsidian fortress rose so high into the air that she couldn't see the top of the spiky towers.

A muffled cry brought her attention snapping down to the wide black curved steps and the tall arched entrance of the fortress.

Veiron.

Erin ran forwards across the black paved courtyard.

A man stepped out from behind Veiron and hauled him up, holding him suspended off the steps by his neck. The man's golden eyes slid to her and his handsome pale face contorted into a cruel smile.

The Devil.

"Leave him alone!" Erin shouted even though she knew it was useless. Her gaze flicked back to Veiron. Black ribbons of smoke held him now, threaded around his arms and legs. They slowly tightened and she gasped as they cut into his flesh and crushed his obsidian armour against his chest, forearms and shins. Blood streamed down his limbs and dripped to the floor beneath his feet. Erin kept running, heading straight for him.

She hit an invisible wall just three metres away from the steps.

"Please... you're hurting him!" Erin rained her fists down on the barrier, tears filling her eyes.

The smoke dissipated and Veiron crashed to the floor, hitting the curved black steps at a vicious angle. He tumbled down them and lay close to her feet, broken and bleeding, barely breathing.

Erin crouched and pressed her hands against the invisible wall that separated them.

"Veiron?" she whispered and her tears cut down her cheeks, hot and fierce. Her heart ached so painfully that she couldn't breathe. "Please wake up. Let me know you're alive."

He wheezed. The action caused blood to pump from the slices across his stomach. It poured over his skin and pooled beneath him, spreading outwards towards her. Her heart wrenched when he moved, slowly pushing himself up onto his elbows, and tore his battered chest plate away. It clattered across the black paving and landed at the Devil's feet.

The Devil stepped over it and approached, neatening the cuffs of his black jacket and shirt, so casual that she wanted to punch a hole in his head to wipe the snide look off his face.

Veiron almost made it into a sitting position, swaying violently all the while. Erin flinched when the Devil pressed one polished leather shoe against Veiron's chest and slammed him back down with such force that the black paving splintered beneath him.

Veiron choked up blood.

"Leave him alone!" Rage curled through Erin's veins, heating it and driving her to action. She smashed her fists against the barrier and let out an inhuman growl. "I swear I will kill you if you hurt him."

The Devil didn't heed her words. He stepped up onto Veiron's chest and positioned his other foot against Veiron's chin. He was going to snap his neck.

Fear pounded in Erin's blood, her heart beat violently in her chest, and dark red flames flickered over her hands and licked up her arms.

The sight of them seemed to please the Devil.

He smiled at her, a glimmer of sick satisfaction crossing his face, and then shoved his foot forwards.

Erin screamed, threw her hands out in front of her, and everything exploded into a bright crimson fireball.

She shot up in bed.

Darkness surrounded her.

Erin breathed hard, pulse racing and limbs trembling, cold sweat trickling over her bare skin. Her stomach twisted and turned, and she doubled over, fighting the urge to throw up. It wasn't real. It wasn't real. It was just another bad dream. She could still smell the stench of burning flesh and Veiron's blood.

Could hear the Devil laughing.

The door burst open, flooding the room with blinding white light, and Erin threw herself away from it. Her heart leapt into her throat, her legs tangled in the sheets and she hit the floor. She clutched the green bedclothes around her, shaking all over, and peered over the top of the mattress to the door.

A shadowy figure stood in the bright doorway, a long blade in one hand.

It reached into the room.

The light flicked on.

Veiron.

His bright crimson eyes scoured the room, as though looking for an intruder, and then settled on her. They widened and concern filled them.

"Erin?" He stalked into the room. "I felt you panic and I thought someone had come for you. What's wrong?"

She couldn't look at him. She felt so stupid. It had just been one of her usual nightmares and he had come rushing in like the cavalry, sword in hand, ready for battle. She picked herself up off the floor, weak knees threatening to give out, and pulled herself back onto the bed. She didn't stop shaking.

What on Earth did she look like? She was soaked with sweat, trembling, and her heart was still pounding against her chest.

"Turn out the light." She burrowed into her knees, feeling like a fool for getting so worked up over a dream. "I look like a mess."

"I don't care what you look like." He walked into the room and stopped at the edge of the bed. "I just need to see that you're all right."

She had to smile at his blunt honest words. "Can you at least give me some dignity and use the table lamp instead?"

He nodded. The light turned off by itself and the table lamp came on. She was never getting used to his tricks. He waved a hand towards the door and it closed.

Veiron sat beside her on the bed, facing her, and she noticed for the first time that he was fully dressed, wearing a black dress shirt that emphasised the breadth of his muscled chest and stretched tight around his biceps, the sleeves rolled up his forearms, and black jeans. He pressed his left hand into the mattress and reached across with his right. Erin stilled as he brushed his thumb across her cheek and she realised that she had been crying too.

She hated that she probably looked truly weak to him now, shaken by a dream. He had called her weak when they had been in Hell. What was he thinking about her now?

He opened his hand and cupped her cheek in his large warm palm.

"Do you want me to stay?" he whispered and relief washed through her, steadying her heart and stopping her trembling.

Erin nodded.

Veiron stood, set his blade down, and removed his boots. He rounded the bed to her right side and laid on the mattress beside her, his head propped up on the green pillows, and rolled onto his side to face her. He stretched his left arm out. Erin stared blankly at it.

"Come," Veiron husked and Erin settled on her side, facing him, and rested her head on his upper arm.

She stared into his eyes, his face illuminated by the bedside lamp behind her. It was so peaceful. Her heart remained steady, drumming softly against her chest, and her eyes remained locked on his. They were dark and gentle, no trace of red in them now. Her breathing slowed to match his.

Comforting.

It had been a long time since she had felt so at ease and safe.

Veiron made sure that feeling ran deeper, until she felt calm to her core, by curling his arm around her. His hand settled below her ribs and he held her.

"You can talk to me about it," he whispered, soft voice warming her and backing up his words. "I'm here for you, Erin."

She couldn't remember the last time she had talked to someone about the things she saw in her dreams. She had stopped speaking to Amelia about them after their mother had died. She didn't know why. She had just closed herself off.

Erin dropped her gaze to his chest, staring at the small V of skin and muscle she could see beyond the open top buttons of his black shirt.

"It's been a while since I had two dreams back to back." She toyed with the first closed button on his shirt, rolling it between her fingers, focusing on it. "I saw

London burning. I thought it was Hell, but it wasn't. Someone was carrying me... an angel."

"What did he look like?" Veiron murmured and moved his hand to her hair, stroking the short black lengths and soothing her rising panic.

"White hair and green eyes, and he wore armour like yours but it was blue and silver. He said that he was my guardian angel." She looked up into his eyes to see if it was possible that she had a guardian angel.

"I wore armour like that once." He smiled but there was sorrow in it.

"You wore it in my dream too... and you had short hair and no tattoos. You attacked the angel and he said something... what was it... something about he should've put you down before." She didn't like the thought of that or what had happened afterwards. She wanted to close herself off to him again, didn't want to talk about what had happened and dredge up the pain she had felt in her nightmare.

"It sounds like me." His smile held more warmth this time and she knew in her heart that he was trying to cheer her up.

She wished she could smile too.

Erin dropped her gaze back to her hands and flipped the collar of his shirt back and forth, trying to find her voice again. It was hard. The wave of emotions she had felt in her nightmare pressed down on her and her pulse spiked again, fingers shaking and cold sweat prickling down her spine. Veiron held her closer, his strong hand clasping the back of her head.

She slowly undid two more buttons on his shirt and parted the material with her fingers. She stroked the smooth skin of his pectorals. There were no marks on his flesh but sometimes when she blinked, she saw him cut and bruised, bleeding.

"You were you again in the next part. There was a huge black fortress and this sort of amphitheatre or something around it. A wall of black spires. The Devil had you and I couldn't get to you. He hurt you, Veiron, and I tried to make him stop, but he—" Erin cut herself off, unable to go on without breaking down.

"It's okay, Erin," Veiron murmured and stroked her hair. He pressed a soft kiss to her forehead. "It's okay."

"No, it isn't... I fought back. I did something... I don't know what it was but it scared me." She pressed her hand to the bare patch of his chest and felt his heart beating steadily against her palm. It comforted her. Veiron was strong. It was just her feelings for him that made her fear that someone would hurt him. Wasn't it?

"Have you ever dreamed things that have happened later?" Those words chilled her.

"No... maybe," Erin said and undid another button on his shirt, revealing the first muscles of his abdomen. "There are times when I see things in my dreams that do happen, but they're always a little different. Recently, my dreams have all been strange... about my sister and a man."

"Marcus?"

"I don't know. He's tall and has dark hair and pale blue eyes, and has wings tattooed on his back."

"That's Marcus. He was an angel sent to watch over your sister."

"A guardian angel?" She looked up into his dark eyes, torn between pursuing discovering more about Veiron and the man called Marcus, and asking him whether he honestly thought that she had precognitive dreams. "Like that other man in my dream and you?"

He smiled and stroked her cheek, but his tone turned emotionless and detached. "I haven't been a guardian in a long time, but I started out like Marcus and then we went our separate ways."

There was pain in his eyes as he said that, a haunted look that told her not to ask about it. She touched his cheek but the barriers had come up again, shutting her out. Whatever had happened to him, he didn't want to remember it or feel anything because of it. He had buried his pain deep.

A noise sounded from below and Erin tensed.

Veiron brushed his knuckles across her cheek, drawing her back to him. "Don't worry. I won't let anything happen to you."

She stared up into his eyes, her fingers stroking his chest. "What about you and what I saw? If I... if my nightmares are things destined to happen... then... Veiron, I don't want that to come true."

"I won't let that happen either. You don't have to worry, Erin. We will find out more about this power of yours and we will find a way to change things. You might see only the future as it stands now. It is constantly changing. The slightest action might alter it completely."

That was comforting. There had been times when she had thought her nightmares and dreams were more than just her imagination running wild, instances where things had happened that had been very close to what she had seen during her sleep. She had never imagined that she would be lying in the arms of a fallen angel, a demonic angel, when she realised that what she had was a power.

Erin only wished that her power had been as useful and fantastic as some of the ones Veiron had. The knowledge that she could see the future in her dreams left her cold to the bone and she never again wanted to sleep without Veiron close to her.

Erin looked into his dark eyes for long seconds, and then whispered, "Can I see your eyes again?"

He didn't hesitate this time. His irises changed, glowing like embers in the low light.

"They're amazing." She stared at all the threads of gold in the crimson, making them her sole focus so she could push away the creeping fear about what Veiron had called her power and the things she had witnessed. "They're like fire... can I see your wings too?"

Veiron nodded. He slipped his arm out from beneath her and she sat up with him. He moved to kneel in front of her, unbuttoned his black shirt, and peeled it off. His body distracted her, all delicious hard muscle and masculine strength that she wanted to run her hands over and kiss. Erin dragged her gaze away from it, back to his eyes. His wings slowly appeared, growing out of his back, the crimson feathers shining in the light. He stretched them, flapped once, and then brought them to rest. The longer feathers brushed the mattress on his right side and the floor to his left.

Erin held the covers around her with one hand and reached out with her other. She ran her hand down the soft feathers of his left wing, following the curve. Veiron closed his eyes and sighed.

"Does that feel good?" she whispered, shaky and nervous. It looked as though it did. She'd had a few lovers in her time but they had all been human. Veiron was an angel, whether he was in service of the Devil or not. She wasn't sure what angels liked or what sort of things would give him pleasure. If he could feel such a thing. The blissful look on his face said that he could and the woman on the floor below, his ex-lover, had told her that Veiron was a fantastic lover, and a very protective male. That had left Erin feeling a little ill. She didn't like the thought of Taylor with Veiron, or the thought of trying to best that woman. If Veiron had left Taylor, how was she supposed to find a way to convince him to stay with her?

"I haven't been touched like this in a long time," he murmured and swallowed when she flattened her palm and stroked the layers of his feathers.

"Since Taylor?" She hated that thought.

Veiron's red eyes flicked open. He shook his head. "Before her. She never touched me like this. I don't think anyone has ever touched me the way that you do."

Erin swallowed, suddenly aware that the only thing that stood between them was a thin duvet. Her pulse raced and blood heated. She kept stroking his crimson feathers, feeling their softness and warmth, savouring the way her touch had Veiron struggling to breathe. His chest heaved, muscles straining, and his eyes burned into her, hot with desire, pupils dilated and reflecting the hunger that she felt within her.

She shook, afraid of where this was leading but unable to bring herself to stop. Veiron was so handsome and strong, so masculine and powerful, immense, and she had felt drawn to him from the moment they had met. Taylor was right about him, but the woman didn't know the depth of his feelings and warmth. Erin knew. When this man loved, he gave all of himself, and would do all in his power to protect the one he cherished.

Erin wanted to be that one for him.

She wanted to be the one who held him and gave him strength, and made him feel it was all right to let down his guard with her because she would never hurt him. She would cherish him, would do all in her power to protect him, just as he would her.

He reached out to her and she inhaled sharply as he caught her arm. He moved it aside and the covers fell away to reveal her bare breasts. Erin closed her eyes and swallowed when his hot hands moulded over her breasts and he groaned.

"I want you," he husked and she moaned, nodded, shivered right down to her soul.

"I want you too." She barely finished her sentence before his mouth swooped on hers and he had her pinned to the bed beneath him, kissing the breath from her.

CHAPTER 12

Veiron's hands came to rest on either side of Erin's head and pressed hard into the mattress, his body poised above hers. Erin lay beneath him, her eyes fixed on his, mesmerised by how the fiery flakes swirled against their blood red backdrop. Strands of his crimson hair fell down to brush his cheek and caress his forehead, giving her an excuse that she was quick to take. She raised her hand and swept them away, her fingertips lightly brushing his golden skin.

Crimson wings framed him, spread wide so they drifted down on either side of her, blocking her view of the room and keeping her focus solely on Veiron.

He was beautiful.

Black pupils swallowed some of the colour in his irises, conveying his desire as clearly as the rigid length pressed between her legs. All that separated her and his delicious body was a thin sheet and his jeans, and Erin wanted to tear both items away. She ached with the hunger to run her fingers over every inch of Veiron's bare flesh and to follow her hands with her mouth, tasting his skin and putting all of him to memory. She burned to explore him and seek out the things that gave him the most pleasure. What would make him close his eyes and hiss in satisfaction? The brush of her nails over his pebbled nipples? The swirl of her moist tongue over the soft blunt head of his cock? A rough thrust of her hand down his rigid length? Did he like a gentle lover or a savage one?

Erin wanted to know it all.

She wanted to know all of him.

Veiron leaned down towards her, his long dark lashes falling to shutter his beautiful irises. Erin raised her hands and gently ran her palms down the arch of each crimson wing, delighting in the softness of his feathers. Veiron stopped dead, his breathing a trembling unsteady sound that equally delighted her. Taylor was wrong about this man. He didn't need a strong lover, not in the way Taylor had meant. He needed someone strong of heart, someone who shared the depth of his emotions and his need for more than just physical contact when making love.

He needed someone who accepted all of him, who felt as strongly as he did, ruled by their emotions and desires.

Erin was that woman.

She lowered her hands, brushing his feathers, and dropped them to his shoulders. From there, she coursed them up his strong thick neck to his cheeks and settled them close to the straight cut of his jaw and held him, waiting for him to emerge and look at her. His lashes slowly lifted, revealing his breathtaking eyes, and they locked with hers.

Erin gently drew him down to her. He moved slowly and with infinite care, lowering himself to his elbows and supporting his weight off her. She held his gaze, bringing him closer, until his breath mixed with hers and she could no longer focus on him. Then she closed her eyes, raised her head and swept her lips across his.

He moaned and shuddered, his reaction more intense than when she had touched his wings for the very first time.

Erin kept her hands against his face, holding him at a distance, stopping him from seizing control of the kiss. She had no doubt in her mind that he could if he truly wanted to, but he seemed content to let her have her way. She lightly brushed her lips across his, teasing him with the whisper of contact, and savoured the taste of him, all masculine heat and spice. He groaned, fisted his hands in her short dark hair and ground against her. That was cheating. Erin's attempt to keep things high in the emotional side of intimacy failed. She swung straight over to the physical, driven by the feel of his long hard cock rubbing between her thighs and his fingers tangling in her hair. She tried to keep the kiss light but slipped and found herself craning her neck and plunging her tongue into his mouth.

Veiron snarled, tugged her head back and kissed her. Really kissed her.

Erin couldn't remember the last time a man had dominated her and she had enjoyed it so much. His tongue thrust past her lips and teeth, hot and probing, forcing her into submission and stealing her breath. One strong hand left her black hair and pushed beneath her, settling in the arch of her back. He dragged her up to him, so hard that not a wisp of air remained between them and she could feel every sexy inch of naked steely muscle pressing against her bare flesh. His fingertips dug into her back, his grip sending thoughts of him holding her forever and never letting her go through her mind.

Possessive.

It thrilled her.

Veiron slanted his head and kissed that thought away. Every rational thought left with it, vacating her head, forced out by an intense need to surrender to her passion and desire for this man. If she did, it would be the most incredible experience of her life.

"I need to taste you," he whispered against her lips, voice roughened by passion, hunger filling each syllable.

Erin could only moan her response, feeling his need echo deep in her veins. She needed to taste every inch of him too.

He devoured her jaw, mouth hard and rough, and followed the line of her neck. He paused near her collarbone, licking the flickering pulse point on her throat. Erin shuddered and couldn't stop herself from wrapping her legs around his hips. He groaned and she tightened her grip, thighs pressing hard against his hips, feet hooked over his backside.

Veiron pulled on her hair again, bending her head right back, and pressed his tongue into her vein.

"Fuck, I need to taste you." He growled and wrapped his lips around her throat, tongue laving and teasing, hot and wet against her flesh.

A light clicked on in Erin's head. He wasn't talking about the sort of tasting she was. Simple licking and kissing, and maybe the odd nip with blunt teeth wasn't at the forefront of his mind.

Veiron wanted to bite her.

Taylor had never mentioned Veiron doing such a thing during lovemaking. Had he never done such a thing with her?

Erin swallowed and didn't respond, fearing that if she so much as moaned at the wrong time he would take it as an invitation to sink razor-sharp red teeth into her flesh and suck her blood.

He moved on, kissing down her chest, descending towards her breasts. He groaned when he reached them and released his grip on her back and her hair, sending her sinking into the mattress. Erin idly stroked his wings, her knees against his waist, and watched him as he pulled one beaded nipple into his mouth and covered her other breast with his hand. He squeezed and kneaded it, all the while suckling her other nipple, a look of sheer bliss on his face.

What was wrong with this picture?

Erin wouldn't have thought it but the wings put it right there in her head.

An angel lay between her thighs, devouring her breasts, worshipping her body. Seeking pleasure.

It should have made her feel something. Guilt. Wickedness. Evil? It didn't. She felt alive for the first time in she couldn't think how long. Veiron brought her to life, filled her body with light and pleasure, with passion and desire, and lit her up like the fifth of November. Every fibre of her being was aware of him, crackling with electricity and need, hunger only this man could sate. She wanted him. Only that want was never satisfied. She could touch, taste, and make love with Veiron until her body could take no more and every ounce of her energy was depleted and she would still want him, still crave him with the same ferocity, as though he was something as necessary to her as her heartbeat.

He bucked as she grasped his wings and sucked hard on her nipple, sending sparks shooting outward across her skin.

"Erin," he moaned against her breast and it was the sweetest thing she had ever heard. She arched into him, clutching his crimson wings, focusing on him and what he was doing. He moved lower, kissing downwards, flicking his tongue over her ribs, across her stomach and around her navel. "Fuck, I need you so much."

There was such honesty in those words, such brutal honesty. It flattered her. She felt that same need burning within her, was a slave to it just as he was. She rocked her hips against him, trying to encourage him to keep going, to touch her where she needed him most of all.

Veiron tugged the sheet covering her lower half away and hissed through his teeth.

"God Almighty, you are beautiful." He kissed below her navel and glided his hands over her breasts, down her waist and across her hips. "Let me see you."

Erin didn't hesitate. She spread her legs for him, heart hammering against her chest, body ignoring the quiet voice at the back of her mind that kept shrieking that he was an angel. A Hell's angel. A fallen angel.

She didn't care.

The first brush of his tongue over her most sensitive flesh had her flinging her head back and crying out his name.

It had been too long since she had been with a man and Veiron felt too good between her legs. His strong shoulders braced her thighs apart and he slid one long finger deep into her moist core. A second followed it, pumping in and out, heightening her arousal. She wasn't sure how much she could take.

She scrabbled, grabbed his wing with one hand and buried the other in his hair. She arched her back, pressing her shoulders deep into the mattress. Veiron groaned into her, tongue flicking and teasing, fingers pumping. She really didn't care about the wings. She trampled the voice out of existence and rocked her hips against his face, moaning each time he sucked her clitoris or thrust his fingers deep into her core.

"Veiron." It came out as a husky murmur that shocked her. She had never sounded so hungry before, so lost to her desire and need.

Her throaty plea elicited a moan from him and he spread his wings over her like a hawk over its prey, covering her. His feathers tickled her bare skin, the touch of them too light for her to handle when she was so alive with sensation.

She giggled and then groaned, flitting between the two. He shifted his wings and she laughed again, her body clenching around Veiron's fingers and knees tightening against him.

Veiron growled and was above her in a flash, his red eyes locked on hers, bright with the intensity of a thousand setting suns and so focused that she trembled.

"I must have you."

Those were growled words, so low she barely heard them. They spoke to her soul, stripping her bare and leaving her open to him. His need for her was primal, something beyond his control. The same as hers was for him.

His wings began to shrink, his focus intensifying, a frown darkening his eyes. She watched them, marvelling as they gradually disappeared into his back.

Suddenly they were gone.

Erin brushed her fingers over his strong shoulders, following the sweeping curves of his tattoos.

She ran her hands under his arms, stroked the muscles over his ribs, and held his gaze as she quested onwards, heading towards his jeans.

Erin paused.

"Don't stop," Veiron breathed, voice low and tempting her to continue, eyes hooded and black with desire.

Her cheeks heated and her heart hammered against her chest.

His gaze met hers. "Is something wrong?"

The look in his dark eyes turned from passion to pain and Erin wanted to kiss him again and tell him that she hadn't changed her mind and she still wanted to do this with him, more than anything. There was just one tiny problem.

"Well... it's just... I was in Hell for weeks, and it's not as though I had my, you know... special pills... on hand when I was down there." Erin closed her eyes and cringed. Way to sound all womanly and take charge. "Total mood killer... but I don't suppose you're carrying protection?"

And what was she supposed to make of it if he was? It would lead to more questions and ones he probably didn't want to answer.

"I'm not fertile." Veiron's voice seemed impossibly loud in the darkness of her closed eyes. She cracked them open and peered up at him. "Angels are sterile. We can't procreate."

"Oh." So he basically didn't have to worry about protection at all, which meant he could bang any woman that took his fancy. The voice in Erin's heart told her that he wouldn't. Veiron wasn't that sort of man and she knew it. She was just scared that whatever was happening between them might not end the way she wanted it to. "So..."

He smiled. "How long has it been? Double figure years that take us back to before you were born. Don't give me that look. I am an angel... immortal? Ring any bells?"

"Just how old are you?"

He dipped down and pressed a brief kiss to her lips. "Around two thousand and something. You lose track... and now I'm losing track... I haven't been with anyone in a very long time. My focus has been on finding a way to escape the service of the Devil and have my revenge on him, and on Heaven. I hadn't so much as looked at a woman until I saw you in that cell, and I knew that very moment that I wanted you."

"You did?" Erin looked up into his dark eyes and found them warm and full of affection mixed with desire, a dangerous combination that had her melting into the bed and forgetting her worries. Except that bit about him being two thousand years old. Talk about an age gap.

"I did... I still do. I want you."

Her fingers brushed his belt and suddenly it was gone too, and so were his jeans. She looked down the length of him, between their bodies, and her eyes widened at the sight of his thick cock.

"And I will have you." Veiron growled the words in the sexiest, most possessive and bone-melting snarl she had ever heard.

Her heart leapt into her throat and everything that was woman in her came alive and reached for him.

"So have me," she whispered and his eyes narrowed on hers.

He settled his weight on her, hips nestled between her thighs, and shifted backwards. Erin held her breath. Veiron knocked it out of her. He entered her in one swift deep stroke, neither brutal nor gentle. Erin grabbed his shoulders. Veiron slid one hand beneath her, holding her body against his, and grasped the nape of her neck with his other, cradling her head. He kissed her as deeply as he thrust into her, claiming all of her, stealing a piece of her with each primal meeting of their bodies.

Erin shifted her hands to his hair, twining her fingers in the long red lengths and holding him to her. She hooked her feet around his backside, moaning with each deep plunge of his cock. In. Out. Shattering her. She couldn't think. Couldn't do anything but react and feel.

Veiron moved above her, his groans deep guttural growls in her mouth, his hands clutching her to him, cock stroking and filling her, plunging to the hilt until his balls brushed her and his pelvis slammed into her clitoris. She had never made love like this. She had never felt so completely possessed by a man, so deeply connected to one.

She kissed him, tasting his passion, letting it flow into her as hers flowed into him. Every time she tightened her grip on him or obeyed her instincts to shift her hips against his, to ride his cock each time it glided into her and withdrew, he groaned into her mouth and held her closer. If that was even possible.

Erin lost herself.

Moving in time with him, kissing him, clutching him, there wasn't a place where she wasn't connected to him. One with him.

She writhed beneath him, breathless, consumed by pleasure and racked by bliss, reaching ever onward for her climax, stretching for it. Veiron grunted, kissed her, pumped harder and held her closer.

Mine.

That thought pounded in her head as surely and rapidly as her heart pounded in her chest.

Veiron belonged to her. They had been made for each other. Fit so perfectly.

One soul in two bodies.

He groaned and buried his head in her throat, clutching and squeezing her, hurting her with the ferocity of his grip but she didn't care. She felt only pleasure. Endless. Engulfing. She drowned in it, in the way her sweat-slicked skin stuck to his as they shifted against each other, thrusting and pumping, lost in each other.

"Erin," he growled into her throat and kissed it, and then bit with blunt teeth. The delicious pressure of his teeth against her flesh tore a moan from her. He curled one hand over her shoulder, holding her in place as he deepened his thrusts, long strokes of his cock that had her groaning louder and louder. She didn't even care if anyone heard her.

Nothing mattered except finding release with Veiron.

"Veiron." His name fell from her lips in a whispered plea that he answered by thrusting harder, deeper, pinning her body against his and taking her. He growled and snarled, a beast in her arms, primal and strong, wild and untamed. Everything she had begun to love about this man.

Erin tipped her head back and surrendered to him, letting him have his way with her, body filling with pleasure that threatened to sweep her away if she didn't find release soon.

Veiron gave it to her. He withdrew and with the next hard plunge of his long cock a dazzling burst of white-hot fire exploded from her core, coursing through her veins and carrying her away into an endless sea of warmth and hazy bliss. She couldn't remember if she had cried his name, or jerked against him. The sensations he ignited and detonated within her swamped all physical awareness of her body, leaving her floating on an emotional plane of existence.

Veiron growled something that she hazily thought sounded like 'mine'.

His cock throbbed, shooting his hot seed into her quaking core and he stilled above her, hands pressing hard into her flesh, clutching her to him as his body trembled.

Erin felt too sated too move, too boneless and warm. He settled above her, body pressing into hers, and she realised that he was shaking too. His breath skated across her cheek and washed her face with heat. Erin opened her eyes and looked up into his, and found them dark and fathomless, but not cold. There was such heat in them. Not passion but something stronger, something that echoed within her.

Before she could figure it out, he closed his eyes and rolled onto his back, bringing her with him.

He settled with her on his chest, her cheek pressing against it, and his large hand covered the other side of her head, keeping her there.

She listened to his heart pounding, a fast drumming that matched his breathing, and closed her eyes.

She had never experienced anything so primal in nature. She'd had some wild sex in her life, even some risky out in the open sex, but she had never felt as she had just now with Veiron. It invaded her afterglow, leaving her mind churning.

Erin focused on his breathing and heartbeat, battling the rising desire to sleep in his strong arms, safe from her nightmares. She wanted to unravel the puzzle, wanted to know what it was about Veiron that had her feeling so connected to him, if it was anything at all. Maybe they were just a perfect fit.

Made for each other.

Veiron wrapped his arms around her, pulled her up to him so his softening cock slipped free of her body, and then dragged the flimsy blanket over them both.

He stroked her hair, the motion soothing, luring her to sleep.

She fought it.

He sighed, as though he had felt her battling her need for rest.

"Sleep," he said, sounding tired himself. "I'll watch over you. No beasties will come near you."

"What about in my dreams?" she whispered, feeling like a child for mentioning it and admitting she was scared of her nightmares.

"Dream about me... like you were in the cave."

She tensed. How had he known she had been dreaming about him then? Her dream hadn't compared to the reality. Not even close. That had her feeling awake again, aware of the naked man beneath her, wanting another go with her on top this time.

"No denial?" There was a smile in his voice. So he had been guessing after all and her reaction had given her away. He chuckled and she liked the sound of it. It relaxed her. "You had good dreams both times you've slept in my arms. I don't know how it works, but I swear to you, if I make the bad ones go away somehow, I will do it again for you now."

That was sweet of him. Noble. Protecting her even in her dreams.

But she didn't want to close her eyes and go there again.

"What if something happens and you have to go away to speak with Taylor or Einar?" she whispered and circled his pebbled nipple with her fingertip. "I don't want to dream like I did just an hour ago. I don't want to see that again."

"I swear, Erin," he said on a sigh and stroked her hair. "That I will not leave your side until you wake."

That comforted her but she read into his words. He wouldn't leave her until she woke. He was still planning to leave her then. She had felt it a few times now, an awareness of his intentions followed by a soul deep need to make him stay somehow.

"Sleep, Sweetheart," he whispered and held her head to his firm chest. His breathing soothed her, soft and steady, and she looked up at him to find him watching her, his eyes as tender as his touch. "If something happens, I'll wake you. I promise you, I won't leave you alone again."

Erin felt that promise deep in her heart. He meant it. He would stay with her, never leaving her side, at least until he had reunited her with Amelia. She would take that much for now, but she wasn't giving up on him.

She would find a way to make him stay with her.

She would never let him go.

He was hers now.

A single word echoed through her mind as she drifted off to sleep, Veiron's arms wrapped around her, holding her close to him, protecting her. Whether the word came from his half of their soul or hers, she would never know, but it was something she felt in every fibre of her being, and it was something she knew she would never feel with anyone other than Veiron.

Mine.

CHAPTER 13

Mine.

Veiron had fallen asleep after thinking it for over an hour whilst watching Erin sleeping in his arms. That single word had been in his head, ever constant, never fading. Whenever he looked at her, it screamed in his mind, beat in his veins, drummed in his heart and awoke in his soul. A deep, unrelenting need to shout it at the top of his lungs so the whole world would hear and to whisper it into her ear so his whole world would know it, rode him all through the time he had spent sleeping with her in his arms.

Sleeping.

He couldn't remember the last time he had slept with a woman. He wasn't talking about post-sex sleep where he couldn't help crashing on his front and snoring up a storm. He was talking about laying with a woman in his arms, holding her flush against his body, aware of her even in sleep. He was talking about sleeping after making love, contented, both his body and his heart sated by a shared intimate moment.

When was the last time he had made love?

He was sure it might have happened with Taylor, but she had always been about the wicked and wanton rather than the deep and soul-searching. What he had done with Erin had gone beyond physical connection and release.

And that was a grand fucking mistake.

His biggest one yet.

He had thought that by sleeping with her, scratching the itch he had to get down and dirty with her, he would satisfy the desire he felt for her, the pull and the deep need.

He couldn't have been more wrong.

What they had experienced together hadn't got her out from under his skin. It had only made his need for her burrow deeper into his flesh and he had a terrible feeling it was heading straight for his heart.

He couldn't stop thinking about her. Even when she was out of sight. His hunger to see her and have her close to him only worsened then.

No good was going to come of this.

She might have accepted a side of himself he had thought she would reject, but she was still mortal and fragile, and he was still a wanted man. He wasn't right for her. She needed someone safe, someone who would protect her. He could do the latter but he wasn't the former. Danger followed him everywhere and until he'd had his vengeance, it wasn't going to go away. Afterwards? Well, he didn't think the Devil and God would take his insubordination lying down, and he was probably unlikely to see such a thing as afterwards. They would kill him before he could do much damage. Even if he had an entire army of angels at his back and all the legions of demons in Hell under his command, he wouldn't be able to defeat the Devil or his purer counterpart on high. Neither of them ever flexed their muscles but they would if Veiron proved a threat. It would only take a flick of one finger against him to shatter every bone in his body and reset his position on their chessboard.

"You're thinking a lot today," Erin said, voice soft and luring him back to the world. She walked beside him, milky evening winter sunlight streaming down on her, casting highlights in her cropped black hair and causing the lilac stripe down the right side to shine vividly.

He shouldn't be out in the open with her but it seemed he lacked an ability to voice the words in his head when it came to her. Everything came out the opposite of what he intended to say.

When she had woken, refreshed from close to eleven hours of nightmare-free sleep, and had eaten a small bowl of fruit, she had asked him to take her back to her apartment so she could gather some clothes. Every instinct had told him to say no. His mouth had said yes.

Instincts meant nothing when it came to Erin. His heart overruled them all, forcing him to let her have her way, indulging her even when it was dangerous.

He had tried to take it back and convince her that going to her apartment was asking for trouble, especially when they had encountered Hell's angels barely a day ago and reinforcements would be looking for them. Erin had listened to none of it. She had shot down every excuse with a sweet smile and a reminder that he was more than capable of protecting her.

While he enjoyed her faith in him and his abilities as her protector, he didn't enjoy her rubbing his ego to manipulate him into doing what she wanted.

Neither did he enjoy the fact that it didn't even take much of a rub to force his agreement. He was too pliant when it came to all things Erin, too eager to please.

Where was the soulless and merciless warrior now?

He had hardened his heart to females, to everyone, focusing entirely on his need for vengeance and his mission. He had vowed not to stop until he had fulfilled that mission and he was free of what felt like a curse. No woman, no man, nothing would stand between him and success or divert his attention.

Erin had softened him. He had tried to fight her, had closed himself off repeatedly, shutting down his emotions and hardening his heart once more, but whenever she was near to him, her fragrance filling his senses and making him hunger for her, he softened again.

"Veiron?" she whispered and he cast a glance across at her.

Her amber eyes were luminous, wide and full of something that looked a lot like guilt.

"Are you upset with me?"

What had given her that impression? His brooding silence, the way he trudged beside her with his gaze scanning and eyes promising bloody murder, or the fact he hadn't looked at her since leaving Taylor's house this afternoon?

He didn't feel like lying to her so he nodded.

Her eyes went a little wider and then she cast them down to her feet. She jammed her hands into the pockets of her borrowed black jeans. The action made her look small and ramped up his need to protect her, to defend her against all the evil in the world around them. Veiron moved closer to her and struggled with himself. She was wearing his leather so he had no excuse that he was keeping the chill off her when he slung his arm around her shoulders. It was a purely possessive move, primal in nature, an instinct that he couldn't ignore. His fingers closed around the cold black leather over her shoulder and he pulled her into his side.

Erin glanced up at him. "Not mad at me?"

He grunted.

She stopped, turned into him and pressed her hands against his chest, burning him through his black shirt. Her tongue swept out, teasing him as it caressed her lips, readying them for a kiss that he too willingly took. He dipped his head, dropped his hands to her backside, and raised her up his body so her sweet lips easily met his. The kiss warmed him deep into his bones, a soft reaffirmation of her desire and his, a mutual understanding and need to know everything was on an even keel between them.

Erin drew back, her smile impish and sweet, contradicting the hunger that swamped her eyes and turned them wicked, promising that she wasn't done with him yet. She was so small in his arms, so light and willowy. He held her to him, clutching her bottom, aware that the people passing them by on the shopping street were staring.

She brushed her knuckles across his cheek, her eyes holding his, claiming his attention. He had never met a woman who could do that to him. When Erin looked into his eyes, the whole of his focus zoomed to her and he lost track of his surroundings. Anyone could have snuck up on him and stabbed him.

But no one could have snuck up on her.

Veiron felt sure of that. He was so focused on her and keeping her safe that he would sense any attempt to attack her before the enemy came within striking distance. She was his to protect.

Mine.

He thought it as he stared deep into her eyes, a feeling of connection blossoming between them again. He wanted to say the words and punctuate each one with a kiss that would brand his name on her soul.

You. Are. Mine.

Forever.

Veiron tensed at that addition.

Not forever. Just for now. He would have to leave her when they eventually found Amelia. It was for the best, no matter how much his heart ached at the thought of never seeing her again and rebelled against his better judgement. Sweet Erin. Would she ever forgive him?

Forget him?

That thought made him want to cling to her, to hold her close to him and snarl at any who tried to take her from him.

She was his.

She ran her fingertip lightly across his lower lip, sending it tingling, and stared deep into his eyes, hers full of warmth and what looked like understanding.

He wasn't guarding himself well. Could she see the battle raging in his heart through his eyes? Leaving her warred with needing to stay.

Veiron closed his eyes and lowered her to the pavement. He withdrew his hands and took a step backwards, placing a small distance between them. When he opened his eyes, she had her back to him and he could feel a glimmer of her hurt beating in his own heart.

It had to be this way. He couldn't keep her. Couldn't she see that?

He raked a hand over his scarlet hair.

Couldn't he see that?

Every fibre of him rebelled against the thought of leaving her, beating down the need and the reasons, screaming and railing against them.

Veiron closed his eyes and sighed. Fuck. He needed to get his head straight and kick his heart into line.

First, he needed to get Erin off the street and get this crazy mission of hers over with.

He grabbed her hand. He had meant to hold it in a friendly fashion, forcing her to move forwards and lead him to her apartment. Instead, he interlinked their fingers, clasping her hand tightly with her palm pressing against his. Erin's gaze returned to him but he didn't look at her, wouldn't while he was still trying to get at least his head straight.

"We need to keep moving," he said, gruff and commanding, no hint of warmth or apology.

His heart gave one to her wordlessly.

It made him squeeze her hand. A slight switch in pressure. A silent reassurance.

It spurred her into motion. She began walking again and less than ten minutes later, she stopped outside an old brick apartment building in one of the London suburbs he was less familiar with.

It seemed safe enough, but part of Veiron still didn't like the thought that she had lived here alone.

A man left the building, pushing the brass-edged glass doors open. He smiled at Erin and held them for her. Too familiar. Veiron wanted to tear his head off. He must have let a growl slip because the man's focus shifted to him and his smile fell away. Veiron straightened to his full height and glared down at the mortal.

He left quickly.

Veiron smiled to himself. Smug and satisfied. Both feelings faded when he looked at Erin. She stood in the centre of a low-lit foyer, a frown on her face. Unimpressed.

"Are you going to go caveman on every man in my building? I do have to live here, you know?"

No. She didn't. She wouldn't. At least not alone. Not without protection. His protection. He snarled, a possessive growl designed to release his fierce need to protect his female and let everyone in the building know it.

All it seemed to do was startle Erin.

And then a slow smile spread across her pretty face.

"You know, I think I like you jealous. I might flirt with the guy who owns the other loft apartment just to see you all growly again."

Veiron glared at her, aware that his eyes were shifting, burning red, and the skin around them was darkening. His muscles itched, bunched, stretched and began to lengthen as his bones creaked and started to grow.

"I didn't mean it." Erin rushed towards him, panic in her wide eyes, her hands fluttering wildly in front of her. She settled them against his chest and he realised that he had already grown over a foot. His heart pounded, accelerated, emotions fuelling the change. "I take it back. I won't flirt with anyone... so it's all good, right? You can stop going all demonic. I don't want company."

That tossed a bucket of icy water on the fire of his emotions.

Veiron instantly shut down his hunger to unleash his temper on a man he had never even met and focused on Erin, using her as an anchor. It was hard to switch halfway through a change but he managed it, using his need to protect her and keep her safe, and not give away their location, to calm his darker side and bring it back under his control.

"Fuck," he growled, grabbed Erin and threw one hand out in front of him.

She gasped as a blazing white portal appeared. "What about my stuff?"

"Quiet," he snapped and leapt into the portal. He appeared a few hundred yards up the street with her, landing hard in a narrow alley. Another shimmering wall appeared before his outstretched hand.

He didn't go through this one. He lowered Erin to the pavement, seized her hand and turned with her, walking back to the main street. He jogged along it and when she limped, he remembered that her feet were still sore. Einar had healed the injuries given to her by the Hell's angel but Veiron had neglected to mention the cuts on the soles of her feet, something he would rectify when they returned to the safe house.

Veiron scooped her up into his arms, carrying her nestled safely against his chest, and didn't slow until he was back at her building.

"Now the door is locked and I don't have a key." Her matter-of-fact tone didn't sit well with him.

The enemy couldn't tell the time at which he used his powers. They just sensed it happening and it was usually a delayed feeling. He waved his fingers towards the door and it opened. They wouldn't be able to distinguish it from the other times he had used his powers in the area.

Veiron carried Erin across the false marble floor to the lifts and pressed the button to call one. When it came and the brass doors had opened, Veiron stalked inside and set Erin down. She pressed the button for the top floor.

Could he risk using his powers to open the door to her apartment when they reached it?

He pondered that as the lift rose, carrying them high into the building. It stopped and the doors pinged and slid open.

Erin exited ahead of him. Veiron growled, a warning shot across her bow, and pulled her back to him. He held her close, clutching her arm, and prowled forwards, gaze scanning and senses on high alert. She didn't protest. Her free hand wrapped around his arm and she held it, her body pressed against its length. He liked the feel of her there, close to him, needing him. He liked it a little too much if he was feeling honest with himself.

"Wait," she said and he stopped halfway along the stark white corridor. She turned towards a door. Hers? She knocked. Not hers. If she was planning on going through with her threat to flirt with the other occupant of this floor, he was going to be more than angry.

The door opened and a smartly dressed man stood in the doorway, his sandy hair slicked back as though he had just had a shower. The deep blue shirt and dark charcoal trousers did nothing to conceal his physique.

Veiron barely held his growl inside when the mortal's blue eyes settled on Erin and he smiled.

"Good Lord above, I haven't seen you in weeks." The man pulled her into a quick hug that set Veiron's blood on fire. "Allan will be so relieved. He's been fretting. We thought something had happened to you."

Erin shrugged. "I've just been busy with work and haven't been out much other than to stay with my boyfriend."

The mortal male's blue eyes shot to him. His smile was nothing short of flirtatious.

Veiron stiffened.

"Well, hello handsome."

Veiron took a step backwards and the man chuckled, his attention returning to Erin. "I take it he isn't into same sex partners?"

Erin shook her head and looped her arm around Veiron's. He was still trying to catch up. This was the man who Erin had said she would flirt with to make him jealous? A man who had a partner called Allan and who was looking at him as though he was a wet dream come true?

"He's one hundred percent straight and one hundred percent mine," Erin said on a smile and Veiron's gaze shot to her, his blood burning for a different reason now.

Mine.

You. Are. Mine.

He wanted to growl it and kiss her, to reach right down to her soul and shake her to her core so she knew it. She belonged to him now.

And forever.

"I didn't call by to show off my new toy though. I forgot my keys at his house and need to get into my flat. Can I have my spares?" Erin stroked his arm and Veiron couldn't take his eyes off her, or his mind off that one word as it hammered inside his skull and beat in his blood.

Mine.

She had said it too. Did she feel the same way as he did? Did her blood heat in her veins whenever their eyes met and her heart pound whenever they touched? When they had made love last night, had she felt connected all the way down to her soul, as though they were made for each other?

The man disappeared, shifting to the periphery of Veiron's senses. He jingled as he returned and held out a set of keys to Erin.

She took them with a smile, said something Veiron didn't hear, and took her leave. Veiron followed her, hazy and lost in his thoughts, trying to decipher whether Erin had experienced the same depth of feelings as he had in her arms.

Had she meant what she'd said or had it just been an act?

He needed to know.

She unlocked a plain white door and pushed it open. Veiron caught her arm when she went to walk straight in, pulled her back in line with him and turned her to face him.

"Wait here," he said and stalked into the apartment. It was spacious and open plan for the most part. There was a wall on the right of the huge white room, dividing what he discovered was the bedroom. Massive windows to his left let the fading evening light flood into the equally white room. The only colours were the rich purple covers on the double bed in the middle of the room and a wall of lilac glass blocks to his right that separated the bathroom from the bedroom.

Veiron turned on his heel and backtracked into the main room of the loft apartment. The ceiling was open and industrial, all silver pipes and dark concrete, and a contrast to the pale wooden floor and the crisp white walls. A bright red sofa stood in front of a large flat screen television screwed to the wall of the apartment nearest the door. At a right angle to it was a black chaise longue scattered with paper and books. A glass coffee table equally swamped with books filled the space between them.

He cast a quick glance at the open kitchen. The cupboards lining the wall and floor were a shocking shade of pink that matched the island that formed a barrier between the kitchen and living room. That was the only startling thing in the apartment. He had never figured Erin as a Barbie pink sort of woman.

No one was here.

He nodded to Erin.

She entered and closed the door behind her. A flicker of nerves shone in her eyes, a potent reminder that the last time she had been here, one of his kind had come and dragged her down to Hell.

Veiron felt sorry for her as she moved around the apartment, cautious, alert, and afraid. This place was clearly her home but she obviously no longer felt that way. What had happened had left her feeling wary of the place, scared that something bad would happen to her again.

"I'll just get some things together and we can go," she said and hurried into her bedroom.

Veiron occupied himself by looking around her apartment. The sun had set beyond the bank of windows along one wall of the expansive room. He strode over to them and looked out at the hotchpotch rooftops, and then at his surroundings. It was a beautiful apartment, modern and clean. He was surprised when his gaze fell on an area close to the windows. A large monitor took up most of the space on the white desk against the wall that closed off the bedroom. It was almost as big as the television. Other equipment filled the rest of the desk. Some large black flat thing with something that looked like a pen resting on it. A wire attached it to the computer tower beside the monitor.

What really took Veiron's breath away was the stack of canvases leaning against the wall next to the desk. He picked one up and couldn't stop there. Each one was more beautiful than the last, scenes of incredible alien lands and enchanting forests and mountains. The colours in them vibrated, bursting with life.

In the corner of each, small neat letters formed Erin's name. These were her paintings. There were no art materials in the room though. Had she painted them elsewhere? He looked closer at the canvases and realised they were printed. His gaze slid to the wide black thing on the desk and the pen. Had Erin drawn these on her computer?

He had never seen such vivid imagery captured by the human hand before. It looked so real, as though he could step into each painting and find himself in that world born of her imagination.

"Veiron, I just want to—" She stopped dead in the doorway of her bedroom. "What are you doing?"

He frowned when she hurried over and tried to take the canvas from his grip. Her cheeks blazed red. Was she angry?

"I didn't mean to upset you. I just saw them and I couldn't help taking a closer look."

"I'm not upset, really... they're silly... just... give it to me please?"

Not angry. Embarrassed. Why? They were amazing.

"They're beautiful, Erin. Did you do all of these?"

Her cheeks burned a deeper shade and she averted her eyes. The smallest nod in the world was her answer. An artist who couldn't take compliments. Or perhaps it was because he was the one complimenting her that she blushed so deeply.

He smiled to alleviate her nerves. "If I had an apartment like this, I would want art like yours on my walls. They really are beautiful. You're very talented."

She nibbled her lip and came forwards, standing close to him so she could see the one he admired. It was a dragon curled around a spire of rock, its leathery wings furled close to its spiky back. A wintry landscape stretched far beyond it. A white castle loomed in the distance, and snowy pines stretched high and dark to the left, filling the middle of the painting and enclosing the castle on one side and a lake on the other. Pale sunlight streamed down through broken clouds and made the frozen lake in the foreground twinkle.

It was the dragon that fascinated him though. So much detail. Its scales sparkled, iridescent like a beetle's shell, a multitude of colours. Its eyes were amber and bright, red flecks burning in them. Smoke curled from its crocodilian jaw, escaping from between sharp hooked teeth.

"It's one of my favourites," Erin whispered and then stepped away from him. "I have the dragon tattooed on my back."

She turned around, removed his leather jacket, setting it down on her desk, and then tugged her black baby-doll t-shirt up to reveal her back.

Veiron put the canvas down with the others and stared at her back. He ran his fingers over her soft skin, following the elaborate design of the dragon that curled around her spine just as the one in the painting curled around the rock. It disappeared into her flesh and reappeared further down, as though it really was wrapped around her spine, a part of her. This one had its wings spread though, stretched across her shoulder blades.

Wings like his.

He traced them and she shivered, and he felt the mood shift and his desire rising.

It didn't stop him. Nothing could. Not even Hell erupting on Earth.

"It's beautiful," he murmured and she looked over her shoulder at him, her eyes dark with arousal. "You're beautiful."

Erin turned to face him. She smiled, wicked and mischievous, bewitching, and took hold of his hand. She walked backwards, bringing him with her, leading him towards the bedroom.

"Where are we going?" he said, eyes on her and only her.

Her smile hit him hard. "You're dirty... I think we need to scrub you clean."

Oh, he was dirty all right. His mind homed in on her suggestion and it only made him dirtier. Erin. Naked. Shower. Wet. So damn hot.

So everything he needed right now.

CHAPTER 14

Erin stripped as she walked through the bedroom, Veiron hot on her heels, his gaze following her every move and drinking in each inch of skin she exposed. He unbuttoned his black shirt and cast it off. Undressing manually was torture but one he endured. He couldn't use any more of his power, not without alerting scouts who were probably in the area by now, looking for him and Erin. That thought made him reconsider what they were doing, but only for a split second, a flash of time before his mind said to go for it and screw the consequences. If someone dared interrupt them while they were in the shower, naked, writhing against each other, he would separate them from vital parts of their anatomy with his bare hands.

He growled and Erin paused on the threshold of her bathroom. She looked over her shoulder at him, a coy smile on her lips, and he growled for a whole other reason.

Veiron reached out, grabbed her wrist and spun her into his arms. She gasped, the sound music to his ears, and her eyes widened. They met his and he drowned in them, in the desire they showed him, like windows right into her emotions. He slid one arm around her lower back and splayed his other hand out between her shoulder blades, anchoring her to him, and kissed her, claiming her lips with his own. His. She was his woman. His Erin.

God forbid anyone try to change that.

He kept kissing her as he moved with her, taking her into the bathroom. Her bottom hit the vanity unit directly opposite the door and he grasped her waist and lifted her onto it. She had managed to get out of all of her clothes except her jeans. He made fast work of them, his fingers undoing the belt and then the button and fly, his mouth working against hers at the same time, savouring her taste and her warmth. She moaned and then gasped again when he yanked her jeans, whipping them out from under her backside. Her giggle echoed around the white tiles and she lifted her legs. Veiron snarled and pulled her black jeans down them, and tossed them over his shoulder.

Erin ran her bare feet over his chest and he caught her ankles. He frowned and rested one of her feet on his shoulder, turning all of his attention to her other one. He stroked the sole of her foot, following the arch, and she giggled. Veiron remained serious. She was healing, the cuts and scratches already past the scab stage, but the scars were red, angry. He kissed them, lavishing each one with care, as if that alone could heal them completely and take her pain away. He wished it could.

When he had kissed every scar on that foot, he moved to the other, giving it the same attention as the first. Erin sighed with each kiss and the mood shifted again, away from a dark hunger to have her to an equally black need to protect and care for her.

She took her leg from him and settled them on either side of his hips. He looked down, eyes drifting over the dusky pink buds of her nipples that tipped her beautiful small breasts to the flat plane of her stomach and down past her navel to his new heaven. Lilac knickers. Definitely hers and not borrowed from Taylor. He liked seeing her in something that belonged to her. This was Erin. Colourful inside. Full of vibrant life.

It was almost a shame that they had to come off.

He hooked his fingers into the waist of her flimsy lace underwear and she raised her bottom off the vanity top. He slid them to her thighs and then tugged them over her knees and down her calves. He tossed them onto the floor with the rest of their clothes. Before he could set to work on making Erin scream his name again, she was undoing his belt and his jeans, pushing them down to his knees and freeing his raging erection. She dropped to her knees before him and he hissed through his teeth at the first contact between her soft mouth and his hard flesh.

Erin moaned, deep and throaty, a sound that vibrated down the length of his cock.

Veiron tipped his head back and struggled for control, mind overloading from the way she moved her mouth on him, up and down, teasing the crown with her tongue, swirling it in the most delicious way. He groaned and fisted his hand in her black hair, guiding her on his cock. The groans soon reduced to guttural grunts, animalistic sounds but he wasn't capable of doing anything more civilised. He pumped his hips, gently rocking his cock into her warm wet mouth, imagining it to be another part of her.

Fuck, he needed to get back inside her.

Veiron grabbed her arm, dragged her up to him and kissed her hard. She moaned, her arms instantly looping around his shoulders, short nails scoring his back. He angled his head and deepened the kiss, claiming possession of her mouth, seizing control of the moment. Erin's clawing subsided into stroking.

She ran her fingertips down the lines where his wings hid and they erupted, springing from his back so quickly that he didn't have a chance to stop them. They smacked into the wall on one side and the shower cubicle on the other, and an ache raced up their bones.

Fucking fuckety fuck.

That wasn't good.

"Shit... sorry," Erin whispered and bit her lip as he stepped back and quickly focused, forcing his wings away and praying that he hadn't just made an army of heads snap in his direction. If there were any Hell's angels in the area looking for him after his earlier outburst, they would know that he was here still.

He stared at Erin, torn between stopping and continuing.

Continuing won.

But the shower would have to wait.

"Need you," Veiron said, more a statement than a request for her permission.

Erin blushed delightfully and held her arms out to him again. He growled and stepped into her, pulled her flush against him and kissed her again, losing himself in how good it felt. She wriggled against him, moist centre against his hard cock, torturing him. He groaned and grabbed her bottom, and lifted her off the vanity.

She mewled a protest when he turned not towards the shower but the bed. It was hard to move with his jeans around his ankles but he made it to the purple double bed and fell onto it with her. She laughed when he growled at his jeans, trying to kick them off without releasing her. He gave up, rolled off her, and managed to toe his boots off and shuck his jeans in record time.

Erin crawled backwards on the bed, her wicked smile still in place, bare body calling out to him. He knelt on the mattress, grabbed her ankle and pulled her to him. He caught her wrist, tugged her up into his arms, and crushed her lips with another hot demanding kiss. She moaned and wrapped herself around him, straddling his knees as he knelt on the bed. Veiron couldn't wait. Her heat pressed against him, slick and ready, and a need to have her right that moment drove him to comply. He raised her up his body and then slowly lowered her onto his cock. He entered her gently this time, breathing hard with her, savouring how good it felt as he inched into her warm depths.

"Veiron," she whispered into his mouth. A plea. A command. A praise.

"Erin," he murmured against her sweet lips, grasped her hips and rocked with her, as slowly as he could manage when the feel of her pushed him to take her completely and let her know that she was his, that he inside her was more than sex. It was possession. Plain and simple. A claiming.

His woman.

He kissed her, focused on her sliding up and down, taking him into her body, welcoming him and giving him bliss in return. She moaned, sighed, and whispered his name in a broken voice that made his heart rejoice. He laid her down and covered her body with his, held her as he kissed her and rocked into her, slow and steady, long and deep, stretching out the moment. Not sex. Making love.

He had expected their second time to be less explosive than their first but he was wrong. It went deeper this time, the connection between them searing him beyond his soul, stamping her name on every inch of him as he sought to brand his on every fibre of her.

She moaned and sighed again, held him to her, her hands gentle on his back now, swirling and shifting, caressing. She raised her hips to his, granting him deeper access, tearing a groan from his throat. He wanted this to go on forever.

Veiron kissed her lips, her cheek, her throat. Every inch of her that he could reach without breaking his stroke. He worshipped her, savoured her and lost himself in her, until he felt as though they had blended, linked by their desire and passion, slaves to sensation. She peppered his throat with licks and kisses, buried her face in his neck as she arched up and groaned, her feet hooking over his backside. He pumped her harder and deeper, filled with a need to possess her, to utter words in her ear that would be his downfall. He could never leave her if he said such things to her, not without breaking her heart, not even when they were true.

Erin was his everything.

How it had happened, he didn't know, but happened it had.

He kissed her, tongue tangling with hers, tasting her and claiming her lips as surely as he claimed the rest of her body.

And she claimed his.

He was no fool.

The possession thing worked both ways. He was a slave to her, a warrior at her command, a beast at her beck and call.

She rolled them over, landing atop him, not breaking their slow deliberate stroke. He ran his palms up her thighs to her hips and guided her on his cock, staring deep into her eyes. Her hands settled on his chest, flat against it, so hot on his skin, and she rode him.

A woman had never looked at him the way Erin did, as though she could see straight down into his soul and cherished what she saw there, thought he was strong because of it not weak. Loved him for what he was.

The look in her amber eyes promised him that she would always look at him this way, as though he was the centre of her universe, regardless of what he did. She knew. She knew all of him, every facet of the man that he was—the killer, the warrior, the protector, and the demon. She knew the good and the bad in him, and she accepted it all.

And by God did he love her for it.

Erin threw her head back and moaned his name, the sound so utterly delicious that he moaned too, thrilled by the pleasure he heard in it.

She bit her lip, white teeth sinking deep into soft flesh.

Veiron growled.

His focus zeroed in on her teeth and her lip. He wanted to bite her.

Her eyes fluttered open and dropped to meet his. No fear in them. Just quiet acceptance as she nibbled her lower lip and stared down at him, rocking her body on his cock, flooding him with heat and emotions that he had tried to stamp out so many times in the past few days.

He couldn't break the spell she had placed on him.

His addiction to her ran deep in his veins, in his soul and his heart, and he couldn't fight it. All he could do was hope that he wouldn't lose her, that nothing would take away this woman that had become his life, because he would die without her.

She leaned over him and he raised his hips, clutching her bottom as he slid in and out, thrusting deeper as he captured her mouth again. Her moans deepened, filling his ears, mingling with his own. He needed more of her. All of her. He couldn't get enough.

Erin gasped into his mouth and jerked, her body milking him, quivering and trembling around his cock. He groaned and moved her harder, plunged deeper, his possessive streak taking control again. He wanted to brand her body. Claim it as his and his alone. No other man would touch her. Never again. Erin was his now. No doubt about that. He would kill anyone who so much as looked at her.

She tensed her body around his and he groaned, his balls tightened and he thrust deep into her core, jetting his seed into her. He throbbed discordantly to her, each pulse stealing a little of his tension until he was limp beneath her, sated for now, but not for long. At the back of his mind, he already wanted her again, needed to have her in a different way, in every way imaginable until she knew that she belonged to him.

Erin settled on his chest, a contented sigh escaping her lips and making him smile.

Awareness of his surroundings slowly returned and with it came a cold prickling down his spine. Was five minutes to bask in their afterglow too much to ask?

"We need to move." He tried to rouse her but she moaned and scrunched her nose at the order before curling up. "Erin. It isn't safe here. We're moving. Now."

He didn't give her a chance to respond. He lifted her off him and gathered their clothes, tugging his on as he went and tossing hers at her. She sat up on the bed, alert now, the post-sex haze gone from her amber eyes. She hopped off the bed and went into the bathroom. Veiron finished dressing, grabbed his leather jacket from the desk and slung it on.

Erin appeared a moment later, a black holdall in her right hand and a pair of black army boots in the other. She dropped the boots and slipped her feet into them. Veiron paused to watch her, losing track of his surroundings as he set eyes on the real Erin for the first time.

She wore a purple tartan pleated short skirt over black leggings, a black baby-doll t-shirt trimmed with lace, and a black flared winter coat that only reached to the bottom of her skirt. Impish. And boy did he love it.

"Ready," she said and straightened, and caught him staring. He expected her to blush and look away, to react the shy way she had when he had complimented her artwork. She didn't. She twirled on the spot, one foot coming up off the floor, her coat flaring outwards, and stopped facing him. She smiled. "You like?"

Veiron growled his appreciation and then showed her just how much he liked her in her own clothes. He stalked towards her, slung his arm around her narrow waist and dragged her up to him for a long deep kiss that threatened to take them back to square one and back into her bedroom.

"Mmm," she murmured against his mouth and he pulled back. Her smile was brilliant. "As much as I want to get wicked with you again, shouldn't we be making tracks?"

Tracks. Right. Fleeing. Something that didn't sit well with him but was necessary. He couldn't fight without placing Erin in danger. He wouldn't make that mistake again.

He took her black bag from her and slung it over his right shoulder, and held onto her with his left. He guided her out of the apartment, waiting while she locked it and made sure it was secure, and then led her down the white hall to the lifts. They would be too obvious, so he took the stairs with her, his boots and hers pounding the concrete steps.

Veiron kept his senses on high alert. The prickling feeling of awareness was growing worse, meaning whatever was nearby was getting closer.

They reached the foyer without incident, crossed it and broke out into the night. The number of people on the streets had dropped but there were still enough that they could blend with them. He turned to his right, intending to head back the way he had come with Erin.

No sign of one of his kind.

What the hell had his senses blaring then?

Erin gasped and stopped dead, yanking back on his arm to stop him too.

Her eyes were wide when he looked at her, fixed beyond him. Veiron looked at the people milling around, going about their lives. No Hell's angels. Just mortals.

A man raised his head and looked over the mortals at him.

White hair. Green eyes.

Those eyes flashed brightly and then a frown darkened them.

The man from Erin's nightmare.

Her guardian angel.

CHAPTER 15

Erin didn't wait to see if the man was friend or foe. She pulled on Veiron's arm and ran in the opposite direction, heart pounding and lungs squeezing. Veiron grabbed her around the waist, swore a black oath under his breath, and leapt. He cleared the heads of the crowd, causing a stir. His right boot hit the roof of a parked car and he pushed up into the air.

Erin expected to fall.

Instead, they lifted off and she looked back to see that Veiron had unfurled his wings and was now wearing his armour. Her bag was gone too. Where?

He beat his crimson wings and shot higher with her. Erin looked down as the ground fell away and her eyes widened.

"He's following," she shouted over the wind and Veiron swore again.

She looked at his hands on her waist and the city below her. The exact same view she had seen in her nightmare only London had been burning and it had been the other angel holding her, flying with her, not Veiron.

What did that mean?

Had they already done something to change that future into this one?

Veiron set her down on the same rooftop as the other angel had in her nightmare and she trembled, shaking down to her bones, and scoured the sky. She tried to remember what had happened. The man had wanted her to go with him and Veiron had appeared behind him, high in the air and coming down fast to attack the man.

"Veiron!" Erin sprinted for him where he stood in the middle of the flat black roof and he turned towards her.

Giving his back to the angel who appeared behind him, silver-blue wings bright in the crisp moonlight, his sword flashing as he raised it above his head.

Erin reacted on instinct.

She ran at Veiron, grabbed his arm and pulled him behind her, placing herself where he had been. The angel's sword came at her and her heart stopped, eyes as round as the full moon suspended above her. Before it could strike her down, Veiron's red curved blade was there, blocking its path to her.

"I should have put you down when I had the chance," Veiron snarled and shot past her, clashing with the angel in mid-air.

This was all wrong.

The angel knocked Veiron aside and then kicked him hard in the chest, sending him crashing into the roof. He tumbled across it, wings bending at angles that made Erin flinch, and hit the low wall near the edge.

"Veiron," Erin whispered and raced towards him.

The angel followed, landing hard on the roof and stalking towards her. She wouldn't let him attack Veiron again. Veiron pushed himself off the black tar and growled, shaking his head as though trying to clear it.

Erin had to protect him until he was able to fight again.

She did the only thing she could.

She picked up Veiron's double-ended black and red spear and faced the angel.

The man halted and stared at the weapon in her hands and then at her, a frown drawing his pale eyebrows together, confusion in his jade irises.

Erin braced her feet shoulder width apart, a warrior's stance that Veiron had taken many times in her presence, and held the short staff in both hands. It was heavy. Incredibly so. She wasn't sure how Veiron could wield it so easily. The broadsword weighed nothing compared to this weapon.

"You will fight me, Erin?" the man said, voice as cold and emotionless as it had been in her nightmare.

She nodded. "I will if you try to harm him."

This didn't seem to make sense to the angel. He frowned again.

"You would choose to side with evil over good?" His fingers flexed around his sword, the action causing the muscles in his toned arms to ripple. He drew a deep breath, raising the rich blue chest plate of his armour. The moon glinted off the silver edging.

"I'm not siding with good or evil. I'm siding with Veiron over you." She held her ground. A shuffling noise behind her signalled that Veiron had found his feet as much as the black glare the angel directed over her shoulder.

"I came to assist you," the angel said, calm and sweet now. He had clearly spent a lot of time practising his charming voice, the one designed to make mortals comply with his every command and believe in him.

It didn't work on Erin.

He frowned again. "Step aside and I will slay the Hell's angel."

Erin shook her head. The staff in her hands suddenly shot outwards, until it was four times its original length. The red blades at either end gleamed wickedly. She looked down and saw Veiron's hand on it, close to hers, and relief burned through her.

He stepped up behind her, until their bodies touched.

"How about I slay you?" Veiron said, all darkness and menace, a black promise that she knew he would keep if she let him. He would fight this angel, not because he was a threat to himself but because he was a threat to her.

"You had your chance when we were in the street and I had not noticed you." The angel lowered his weapon and turned his attention back to her. He actually smiled. "I mean you no harm, Erin. I am here to protect you. I am your guardian angel."

"You keep saying that but I don't believe it." Erin straightened and tipped her chin up, anger pouring like acid through her veins now. "If you are my guardian angel, where were you when I was taken to Hell?"

He flinched as though she had slapped him and recoiled. "I would not set foot in that realm, not even if my master commanded it. I was given orders to wait. It had been foreseen that the demon would seek to rescue you and would succeed, and that I would be granted this opportunity to take you into custody."

Custody. That was a strange word to use. Just as she had felt there was something wrong about him in her dreams, she felt it again now.

110

"Take me into custody?" She tightened her grip on Veiron's weapon. "By force, I presume?"

"If necessary."

"Do not listen to him, Erin." Veiron banded his free arm across her chest. "He speaks foul words."

"Quiet, Demon," the angel snarled, as vicious and dark as Veiron had ever been. He smiled again when he returned his attention to her. "I am your guardian, Erin. I only desire to protect you."

"You will have to get through me first." Veiron tensed and tried to take the weapon from her but she gripped it harder, refusing to let him fight. He growled but she didn't heed it.

"Easier done than said." The angel smirked at him. "I have orders to kill you anyway. Heaven desires you dead. You and those you have collaborated with. The female and Marcus."

Female? Amelia?

Erin was the one to growl this time. "You stay away from my sister!"

"Your sister?" The angel turned his smile on her, genuine amusement in his jade eyes. "My, we have been deluding ourselves."

"What do you mean?"

"Don't listen to him, Erin. Amelia is your sister, but she is a reincarnated angel. The original angel. Heaven and Hell sought her blood to seal the other realm. It is all a vicious game. She survived with the help of Marcus, and myself and others." Veiron's words weren't a comfort.

"And now you are all wanted men. I will fulfil my orders, Demon, starting with you." The angel launched himself at them, his sword a bright silver arc.

Veiron snatched the spear from her and attacked, evading the angel's strike and knocking him backwards. They clashed again, harder this time, each slashing and snarling with effort, taking their fight high into the night sky. Erin couldn't watch but she couldn't take her eyes away either. Her heart lodged in her throat and a strange sensation settled in her fingertips, heat prickling there.

The angel beat his wings, slammed into Veiron and sent him careening backwards through the air.

Erin's heart beat harder.

Her hands grew hotter.

The heat stole into her veins, until her arms were burning, boiling, and her head felt fuzzy. Her vision blurred but focused as the angel struck at Veiron, cutting across his obsidian chest plate and catching his arm. The smell of his blood hit her, the sight of it spilling down his arm and the smug look on the angel's handsome face causing rage to coil in her chest.

"I told you," Erin said and breathed hard, struggling to contain the heat blazing out of control within her. "If you harmed him... I would kill you... bitch."

The angel looked at her, the expression on his face saying he was going to laugh at her threat. His smile faded. Veiron looked at her too.

Erin felt dizzy.

She looked down and her eyes shot wide, her heart leaping high into her throat. Dark red flames licked up her arms and fluttered over her hands. She swiped at them, trying to put them out, afraid they would burn her, and then calmed.

Not burn her.

They hadn't in her dream.

She had used them as a weapon.

Her weapon.

Erin screamed and launched her hands forwards, towards the angel where he hovered ten metres above her. A dazzling crimson ball of fire blasted from between her palms and shot towards him. White light filled her vision, shooting down from the starry sky, and the world exploded so brightly it blinded her.

The light faded. Erin's head spun and she shivered, so cold that her bones ached and her fingers were stiff.

"Erin?" Veiron's deep baritone soothed her ears and warmed her from the inside out.

She slowly opened her eyes to find him above her, looking down at her, concern in his red eyes. Fear too. She scrambled up in his arms, her backside hit the flat roof and she threw a glance around, searching for the angel. Gone. The sky was black and still, the moon bright and drowning out the stars so they were faint. The city lights cut upwards around the building, glowing orange, and the sound of cars and people rose from below.

"What happened?" she said and swallowed to ease her dry throat. She thought back. Veiron had fought the angel. The angel had hurt Veiron. She had lost her temper and somehow called some sort of fire that she had used to blast the angel away. "Is he dead?"

Veiron shook his head. "He called a pathway to Heaven before you hit him with... whatever that was. What was that, Erin?"

"I don't know." She sat up and stared at her hands, trying to call the flames again and failing. "A power?"

She looked over her shoulder at Veiron. He frowned, red eyebrows pinched tightly above narrowed eyes that were focused on her hands. He took hold of them, turning them over, inspecting them. Her fingers warmed in his.

"Amelia can produce blue balls similar to that which you made." He sounded distant. Thinking aloud. It comforted her that Amelia had a power like she did and she clung to that as the explanation she desired.

"So I'm like her? An angel?" It sounded incredible and too good to be true.

Veiron reinforced that feeling. He shook his head. "I don't know what you are, Erin, but you're not like Amelia. Amelia is the reincarnation of the original angel. Only one was created before Heaven realised its mistake and created my kind instead, granting us less power and less freedom."

"So what am I?" Her voice shook and she cursed it for making her sound weak. She trembled inside, afraid of what was happening to her. "If I'm not like Amelia, what am I?"

"I don't know." Veiron rested his palm against her cheek, the soft look in his eyes conveying how much he wished he had answers for her. His hand was hot against her, calming her and soothing her pounding heart as much as the tenderness in his gaze and the knowledge that he wanted to help her. "You're something else... but we'll find out, I promise you. Was this what you did in your vision that scared you?"

Erin wished he wouldn't call her dreams and nightmares that. It made her recall what had happened in the second nightmare. She didn't want to have to watch Veiron dying before her eyes and be unable to do anything to stop it from happening. The whole scenario this evening had been similar to the first nightmare but all wrong, with the world different and the angel and Veiron's roles reversed. She hoped that meant that the second one would be different too now.

She nodded and he wrapped his arms around her. Erin leaned her head against the cold black armour protecting his chest and sighed. "The Devil hurt you and I wanted to stop him. I was so angry... consumed by rage... it was instinct."

"Just as it was earlier?"

Erin looked up at him and nodded. He was right. The angel had threatened those that she loved, had hurt Veiron, and a boiling abyss of rage had opened within her heart, all of it directed at the disgusting creature that had dared ignore her warning. Cold wind buffeted her, chilling her skin through her clothes, freezing her heart. She cuddled closer to Veiron, afraid of what it all meant and where her power came from.

Veiron rubbed her back, holding her against him, and pressed his lips to her forehead. He sighed.

"I will do all in my power to find out where your newfound abilities come from, Erin. It could just be that you have some power like your sister. It would make sense. You share genes, DNA, scientific shit. It's possible." He sounded as though he was trying to convince himself now rather than her but she appreciated it all the same.

Erin wrapped her arms around his neck and curled up on his lap, clinging to the one thing that felt solid in her world right now.

"I want to see my sister," she whispered against his throat and he stood with her, one arm behind her back and the other hooked under her knees.

"You will soon, Erin. I swear to you. We'll arrange a meeting place and leave immediately. We'll find out what's happening and I won't let anything happen to you. I will keep you safe." He pressed his forehead against hers and she nodded, believing every word he said.

Veiron spread his wings and flew with her. Erin looked over his shoulder at the place where he had fought the angel. At the place where she had unleashed a fireball straight out of her nightmares and tried to kill a man because he had harmed Veiron.

If she wasn't an angel like her sister, what was she?

CHAPTER 16

The hot sun on his back did nothing to improve Veiron's mood. Ever since the fight on the rooftop three nights ago, Erin had been quiet and brooding. Her smiles were false and she was keeping her distance from him. She had slept in his arms each night but they had only made love once, the same night as she had used a power neither of them knew anything about. He wished he had answers for the questions she refused to voice. He had explained things to Einar and Taylor but neither of them had been any help. Einar did share his opinion though. Whatever Erin was, she wasn't like her sister.

As far as he knew, Amelia hadn't exhibited any powers before dying and reawakening as an immortal, an angel.

Erin had been having visions for her whole life, and now she could use a devastating power that was on par with her sister's one. All without dying.

If it plagued him, he knew it plagued her a thousand times worse. She had little knowledge of his world, was only just becoming accustomed to there being a Heaven and Hell, angels and demons. He wanted to find the answers to her questions, wanted to convince her to speak to him about it rather than brood in silence, stewing over what had happened and trying to keep it all to herself. He was sure that by speaking to him about it, she would feel better. He could at least say something that might inspire more positive feelings in her heart.

"Not long now," he said and drew her closer. She bounced against him in time with the speedboat.

Her mood had brightened since the plane had set down and they had disembarked with their two black holdalls and headed for the dock. Her amber eyes shone as she looked up at him, a glimmer of excitement in them that warmed his heart and gave him some relief. Perhaps she would get over her fear in time, and in the arms of her sister.

Veiron had failed to soothe her. He hated that almost as much as he hated the divide that had grown between them.

"I've always wanted to go to the Maldives," she said, sounding as excited as any of the other mortals occupying the speedboat with them. Three other couples in total. One of them newlyweds.

According to the passports that Einar had arranged, he and Erin were also newly hitched.

That and the fact that Wingless had also booked them into the resort as freshly married and on their honeymoon didn't amuse Veiron in the slightest.

Erin leaned into his side, her black linen shirt blending into his tight t-shirt. They were the odd couple in the boat. The other six occupants were all wearing minimal clothing, as though it was optional, and all of it brightly coloured.

He and Erin were head to toe in black and both of them still wore their boots. No sandals for him. He had noticed a pair in Erin's luggage though and had smiled to himself. After everything that she had been through, she needed a vacation. He hoped that she found some peace on the island, with her sister.

He wasn't sure if he was staying or leaving on the next flight.

When he handed Erin over to Amelia and Marcus, his mission was finished. He had no reason to remain. She would be safe. He could return to nursing his need for revenge.

Couldn't he?

Veiron didn't think he could. He didn't want to leave Erin's side, not while she still had so much to deal with.

Not ever.

Veiron stared down into the dark calm sea below them. Erin moved away and he felt her eyes on him.

"You look as though you're trying to see back into Hell." She whispered it so quietly he barely caught it.

He smiled. "Maybe I am."

A pause.

"Why would you want to do that?" she said and he couldn't miss the darkness in her usually light voice. He glanced up from the water to find her scowling down at it. She wrapped her arms around herself. "I hate it down there... I hate everything about it. I want nothing to do with the wretched horrible place... I thought I was going to die surrounded by that stench and all that evil."

Veiron's frown intensified with each word she said, every one of them cutting at his heart, forming another wound in it that bled and wouldn't stop.

All. That. Evil.

Evil like him?

"There's nothing good in that place..." She lifted her head, smiled and touched his cheek. "Thank you for saving me."

Veiron grunted and turned away from her to stare at his boots. Her hand fell from his face and she shifted away from him. He ignored her as she prattled on about the island, his focus on his battered boots. Boots that had trekked through Hell to save the beautiful woman beside him.

From all that evil.

Nothing good in that place.

Nothing good. All evil.

He fisted his hands and then opened them and settled them on his knees, gripping them so tightly his knuckles bleached.

"Look." Erin nudged him, obviously oblivious to the harm she had done with her careless words.

He glanced up to see what all the fuss was about. A lush green island rose from the water ahead of them. Water that gradually lightened, turning as bright and clear as a jewel around him. Large villas lined the white shore, shaded by towering palms. Three of the single storey dwellings were reserved for them. One for him and Erin, one for Marcus and Amelia, and one for Einar and Taylor. They were due to arrive two days from now.

Erin looped her arm around his and he reacted on instinct, tugging his free. She looked at him and he felt the pain beating in her heart. Good. Perhaps now she knew how he felt. He stared at the water, ignoring her look, knowing that she wanted him to explain. She could figure it out for herself. She was a big girl.

She didn't need him to explain everything for her.

Or take care of her.

The water began to pale and Veiron was tempted to leap overboard and swim the rest of the way to shore, desperate to get away from Erin and get some air. He needed some space to recover from the verbal kick in the balls she had just delivered.

Evil.

"Veiron?" she whispered and touched his arm.

The boat docked, giving him a reason not to acknowledge her. He breathed hard, struggling to keep it together. He couldn't lose control, no matter how much he wanted to fling his head back and roar his fury at the bright blue sky.

Evil.

It chanted inside his head. Tore at his soul.

Erin thought him evil. Nothing good. Everything bad. Spawn of a place that had left her tortured and scared. Servant of a man who had abducted her and tried to bribe her.

His mind tormented him, throwing flashes of her reaction to the fact that he was a Hell's angel.

He grabbed her arm, ignoring her gasp of pain, and dragged her from the boat. Red bled into the edges of his vision as he stalked along the jetty, his heavy footfalls shaking the weather-beaten timbers.

"Veiron?" she said again, louder now, as though volume had been her failing the first time.

He prowled onwards, casing the island and everyone on the jetty. They moved out of his way as he approached. Wise. The mood he was in right now, he was liable to beat the crap out of anyone who so much as looked at him the wrong way.

"You're hurting me." Those three hoarsely spoken words had him loosening his grip and stopping in the middle of the narrow jetty, blocking the path for those behind them.

He turned towards her and bit back his desire to say that she had hurt him first. He just stared at her instead, trying to remain unaffected by the tears that beaded on her dark lashes, hoping she would see his pain in his eyes and realise why he was suddenly upset with her.

Erin soothed his savage side by stepping into him, tiptoeing and kissing him. Sweet mercy. He couldn't stop himself from snaking his arms around her waist and drawing her closer, kissing her deeper and trying to steal a piece of her.

"I wasn't talking about you," she whispered against his lips and slowly drew away, her eyes meeting his. "You know that, right?"

He shrugged. "Right."

"No, you don't..." She sighed and trailed her hands down his arms to his elbows. "Am I ever going to stop messing things up with you?"

Only she had the answer to that question so he didn't bother to answer it for her. Maybe it was for the best that she said things that drove him away and hurt him. Maybe this was some sort of subconscious defensive tactic to get him out of her life or perhaps it was just fate giving him a helping hand so he could continue his mission.

Either way, it sucked.

Veiron took hold of her hand and led her to the thatched main building. The resort was glamorous, a beautiful pristine island with limited and spacious villas on the shore, a small block of apartments off the main set of buildings, and smaller huts that lined a jetty over the water. Whenever he had met Amelia and Marcus in the past, it had been at remote islands with no facilities, all of them uninhabited. It was a nice change to have a bar and restaurants on site, but it also increased the risk of discovery. Or worse, it increased the risk of mortal casualties should they come under attack.

He checked them in at reception, ignoring the congratulations that staff tossed his way but taking the champagne flute they offered him. Erin sipped hers. Veiron necked his.

The moment Erin had finished her drink, he led her away, passing a huge pool with only a few couples occupying it, sitting in the water at a small bar that lined the edge in one part. He crossed the patio and headed towards the beach and their villa. It was the first in the row of detached single storey thatched cabins, larger than the rest.

He unlocked the wooden door and entered ahead of Erin, gaze scanning over everything. No sign of trouble in the large apartment style villa. The bedroom was at the back, a sliding glass door looking out onto the deck and the sea beyond. Everything was wood. The floor, the walls and the ceilings. All rustic and what he supposed was meant to be appealing and natural. Considering his home in Hell was a black hut with no electricity and a stone slab for a seat, everything in the mortal realm looked luxurious and appealing to him. He opened the patio door and checked out the deck.

There was a hot tub set into it, partially hidden from view by a short wall that covered half of the deck on either side. Thoughts of kicking it into life and soaking with Erin under the stars filled his head. Pleasure later. Business first.

He slid the glass door closed, turned back around and walked through the bedroom to the living area off to the left. A small kitchen occupied one end of it. Closer to the entrance was an enclosed bathroom.

Erin was still standing outside.

"Something wrong?" He stepped outside and looked around in case she had seen something that had made her nervous about the whole location. Mortals were coming and going along the path between the back of the villas. No danger.

Erin cleared her throat, rocked on her heels and shot an expectant look between the door and himself.

He didn't get her problem. "It's safe. I've checked it over. No beasties."

She sighed and flicked her black hair from her face. "I thought we were just married?"

"Only in Einar's head. Fuck knows what the man was thinking."

Her face fell and then she rallied. "I take it you won't be carrying me over the threshold then?"

Veiron laughed. So this was her problem? Her doting husband wasn't doing much doting or following tradition.

"I carry you everywhere else, why not into the villa, eh?" he said and she didn't look as though she appreciated the reminder that she had spent more time in his arms than walking recently. He went to grab her and she evaded him.

"I've changed my mind." She turned her nose up at him. He was coming to hate it when she did that.

When she tried to pass him, Veiron grabbed her around the waist and hauled her over his shoulder. She punched his backside and flailed, and he clamped one arm down over her bottom and wrapped the other across the backs of her knees to hold her in place.

"Put me down!"

Veiron laughed again. "I thought you wanted me to carry you? Make up your mind, woman."

He ignored her as she cursed him and carried her inside, kicking the door closed behind him. He trudged forwards, heading for the bedroom.

"You can put me down now," she said and he shook his head.

"Not yet." He entered the bedroom and grinned at the huge white bed. "Now."

Veiron dropped her onto it and covered her body with his, pinning her to the soft mattress. She gasped.

"Mr... Veiron? I don't suppose you have a last name?" she said and smiled up at him.

Veiron shook his head. "You'll just have to settle for Mrs Veiron."

She giggled and twined her fingers through his hair. "I don't recall us having our first kiss."

"I thought we had that on the dock."

She frowned. "Stop spoiling my fun and kiss me."

Veiron grinned. "Yes, Wifey."

He lowered his head and closed his eyes.

The patio door slid open and a gasp broke the silence.

"What the hell are you doing to my sister?"

Veiron grimaced and then cracked one eye open and looked at Erin beneath him. Her cheeks had turned deep pink and she was cringing too. She bit her lip, turned her head to her left, and smiled.

"Hi, Amelia."

He thought she would have waved had she not still had her fingers tangled in his hair. Amelia stormed into the room and shoved Veiron so hard that he hit the pillows and slammed the headboard against the wooden wall.

"Fuck, woman... put a leash on that temper." Veiron glared at her and sat up. "It's not as though I was doing anything against her will."

Erin lay on the bed staring at Amelia, a puzzled look on her face. Amelia turned her black look on her sister.

"Is he telling the truth?" Amelia said, her voice higher than Veiron had ever heard it, a squeak that blended horror with anger into something that sounded a lot like outrage and disbelief.

He had been working with Amelia and Marcus for over a year and a half and she still didn't trust him. That was nice. He had thought that throwing himself into Hell on a suicide mission to save someone precious to her might have gained him a little favour from the angel.

"What happened to your hair?" Erin said, her frown sticking, and sat up on the bed, propping herself up on her palms.

"Answer my question." Amelia looked ready to pull rank in the age stakes. Her grey eyes flashed brightly, a sign that she was losing her temper and liable to change at any moment. He just hoped she didn't deem him worthy of having a blue fireball tossed at him.

What she had seen was nothing compared to what she could have walked in on if she had given them five minutes more. He had intended to have her little sister naked and sweaty by then.

Erin nodded. "Of course he is. He's not a liar, Amelia. Apparently we're newlyweds."

Amelia gaped in horror, her silvery eyes as wide and luminous as full moons. "What the fuck, Veiron?"

She was across the room in a flash, grabbing him by the collar of his t-shirt and hauling him onto his feet.

"What the hell do you think you're doing with my sister?"

"Lay off, Amelia." He grabbed her hand and yanked it off him. "It was Einar's idea of a twisted joke. He signed us in as newlyweds. Jesus. Get off the power trip before I knock you off it."

The edges of his vision bled into red and he towered over her. Amelia looked as though she was going to square up to him and then backed off a step and returned her attention to Erin.

Who was smiling.

"You think this is funny?" Amelia snapped.

Erin's smile faded and then came back broader than ever. "You have to admit you are flying off the handle a bit."

"He's a Hell's angel, Erin... a demon!"

Erin gasped and turned horrified eyes on Veiron. "You took my virginity and wed me and you're a demon?"

Veiron laughed. Amelia didn't look amused.

"Now I know you're being stupid." Amelia folded her arms across her chest, squashing her breasts together in her pale cream summer dress.

Marcus poked his head around the door. "I take it the family reunion is not going well?"

"He was about to kiss her, Marcus," Amelia said, pinning Erin and then Veiron with a vicious glare.

Marcus turned silver-blue eyes on him, looking a little lost as to an appropriate response.

Veiron shrugged. "It could've been a lot worse."

"Gross." Amelia grabbed Erin's hand and pulled her onto her feet, dragging her towards the deck. "You have a lot of explaining to do."

"You're not my mother, Amelia," Erin groused and tried to get her hand free. "And he's smexy as hell... and really nice... and will you let me go... and why is your hair silver?"

Veiron wanted to follow her but the look in Marcus's eyes said to give them a moment alone to catch up and argue it out. At least the former guardian angel wasn't giving him the third degree about what had clearly happened between him and Erin.

Marcus nodded towards the deck and turned away, and it was then that Veiron noticed what he was wearing. Or not wearing. The man was dressed in nothing but a pair of black swim shorts. That was a little too much Marcus on show for his liking. Whenever they had met in the past, Amelia had been wearing a summer dress and Marcus had been wearing linen trousers at worst or trousers and a shirt at best.

Marcus sat down on the edge of the wooden deck, legs dangling over the short drop to the white sand below. His dark hair was wet and slicked back from his face. Come to think of it, Amelia's hair had been wet too. Had they been swimming together when they had sensed his arrival, or in the hot tub at their own villa?

Veiron looked down at the one on his deck, wishing he'd had a few minutes alone with Erin so they could have tried it out before her sister had invaded their lives. He sighed, toed his boots off and removed his socks, and then yanked his black t-shirt over his head and tossed it onto the bed. He stepped out onto the deck, the boards warm beneath his bare feet, and sat down next to Marcus.

"You are in trouble." Marcus glanced across to his left.

Veiron followed his gaze to the next villa. Erin and Amelia were sitting on the chairs on the deck there, having what looked like a heated debate rather than a sisterly catch up session full of 'I missed you' and 'I'm glad you're safe'.

"Don't I know it?" Veiron sighed and pressed his palms into the wooden boards of the deck, curling his fingers over the edge. He stared at Amelia and Erin, his gaze constantly wandering back to his impish beauty. "I'm always in trouble one way or another. I thought I would at least get a thank you."

Marcus settled his hand on Veiron's shoulder and Veiron tore his gaze away from Erin. "Amelia came over with the intention of thanking you but whatever she walked in on, she wasn't expecting it. What were you doing to Erin?"

"Exactly what Amelia said. I was kissing her... or about to."

"That doesn't sound too bad."

"She was beneath me on the bed at the time."

Marcus's black eyebrows rose. "Ah."

"It could have been far worse."

Marcus's expression said it all. "At least you didn't barge in on us."

Veiron chuckled and Marcus laughed along with him. "A pot and kettle situation then. I wonder if Erin knows it."

He looked back across at her. The heat seemed to have subsided and the two women were now chatting animatedly, Amelia toying with her silver hair and waving her hands around. Was she explaining everything to her sister? He hoped so. Erin deserved to know everything.

"Marcus." Veiron turned back to face him. "There's something different about Erin."

"Different how?" Marcus frowned at him and then looked beyond him to the women. Veiron didn't need to look back at them to know that Marcus's gaze was locked on Erin rather than Amelia. "She's mortal."

Veiron nodded. "She is, but she's had visions her whole life... and a few days ago she fought back against a man claiming to be her guardian angel."

"Visions aren't that uncommon."

Veiron frowned at the white sand and then at Erin, and finally at Marcus. "No... but hurling fireballs is."

"Fireballs?" Marcus's focus shot back to him. "Like Amelia can use?"

"No, different somehow. They are almost the same but they're red and they're damn powerful. She almost took him down but he did the disappearing trick." Veiron glanced back at Erin. "Another thing... the little fucker came to her in Hell. He must have wanted to bargain with her about something. I've had Hell's angels on my arse since leaving it. I use one iota of my power and they're coming for me... for her. She was more than bait, Marcus. I know the Devil. If she was just bait, he wouldn't have tried to bargain with her and he would have changed tactics once she escaped Hell. He wouldn't send his men after her every time we popped up on his radar. He would've waited for her to meet Amelia."

Marcus frowned. "What are you saying?"

"He was trying to take her back." That thought left Veiron cold inside. It was the only logical conclusion. It hadn't made sense before but now that he knew Erin had a power of her own, one that could challenge Amelia's, it was something he couldn't deny and something that turned his blood to ice.

"You think he wants her power?"

"It's a possibility, and not one I enjoy entertaining." He stared across the open stretch of beach to her and she looked over at him, her smile quick to come but just as quick to fade when she saw how serious he looked. "We need to figure out where her power comes from, why she has her own guardian angel, and what the fuck the Devil wants with her."

"Easier said than done," Marcus murmured and cast a glance around them. "And this isn't exactly the place for it. I know one thing though... if Heaven assigned her a guardian angel, then they knew about this power."

"The angel didn't. It shocked him."

"Why does that not surprise me?" Marcus practically growled the words. "I swear they enjoy keeping us in the dark so we obey them. My only wish is that we could expose the whole thing and make the angels see we have all been used by Heaven and Hell."

"I hear you," Veiron snarled and glared at the horizon. "I want nothing more than to end this crap."

"Soon." Marcus squeezed his shoulder, a show of solidarity that warmed Veiron and thawed his blood. When the time came, Marcus would stand beside him. Would Amelia too? The others? Erin? Together they could form an army and could perhaps recruit other angels into their ranks. Amelia was Marcus's new master and had made him like her. It was possible that she could do the same with other angels. "First we need to learn what the Devil wants with Erin and why Heaven has her under the protection of an angel."

"Erin saw something in a vision. I need to go to Hell to see if it will come to pass and I'll poke around while I'm down there, see if I can figure out what the Devil really wants with Erin." The thought of leaving her didn't sit well with him but Marcus and Amelia would protect her in his absence, and Taylor and Einar would join them soon.

"Not yet," Marcus said and scrubbed a hand across his face. "Give her a day to settle in with Amelia again and then go if you must."

Veiron frowned. He was sure that Amelia would prefer him out of the way given the fact that she had discovered he was intimate with her little sister. Was Marcus willing to go against the wishes of his woman for Erin's sake or Veiron's? He couldn't believe it would have anything to do with him so it had to have everything to do with Erin. Veiron despised the thought of Marcus becoming protective of Erin. That was his job, not the angel's. He couldn't protect her from Hell though and she needed to remain here on the island, hidden from his world and that of Heaven.

"What about Heaven? If they have a guardian watching her, he will know where she is. We can't hide her from him... and that means he knows where we are if he turns his attention back to her," Marcus said, his face a picture of darkness as he scowled up at the blue vault above them.

"Shit... I wasn't thinking. I should have delayed our meeting. I'm sorry... I fucked up. I just—Erin was in danger and I had to get her out of there. I thought only about the Hell's angels and getting her to Amelia so she would be safe."

Marcus patted Veiron's shoulder again. "Don't beat yourself up about it. Erin sent the angel running, so there is a chance that he is licking his wounds and will not be looking to come back down and confront her until he has more information about her and her powers from his superiors."

"What if he gets that information... what if he tells his bosses about what happened and they send a whole bloody army to retrieve her and take her into custody for questioning?"

Marcus's expression turned grim, his eyes brightening and swirling, rich blue puncturing the paler silver in his irises. "They took Amelia from me like that... I will not let them take Erin. With you, myself and Amelia here, and Erin exhibiting a power of her own, it would be foolish of them to try to take her from us, and it would take more than an army to achieve it."

Dark words from a man who had once upheld everything that Heaven decreed and obeyed his master without question. The game that Heaven had played with Marcus, forcing him to do things against his will, had broken him but Amelia had given him a new life.

That same game had broken Veiron too and he hadn't felt whole again, hadn't truly felt anything, until Erin had entered his life and shaken his black world to the foundations and given him a new purpose and reason to end the game and seize his freedom.

"Taylor and Einar will be here in a couple of days. Once Taylor comes, I will make her send Erin to sleep so she drops off the radar." Veiron dug his fingers into the edge of the deck. They still had to make it to then though. He wasn't sure what would happen should the guardian angel make an appearance before they could conceal Erin's location. It would be war. Amelia wouldn't stand for her little sister coming under fire from the realm that had tried to force her lover, Marcus, to murder her and spill her blood. "What we really need is someone who can go up and see what's happening up there."

Marcus tipped his head back, the unruly waves of his short black hair brushing the nape of his neck. "Impossible. Lukas is the only angel left among us who could enter Heaven without raising suspicion and he has his hands full as far as I know. Annelie and Serenity are going through the trials."

"They want to become immortals?" Veiron found that difficult to digest. The trials were diabolical and few survived, but they were the only way for a mortal to achieve a lifespan long enough to match an angel. If a mortal was serious about their love for an immortal, like an angel or a demon, then the temptation of the trials was probably too great to resist. Immortality and an end to their aging were the rewards if they survived.

He had always thought it was a foolish thing for a mortal to do and that the immortal they loved was cruel to ask it of them rather than convincing them to part ways and give up on their dreams of a future together. Mortals were so fragile and fleeting.

Veiron looked across at Erin, watching her talk to her sister, feeling it right down to his bones. She was mortal. He had never desired to involve himself with them before. In barely two decades, she would look so different, and he would not. She would come to despise him and what love could survive that?

The voice at the back of his mind said again that it was better to end it now, before he was in too deep to save himself. Two decades was a blip in his existence and the thought of watching Erin die, either because of old age or because she decided to face the trials and failed, was too painful to contemplate.

What future was there for them? Even if aging wasn't an issue, he was. She tried to hold her tongue around him but she had shown the feelings for his kind that she hid in her heart, and he couldn't blame her for hating them. Hell's angels had abducted her, tormented her, hurt her and chased her. They deserved her wrath and her hatred.

She would always hate them.

And that meant a part of her would always hate him.

It hurt whenever she turned on him now. It would tear him apart if he let himself fall in love with her.

"We should join the females." Marcus dropped to the sand below them.

Veiron nodded, shook away his painful thoughts, and followed him.

He would do as Marcus had asked. He would wait a day and then he would leave Erin and return to Hell.

He had to. Not to continue his mission, but to discover his fate and the truth about Erin.

She needed answers.

And he would get them for her.

CHAPTER 17

Erin had barely seen Veiron since Amelia had come in unannounced and interrupted what had promised to be another very wicked moment with her demonic angel. A moment she had needed with every ounce of her being and all of her heart.

Things had been off kilter between them since she had unleashed some sort of power on the rooftop back in London. She had tried to get it back on track, tried to shove her worries to the back of her mind, and had even tried to speak to Veiron about them a few times, but none of it had worked.

How could she have been so stupid as to say all that stuff on the boat? She hadn't been thinking. Sometimes, it was so easy to forget that Veiron was from Hell, that he lived there and was a part of that place. She needed to start watching what she said around him or he was going to end up leaving her. Now that she was back with her sister, it was only a matter of time before Veiron made his excuses. Her heart ached at the thought of him leaving, casting aside what they had together, but her conversation with her sister had given her a clearer understanding of his reasons for trying to keep some distance between them and wanting to leave.

He had a mission, a vow to destroy the game that Heaven and Hell was playing with him, Marcus and Amelia, and to free himself of it forever.

From what Amelia had told her and what she now knew of the Devil, Erin wasn't sure that was entirely possible. The Devil was powerful. He had killed a demonic angel right in front of her and hadn't even broken a sweat, and the man had been strong and huge. If Veiron went after the Devil, things would end as they had in her vision, and that was something she didn't want.

Marcus talked to Veiron at the edge of the deck of his and Amelia's villa. It was smaller than the one she shared with Veiron but it had the same luxuries. Amelia had offered to share a dip in the hot tub with her but Erin had turned her sister down. She wanted to take a dip, just not with Amelia.

Her gaze roamed over Veiron and she made the appropriate murmurs and grunts as her sister continued to speak to her, telling her all about everything that had happened.

Marcus was good-looking, tall and athletic, his muscles honed to the point where he looked like a fitness model on the cover of one of those health magazines in his black shorts. He wasn't a patch on Veiron though. She loved Veiron's dark sensuality and his possessiveness. She was sure that Marcus was just as lethal as the man stood beside him, but Veiron broadcasted danger and it drew her to him.

The only thing she didn't like about Veiron was his mood swings. It annoyed her when he shut down his feelings around her and turned cold, especially when she was burning for him.

Veiron glanced at her out of the corner of his eye. Erin smiled at him, gaining a tight smile in return. Whatever they were talking about, it had Veiron on edge. Or maybe that was her. She hadn't exactly started off their time on the island in a good way and she had wanted to tell him that, and apologise, but she had ended up kissing him instead. When she had tried to offer up a heartfelt apology and an explanation, it had come out sounding weak. After that, he had joked with her as though everything was fine but she had seen his playfulness for what it really was—a way of covering his hurt.

She longed to escape Amelia and take Veiron somewhere quiet so they could talk but it wasn't going to happen anytime soon. Whenever she so much as looked at Veiron for longer than a few seconds, Amelia started reminding her that he was a Hell's angel, as though she cared about that.

Veiron was a good man.

He had protected her, had been gentle with her for the most part, and had even saved her life.

She didn't care what Amelia thought about him. She only cared that she was falling in love with him.

Erin turned away to talk to Amelia where she sat beside her on a reclining lounger and felt Veiron's gaze shift to her entirely. She wanted to look at him again but settled for enjoying the feel of his eyes on her, locked and focused.

"I'm never getting used to the hair." Erin combed her fingers through Amelia's long silver ponytail. It was like looking at a different person. "It doesn't suit you, you know? It's too wild for you."

Amelia smiled. "You're one to talk. When did you do that to your hair?"

Erin fluffed up her own much shorter black hair. "About a year ago now. You don't like it? Dad loves it. He says it makes me look artistic."

"How is dad?" There was a sombre note to Amelia's voice and it was there in her grey eyes too.

When Amelia had first told her about everything that had happened, she had felt a little jealous of her sister's powers and the fact that she could fly. Now, Erin didn't envy her at all. Amelia was constantly on the run with Marcus, moving from one hideaway to the next, hoping to live to see another day.

Was that how Veiron had been living since turning his back on his master and siding with the enemy?

Her gaze slid back to him. Amelia patted her knee.

"I was speaking?" she said and Erin smiled, returning her attention to her older sister.

"He's good. I tell him whenever I hear from you. He thinks you're off travelling, which I guess you are. It must be a nightmare."

Amelia shrugged and cast her gaze downwards. She picked at the hem of her pale dress and sighed. "It's been difficult. Marcus takes care of me though. I'm lucky to have him."

As if he had heard her, Marcus looked across the deck at Amelia. Erin looked to Veiron to find him walking down the wooden steps to the beach. The sun was setting now, sinking towards the infinite horizon, and it cast warm light over him. Erin went to stand but Amelia's hand on her arm stopped her.

"We're still talking."

Erin frowned at her and then at Veiron as he strolled along the shore, heading away from them. She wanted to go to him. Couldn't her sister see that and let things be? Couldn't she see that Erin was happy with Veiron?

Marcus dragged a chair across the deck and set it opposite her and Amelia. He sat down in it and leaned forwards, resting his elbows on his bare knees. "Veiron says that you have some powers."

Erin swallowed. "I do. I don't know what they are or where they came from. I had thought maybe I was like Amelia, but Veiron says that isn't possible."

Marcus shook his head and a lock of his dark hair fell down. He preened it back. "It isn't possible. There was only one female angel. Veiron would know if it was any different."

"How?" Erin said and found herself leaning forwards too. How much did Marcus know about Veiron and how much would he be willing to tell her? Taylor had told her things but nothing about his past.

Marcus looked as though he wouldn't answer.

"Please... tell me how he would know such a thing. Is it because he's fallen?" She reached out to touch his hand and then thought the better of it. If Amelia touched Veiron, she would probably kill her sister in a fit of jealousy. Amelia might feel just as strongly about Erin touching Marcus.

"When angels die, we are reborn in the same physical form but everything else about us is wiped clean and often our positions alter. Mine does not. Neither does Veiron's. Whenever he dies, he's reborn as a guardian angel." Marcus drew in a deep breath and exhaled it on a sigh.

"You make it sound as though he dies quite often, and that he isn't an angel when it happens."

Marcus frowned. "Erin... whenever Veiron is reborn, he is destined to become a Hell's angel. It is part of the game. He is the Devil's knight... and I am God's. It doesn't matter what he does in his time as an angel, or how dedicated he is to his duty... he will fall."

That was terrible. Her gaze sought and found Veiron standing on the shore with his back to her, the water lapping over his bare feet. What was he thinking as he stood there alone staring out at the ocean? Did he want her there with him, holding his hand, speaking to him? She wanted to be there with him. She wanted to hear these things from him but she knew that he would never tell her. If she asked him, he would close himself off and push her away.

"When Veiron found me in Hell, he said that Amelia couldn't come to get me because if she died, he would die too... when I pressed him to explain that to me, he said he meant it literally." Erin's heart thumped and she swallowed to clear the dryness in her throat. "Is it true?"

Marcus nodded. "If Amelia were to die, then both myself and Veiron would die too. The game would be reset and because we had been reborn, we would not remember anything that had happened."

Erin felt sick. Being reborn on death hadn't sounded too bad but coming back into the world without knowledge or memories of things you had done in your previous life? That sounded horrible and she couldn't stop her mind from chanting a single question.

If Veiron died, would he forget her?

Images from her nightmare flashed across her eyes. Veiron bloodied and beaten, lying broken under the Devil's feet, watching his master as he came to end him and trying to fight for his life. Her blood sank to her toes.

Erin shot to her feet. Amelia's hand circled her wrist and held her firm. She looked down at her sister, the low light from sunset barely illuminating her face, and silently pleaded her to stop trying to intervene in her relationship with Veiron. It wasn't protecting her. It was just hurting her. She needed to see him. Couldn't her sister see that? The thought of Veiron dying tore at her soul, cleaving her heart open until she felt as though she was bleeding inside, and only looking into Veiron's eyes and hearing him tell her that everything was going to be fine would heal her.

"Amelia," Marcus said and her sister looked across at him. Whatever look he gave her, she would have to thank him for it later, because her sister released her hand.

Erin hurried down the steps to the white sand. She had removed her boots and socks while talking to Amelia and the sand was soft between her toes, still warm from the day. The sun had set and the sky was already turning inky above her, the moon rising higher into it to shine down on the island and light her path. Erin rolled her jeans up and headed towards Veiron where he walked the shore.

He stopped as she approached but remained with his back to her. He must have sensed her because her footfalls were silent and she was barely breathing, her chest too tight and throat too dry.

"Veiron," she whispered and he slowly turned to face her, his expression as dark as she had ever seen it.

"What is it?" he snarled and she froze mid-step, confused. Was he still angry because of what she had said earlier?

She took another step towards him and wasn't sure what to say to him or where to start. The muscle in his jaw tensed and the edges of his irises burned crimson.

"Nothing," she said and felt weaker than she had ever been. She straightened a heartbeat later and looked him in the eye. "What's wrong?"

"Nothing," he parroted and she frowned at him, unwilling to take that as his answer. He looked away from her, towards the sea and the dark horizon.

"You left us."

He shrugged. "I wanted to walk... I needed some space."

Space from her? She reached out to take his hand but he moved, angling his body so her attempt failed.

"I thought I would enjoy what little time I had here," he said. "No offence to Marcus and Amelia, but I'm not exactly interested in going over old ground with them."

Erin had failed to hear what he had said after his first sentence. "You're leaving?"

Her heart pounded in her ears, loud enough to drown out the sound of the gentle waves breaking against the shore.

"I have to."

Erin grabbed his hand this time and forced him to face her. If he was going to leave, he could at least do her the courtesy of looking her in the eye and telling her why. It wasn't as though they were just friends. The time they had shared with each other had to mean something to him. It had to. It hadn't just been casual sex that had meant nothing to him, or her. It had been something incredible.

"Why? Where are you going?" she said and he looked down at his feet and then finally met her gaze.

"Home."

Erin dropped his hand, shock rippling through her. "You can't go back there! What about what I saw?"

Veiron stared into her eyes, cold and emotionless, as distant from her as he had ever been. Erin took deep breaths to calm her rising anger. In. Out. Steady. It wasn't working. She wanted to scream and rant at him, to beat her fists against his bare chest until he said that he had only been joking to wind her up and that he was staying.

"That's why I need to go back. I have to see what happens in my future." Not the answer she had wanted.

Tears threatened to fill her eyes but she sniffed them back, unwilling to look weak even when her heart felt as though it was going to break.

"How?" she said, the barest tremble in her voice. She had known he wanted to leave. She should have been more prepared for it when it came. Would have been, but she had thought she had more time to work on convincing him to stay. The way Veiron looked right now, she felt as though he was going to fly off at a moment's notice and she would never see him again.

"There is a pool in Hell that can show the future. I need to go there." The uncertain look in his eyes, the trace of fear she easily spotted in them, made her heart skip a beat.

"Where is this pool?" Her voice trembled fully now. Her eyes widened. He didn't answer. "God... no, Veiron... don't tell me that it's near that fortress I saw."

He looked away from her. It was all the answer she needed. Erin grabbed his arms and shook him until his dark gaze slid back to her.

"You can't go there alone!" She gripped him close to his elbows, squeezing so tightly that she felt sure she was hurting him. He didn't show it if she was. His gaze remained dark and cold, void of feeling. Erin clung to him, afraid that if she loosened her grip, he would create one of those portals and beam himself straight to Hell and the Devil. "I won't let you go alone. I'm coming too."

Veiron laughed and then frowned at her, as though he had thought she was the one joking now. "No. It is too dangerous... and I don't need your help."

That one stung. "I won't let you go alone, Veiron. I have my powers."

"Powers you do not know how to use," he growled and Erin flinched. There was no need for him to throw that one in her face. She could figure out how to use them as they travelled. She could help him. "You are back with your sister now and that is all that matters. My mission here is done, Erin. Let me go."

"No!" Erin didn't care if he meant let him go forever or just release him. It wasn't happening either way.

"You must. Stay here with Amelia and Marcus. They'll take care of you."

Erin swallowed. "I don't want them to take care of me."

He yanked his arms free of her grip. "I can't be the one to do it."

Erin bristled and glared at him. "I can take care of myself!"

Veiron just stared at her. She damn well could take care of herself. She could master this power of hers, whatever it was and wherever it had come from, and she would.

"If you go down there, so help me God, Veiron, I am coming with you and you can't stop me."

He gave her a look that said he could easily stop her.

Erin squared up to him, ignoring the fact that he stood almost a foot taller than she was, set her jaw and clenched her fists. Her fingers began to tingle and heat and she felt queasy. "I will not let you go alone."

"What do you care if I go back to Hell where I belong? You have your sister now. Marcus will take care of you both."

Erin unclenched her hands and sagged, the fire draining from her and leaving her cold. It wasn't the first time he had mentioned that she had her sister and Marcus, and something told her that he wasn't mentioning it because it meant his mission was a success. Amelia had kept her away from Veiron and had treated him poorly. She had told Erin countless times that he wasn't worth her attention and was a bad man. Was part of Veiron's desire to leave because he felt her sister would never accept him as Erin's lover?

"Veiron," Erin whispered and tried to touch his hand but he moved it out of reach. She smiled briefly and then looked up into his eyes, tears filling hers. "I care... you're the only thing I care about... can't you see that? The thought of you going down there when you know you might die... that kills me. Please don't go."

"I must."

"Please." She wasn't above begging if it came to it, anything to stop him from going off to Hell half-cocked and looking for a fight because of the things her sister had said and the things that she had said too. "Stay."

"No." He turned away from her. "Go back to your sister, Erin. Nothing you could say will change my mind."

"Fine. Be like that." Erin backed off a step. "Maybe she's right and I'm wrong about you."

He hung his head and sighed, his broad shoulders heaving with it. Erin hesitated, torn between touching him one last time, swirling her fingers around his tattoos, and remembering him with a final kiss, and walking away.

She opened her mouth to speak.

"What's wrong?" Amelia said, appearing out of the darkness. She took one look at Erin and settled her arm around her shoulders.

Erin wanted to shirk her touch and shout at her. This was all her sister's fault. Things had been going fine, except for the occasional hiccup on her part, between her and Veiron and Amelia had wrecked it. She was sure of it. Amelia had kept her away from Veiron all day and she had thought nothing of it until now. She stared at Veiron's back, willing him to turn around and see in her eyes that she was sorry and that she wanted to be with him. He had to stay.

"Veiron is leaving," Erin said.

"I know." Those two words leaving Amelia's lips made her frown and she turned it on her sister. "Marcus told me he intends to go to Hell to find out more about what the Devil wants with you and something about his future."

More about what the Devil wanted with her? Why hadn't Veiron told her that? If he had, she might not have felt so certain that she would never see him again. Now she felt as though he was going back to Hell for her sake, to bring her answers. If he believed the Devil wanted her because of her power, then perhaps the Devil knew where her power came from. But Veiron would have to speak to the Devil, and the Devil wanted him dead.

It would end as she had seen in her nightmare.

"Did Veiron also tell Marcus what I saw in my vision?" Erin looked from Amelia to the dark-haired man in question. Marcus shook his head. "The Devil kills him... and I'm there... and I unleash the power I have on him. If Veiron goes to Hell, he'll... he can't."

"Veiron can take care of himself," Amelia said and Erin caught the words she didn't say hidden in her tone.

Veiron wasn't worth her concern.

Erin broke free of her sister's grip and stared at the back of Veiron's head. "I won't let you die... and I know you can hear me. I care about you, Veiron. If that means I have to go into Hell again to make sure you survive, then I will do just that. I'll do whatever it takes to make sure you're safe and to keep you with me."

Veiron's shoulders shifted in a deep sigh and he ran a hand over his hair, settling it at the back of his head, close to his ponytail.

Silence reigned.

Marcus broke it. "If Veiron will be in danger by travelling to Hell and you are concerned about his safety then I will go with him."

"No!" Amelia snapped and Erin wanted to remind her that she didn't have the right to get upset about Marcus going to Hell when she had been telling Erin just a few seconds ago to let the man she loved travel to Hell and not worry about him.

Loved.

Not falling then. Fallen.

Marcus sighed as Amelia glared at him. "Einar and Taylor will arrive soon. When they do, Taylor can hide you and Erin. I shall go with Veiron to Hell, and everyone is happy."

Erin was certainly happier with that as it gave her more time to convince Veiron that she loved him and didn't care about what everyone else said about him, and it threw Marcus into the equation. She wasn't going to give up on accompanying Veiron though. Unless Marcus being there and her not being there would mean that her vision wouldn't come true.

"Veiron?" Erin said, needing to hear him say that he would stay and wait for the others to arrive, and then he would go to Hell with Marcus.

He grunted and kept his back to her.

"At least think about it," she said and Amelia slipped her arm around her shoulders again.

"Fine," Veiron grumbled. "I'll think about it."

Erin smiled.

Amelia squeezed her shoulders. "Why don't we hit the bar and Marcus can talk to Veiron? I don't know about you, but I could use a cocktail or two."

Or ten. The mood Erin was in right now and the all-inclusive package they were on, she would be hitting the bar as hard as she could and not stopping until Veiron came to tell her that she couldn't look after herself after all and carried her to bed.

She wanted to stay and convince Veiron herself, but Amelia was right. Veiron wasn't listening to her but he might listen to Marcus.

She hoped that he did.

Because she had the terrible feeling that if he went to Hell alone, she would never see him again.

CHAPTER 18

"I thought we had agreed you would wait?" Marcus said and Veiron ignored him and stared out at the black moonlit sea.

They had but seeing Erin with her sister had changed his mind. He knew when he wasn't wanted and Erin's impassioned speech hadn't convinced him to stay. As soon as he was able, he was leaving, whether that was when Taylor arrived or before then. He would rather face the Devil alone and cause the future Erin had seen to happen than hang around watching Amelia poison Erin's mind and watching Erin drift away from him.

She hated his kind. How long would it be before she hated him too?

Marcus sighed. "You like her... do not deny it. I might be new to love but I am not blind to it. If you like her so much, why are you in such a hurry to leave?"

Veiron closed his eyes, wishing he was a thousand miles away and wasn't getting interrogated by a man who had apparently had one love and one woman in his current lifetime. What did Marcus know about the difficulties of love? He had been a guardian angel, one of the good men. Amelia had probably thrown herself at his feet on discovering that.

Although, Marcus had tried to kill her.

If Erin was as tough as her sister, there was a chance that she might get over the things that his kind had done to her, just as Amelia had gotten over what Marcus had done.

But that counted on her sister changing her mind about him and stopping her assault on their relationship.

"I know when I'm not wanted," Veiron said, opened his eyes and glared at Marcus.

It killed him to leave. Is that what Marcus wanted to hear him say? He didn't want to, not in his heart. He wanted to stay with Erin and protect her from whatever came after her. They had shared so much in their time together and he didn't want to let her go. The thought of it wrenched at him, sinking claws into his heart and threatening to tear it from his chest. He needed her, had never felt so hungry for someone before, so possessive and protective, and unwilling to allow anyone near her.

Even seeing Marcus close to her had made him want to growl and fight the man.

"I really don't think you do." Marcus moved around him and looked up the shore towards the resort complex, his back to the ocean. "I know Amelia isn't handling this very well and I will speak to her about it."

Veiron appreciated that but he still wasn't going to change his mind.

He envied Marcus for having Amelia and having contracted with her. Amelia was his master now and Veiron felt sure that if he died and Amelia lived, Marcus would be reborn as he was now, not as a guardian angel. If Veiron died, he would come back as an obedient soldier of Heaven and wouldn't remember anything about his past lives until he inevitably fell and pledged himself to the Devil. He wouldn't remember Erin, and that killed him. What sort of life could they have together?

Nothing but one filled with heartache and misery.

It was better this way. She didn't need him. He was no good for her and would only end up hurting her. She had her sister now and Marcus, and as much as it hurt him, they would protect her in his stead and keep her safe from his kind and the angels. He couldn't do that. He wasn't strong enough. Amelia's power far surpassed his own.

He would fail Erin and he couldn't bear the thought of seeing her die. When she had been bleeding in his arms after the Hell's angel had attacked her, it had felt as though his whole world had been falling apart before his eyes. He had felt as though he was dying.

He couldn't go through that again. He couldn't fall in love with her. No good would come of it. He needed to protect her and himself, and the only way for that to happen was to leave her.

"Veiron?" Marcus whispered.

Veiron shook his head. "I know you will take care of her, Marcus. You and Amelia both. She needs you, not me. I'm no good for her and we both know it. She's better off without me."

Marcus gave him a tight smile. "Are you trying to convince me or yourself, Veiron?"

Veiron frowned. "We both know it's true. If she's with me, she is constantly in danger, and I certainly don't need the complication of having to babysit a mortal. She doesn't belong with me. I will only get her killed... if not by giving away her location to those after her... then by my own hand. The Devil can use me against her... fuck, I don't think I could handle that... and I don't think I would be strong enough to fight him."

Marcus made a low growling noise under his breath and his eyes brightened, beginning to glow an eerie blue in the dim light. "You think I did not fear for Amelia's sake when I was falling for her? My mission was to protect her and I got her killed by Apollyon... and then I almost killed her myself... but the depth of her love for me and my love for her stopped me."

"Erin doesn't seem to like me that way, so let's not go there. She's barely looked at me since seeing Amelia again."

Marcus scowled. "They haven't seen each other in years and she is just discovering what happened to her sister. It is reasonable for the females to get wrapped up in each other... and I acknowledge that Amelia is not helping matters. She has stopped Erin from going to you several times this day... but Erin never stopped wanting to be with you. She did stop you from leaving, and I believe that what she said is what she feels. She cares about you."

Veiron closed his eyes and pinched the bridge of his nose. Marcus had a point and Veiron believed Erin too. She did care about him, and he cared so much about her that he wasn't sure what he was meant to do or how he was supposed to react. The sight of her with her sister, the fact that she had barely looked at him and hadn't spoken to him all day, had messed with his head, but she had come to him in the end and asked him to stay.

He had felt the truth in her words in his heart. She cared about him and her time with him had meant something to her, something strong and deep enough that she had gone against her own flesh and blood in order to come to him. She wanted to be with him.

He wanted to be with her.

It was no use fooling himself into thinking any other way. The truth bled through each time and Marcus was right, he was trying to convince himself that Erin didn't need him and he didn't need her, and he was failing dismally at it.

"Speak to her," Marcus said and blew out a long sigh. "And do not let Amelia's actions or anything colour your judgement. Just speak to her and see where it takes you."

Veiron nodded and walked up the beach with Marcus, heading for the complex. Warm lights lit the path to the brilliant blue pool and the bar next to it. Erin sat on one of the stools lining the oblong thatched building with Amelia next to her, nursing a brightly coloured drink and wearing very little. The sight of Erin in nothing but a black bikini top and a pair of black shorts heated his blood but it was the way the men coming and going between the bar and the tables on the patio were ogling her that sent his temperature soaring. If it hadn't been for Marcus walking beside him, his eyes glued to him, watching him, Veiron might have completely lost his head.

As it was, he had to fight hard to quell his raging desire to slaughter them all for looking at Erin with lust in their eyes.

Impulse control. He really had to work on it because with things so fragile between him and Erin, one wrong move would destroy everything they had built with each other. He didn't think she would like it if he flipped out, unleashed his darker side, and savaged every mortal male who had dared to glance her way in the past few minutes, let alone the fact that he would alert the Devil to her location and likely bring some unwanted visitors to the island.

Veiron settled for glaring at them all whenever they looked at him, pinning them with dark looks that conveyed every bone-crushing and bloody thought filling his mind.

He slid onto the padded stool next to Erin at the bar. Amelia looked across her at him and then over her shoulder. Marcus played his part and lured her away, leaving him alone with Erin.

Erin continued to suck on the straw in her cocktail, her amber eyes fixed on the bar and head lowered enough that the short lengths of her black hair fell forwards and concealed part of her face.

Veiron wasn't sure where to start. Speaking to her had sounded like a good thing and he had hoped to be calm and rational about everything but the sight of so many men looking at her had him riled and snappish. Not the best of moods for a heart to heart.

"Be careful when you go back," she said without looking at him. "I don't like the thought of you going down there, not after what I saw, but I won't try to stop you."

"I can take care of myself. I have done for centuries." Veiron shrugged and leaned one elbow on the bar and swivelled to face her.

She didn't move to face him. Her gaze stayed glued to her drink and she prodded at the ice and chunks of pineapple with her black straw. Not quite the response he should have given her. He should have told her that he would take care and that he was going there for her sake as much as he was for his. She needed answers and he would get them for her. She might have liked to hear that. Maybe he could have hooked her hair behind her ear and touched her cheek too. It would've been better than sounding like a heartless bastard.

"I don't care," she whispered and then sighed. "I just want to hear you promise you'll be careful."

Veiron shrugged. "I'm a demon. We're not big on promises."

Erin sighed again, her bare shoulders lifting with it. He wanted to kiss that milky patch of skin, desired to worship it and ease her pain. If he did, she would know that he felt something for her and that leaving her was the last thing he wanted to do, but he wasn't sure what he was doing or how he was feeling or what were the right reactions to it all.

"I had that one coming." She lifted her head and looked across at him, her eyes full of hurt that he had heard in her soft voice. "I forgot where you were from and I shouldn't have said all those things about your home. I wasn't thinking. It's just... you're nothing like the ones who held me captive and I don't think of you as one of them, so I didn't think that what I said was going to hurt you... but I should have... and I'm sorry I said it."

Veiron stared at her in silence. She swallowed and her gaze slowly fell to her drink again, and she started poking it with her straw.

"Don't worry about it." He brushed the hair from her face, tucking it behind her ear and savouring how soft her skin was beneath his fingers. Skin he wanted to kiss every inch of so she would know that she was precious to him and he couldn't get enough of her. "You've been through a lot and you're entitled to your opinion. I don't hold it against you."

Much.

He shouldn't hold it against her at all but he couldn't shake the voice that kept telling him that whenever she cursed Hell and his kind, she cursed him too.

"But I hurt you."

Veiron didn't acknowledge that. She already looked miserable enough without him adding to it by confirming that she had wounded him with her thoughtless words.

He flagged the bartender instead. "Double whiskey."

The man poured it for him and slid it across the bar, all without his gaze straying to Erin. Wise man. Never a wiser one in existence. A fight, even one using mortal strength, would make Veiron feel a whole lot better right about now and he would be quick to take anyone up on the offer they made by looking at Erin.

Wouldn't that just impress the beautiful woman beside him?

He would probably seal his fate if he lashed out at any of the mortal males in the vicinity, even if he did withhold most of his strength. Erin would think him a monster.

"I thought you wouldn't be able to drink," she said, oblivious to the dark thoughts that were probably showing in his eyes, ringing them with crimson.

Veiron laughed. "I refer you back to my earlier comment. I'm a demon."

"A demonic angel."

Veiron swirled the whiskey around his glass, staring at the amber liquid. "Something like that... I think the popular term is Hell's angel... most just call me a demon."

Erin flinched. "I'm sorry."

"About what?" He looked across at her. Something told him she wasn't apologising for her outburst on the boat now.

"About letting Amelia keep me occupied all day when all I really wanted to do was take you back to our villa and get wild with you." She smiled but it was short lived. "She kept telling me things and I think they were meant to drive a wedge between us but they only made me want to see you and be with you even more."

Veiron smiled now. That sounded like his Erin, the rebellious woman who probably liked him more because of the bad things he had done. He kept trying to be a good man for her, to prove he had a good heart and was what she needed, and it turned out she wanted the bad boy instead.

"What did she tell you?" He sipped his whiskey and enjoyed the burn as he swallowed.

"She told me about what happened to you all and then Marcus told me more... about what Heaven and Hell did to you... and I understand why you want to get your own back." She took another long suck on her straw, draining the last of her cocktail. "I'm worried about you, Veiron, and I know you'll just tell me not to in that gruff way of yours and that you can take care of yourself, but that isn't going to stop me from worrying when you go to Hell... I need to know that you'll be safe because I... I care about you... a lot."

Veiron's eyes widened. Was she saying what he thought she was? He stared into her eyes, trying to see it in them, but she lowered them to her bare knees.

He smiled even though she wouldn't see it. She didn't need to feel awkward about what she had said, but if it made her feel better, he could confess his feelings in a roundabout manner too. "You know, I thought you hadn't been wearing much when I first met you but this little number... fuck, do I want you when you look so sexy... and I want to kill every man who is looking at you... because you're mine, Erin."

She blushed and bit her lower lip, a beautiful touch of shyness that tugged at his protective side before she lifted her eyes and met his, sending a hot jolt through him that rocked him to his core. Damn, he wanted her right here and right now, regardless of the audience.

Erin reached across, all hint of shyness gone as her pupils ate up her irises, swamping her eyes with desire and passion that he had tasted firsthand and wanted to taste again, craved like a drug. She laid her palm on his bare chest and his heart beat wildly, blood rushing through his veins. Her caress was fire and what she said knocked the air from his lungs and made him want to wrap her in his embrace and fly away with her.

"You're mine, too, Veiron," she husked and dropped her gaze to his lips before dragging it back up to his, sending another white-hot bolt of hunger through him. "And I'm never letting you go."

Veiron growled, wrapped his arm around her back and dragged her off her stool and into him. He claimed her mouth, crushing her lips with his and kissing her with all the force of his desire and need for her. She moaned, her hands pressing against his bare chest, searing him down to his soul.

Mine. She belonged to him now, hadn't denied him and had claimed him as hers too, and had vowed to keep him.

He wanted to be hers.

Needed it.

He would give all of himself to her and take all of her in return, and nothing would stand between them.

Not even the Devil himself.

CHAPTER 19

Erin walked the shore hand in hand with Veiron. She had wanted to go straight back to their villa and make love with him but he had insisted that they walked a while, and while she had been annoyed at first, she was glad that he had suggested it. It was strangely peaceful on the empty beach under the moonlight, Veiron's fingers locked tightly with hers, his large hand engulfing her smaller one and keeping the chill off her skin. Palms fringed the sweeping shore and the warm water washed over her feet, the sound of the shallow waves steadily puncturing the near silence. The noise of people at the complex was nothing but a distant hum this far along the beach. The only competition the waves had was the occasional party at one of the villas and they had left the last of them behind a few metres back.

A breeze blew in off the ocean, carrying the scent of saltwater, and Erin shivered.

Veiron stopped, untangled their hands, and wrapped his strong arm around her, pulling her against his bare chest. Erin snuggled into him and looked up, meeting his gaze. His eyes were black in the moonlight but not dark. They were warm and soft, full of feelings that she felt mirrored in her own heart.

She lifted her hand and cupped his cheek, sweeping her thumb over his lower lip. She wanted to tell him again to be careful when he went to Hell but couldn't find her voice, didn't want to spoil this moment between them. It wouldn't be their last. Nothing would happen to Veiron. Marcus would go with him and together they would be safe.

Erin kissed him instead, tiptoeing and gently capturing his lips. She kept it light, bare brushes of her lips against his, her emotions running wild with her. Veiron surprised her by doing the same, sweeping his mouth over hers and holding her close to him, his hands gentle against her back.

He drew away, breathing hard as though he had run for miles rather than stood still on a beach and kissed her. She was breathless too, alive with emotion and warmth, with all of her feelings for Veiron.

"I keep thinking about something," he said and he sounded so serious that she pulled further away so she could see his face. He smiled wickedly. "Hot tub."

Erin laughed. "It's like you read my mind."

His smile became a grin and he slipped his hand into hers, entwining their fingers, and started back along the shore with her. She walked beside him, letting the waves lap at her feet. Obviously she wasn't walking quickly enough for Veiron's liking because suddenly the world spun before her eyes and she was staring at his backside.

"Hey." Erin punched his bottom and sighed to herself. So firm. The man had buns of steel.

"You're slowing me down again," he said with a smile in his voice.

His backside shifted as he strode purposefully along the beach with her slung over his shoulder and the cute dents either side of his spine on his lower back called to her. Erin hooked her hand into his belt, pushed herself up to relieve the pressure on her organs and fingered one of the dips with her free hand. Veiron practically purred.

The world whirled past her again and she was in his arms, cradled close to his chest.

"Damn, woman, you drive me crazy," he growled and then kissed her, hard and rough, so passionate that her knees would have buckled had she been standing.

Erin wound her arms around his neck and returned the kiss, trying to make him growl again. He kept striding onwards and she had to wonder how he knew where he was going. Some sort of supernatural awareness of his surroundings?

He cursed under his breath and she looked down to see he was knee-deep in the sea. Maybe not. Erin giggled. Veiron growled. Not the sort of one she had wanted to hear. This one was born of frustration rather than desire.

"I said you drive me crazy, that includes scrambling my senses until I can't think straight around you... fuck, I need you, Erin... tell me you're mine. Tell me you're only mine and I'm the only one you want in all the three realms." The look he gave her was pure animal hunger and Erin melted, her blood heating to a thousand degrees, burning for him. "Tell me and I will swear to you that I am yours, now and forever."

Heavens, could this man get any better? He growled, snarled and fought like a wild thing, like a warrior, but he had the heart of a poet. A heart that she was beginning to think now belonged to her.

"You're the only man I want, and the only one I need." Erin stroked his cheek, clearing a rogue strand of crimson hair from it, and looked deep into his dark eyes. They blazed red at the centre, highlighting his dilated pupils, a sign of his desire.

"Say it," he growled, a command this time, one that made her heart flutter.

"I'm yours, Veiron, and only yours... now and forever... and you are mine." The way he looked at her made her feel as though she had just made him the happiest man in what he had called the three realms and left her feeling as though they really were newlyweds, only they had just wed each other on this moonlit shore with words that promised eternity.

A dark possessive snarl curled from his lips and he kissed her, the softness of it surprising her when she had expected hard and passionate. He kept kissing her as he walked up the beach, heading towards their villa. Erin wriggled, anticipation making her restless. She wanted Veiron naked and in the hot tub, water frothing around them, and the wall that concealed the half of the deck nearest the villa hiding them from prying eyes.

She could barely contain herself as he took the wooden steps up to the deck and set her down. Erin swept her hands over his chest and down the ridges of his stomach, licking her lips the whole time. His eyes narrowed as she tugged his belt open and then set to work on his jeans, slowly popping each button.

"I didn't bring any shorts," he said, his deep voice stirring heat inside her. She wanted him to whisper things against her skin as he kissed it and into her ear as they made love. She craved the feel of his strong hands on her body and the bliss of being one with him again.

Erin pushed his jeans down to his knees, so he stood on the deck in his black trunks. She could let him go in the hot tub in his underwear but that would spoil the fun. "That's a shame... you'll just have to go in naked."

"If I'm going in naked, so are you."

Erin could go along with that. She went into their villa and grabbed the two white robes from the large bathroom. When she came out, she found Veiron in the bedroom, stripping off his jeans and his underwear. My, she was never getting used to how delicious he looked naked.

His cock was already hard, jutting out thick and long from a nest of deep red curls.

Erin wanted nothing more than to sink to her knees and worship him right there in the middle of the bedroom, but the words 'hot tub' kept spinning through her head and she knew if she took him into her mouth, they would never make it there.

She tossed one of the robes at him and stripped out of her shorts and bikini. Veiron growled at her, his hands tightly clutching the robe in front of him, every muscle on his broad body delightfully taut and pronounced. She wanted to lick him all over when he looked like that, so delicious and tempting.

He crossed the room to her and before he could grab her and kiss her, she ducked under his arm and threw on her robe. She reached the deck before he caught her, pulling her back against his front. He swept her hair aside and kissed her throat, licking and nipping it with blunt teeth.

"I want to taste you." That wasn't the first time he had said that and it wasn't the first time she had reacted to the words with a flush of prickly heat and a momentary desire to agree and let him bite her.

The thought of Veiron taking her blood, tasting her, and marking her flesh had her tingly in all the good places.

"Let me taste you," he husked into her ear and she moaned.

"Have you ever?" She couldn't finish that sentence. Fear of what his answer might be stole the rest of it.

"Never," Veiron breathed against her throat and kissed it again. "I have never wanted to do such a thing with anyone else, but the thought of tasting you, sinking my teeth into you... fuck, Erin... I think I might blow my load just imagining it."

He ground his erection against her backside through her robe and she moaned again, groin pulsing in response and nipples tightening into hard buds.

"I want to mark you, Erin... I need it." He rubbed against her again, hands holding her hips, harder this time, eliciting another heated moan that she couldn't contain.

Erin nodded. She wanted it too. The thought of Veiron biting her, staking such a claim on her, had her heart pounding and knees trembling.

"Now?" she whispered, aware she sounded needy but too far gone to care.

"Soon." He pressed another kiss to her throat and then released her.

Erin almost collapsed into a boneless heap on the wooden deck. Veiron stalked back into the villa but she didn't follow him. She crouched by the hot tub set into the deck and pressed buttons on the panel until the lights came on and the water began to bubble and heat.

The tub was only shielded from view on three sides but there was no one on the beach and even if there were the odd couple strolling along it, it wouldn't stop her from doing this with Veiron. She waved her hand through the water, feeling it growing warmer, her mind racing forwards to imagine making love to Veiron in it. She had never made out in water before and had never been in a hot tub.

When it was warm enough, she slipped out of her white robe and into the water. She sank down into it, so it lapped at her shoulders. The heat of it was wonderful but not quite blissful. She was missing a vital ingredient to make this one of the best nights of her life.

Where was Veiron?

She turned and leaned her back against the side closest to the beach, studying the dark villa for a sign of him. He emerged out of the shadows wearing the white robe and carrying two champagne flutes in one hand and an open bottle in the other. His gaze fell on her and he stopped dead.

"Damn... you look wicked," he breathed and she raked her gaze over him, settling it on the tented robe in front of his hips. Clearly, she looked wicked and he liked it.

Veiron set the two glasses and bottle down, stripped out of his robe and stepped into the tub beside her. Erin swept her tongue across her lips, tempted to cross the water to him and lick every inch of his erection to bring him to his knees.

Why not?

He went to sink into the water but she beat him to it, settling her hand around his rigid length and running her tongue up it from root to tip. He groaned and trembled, muttered something about people seeing. Erin didn't care. She wrapped her lips around him and sucked, pressing her tongue along the underside of his cock. He moaned again, hands clamping down on her shoulders, breath coming hard and fast.

"Erin," he whispered and then groaned, hips bucking. "God, woman, the things you do to me."

Erin smiled around his cock and sucked the soft head, flicking her tongue over it. He groaned and then shuddered and pushed her backwards.

She looked up at him, water bubbling around her breasts, her hands on his hips. Veiron loomed over her, the hot tub casting blue light up the length of his body and illuminating his face, revealing his hunger to her. She had never seen him looking so hungry before. It thrilled her.

He sank into the tub beside her, still breathing hard, and settled his arms on the lip of it, stretching them out to follow the curved shape. She smiled when he closed his eyes and tipped his head back.

Inching through the water, she kept her eyes on him, trying to move silently. It didn't work. He snapped his eyes open before she reached him and stared at her.

"Champagne first," he said and scooted to the side closest to the villa. He poured two glasses and handed one to her. She took it, raised it and knocked it against his.

"Cheers." She sipped it, the bubbles exploding on her tongue, and watched Veiron do the same. "So is this a romantic gesture, or is this to give me some false courage so I don't go back on the whole tasting thing?"

Veiron laughed. "I was being romantic, but if you want to believe I have an ulterior motive, go ahead... I don't think I need you drunk for you to let me bite you... I think you want it just as much as I do."

He couldn't have been more right but Erin didn't let him see that. She closed her eyes, drained her champagne glass and handed it back to him to refill. He poured her another glass and she sipped this one.

Veiron caught her other arm and dragged her across to him. He turned her and pulled her onto his lap, so she was sitting on his thighs with her back to his front and one of his arms banded across her chest. She sipped her drink and gently paddled with her feet, staring out at the black ocean and enjoying the moment. Moonlight rippled across the sea. The world had gone quiet, only their breathing and the waves breaking the silence.

When she had dreamed about coming to the Maldives in the past, it had always featured a man and had always been a romantic getaway, but she had never imagined it would be like this. It was perfect as she sat on Veiron's lap, the hot water bubbling around them, sipping champagne and enjoying the silence. Enjoying just being together. She had never imagined she would find a man like Veiron, one who was strong and capable of taking care of her and himself, but romantic and poetic too.

Erin stared at the shore, at the place where she had practically exchanged vows with him. She smiled to herself and leaned back into him. He held her closer and pressed his lips against her bare shoulder.

"What are you thinking?" he husked into her ear and she shivered at the feel of his warm breath caressing her damp skin.

"Just how perfect this is." She paddled her feet and sighed, tipping her head back and resting it on his shoulder. "I wish we could stay like this forever."

He chuckled. "I would like that too."

A chill washed over her skin. "But we can't... can we? You need to go to Hell and sooner or later we'll have to leave this place."

Veiron shifted behind her, causing small waves to cascade across the water, and she heard him set his glass down. He wrapped his other arm around her, holding her tight against him, and rested his chin on her shoulder.

"I have to go... you know that. I'll be careful. The little fucker won't get me. Promise." He kissed her cheek and Erin wished that promise had chased the cold feeling from her but it hadn't. She understood that Veiron had to know what his future held and that he was going to Hell for her sake too, but she hated the thought of him returning to that realm and placing himself in so much danger.

Her vision hadn't shown anyone other than her, Veiron and the Devil, but she couldn't take comfort from the fact that Marcus would be there and she wouldn't. Her vision had shown something different to what had happened on the rooftop in London too. They were screwy. What if Marcus only took her place, trying to stop the Devil from killing Veiron?

"Don't think about it," Veiron whispered and stroked her arms under the water. It felt cold against her now. She tried to shake off her bad feeling but it refused to go.

"I don't want to... maybe you need to take my mind off it."

Veiron chuckled again and kissed her cheek. "I can do that."

He settled his hands on her hips and ground his hard cock against her bottom. She moaned and bit her lip, the thought of making love with him again chasing away some of her fear. She needed this moment with him, this calm before the storm. She had never needed anything so much.

Veiron peppered her cheek and throat with soft kisses.

"I want to touch you while I'm inside you... one with you," he murmured against her cheek and it flushed, hot from the thought of him doing that. She wanted it too.

He took her glass of champagne from her and set it down beside his. His hands claimed her hips again and he easily lifted her from the water. Her heart fluttered when he positioned himself and slowly eased her down onto his length. It felt amazing as it stretched her, filling her and joining them once again. She moaned as he shifted his hands to her thighs and spread them, so her legs dangled either side of his. The first brush of his fingers over her clitoris tore another breathy moan from her throat and she closed her eyes, leaning her head back against his shoulder. Veiron moaned into her ear.

"Feels so good," he whispered and kissed her shoulder, worshipping it as his fingers toyed with her bundle of nerves.

Erin wanted him to move inside her, to thrust deep, but he remained still, just filling her as he pleasured her. She writhed, shifting on his cock, hungry for more than just his touch. He caught her hip with his free hand and made her still. She whined.

"I just want to feel you climax," he husked into her ear and she moaned, heat flashing through her over how needy he sounded, as though it was vital to him.

She settled on him, focusing on the feel of him inside her, joining their bodies, and the way his fingers danced on her clitoris. Each stroke and swirl cranked her tighter, until she was moaning breathily, tensing and wriggling, losing control of herself. She needed more.

Erin slipped her hand under the water and settled it over his, wanting to feel him touching her. She arched forwards and her breasts cleared the surface, the cool night air causing her nipples to pucker. Erin couldn't resist. She lifted her other hand and toyed with one of her nipples, playing with it while Veiron did the same to her nub. She clenched her muscles around his cock, drawing him deeper, pushing down on his impressive length. Veiron groaned and his free hand joined hers, teasing her other nipple. He pinched and tugged it, gently swirled his fingertip around it, and then rolled it between his fingers. Each action elicited another moan from her, winding her insides and bringing her one step closer to orgasm.

The feel of his strong hand teasing her clitoris, his long cock filling her, and his fingers toying with her nipples was all too much. Erin bit her lip, shifting on his cock, trying to keep still but unable to control her body as she sought her climax.

Veiron grunted each time she lifted off him and forced her back down, pinning her there for a few seconds before teasing her nipple again. She screwed her eyes shut and he squeezed her clitoris, and the tension inside her exploded, her body quaking around his, milking his length as she came.

Veiron moaned and held her against him, as though savouring the feel of her body trembling around his, squeezing and clenching him. Erin collapsed back against him, heat chasing over her skin and her entire body shaking. She breathed hard, bringing herself down little by little. As the haze of her orgasm began to clear, she focused on the feel of Veiron still inside her, and her desire spiked right back up.

He had given her pleasure and taken none for himself.

Erin was determined to change that.

CHAPTER 20

Veiron groaned as Erin raised herself off his erection and turned to face him, settling herself straight back on it. He clutched her bottom and kissed her, pouring out the hunger that had steadily built inside him while he had been pleasuring her. The feel of her climaxing on his cock had been delicious, cranking him tight with need, until he had been close to coming too. He didn't think he would last long if she turned the tables on him now.

He kept kissing her, keeping her hips still so she didn't try to ride him, buying himself time to calm down so he would last longer than a few seconds. That would hardly be the perfect end to what was becoming a perfect evening. He was fucked if he was going to shoot his load like a virgin. He wanted to make love to his woman, wanted to pleasure her again and spoil her to all others.

Mine.

She had consented to it and it had awakened some deep primal male side of him. What he felt for her now went beyond possessive. She was his woman. His to protect and love, to cherish and to pleasure. And he was hers.

He was sure that there had been a time not so long ago when he had told himself not to go here, that she was mortal and things would never work out between them. Erin was mortal and he didn't care. He would either find a way to make her immortal or he would find a way to make himself mortal. He wanted to live with her for the rest of her days and die with her. He wanted nothing to come between them.

Erin sat back on him and he grunted, the change in position making him aware of where his cock was again. She was so hot and wet, so relaxed and ready for him to pump into her. He groaned and tried to kiss her again, but she ran her hands down his chest and leaned back, making her body tighter around his.

She picked up her glass of champagne and sipped it. Veiron groaned again. She couldn't seriously be suggesting they drink and chat while he was buried deep in her heat.

Veiron took the glass from her, set it back down, and snaked his arm around her waist. She giggled when he dragged her against him and kissed her, hard and fierce, a rough meeting of their mouths and tangling of their tongues.

Erin raised herself up and then sank down on him, and his hands shot to her hips. He guided her on his cock, pumping deeply and slowly into her, savouring the heat that steadily built between them. She clutched his arms and moaned into his mouth, tongue brushing his and teasing him. He slanted his head and deepened the kiss, needing more of her.

Veiron tensed his bottom, thrusting his cock up each time she sank down, their movements causing waves in the hot tub. Erin moaned and tightened her grip on his shoulders, holding him so fiercely that it bordered on painful. It only added to his pleasure. He groaned to let her know that he liked this side of her, this commanding and passionate woman. Her pace quickened until she was riding him hard and moaning into his mouth each time their hips met, her body rubbing against his. Veiron grasped her bottom, pressing his fingers in, guiding her and matching her pace.

Her body was so hot around him, so wet and sweet. Her hands literally branded his flesh as she held him.

The passion and desire clouding his mind cleared enough for him to realise that something was wrong. He broke away from Erin and looked down at her body. Water droplets fizzled on her skin and heat rose from the water around her. Hot.

"Erin?" Veiron said and she moaned, writhed, and rode him harder.

"Don't stop," she groaned and screwed her eyes shut. Her pulse hammered in her throat and Veiron felt a deep urge to bite her.

It wasn't the only urge he was feeling. She felt amazing as she bounced on his cock but whatever change was coming over her, it was affecting him too. It called to his darker side, the demon within him, and drew it to the surface, luring him into changing.

His nails sharpened into black claws and Erin moaned, throwing her head back and arching into him. He grunted and swallowed, tried to keep his focus but it was impossible. Everything in him said to forget his concern and just go with it, go along with the incredible heat and pleasure flowing through him. He couldn't get enough of her as she rode him, clutching him and moaning so sweetly.

"Veiron," she breathed, passion and hunger roughening her voice, and his teeth began to sharpen. She moaned again, as though she had felt the change and liked it. That only made the demonic side of him push harder.

When his teeth finished sharpening, she cried loudly and responded by lifting almost all the way off his cock before sinking back onto him, hard and fast, rough and passionate. He groaned and held her hips, keeping her moving on him, too far gone to stop now. She felt too good around him.

Erin didn't slow her pace. She kept riding him, undulating her hips, milking his cock as though she couldn't get enough of him. He wasn't sure how much longer he could last. His balls were tightening, body tensing and readying for his climax. He groaned and breathed hard, struggling against his desire to change completely. He couldn't. He would tear her apart if he did. He tried to tamp it down and keep control. Erin rocked on him, moaning and writhing, her head thrown back and breasts glistening under the moonlight. Steam curled around her, her heat invading him now, turning his blood to fire.

"Veiron," she whispered and snapped her head down. She kissed him, devouring his mouth, her taste so sweet and hot. "Keep going. It feels so good."

He thrust into her, countering her movements, losing himself in the moment again. She moaned with each plunge of his cock into her welcoming heat and each one made him thrust harder, pump deeper, until he was pounding into her. Her breasts bounced with each hard meeting of their hips and she cried out with each one, calling his name. He didn't care if anyone heard them. All they would know was that Erin belonged to him.

"Feels so good," she murmured breathlessly and moved her hips in a figure of eight, her hands tangling in the short lengths of her black hair. "I want to feel you climax."

Veiron growled and dragged her against him, sucking her nipple and teasing it with his sharp teeth as he plunged into her, eliciting another high groan from his woman.

She buried her fingers into his hair, clinging to him, and her skin heated under his lips. He didn't understand what was happening and then it didn't matter.

She convulsed against him, her inner walls clenched him and she cried out as she climaxed. Heat flashed through his body, burning up his blood, sending his head spinning and he couldn't hold back. He shoved her down onto his cock, impaling her, and came hard. His balls throbbed, every muscle in his body twitching, and he groaned. He couldn't stop. He shot his seed into her and her body milked him, drawing his orgasm out, until she moaned his name and climaxed again, and so did he.

Veiron collapsed against her chest, leaning over her, breathing hard and struggling to remain conscious.

Erin shifted on his still-hard cock and pushed him backwards.

His gaze flickered to her throat and the pulse beating there. An urge to bite her overtook him and he couldn't stop himself this time. He grabbed her, dragged her against him, and sank his sharp red teeth into the smooth unmarked skin on the left side of her throat.

Erin cried out again, shouting his name to the heavens.

Veiron trembled, heat rushing through his veins as the first drop of her blood touched his tongue. It flowed into him, bringing incredible fire with it, an inferno that made him feel as though he was going to burn to ashes and that unleashed his darker side. His eyes changed and he growled against her throat. Erin quaked in his arms, clutching his head to her and her body throbbing around his.

He took barely a sip of her blood before he pulled away, awareness of what he had done dawning on him. Blood marked her throat, dark in the low light. It beaded on the rows of puncture wounds. He shouldn't have bitten her. He had no way of stopping the cuts from bleeding. He leaned in and licked the wounds, and Erin moaned and shivered again, the sound so light and breathless that he groaned in response. He licked the marks again, tasting her sweet blood, and then drew back.

No new blood blossomed on her skin.

He frowned and looked closer. The marks looked smaller. Was she healing them somehow?

Veiron looked at her. She smiled shyly and touched the marks on her throat.

He was still trying to catch up with everything when she curled up against him and settled her head on his chest. She stroked it with her left hand, drawing wet patterns on his skin, and murmured contentedly.

Veiron touched her back and frowned. She was ice cold. He went to lift her up and she moaned.

"Don't move, not yet... I just want to lie like this a while." She held onto him and he relented and settled with her, sinking lower in the water so it covered her shoulders.

He held her, his body still inside hers, and stroked her wet hair.

"What the fuck just happened?" he whispered, needing to ask even though he knew she wouldn't be able to answer that question. He just needed to hear that she was aware things had gone severely into the weird just now.

"I don't know," she said and her hand stopped and rested on his chest. "I just did whatever my desire said to do... and then I felt so hot... and every time you showed a little more of your demonic side, I... you know."

He did know. She had responded to it, as though she had been feeding off his change, gaining pleasure from it.

"You were hot," he said and she curled up closer to him, and he felt her fear.

"It was my power. I could feel it inside me... growing... pushing." Those words were quietly spoken and small sounding, as though she hadn't wanted to say them because doing so would be admitting that it had controlled her to a degree.

"It's okay, Sweetheart." Veiron wrapped his arms around her and held her tightly, letting her know without words that he was there for her and nothing was going to change that. She didn't need to fear. "My power is the same. Sometimes it feels as though it isn't a part of me. There's nothing to be worried about."

"Promise?" she said and he nodded.

"I promise."

"I thought demons weren't big on promises," she said and there was a smile in her voice at last.

He grinned and pressed a kiss to the top of her head. "We're not, but I'll make an exception for you. I swear to you, Erin, I'll find out what your power is and we'll deal with it together. You're not alone and you never will be. I'm here with you."

Veiron held her closer, a need to protect her burning in his heart. He would get the answers for her and would make everything better. He would take care of her because he loved her with all of his heart and her happiness was his.

For now, he would take care of her immediate needs. He reached over to the control panel for the hot tub and cranked the temperature up. He would get her warm and then take her to bed. She needed her rest and so did he.

He would go to Hell with Marcus soon but he wasn't worried about his own safety. He was worried about Erin's.

She had drawn him into changing tonight, enough that he could have revealed their location to the Devil. It was still a day until Einar and Taylor arrived, and Taylor could hide Erin and Amelia.

What if Hell's angels found them before then?

Veiron growled and clutched Erin to him. It didn't matter. If any of them dared to come near her, he would kill them all. He would protect what was his.

He would fight the Devil himself for Erin's sake.

CHAPTER 21

Erin had been on edge since falling asleep in Veiron's arms after their hot tub encounter the day before yesterday. Amelia had flown off the handle again when Veiron had admitted that he may have alerted other Hell's angels to their whereabouts. Erin had backed him up and then left with him to get some space and time alone with him. She didn't get her sister sometimes. Veiron could have kept it a secret but he had done the right thing and warned Amelia and Marcus, and rather than just saying they would deal with anything that happened, Amelia had given him hell.

Who had died and made her big sister boss?

Erin was having none of it. If Hell's angels came, they would probably be coming for her. If she didn't go nuclear at Veiron about what he had done then what right did her sister have to shout at him about it? She huffed and pulled her black shorts on over the bottoms of her black bikini, and then towelled off her wet black hair.

Tired of her sister's god complex, she had spent most of yesterday snorkelling with Veiron, and had avoided Amelia and Marcus by heading back out onto the reef first thing this morning. The house reef at the resort was amazing, full of colourful fish and even turtles. She had never been snorkelling and the closest she had come to seeing tropical fish were her family visits to the London Aquarium as a child.

Veiron seemed to attract some of the scariest-looking fish she had ever seen though, including a small shark this morning. It hadn't bothered him. He had petted them all. Even the shark. It had quickly turned and sped away into the murky distance. Erin had laughed and got a lungful of seawater then, and Veiron had insisted they call it a day and head back to shore.

She smiled at him where he lay on the double bed wearing only his black jeans, skin golden against the white sheets, his eyes closed and wet hair spread around his shoulders.

A sudden pang of uncertainty stabbed her in the chest. In less than an hour, Taylor and Einar would arrive at the resort and Marcus and Veiron would leave for Hell. It turned Erin's stomach whenever she thought about it and she wanted to ask him to stay, to forget about seeing whether his future was like her vision and discovering where her powers came from and why the Devil wanted her.

Veiron's eyes cracked open and he pushed himself up onto his elbows, resting on them. Every muscle of his torso tensed, the thick ropes of his abs luring her gaze downwards, and she wanted to congratulate him for finding a way to make her instantly forget her worries. Whenever he looked so delicious, she couldn't think about anything other than making love with him again.

"I'll be careful," he said and her momentary amnesia brought about by her lust for him disappeared, worry crashing back down on her even fiercer than before. He held his hand out to her. Erin stepped towards him, slipped hers into it, and allowed him to lead her onto the bed. She knelt astride his legs and he tipped his head back, luring her in for a kiss. She went willingly, needing the comfort that came from contact with Veiron, and closed her eyes as she kissed him. He kept it soft and slow, full of affection and reassurance.

Erin wanted to melt into him and deepen the kiss, turning up the heat until she awoke his passion. She wanted to lose herself in him and forget what would happen in only a handful of minutes that were quickly slipping through her fingers. She had to be strong though and burying her head in the sand by losing herself in her desire for Veiron was an act of weakness.

She took what he gave her in his tender kiss instead, letting it soothe away her fears and savouring it and this moment with him. She could feel his love for her in each soft sweep of his lips over hers and how much he needed her, and it brought tears to her eyes. He would come back to her, she was sure of it. He had survived centuries in Hell and had come to rescue her when he had been a wanted man. He knew how to move through that realm without making the enemy aware of him. He could get in and out without drawing the Devil's attention.

"Erin," Veiron whispered against her lips and she drew back. He frowned, concern lighting his dark irises, and swept the pad of his thumb under her eyes, capturing her tears and wiping them away. His hand cupped her cheek and she sighed and leaned into his touch, absorbing the heat of his palm and how good it felt against her.

She could see in his eyes what he wanted to tell her and could see his fear too, and his uncertainty. She knew him, knew that he was a man who loved with all of his heart, but who also believed that no one could love him. He needed to hear her say it first, and she would, because she wanted to prove him wrong about her and the world. There was someone who could love him, who did love him.

"Veiron." She covered his hand with hers, holding it against her face, and looked deep into his eyes, wanting to see right down to his soul, and wanting him to see straight into hers when she said the words. "I love you."

He swallowed hard, slipped his hand around the nape of her neck and drew her to him. He pressed his forehead to hers, clutching her against him.

"I love you too," he husked, voice low and raw, full of so much emotion that she wrapped her arms around him and held him to her. He tipped his head up, captured her lips, and kissed her hard and roughly, his tongue tangling with hers. Every inch of her warmed, not just from the kiss but from his words and the knowledge that he loved her. She melted into him and slanted her head to deepen their kiss, returning it with equal desperation and need, letting him know that they were in this together and she wanted it to go on forever, never wanted him to part from her again. She swept her tongue across his lips, eliciting a deep moan from him that heated her through and made her want to do it again. Before she could, he broke away from her, breathing hard, and growled. "Christ, Erin, I love you so much."

Erin smiled, leaned into him so he collapsed back onto the bed with her lying on top of him, and kissed him again, tangling her fingers in his long wet scarlet hair. Amelia was going to flip her lid but Erin didn't care. In a world where everything felt so uncertain for her, with her strange powers and the Devil after her, Veiron was the one thing she was certain about. She loved him with all of her heart, was so deeply in love with him, and he with her. She wasn't afraid of it or the depth of their feelings. She didn't care that he was a demonic angel. They belonged together.

Veiron rolled her over, pinning her to the bed beneath him, and deepened their kiss, stroking the length of her tongue with his, turning the heat up another notch.

She wrapped her arms around his neck and her legs around his waist, intent on stealing another moment with him.

Someone knocked on the door.

Veiron lifted his head and growled in the direction of the glass doors to the deck.

Erin sighed. At least they had knocked this time rather than barging in. She mourned the loss of Veiron's body against hers as he pushed himself off her and grabbed his black t-shirt from the back of the chair in front of the dressing table.

She sat up and looked across at the door to find Marcus standing there with his back to them. Had he seen them together on the bed and turned his back before knocking and waiting for them to answer? She had only known him a short time but it seemed like the sort of thing he would do. Unlike her sister, he respected her relationship with Veiron and sometimes even backed them up, siding with them against Amelia. Her sister glared at him whenever he did but always stopped her assault. It was good to have her sister's lover on her team.

Erin crossed the room and opened the door to him. He turned and smiled at her, pale blue eyes bright with it.

"I am sorry for disturbing you." His smile held and he raked his fingers through his dark hair. "Amelia wishes to head to the dock to meet the boat. It arrives shortly."

Erin's heart thumped against her chest. So soon?

Marcus's expression shifted to one of concern. "I will take care of him for you, Erin. I will not let anything happen to him."

"Like I need your help," Veiron grumbled and tossed his black holdall onto the bed. "I'll probably be the one taking care of your skinny arse."

Marcus raised an eyebrow and his eyes brightened, the darker flakes in them swirling. "If it were not for Erin, you would be heading down there alone... just remember that."

"Not alone," Erin said, not wanting to intervene in what was fairly standard behaviour between the two angels but needing to speak up. "If you weren't going with him, Marcus, I would be."

"No way in Hell I'd let you go back down there." Veiron continued to rifle through his holdall, his eyes never leaving it. "I don't need a chaperone."

"Well, you've got one, so suck it up." Erin walked up behind him, wrapped her arms around his waist, and rested her head against his back. "It's either me or Marcus. Your choice."

Veiron grunted, was still for long seconds, and then placed his hand over hers where they were locked in front of his stomach.

"I would never risk you," he said and she smiled, warmed inside by his words and the affection in them.

"That's what I thought... so play nice with Marcus. If you're a pain in his arse, I'll never hear the end of it from Amelia."

Veiron sighed and straightened. He caught her right wrist and pulled her around him, turning at the same time. He settled his arms around her shoulders and briefly kissed her, hard enough that her lips tingled when he broke away.

"Fine. I'll be nice. Satisfied?"

Erin nodded, tiptoed, and kissed him again. Marcus cleared his throat. It was a little high-pitched for him. She glanced over her shoulder to see her sister standing in the doorway in front of Marcus, her silver hair up in a ponytail that shone in the strong sunlight and her grey eyes dark.

She had never seen Amelia looking so on edge.

Erin reluctantly slipped free of Veiron's embrace and took hold of his hand. He linked their fingers and squeezed her hand, and she silently thanked him for the reassurance.

They walked over to Amelia, Veiron pocketing his passport along the way, and headed out. The walk to the dock seemed too short, not enough time for Erin to absorb her remaining few minutes with Veiron safe in her grasp. Amelia and Marcus walked ahead of them, hand in hand, talking in low voices. Erin caught snippets of Amelia pressing Marcus to be careful and offering to go with them. Marcus wouldn't hear of it.

It seemed all angels were born heroes, especially when it came to protecting their women.

Erin looked up at Veiron and smiled when he glanced down at her, right into her eyes. She didn't need to tell him to be careful or to get out of Hell at the first sign of danger. But there was something she needed to tell him again.

They reached the dock in time to see the speedboat rumbling up to the jetty. It wasn't hard to spot Einar and Taylor. Both of them wore black and Einar looked huge compared to everyone else in the boat, parked at the back of it with his arm slung around Taylor's slender shoulders. Her blue eyes scanned the dock and settled on Erin. They narrowed and then she smiled, chasing away Erin's suspicion that Taylor still didn't like seeing Veiron with her, despite her claims that she was over him.

Well, if she didn't like that, she definitely wasn't going to like Erin's goodbye to Veiron when it came.

Erin didn't care. Taylor had had her chance with Veiron. He was Erin's now and she wasn't going to let him go. Never. What they had was for forever.

The boat docked and Einar and Taylor were the last to disembark.

"Any problems?" Einar asked, his deep voice growly with sleep. He looked as though he had been awake for three days solid.

"None," Erin said and then added, "How about at your end?"

Taylor patted Einar's forearm. "It turns out that Romeo doesn't like flying. Ironic, right?"

Erin giggled and Einar frowned at her. "Come on, you have to admit it's a bit silly. You've probably been flying in more dangerous conditions for most of your life."

He shrugged.

"It isn't that bad, Wingless. You just sit in the tin can and it flies for you." There was a laugh in Veiron's tone and Einar scowled again.

"Even you have to admit it's much nicer to fly on your own volition."

Veiron gave an easy lift of his shoulders. "I guess. You made your choice though. I don't exactly have one. I fly and all of Hell's legions are after me."

"Or after me," Erin said under her breath and Veiron squeezed her hand.

"I'll take care of the nasties, Baby. Don't fret." He leaned down and pressed a long kiss to her bare shoulder.

Several people passed them, heading for the boat. Erin swallowed. This was it. Time up. Any second now, Veiron was going to have to get on that boat and she would be left to worry over whether she would ever see him again.

"Erin?" Veiron said and she looked up at him, trying to school her features so he didn't see her fear. He sighed and stroked her cheek. "I swear to you, Sweetheart, I will be careful. If I get so much as a bad feeling, I'll get my arse and Marcus's to the nearest gate. Nothing bad will happen to us."

She nodded. She knew that in her head but her heart wasn't getting the message. It scrambled it so it came out reading like Veiron was going to his death and Marcus would die too, and her sister would never forgive her.

"You're not going to Hell?" Taylor's voice was high-pitched and tense. Veiron lifted his head and looked across at her. Her blue eyes widened. "That's insane and you know it. You've got half of Hell looking for your butt and you're going to what, just waltz in there and out again unnoticed?"

"I need to go for Erin's sake and my own. Erin needs to know what her power means and I need to know whether the future she has seen will come to pass." Veiron drew Erin closer and placed his arm around her shoulder, a possessive act if ever she saw one but one that she liked.

"I will go with you," Einar said and Taylor looked horrified.

"Oh no, you won't. This is their problem, not yours. You're not going to Hell."

He frowned. "I am going, Taylor. The more of us there is, the more likely we are to get out unscathed... or at least alive."

Erin wanted to tell him that she appreciated the offer but Taylor looked as though she would bite the head off anyone who dared to back him up.

"I don't want you to go down there," Taylor said.

"I know." Einar caressed her cheek. "But I must. We are all in this together. You stay here and keep Amelia and Erin hidden while we're gone. We'll be back before you know it."

"Fuck... I never thought I'd live to see the day you grew some balls, Wingless." Veiron slapped a hand down on his shoulder. "Good to have you onboard. You sure you're going to be up for a little more time in a tin can? It's a shorter flight from here to the nearest gate in India but it's still flying."

Einar nodded. "Not a problem. If I feel sick, I will make sure I throw up on you."

Veiron grinned. "That's the spirit."

Taylor looked as though she was going to punch Veiron for accepting Einar's offer so Erin caught his attention by squeezing his hand. He looked down at her and his smile faded. He turned to face her, settled his hands on her bare waist and drew her up to him, so her body was flush against his.

This was it.

Everything she wanted to say got stuck in her throat.

"I love you," Veiron whispered and Erin felt Taylor's eyes dart to her. "I promise, I will come back to you."

Erin nodded, tiptoed, and looped her arms around his neck. Veiron shifted his grip to her bottom and raised her up him, so her feet dangled inches off the wooden jetty. She pressed her forehead against his, feeling his warm breath mingling with hers, and told herself that he would keep that promise and everything would be fine.

"I love you too," she said and closed her eyes, lowered her mouth and kissed him. It was slow again, a bare meeting of lips meant to convey all of her feelings to him and back up her words.

The man on the boat called for anyone heading to the airport.

She drew back and stared down into Veiron's dark eyes. A touch of crimson edged his pupils. She loved his eyes. He tried so hard to hide what he was but they always betrayed him and let the truth about him shine through. A demonic angel. The man she loved. He never had to hide the truth from her. She loved all of him, and thought he was gorgeous in both of his forms and everything in between.

Amelia and Marcus moved past her and Veiron finally lowered her back to her feet. He held her a moment longer and then pressed a final kiss to her lips and walked past her.

Erin turned but didn't follow him. She had felt his feelings in his kiss and had seen them in his eyes. He couldn't handle a long goodbye and neither could she. He settled into the boat, in the same place where they had sat on their way to the island. Marcus and Einar sat either side of him.

The man pulled the boat away and Erin fought to hold back her tears. She didn't want to cry. It would be a sucky image to leave Veiron with as he journeyed through Hell.

She held her hand up and then grinned to herself, brought her hand down, curled the fingers of both of her hands over and pointed her thumbs downwards. She pressed both hands together, forming the shape of a heart over hers.

Veiron smiled and mouthed, "Right back at you."

Tears filled her eyes but she held her smile for him, until he was so far away that he wouldn't be able to see her clearly. Then she let them fall.

Amelia came to stand beside her and placed her arm around her shoulders, squeezing them and holding her tightly. She hoped that Amelia wouldn't say anything derogatory about Veiron because she couldn't take it right now. She needed her sister's support and understanding, not her criticism. Amelia sighed and held her in silence, and Erin looked at her, catching the unshed tears in her eyes. She scrubbed her own away and looked across at Taylor.

"How are the cocktails?" Taylor extended the handle of one of the black suitcases beside her. "Because I don't know about you two, but I need a bloody stiff drink."

Erin smiled shakily and Amelia smiled too.

"I think we have time for a few before you send us to sleep." Amelia turned with Erin, leading her along the jetty. When she broke away from her to take one of the suitcases for Taylor, Erin looked back over her shoulder, watching the speedboat disappearing into the distance.

Taylor would keep them asleep until Veiron and the others returned.

She would be with him again before she knew it.

She hoped.

CHAPTER 22

Erin wasn't sure how Taylor's power worked but it was certainly an interesting one. Erin sat next to Amelia on a white painted metal railing that separated a boardwalk from a pristine white beach. Hot summer sun washed over her, easing away her tension, and the sea stretched endlessly into the distance where it eventually met the sky and the line between them blurred.

This wasn't the island. This was some other place. Amelia had explained that it was her inner world and she had once brought Marcus here, when she had been going through everything with him and the game between Heaven and Hell.

It was beautiful.

Tall palms towered above the boardwalk and strings of lights curved between them. It would look even more beautiful at night, with the lights on and the full moon illuminating the world.

They had been sitting here on the chipped railing for over an hour, talking to each other and catching up. Amelia hadn't berated her once about what she had said to Veiron at the dock and Erin was thankful for it. She didn't want to argue with her sister, not when she needed her company to keep her mind off where Veiron had gone.

He wouldn't even be there yet. The plane had left the main airport in the afternoon, bound for Chennai in eastern India. There was a gate a few miles from there that would take them down into Hell close to something called the bottomless pit.

Marcus had explained that the bottomless pit was where the Devil was supposed to reside, trapped by an angel named Apollyon each time he lost their scheduled battles. Erin had countered that the Devil didn't seem particularly trapped to her. He had roamed around quite freely. Marcus hadn't had an explanation for that one, but Veiron had said it was probably because Apollyon was due to fight him again so the effect of the angel's victory and the Devil's consequent containment was wearing off, allowing the Devil to move around in a larger area of Hell surrounding the bottomless pit.

It was reassuring to know that there was a limit to where the Devil could go right now. Apparently, Earth was off-limits.

Amelia had flinched whenever anyone had mentioned Apollyon's name. Erin hadn't had a chance to ask her why.

Until now.

She grasped the pole on either side of her thighs and looked over at her sister. The gentle breeze blowing in from the ocean caused Amelia's cream summer dress to flutter and dance around her legs. Erin had discovered shortly after their arrival in her inner world that Amelia ruled here, and that included her clothing. She was wearing a summer dress too. At least her sister had done the decent thing and given her a black one with deep purple flowers all over it.

"So... um... what's the deal with you and this Apollyon bloke?" Erin watched her sister flinch again.

Her grey eyes slid across to meet Erin's. "He sort of killed me."

"Holy shit... really?" Erin almost fell off the railing. "You died?"

"And awoke as a wholly different person, but I'm back now, just a little improved," Amelia said and then frowned. "It wasn't Apollyon's fault though. He didn't want to kill me. Heaven made him do it, and since then he's been bent on revenge."

"Man, I can relate to that. Heaven really did a number on you and Marcus, didn't they?"

Amelia nodded. "More than a number. They don't care who they hurt in order to get what they want... you do understand that, don't you? If Heaven can control its angels and force them to do things against their will, then Hell can do the same."

Erin frowned. "What are you saying?"

"I'm saying that Veiron might be in love with you, but that might not stop him from trying to hurt you. If the Devil wants you that badly, he will make Veiron obey any and all commands sent to him."

Erin swallowed, trying to wet her suddenly dry throat. Was that even possible? If the Devil could do such a thing, surely he would have done so already, rather than sending his men to retrieve her from Veiron.

Unless he had a reason for wanting her to remain with Veiron.

She looked at Amelia again. Or was it her sister that he wanted her close to so he could track them and find her?

But he hadn't sent his angels after her again and he must have felt Veiron's location on Earth when Veiron's eyes, claws and teeth had changed while they had been making love in the hot tub.

What if the Devil had used the pool in Hell that Veiron wanted to visit and had seen the future in it, and knew that he didn't need to do anything in order to get Veiron down there and out of the way? What if he had seen something else in it?

Like her and Amelia alone and vulnerable.

Suddenly, Erin wanted to wake up. Taylor could use enchantments or whatever to protect their location, just as she had done on her home with Einar. Erin didn't want to be stuck here sleeping, unable to wake, not knowing whether or not someone had already come and captured them.

Her skin prickled and tingled, and her chest tightened, turning her breathing laboured.

"What's wrong?" Amelia laid her hand on Erin's back between her shoulder blades, over her dragon tattoo.

"What if the Devil sends his men for us while we're asleep?"

Amelia smiled reassuringly. "Taylor is setting up protection spells around the villa. We'll be safe."

That was a relief but her panic didn't subside.

The tingling in her fingers turned to heat and she flexed them, trying to calm down. It wasn't her power manifesting. It was just a panic attack because she was thinking it was. It was psychosomatic. She swallowed and kept flexing her fingers.

Her eyes widened. The world around them began to fall apart. Piece by piece, it crumbled and changed. The white sand turned black and formed into sharp jagged rocks. Steam rose from the sea as it began to glow red and turned into a rolling river of lava. The endless blue sky darkened to black and the trees behind them caught fire.

No.

Erin's hands blazed red, ribbons like smoke swirling outwards from her palms.

"What's happening?" Amelia said, voice high with panic. "Erin, why are we in Hell?"

"Vision." Erin forced the word out and shook her hands, trying to stop them from bursting into flames. She didn't want that to happen again. She didn't want this power, whatever it was.

A scream shattered her already fragile nerves, pained and garbled.

Erin's head shot up and her eyes widened. The scenery had changed again, the river of lava now further in the distance and leaving a wide expanse of black ahead of her. Spires of rock rose around her, forming a semi-circle, and her heart stopped.

Not this.

Not again.

She shook her head. "No... no... no!"

She dropped down and the railing disappeared, sending Amelia crashing onto the black basalt. Amelia gasped as the black fortress rose out of the ground, rocks tumbling down it as it reached towards the obsidian vault above, each spire taller and more jagged than the last.

"What the hell?" Amelia pushed onto her feet. "What's happening, Erin?"

"Not this... please, not this."

Veiron, Marcus and Einar appeared in the middle of the courtyard, fighting for their lives against Hell's angels. Amelia went to run forwards, silver wings erupting from her back and eyes brightening, but Erin caught her hand.

"It's no use," she said and shook her head when her sister looked at her, fear written in every line of her face. "Nothing we do will stop it."

"We have to try." Amelia broke free of her grip, took a step forwards and then stopped.

A terrifying roar broke the noise of battle and a black voice boomed out of the distance.

Dark red smoke curled in front of the fortress and then parted to reveal the same handsome dark-haired man she'd had the displeasure of meeting during her captivity.

His eyes burned red as they shifted to Erin.

"Is that another demonic angel?" Amelia asked quietly, as though afraid the man would hear and turn his attention on her.

He smiled at Erin and adjusted the cuffs of his blood red shirt beneath his elegant black suit jacket.

"No... he's something far worse," Erin replied and Amelia stepped back in line with her.

He disappeared in a flash and reappeared in the midst of the fray, taking on two of them at a time. They didn't stand a chance. Erin closed her eyes, not wanting to see what happened next because she knew it would end like her previous vision.

"We have to help," Amelia said and then a gust of wind blew against Erin.

"Amelia, no!" Erin shouted but she was too late. Her sister shot into the battle, barrelling through the Hell's angels and knocking them out of the way with her silver wings.

The Devil caught her by the throat and tossed her aside, sending her careening into the spires of black surrounding the courtyard. He turned his attention on Marcus and Einar next, easily defeating them and leaving his men to deal with them. Erin shook her head when he grabbed Veiron by one of his dragon-like wings, causing him to cry out, spun and sent him slamming into the ground.

Erin moved, rushing forwards, her hands blazing. She wouldn't let the Devil hurt him.

Not again.

The Devil stepped on Veiron's prone form and extended his hand to her.

"I am waiting," he said with a smile curving his sensual lips. "Do not disappoint me, Erin."

Erin growled with effort and threw her hands forwards, unleashing a huge glowing orange fireball at him. The world disintegrated in a blast of white-hot light.

Erin shot up in bed, breathing hard and drenched in cold sweat. Amelia sat beside her, her wide eyes fixed on the far wall of the bedroom and her silver half-feather half-demonic wings out.

"What the hell just happened?" Taylor's voice pulled Erin out of her stupor and she jerked to face her. Taylor looked as shocked as Erin felt.

"We need to go," Amelia whispered, her breathing laboured and fast, eyes still enormous and glowing silver. "We need to go."

Erin nodded. "We do... we will."

"Go where?" Taylor said and Erin wasn't sure how to break it to her.

"I had a vision," she said and that seemed to be all the information Taylor needed.

"Screw this. We're going down there and we're not going alone. We need help and we need it fast, before the boys end up too deep in Hell and we can't find them." Taylor pulled a phone out of her pocket and the screen lit her face as she dialled.

She pressed it to her ear and then took a deep breath when someone at the other end answered.

"Apollyon, we need your help."

CHAPTER 23

Erin paced the moonlit shore, finding it impossible to keep still. Taylor sat on the edge of the wooden deck of the villa. Amelia sat on the steps that led onto the beach and had told her several times to conserve her energy and that Apollyon would reach them soon. The two of them were wearing black jeans and t-shirts and it was hard to make them out in the low light from the moon. Erin wore similar gear, perfect for sneaking through such a dark grim environment as Hell.

She turned and paced back again, ignoring her sister's irritated expression. She couldn't help it. It had been hours since Taylor had called the angel and asked for his assistance. She had expected him to reach them quickly, but it seemed even angels had their limits. Apollyon had left Paris almost immediately, after ensuring that his wife, Serenity, was safe and sound with another angel named Lukas and his girlfriend, Annelie, but it had still taken him hours to cross the world to them. It was gone midnight now.

Veiron, Marcus and Einar would already be in Hell.

Amelia had expressed her concern that Serenity wasn't accompanying her angel. In fact, she had mentioned it several times, so often that Erin had finally succumbed to her curiosity about the woman. It turned out that she was a witch and Apollyon's current master. Erin had recently found an ability to deal with almost anything but the knowledge that there were witches in the world had still astounded her. Amelia had mentioned that she had once shared her surprise, but Serenity was a full-blooded witch. Her reason for not coming with Apollyon had surprised Erin even more.

Serenity and the other woman, Annelie, were undergoing some sort of trial that, if they passed it, would grant them immortality.

Erin liked the sound of that.

They were doing it so they could spend forever with their angels and that was something Erin wanted for her and Veiron too. Lukas had remained with the two women to help them through the trials and take care of them. They were highly dangerous and the success rate for those who entered into them was small, but Apollyon believe that with the assistance and guidance of an angel, they would both make it through.

If Erin took the trials so she could become immortal, would Veiron help her through them? Was his help as good as an angel of Heaven's?

"Here he comes," Taylor said and slipped down onto the sand.

Erin immediately spun on her heel and scoured the distance, looking for a sign of the angel.

She spotted him a good distance out over the ocean and heading directly for them. It was hard to see him. She had expected him to look like the one she had met on the rooftop in London but he was nothing like that. As he came closer, she could make out his dark hair and huge black wings, and the obsidian armour that barely left anything to the imagination.

The closer he came to her, the harder Erin's heart beat against her chest.

It couldn't be.

He righted himself as he reached the shoreline and glided down to land just a few metres in front of her. His keen gaze shifted from Taylor, to Amelia and finally to her, and Erin couldn't breathe.

She caught a flashback of Hell, of a man with huge black wings, obsidian armour edged with gold covering his shins and hips, and wild black hair.

"Good to see you again," Taylor said and added, "I wish it was under better circumstances. We all know you hate going down there."

Apollyon growled low and fierce, "The Devil needs to learn when to stay down."

"Really?" Erin piped in, her voice a high squeak, and trembled when he looked at her again. "You looked pretty pally with him in Hell... you were doing his work, right? Luring me into leaving with you for some reason so he could convince me to help him or something... just stay the fuck away from me. Got it?"

"Erin, what's wrong?" Amelia wrapped an arm protectively around her shoulders and turned on Apollyon. "What were you doing down there? Did you try to hurt my sister?"

Apollyon's eyes widened and he held his hands up at his sides. "I have never met this woman and I have not been in Hell since I was there with Marcus over a year ago now."

"I swear, if you go near my sister, I'll kill you myself." Amelia pushed Erin behind her and unleashed her wings, shielding her with them.

Erin looked over Amelia's shoulder at Apollyon. He frowned, eyes dark and full of violence, and something else. He stepped back and furled his black wings. His hand came to rest on one of the golden swords hanging from his waist and he drew a slow deep breath, as though preparing himself for a fight.

"I have never set eyes on this woman you call your sister. Never." He backed off another step and Erin caught the look in his eyes.

He wasn't intending to attack. He was defending himself, and distancing himself too. She stared at him, gaze tracking over the armour that covered his lower legs, his hips, and his chest and forearms. It was the same as he had worn in Hell, only newer and well maintained.

He looked a little different now too.

While his physical features were the same, his hair was long and tied back in a ponytail at the nape of his neck, and his eyes were dark, faintly glowing blue in the low light from the moon.

It wasn't the same man, but the look in his eyes and his reaction said that he knew the man she had accused him of being. Time to test that theory.

"I saw someone just like you down there... but he had shorter hair and eyes like a hawk. He flew up to my cell and offered to help me escape." Erin stepped out from behind Amelia and his dark eyes followed her, his wary look not shifting.

His hand moved away from the hilt of one of his swords and he closed his eyes.

"What you saw was a copy of me," he said, deep voice low and brimming with resignation edged with something dark. He opened his eyes and fixed them on her again.

"A copy?" That was a creepy thought. She couldn't imagine what it would be like to have a clone of her running around.

He nodded and heaved a sigh. "When the Devil defeated me the first time, he did not put me to my death immediately. He... tortured me... until I lost my mind and then he drew all that was dark out of me and used it to create the angel you saw. In effect, he is my doppelganger, and he is not a man to take lightly. He is dangerous and cruel, and would not think twice about using you for his own gain."

"Einar never mentioned you had a twin," Taylor said and Apollyon's gaze snapped to her, brightening at the same time, a warning not to call this man his twin as though they were siblings. A strange sensation washed over Erin, pressing down on her and making her tremble, and her stomach twisted. Whoever Apollyon was, he was extremely powerful and it probably wasn't wise to piss him off.

"I do not desire the creature's existence to become public knowledge, just as his master hoped it would." Apollyon glared at them all and Erin got the message loud and clear. She wouldn't say a word about Apollyon's evil twin to anyone. "I will deal with him if he ever tries to leave Hell, but so far he has shown no indication that he will. He seems content down there, wreaking havoc for his master."

So, he had been working for the Devil when he had offered to free her. He had wanted to torment her by making her believe she would soon be free and then watch her hope die as she realised she was still his prisoner.

The bastard.

Erin wanted to kill him for that.

"Now that I have proven I am not a subject of the Devil, we should move quickly. What gate were they using?" Apollyon turned his attention to Taylor and Erin held her tongue as the half-demon filled him in on the details. She could tell that this was his way of stopping them from asking any more questions about his clone and she could understand why he needed to talk about something else. She couldn't imagine what he had been through when the Devil had tortured him, or how it would feel to have an evil doppelganger, especially if you were an angel.

Erin continued to stare at him. He was impressive. Tall, well built, handsome in a dark and glowering sort of way, and his black wings were huge even when furled against his back. His armour reminded her of Veiron's, only Apollyon's had gold edging around the obsidian and rampant lions on the cuffs protecting his forearms.

His gaze shifted to her again. "Any idea why the Devil has set his sights on you?"

She shook her head and then hesitated. He had been trusting enough to tell her something he had kept secret for God only knew how long. He deserved a little honesty from her in return. "I do have some sort of power, and I am Amelia's sister. He gave me a choice between playing bait and killing her."

Amelia turned on her. "I think you might have mentioned that to me earlier."

"I said no, so what's the problem? And Veiron's convinced that the Devil wants me more than he wants you now."

"If he wants you rather than Amelia, then your power must be of value to him, which means that it is strong enough to prove a threat to Heaven." Apollyon's dark look didn't make any of what he had said easier to digest.

Was he saying that the Devil thought that her power made her a great weapon against his enemies? Just what was this power that she had and did the Devil really want her so he could use her against Heaven in this twisted game of theirs? Her stomach turned again and bile burned up her throat. She covered her mouth with her hand and breathed slowly to settle her stomach. Losing it now would do her no good. She had to stay strong so she could stop her vision from happening and could save Veiron and everyone else. Amelia gave her a concerned look. Erin set her jaw, straightened, and sucked in a deep breath to fortify herself.

"What are we waiting for?" she said, her determination rising.

Apollyon smiled, as though she had impressed him, and then looked down at his feet and unfurled his black wings. He beat them hard, sending sand swirling in all directions, and lifted off the moonlit beach.

"Step back," he said and Erin, Taylor and Amelia moved as one, hopping up onto the deck of the villa.

Apollyon held his hand out towards the sand and Erin held her breath. A tiny orange spot appeared and then a jagged line cut across the sand in both directions, forming a glowing crack that stretched like a barrier between them and Apollyon. That crack grew, flickering brighter and spreading like lava. It widened and then the middle collapsed, leaving molten fire spilling down into a black chasm.

"It will lead us down to the bottomless pit. The gate the others used is close to there." Apollyon spread his wings and glided down to land on the deck.

"And how do we get down there?" Erin eyed the fault line that stretched over forty feet across the shore and was close to twenty feet wide. Waves rolled up the shore and hissed when they touched the edges of the opening Apollyon had created, steam rising and filling the air with the scent of the sea.

"We fly." Amelia flapped her wings. "Apollyon can carry Taylor and I'll carry you."

Erin could deal with that, as long as Amelia kept away from the edges. She didn't want to burn herself on the way down because her sister couldn't handle her weight. Erin doubted she was as strong as Veiron and could carry her as easily.

"Let's go," Erin said and then froze when heat flashed over her and a sense that she was in danger followed it.

She looked around, the others leaving her behind as she searched for a reason for her bad feeling, and her eyes widened.

"Incoming!" Erin shouted and threw herself at Amelia, tackling her to the ground at the same time as Apollyon grabbed Taylor and shielded her in his arms.

The man who had claimed to be her guardian angel slammed into Apollyon's back, sending him and Taylor flying. They landed hard in a tangle with the angel but Apollyon came out fighting, his formidable height and power an advantage over the shorter pale-haired angel.

Erin was on her feet in an instant. Taylor shot to hers and growled a ripe curse as she held her arm. Amelia muttered something equally as black under her breath.

Apollyon drew one of his swords and clashed with the guardian angel.

"Go," he shouted over his shoulder. "I will handle this."

Erin couldn't move. Apollyon was no doubt strong enough to deal with her guardian angel but this wasn't his fight and he shouldn't have to deal with it for her. Her hands heated and the angel broke past Apollyon, heading straight for her. He didn't get far.

Amelia yelled and barrelled into him, taking him down. Erin had never seen her sister fight but as she watched her unleash hell on the angel she held pinned beneath her, she could understand why Heaven and Hell feared her. Amelia's hands glowed blue and she kicked off the angel, leaving him lying in the sand, and beat her silvery wings. An orb formed between her palms and the angel came to his senses just as her sister released it and it shot towards him. Sand exploded upwards from the spot where he had been.

He let out a frustrated growl from high above them. His silver-blue wings shone in the moonlight and his pale hair glowed like a halo, but Erin felt nothing good in this angel. His expression was blacker than midnight and promised violence and pain.

"I cannot hold the gate open and fight. Get out of here." Apollyon shoved Amelia and she tumbled through the air and hit the sand close to the deck, spraying it everywhere.

"Bastard," Amelia mumbled, righted herself and checked her wings over.

The guardian angel shot towards Apollyon and the dark angel grinned as he beat his broad black wings and rose to meet him.

"Whatever you do, don't let go." Amelia grabbed Erin around the waist with one arm and Taylor with the other, beat her wings and dropped into the black crevasse.

Erin held onto her sister for dear life as they sped downwards. It was far from a controlled descent. They plummeted towards a growing fiery line far below them and she had the terrible feeling that their landing was going to be bumpy at best.

At worst, they were going to crash into what looked like it might be a lake of lava.

Erin closed her eyes and hoped for the best.

CHAPTER 24

No problems so far, but Veiron wasn't going to delude himself into thinking that things would be smooth sailing all the way to the Devil's cosy little home just beyond the bottomless pit. He trudged along a wide black path that wound down from the gate towards the plains they needed to traverse to reach the fortress. The right side of the path dropped straight down to the plain and one of the major rivers of Hell and a tall black cliff rose up on his left. At the top of that cliff was a plateau that stretched for miles and was home to Heaven's only contingent of angels in Hell. They guarded the bottomless pit and the pool that recorded the events of Earth and Hell.

His happy trio had only left the gate behind an hour ago and already they weren't speaking to each other. It wasn't as though they had argued and fallen out. There was a general air of melancholy hanging over them that had one root cause.

Women.

Fuck, he missed Erin.

He wasn't about to voice those words for the other two men to hear but they beat in his heart and his blood, a visceral ache to see her again even though he had only just left her.

What was she doing?

Was she sitting on the deck of their villa waiting for him to return?

Not likely. That didn't fit with her personality. She might be sitting there staring out at a moonlit ocean but she wouldn't be alone, and she would probably be nursing a cocktail and have snacks on hand. The women were probably talking about them, griping about their heroics and not being allowed to participate. Taylor would send her to sleep soon together with Amelia, if she hadn't already.

Was Erin worried about him? He knew the answer to that. Erin always worried about him, and it touched him more than she would ever know. He loved her for her concern and how she placed importance on his feelings and understood him so well. He had never known a woman like her.

He frowned.

Taylor had better be treating her well. He hadn't failed to notice the half-demon's attitude around his little nymph or the look she had given Erin when they had shared that 'I love you' swap on the jetty.

Veiron grinned, unable to stop it from curving his lips.

Erin loved him.

He hadn't realised how much he had needed to hear her tell him that until she had said the words. It had overwhelmed him then, hitting him with the force of a tidal wave, leaving him aching to kiss her and pour out all of his feelings for her so she knew that he felt the same way about her. She was his Erin. His willowy wicked woman now and forever. Yeah, he had reasoned that tacking on forever wasn't a good idea, but a series of bad ones had led him to find the love of his immortal life and since he was on a roll, he figured that he would go with it. Forever.

"Am I the only one who finds that look on Veiron's face disturbing?" Marcus said from beside him, the tall dark-haired warrior frowning across at him and then looking over his shoulder at Einar.

"Why do you think I decided to walk back here?" Einar practically chuckled the words.

Veiron scowled at both of them. "You want me to accidentally lose you in some of the less friendly parts of Hell?"

They shook their heads.

"Shut the fuck up then," he said on a snarl and resumed his grinning.

"It is actually an improvement on his usual expression," Einar said, clearly wanting to be dropped off the tall sheer cliff that edged one side of the path and into the bubbling river of lava hundreds of feet below.

"Listen, I've had just about enough of your shit—" A loud crack echoed around them, cutting Veiron off.

It bounced between the jagged spires of black rock that punctuated the boiling river and rolled like thunder across the plain.

Light suddenly broke through the constant dimness of Hell. Veiron's head snapped up. A huge split had opened in the vault of Hell above them. Above the plateau.

Were angels coming down?

He wanted to call his spear to him but he couldn't risk alerting the Devil to his presence. He stared up at the wide crooked gap in the black ceiling, seeing a streak of inky sky beyond. Part of that streak stuttered, a sure sign that someone was descending, and they were coming down fast.

"Amelia," Marcus breathed and Veiron's eyes widened when he finally made out her silvery half-feather half-leather wings.

She was coming down too quickly, Erin and Taylor hanging from her arms, both of them struggling to hold on and close to falling.

Veiron's crimson wings erupted from his back, tearing through his black t-shirt and he beat them hard, his eyes fixed on Erin and his heart hammering against his chest. He shot upwards, beyond the plateau, heading for her at maximum speed. He could hear Marcus behind him, his wings beating the hot air as urgently as Veiron's were.

Amelia screamed and Erin slipped, almost losing her grip on her sister's arm. Taylor reached for her. Veiron growled and Erin looked at him, her wide amber eyes brimming with fear. He doubled his effort, his wings aching with each beat, and reached for her. She shrieked and slid another few inches down her sister's arm. Amelia rolled that way, dragged by Erin's weight. Erin flailed her legs and closed her eyes. Her hands slipped.

Veiron grabbed her around the waist as she dropped and gathered her close to him, heart racing with the need to feel she was safe in his arms. Amelia used her now free hand to grab Taylor and keep hold of her. Marcus reached them and caught Taylor under her arms, and Taylor released her death-grip on Amelia so she could right herself and fall into a steady glide.

They all drifted down on the hot air to land on the black plateau.

"Everything alright up there?" Einar called, a detached voice curling up from the abyss.

Veiron had forgotten that the angel couldn't fly.

Marcus shouted, "All fine. Wait there, I will come and get you."

He shot off towards the edge of the plateau and then dropped over it.

Veiron looked down at Erin. She curled into him, her eyes still closed and her heart beating frantically against his chest. He sighed and stroked her sleek black hair, paying close attention to the lilac streak down one side. She felt so small in his arms as she shook against him, her fear still palpable. He wrapped his crimson wings around her and held her closer, wanting to reassure both her and himself that she was fine now. He would never let anything bad happen to her.

He would sooner die than let that happen.

He frowned. All this time he had been intent on living and never dying so he couldn't be dragged back into the game through rebirth as a guardian angel. Now he would let that happen if Erin was in danger. He would die to protect her.

"You okay?" he whispered down at her and she nodded and finally lifted her head. Her amber eyes met his and he was glad that the touch of fear that had been in them was gone. He smiled. "So you want to tell me what the fuck you're all doing down here? I take it this visit isn't because you all missed us so much and can't live without us?"

Marcus landed hard beside him, almost dropping Einar. The fallen hunter angel straightened himself out and then wrapped Taylor in his thickly muscled arms.

Marcus frowned, his pale blue eyes intense and hard. "I second that question. What are you doing here, Amelia?"

Amelia looked down at her feet and her wings shrank into her back and disappeared. Veiron focused so his disappeared too. His black t-shirt hung in tatters on his back so he removed it and tossed it onto the ground.

"I had a vision," Erin said and his attention was immediately with her. The fear was back in her beautiful eyes. She pressed her hands against his bare chest and he felt her shaking. "The Devil killed you all. Apollyon came to help us get down here and get you out before anything happened."

"Apollyon?" Marcus said on a growl. "Where is he now?"

"He was supposed to come with us but that guardian angel attacked before we could all come down. He's still up there fighting him. We have to go now."

Veiron stroked her cheek. "We'll go, and when we get topside I will kick that angel's arse so he never bothers you again."

She smiled shakily. "Sounds good to me."

"Change of plans?" Einar said and Veiron nodded. As much as he wanted to see what his future held in store for him and discover more about Erin's powers, he needed to get the women out of Hell and back to safety, and ensure that Erin's so-called guardian angel stopped coming after her.

"We use the pathway that Apollyon opened. All agreed, raise your hand and let's get the fuck out of here."

Marcus actually raised his hand and then scowled at everyone when no one else did. Veiron stifled his laughter. Trust Marcus to think he was talking literally. The former angel still had a lot to learn about the world and mortal turns of phrase.

"I'll take Erin. Amelia takes Taylor and Marcus takes Einar." Veiron stooped, grabbed Erin's bottom, and lifted her. She wrapped her legs around his waist and looped her arms around his neck. She felt so good against him. He was never getting tired of carrying her. His wings grew from his back and he flapped them to get all the feathers into line. "Let's go."

Before he could lift off, the rift above them began to shrink and heal.

That wasn't good.

Einar exhaled a black curse. Veiron looked across at him where he stood in front of Marcus, ready to agree with him, but he wasn't looking at the ceiling and the closing gate to the mortal realm. He was looking towards the edge of the plateau where it dropped into the bottomless pit.

The low thunderous hum of hundreds of wings filled the air.

Veiron turned slowly and swallowed.

A legion of Hell's angels approached and the nearest escape route had just closed. He couldn't create portals large enough for all of them and the gate they had entered through was too far away even by flight. The angels would be upon them before they reached it.

This really wasn't good.

CHAPTER 25

Erin couldn't keep up with the insanity erupting around her. Her heart beat like a jackhammer against her chest, thundering so hard it felt as though it would either break through her ribs or stop. Veiron dragged her with him as he ducked and wove through the battle, one hand on his spear and the other clutching her wrist. He shoved her behind him whenever they came under attack, shielding her with his body as he fought his own kind.

Her amber eyes wildly searched the fight, scouring the chaos for her sister. She spotted Amelia hovering above it all over fifty metres away, unleashing bright blue orbs of power at any Hell's angel who came too close. Marcus had her back, fending off all who tried to attack her from behind.

Below them on the ground, Taylor and Einar fought against a swarm of Hell's angels, each wielding a silver blade with deadly expertise.

Veiron growled and turned, spinning with Erin and slashing at another angel that she had failed to notice. The long thick blades of his black-handled double-ended spear glinted red as he turned with her again, pulling her hard against his chest this time. He swept his spear downwards and the demonic angel blocked it with his own weapon, cutting upwards. Veiron beat his crimson wings and shot backwards with her, narrowly avoiding the blade.

Around them, bright white flashes of light punctuated the fight, blinding her at times. Each Hell's angel that fell disappeared only moments later, leaving the battlefield clear of dead. She wasn't sure why the light took them. Was it Heaven reclaiming their fallen warriors?

Erin shrieked when Veiron spun her again and she came face to face with a Hell's angel. He snarled down at her, towering several feet over her, immense in his black demonic form. Instinct made her raise her hands to defend herself and a fiery orange orb exploded from her palms, hitting him square in the chest. He screamed and glowing red cracks appeared on his black skin and then he exploded into ashes.

"What the fuck did you do?" Veiron snapped and then grunted as he leaned back and threw his weight into his swing. It connected with the demonic angel he had been fighting and the spear's blade cut straight through his middle. The two parts of him fell to the ground and Veiron kicked off, pulling Erin into his arms at the same time.

He beat his wings and rose with her.

"I don't know!" Erin looked down at her hands and wished that she hadn't. Veiron was holding her from behind and she had a terrifying view of a long drop to a painful death. "It was instinct. He was there and it just happened and then he went poof."

"Well... just make sure who you're pointing those hands at before you fire, okay?"

Erin's eyes widened. He was worried she was accidentally going to unleash a fireball on him. Erin looked down at his arms around her waist. His skin gradually turned black and now that she knew he was changing, she could feel him shifting against her back. She looked across and watched his crimson feathers draining to black and then falling away to reveal the leathery membrane beneath.

"I'll just stick to you like glue and then we won't have to worry, right?" she said and cursed herself for not sounding sure. She didn't want to incinerate her lover by accident.

Veiron kissed her shoulder with his wide black mouth and squeezed her as he took them higher. His voice was a deep rumbling purr in her ear. "Absolutely. Ah, fuck."

"What?" Erin raised her eyes and saw what had Veiron swearing.

Another contingent of Hell's angels swarmed towards them. She was beginning to feel as though for every one they defeated, another five took their place. It was an endless surge, a relentless tide of demonic angels. Was there no end to the Devil's army?

Veiron cut down an angel that dared to attack them, smashing his spear into one of his wings and sending him careening down to the ground. He hit with a boom and a bright light engulfed him. When it faded, the demonic angel was gone. How many was the Devil willing to send back to Heaven in order to capture or kill her and her friends?

Veiron beat his wings and shot through the Hell's angels fighting in the air, heading straight for Amelia. Her sister turned as they approached, her silver hair flowing around her shoulders and grey eyes glowing. Amelia raised her hands, a blue orb of light appearing between her palms, and glared at Veiron.

"No." Erin held her hands up.

"Not the enemy, so back off, bitch," Veiron snarled, his voice deeper and rougher than usual. He flapped his wings and came to an abrupt halt close to Amelia, who launched her fireball at another approaching wave of demonic angels. "Like I would let anyone grab Erin. Try to have some faith in me."

"That does not look good." Marcus cut down another demonic angel with one of his curved silver swords and pointed towards the incoming swarm of Hell's angels with the other.

"Not good at all. It's the First Battalion. These boys live to fight, and if they can dismember and torture in the process, all the better. The Devil isn't looking to take prisoners." Veiron shifted his grip on her and Erin swore he was trembling. She glanced at her sister and Marcus. They looked tired too, blood coating them and both of them sporting minor wounds.

"Incoming!" someone shouted and Erin was too late.

By the time she had turned to see what was happening, a huge black blast of energy sent her, Veiron, Amelia and Marcus flying. Veiron tried to keep hold of her but the shockwave tore them apart.

Erin tumbled through the air and hit a demonic angel, taking him down with her. He snarled, exposing sharp red teeth, and barely managed to stop himself from crashing into the ground. Erin pushed away from him before he landed and hit the ground, rolled and grimaced as she twisted her ankle.

Damn it.

She quickly pushed herself up. He would come after her and she didn't have a weapon other than her powers, and she still wasn't sure how to use them. The times she had used them so far, she had been reacting on instinct.

When she had made it a few metres and no one had grabbed her, she paused and looked back at him.

He stood exactly where he had landed, growling as he straightened out his leathery wings and his armour.

Not attacking her.

Erin spun around, searching for everyone. Marcus was back with Amelia, battling on the ground now. Amelia had put her wings away. Had that black blast of power damaged them? Taylor and Einar were fighting close to them, forming a square with them and driving back the demonic angels. She couldn't spot Veiron anywhere but then she hadn't expected it to be easy considering he had gone demon on her.

He would find her, she was sure of it, but until then she was on her own and she had a lot of ground to cross to get to her sister and friends. Erin spotted a discarded sword just a few metres from her and ran for it, keeping low so the Hell's angels flying above wouldn't spot her. Hopefully.

She grabbed the sword. It was smaller and lighter than the broadsword she had once tried to wield but she still wasn't sure she would be able to use it. She had seen plenty of action movies. How difficult could it be? She gave it a few test swings and was surprised by how powerful she felt. Strange considering she had power in her that could do infinitely more damage than a piece of steel.

Erin ran at the nearest Hell's angel, roaring a battle cry at the same time and ignoring the pain in her ankle. He turned sharply and she brought her sword down, intent on cutting him straight across the stomach. He sidestepped her and then evaded her second strike and even her third. Erin blew her short black hair out of her face and growled as she swung again. The demonic angel didn't even block her or raise his own weapon. He just kept sidestepping.

It was frustrating as hell.

She decided to forget him and try another. She ran at her second target, going for a sneak attack this time, and swung so hard she would have fallen over if it hadn't connected with him. The sword sliced into his side and he snarled and turned on her, eyes burning crimson. He raised his own curved red blade and brought it down hard. Crap.

Erin flinched and clumsily brought her sword up, hoping to block his strike. His sword didn't even hit hers.

She peeled one eye open and frowned. He had stopped with his sword mid-strike and was staring at her. Affronted didn't cover how she felt when he huffed, turned away and beat his dragon-like wings, taking off.

What the hell?

Did no one want to fight her?

She tested her theory by strolling straight up behind another demonic angel and kicking him in the back of his left leg, so it crumpled beneath him and his knee hit

171

the basalt. He snarled as he turned and then snorted and just shoved her aside before stalking off towards Taylor and Einar.

Erin's hands burned. No one wanted to fight her. Why?

Heat prickled down her spine. Another black bolt arced through the air. This time it sent a demonic angel flying.

Veiron. It had to be him. He landed hard, spraying fragments of black basalt everywhere. Erin ran towards him, weaving through the demonic angels that were heading for him too. Marcus beat her there, landing hard and attacking with both of his curved blades. The demonic angels shifted backwards and a gap opened, a path that drew her eye and formed a straight line between her and someone she had never wanted to see again.

The Devil.

He sat on a black throne at the periphery of the battlefield, dressed impeccably in a black suit and deep blue shirt, with his legs crossed at the knee and his fingers steepled in front of him. His eyes glowed so brightly that she could feel them on her, burning across the distance. Her hands heated another ten degrees.

This was his doing. Her sister, her lover, her friends were all fighting for their lives because of him. And he had ordered his men not to touch her. There had to be a reason for that. She had to be of some value to him, just as everyone had said, if he didn't want her to come to harm. When he had held her captive in this horrific realm, he had been angry with those who had hurt her and he had treated her well.

If anyone could make him stop this insanity and call off his men, it might be her. Her hands shook, heart trembling in her throat, beating timidly now. The sound of battle and the sight of her friends and Veiron fighting so hard to win against his Hell's angels made her strong though. She straightened, clutched the sword tightly in her right hand, tipped her chin up and strode towards the Devil.

Some of the Hell's angels stopped to watch her pass while others continued the fight. Erin drew slow deep breaths. She had to do this. If the Devil wouldn't call off his men, then she would damn well fight him and make him call them off.

He smiled as she approached, a sensual one full of pleasure. He had been waiting for her all this time, toying with the lives of her friends until she had noticed him and come to him. He had known what she would do. Erin cursed him for that and for manipulating her by endangering those she loved.

Erin stopped directly in front of him, flexed her fingers around the grip of her blade and looked him straight in the eye.

"I want to bargain with you."

His amber eyes sparkled. "I had not expected you to return so soon, Erin. It was very brave of you but also very foolish. Your compassion makes you weak."

No, it didn't. It made her strong. Her love for Veiron and for her sister, and her newfound friends, all of it made her strong.

Erin held her head high, refusing to waver and give in to her growing fear. This man didn't scare her. She wouldn't let him scare her.

"I said I want to bargain with you."

His smile widened. "A deal with the Devil? How cliché. Speak. Ask what you will of me."

"Call off your men."

The Devil didn't seem very interested in doing such a thing. He sighed and looked at his polished fingernails, picking at them.

"Please?" she said and hated that he had reduced her to begging so quickly. The battle raged on behind her, the sound of it shredding her nerves. She wanted to glance around and see if everyone was still fighting, still alive, wanted to reassure herself that Veiron was safe and with the rest of her side at last, but she couldn't look away from the Devil. She could show no weakness. She had to keep calm, play it cool, and keep holding his gaze. He didn't scare her.

His smile returned and he leaned back in his obsidian throne and uncrossed his long legs.

"And what will you offer in exchange?" he said, voice deep and exotic. A voice made for tempting mortals.

"My soul," Erin blurted before she could consider the gravity of what she was offering.

He laughed.

Erin frowned at him.

"Really?" He shook his head, as though the worth of her soul wasn't equal to what she desired. Wasn't a soul the thing the Devil wanted most?

His sensual lips curved into another smile.

"I see that question in your eyes, Erin. If you had a soul I wanted to extract, then I would take it, but I prefer your soul just where it is."

"What do you want from me then?" Had she really just said that? She had sunk below begging to letting him set his own price now and God only knew what he would ask for.

A scream cut through the din of battle. Her heart leapt and she barely stopped herself from looking away from the Devil. At the speed things were going, her side would all be dead before she could get the Devil to call off his men. Maybe that was what he wanted. He wanted to keep her here until she was the only one left and it would have been for nothing, she wouldn't have saved her friends by sacrificing herself.

The Devil lowered his hands to the arms of his throne and slowly stood.

His eyes held hers.

"I want to awaken you."

Erin frowned. Awaken her? What the hell did that mean? Like Amelia had been awakened by Apollyon? Amelia had died.

"You want to kill me?"

The Devil shook his head. "No, I do not wish to kill you. You do not have to die."

Erin's skull buzzed with her rampaging thoughts. If she didn't have to die, then maybe it would be alright. Maybe he just wanted to awaken the power within her and have her use it in some way, as Apollyon had said. Would that be so bad? If she could deal a blow to Heaven then she damn well would, with or without the backing of the Devil. They deserved punishment for what they had done to Veiron, her sister, and Marcus.

"You do not have time to think about it," the Devil said and another anguished cry rose above the noise of the fight, sending a chill down her spine.

"Fine! Call off your men and I'll do it."

The Devil grinned, his white teeth sharp and gleaming, and moved in a blur of speed. He grabbed her wrist, twisted her into his embrace, banded one arm across her chest and swept his other in a theatrical arc across the battlefield.

The Hell's angels immediately stopped fighting, looked across at him, and took off as one, swarming into the black sky.

Erin's heart settled at last.

It was over.

A humming broke the silence, low and menacing, causing the hairs on the back of her neck to rise and her fingers to heat once more.

Veiron stood a few hundred metres ahead of her, chest heaving, back in his human form now and covered in blood. Marcus stood with him, their backs to each other, weapons at the ready. Off to her left, Amelia, Einar and Taylor were slowly turning away from her.

What was coming?

Erin's hands burned again, skin prickling as the fire spread up her arms and through her blood. Something was coming. Something dangerous. She tried to run to Veiron but the Devil tightened his grip on her, dragging her back against him and holding her there, with her back pressed to his front.

Her eyes widened.

Shapes began to form, coming out of the gloom. Black wings beat the hot air. Fiery light from the lakes and rivers of Hell glinted off the gold edging on their black armour and their golden weapons.

Angels.

Was it Apollyon?

Had he come to aid them?

Her heart mocked her, saying that she knew it wasn't. Apollyon was an outcast like Einar, and Marcus, and the one they had mentioned called Lukas. No army of angels would assist them.

They were here to kill or capture them in the name of Heaven.

CHAPTER 26

Erin had been wrong. The fight against the Hell's angels hadn't been insane. This was insane. The black-winged angels of Heaven had come at her side hard, a relentless force bent on killing them all. She struggled against the Devil's grip, kicked him in the shin to try to make him let her go, but he didn't give an inch. He held her against him, one arm across her chest and his other hand holding her jaw, forcing her to watch as her side battled against overwhelming odds.

"Make it stop!" Erin screamed, fingers itching with heat now, skin burning so hot that sweat trickled down her spine beneath her black top. She had tried to use her power countless times but it refused to leave her hands, and she suspected it had something to do with the man behind her. He was stopping her from using her power, forcing her to watch her friends fight.

She elbowed the Devil in the stomach but he merely laughed at her.

"I cannot," he purred into her ear, as seductive as ever, his voice easing away her fear until she realised what he was doing. He was trying to control her. That wasn't going to happen. She struggled again but it was no use. She wasn't strong enough to break free of his grasp.

"Please?" Erin whimpered, tears stinging her eyes as she watched her sister and Marcus desperately fighting against six angels. Her chest ached, a dull throb that pulsed through her, running deep in her marrow. "Make them stop."

"You asked me to remove my forces, and I did. The deal was struck, Erin, and now you must fulfil your side of it." He stroked her cheek with his fingers, his thumb pressing hard into her jaw. She shook her head and he chuckled. "You do not get a choice. You will awaken."

"No," she whispered and he tightened his grip on her jaw, pressing the tips of his fingers into her flesh until it hurt.

She didn't want this. This wasn't part of their deal. Erin stared at everyone as they fought, her tears almost blinding her, fear crushing her heart in an icy grip. She had wanted to save everyone, not condemn them all to death.

"Please," she said again, knowing it was pointless but needing to try. "Help them."

Her gaze leapt between them all, the ache in her deepening with each of them. Amelia, Marcus, Einar and Taylor were all deeply injured, weak and shaking, at their limit, but it didn't stop them from fighting. It didn't stop Veiron either. He was fighting to get to her, each cry of her name a hot sword that pierced her heart and cranked her internal temperature up another notch. Every time he got close to her, the angels knocked him back, tearing at his beautiful crimson wings. It didn't slow him down. He growled at them all, slashing with his blade, and kept fighting to reach her.

Erin's tears fell, cutting down her cheeks, and hitting the Devil's hand on her jaw. He huffed behind her and she half expected him to mention how weak she was, crying because she wasn't strong enough to escape him and help her friends. She wanted to save them and hated that she couldn't. She had failed them all.

She reached for Veiron as an angel swept his legs out from under him, sending him crashing to the black ground. Hot tears burned a constant path down her face. "Veiron!"

Veiron rolled to avoid the golden sword of the angel as it came down hard, sending sparks showering upwards when it struck the basalt. He was on his feet and fighting again before she could blink, his eyes glowing as bright as coals and fixed on her, determination radiating from him.

"Please," she whispered again and leaned into the Devil. "Make it stop. Save my friends."

"Save your friends?" He sounded thoughtful and she dared to hope that he might do as she asked. "Well, this process is going more slowly than I had anticipated and if I do not do something dramatic soon, there is a chance these fools will make me their target too."

Erin's heart leapt, the ache leaving her, and she almost smiled. He would help them. Relief poured through her, melting her bones, leaving her weak and trembling in the Devil's arms.

He released her jaw and waved his hand again.

Amelia disappeared, followed by Marcus. Taylor was next, leaving Einar looking confused and panicked for a brief heartbeat of time until he too disappeared.

Erin's gaze shot to Veiron. He battled three dark angels, fending them off, one arm hanging limp at his side and drenched in blood.

He didn't disappear.

Her heart squeezed. Heat blazed through her bones and erupted from her fingers in flickering red and black flames.

"No," she said and threw her hands forwards in an attempt to use her power. Nothing happened. She growled low in frustration, rage pouring like gasoline through her veins, igniting her blood, and elbowed the Devil with everything she had. He grunted. "You said you would save them all!"

"I did not say any such thing." The Devil caught her jaw again, pressing sharp fingernails into her cheeks, and forced her head around towards Veiron. She stared across the black landscape to him, fear reigniting within her. "You asked me to save your friends. I did so as an act of benevolence. You did not ask me to save your lover."

"Bastard!" Erin got one arm free and sent her elbow smashing into his head. He snarled, dark and unholy, grabbed her arm in a bruising grip and pulled it down, twisting it hard at the same time. She cried out.

"Erin!" Veiron roared and hacked at the angels around him, swinging his spear to drive them away. The moment there was an opening, he ran towards her, one hand reaching for her, all his love for her in his eyes. She reached for him too, tears streaming down her cheeks, wishing that they were miles away from here, that she had never told him about her vision, and wanting nothing more than to touch him again.

A black-winged angel barrelled into him and another two bundled on top, trying to pin him down. He growled and erupted from beneath them, sending them flying. His body shifted, black moving across his skin in a wave as his limbs grew and muscles expanded. The tattered crimson feathers on his wings fell away to reveal scarred leathery membrane.

"Erin," he called again, reaching for her once more. Erin reached for him with both hands, her heart shattering as heat seeped into it, burning her from the inside out, setting her every molecule on fire.

"Please," she whispered, broken and hoarse, and sniffed back her tears. "Save him. Please. He doesn't want to die. Please, don't let him die."

The Devil stroked her cheek and she flinched away as another angel tackled Veiron and punched him before he could get up, hammering away at his beautiful face. Erin's heart burned hotter, fingers tingling and turning numb.

"Please, don't let them do this." She sucked down a sharp breath and couldn't watch as the angels tore at Veiron's wings. The sounds of his screams made her ears ring and her body shake. Her blood rose to a thousand degrees, blazing within her, causing tendrils of red and black smoke to rise off her skin. Her shoulder blades itched and then the feeling shifted down her arms and torso, a slithering sensation under her skin that turned her stomach. "Please. He doesn't want to die again."

"But he must," the Devil said and a fresh wave of tears rolled down her cheeks.

She shook her head, her eyebrows furrowing. "No. You don't have to let them do this. I'll do whatever you want. Just don't let them kill him."

"I cannot do that. I need you to see this, Erin." He held her again and forced her head around. Her eyes flicked open against her will and a terrible chill replaced the heat flowing through her, realisation that she was powerless to stop this from happening and that it was all her fault freezing her and stealing her breath. "I need you to watch your beloved die and feel the endless dark in your veins awaken. You can feel it, can you not?"

She could. It was cold and fathomless, writhing beneath her skin, as black as Hell and as unforgiving and evil as the man at her back. It whispered to her, telling her to seize her desire for violence and destroy those who sought to destroy her love. It terrified her.

"Good... good," the Devil whispered into her ear. "Veiron has played his role in my plan to perfection. Now, I must lose one of my best men in order to gain my best woman."

Erin didn't understand. His words swam in her head, a whisper far quieter than the roar for violence in her blood and her heart. The ringing in her ears grew louder, numbness sweeping over her, fogging her mind. The strange sickening sensation of darkness writhing beneath her skin grew more frantic and she ground her teeth as sharp daggers scraped over her skull.

"Veiron," she murmured and lifted a heavy hand, trying to reach for him.

He broke through his enemies again, battling to reach her, still fighting despite his injuries.

This time he left them behind.

She smiled weakly, heart buoyed by the sight of him running towards her, coming within her reach. Just a few more metres and he would be with her again. They would be together and they would leave this place, and the Devil, and they would never return. He wouldn't die.

Erin stretched both arms out.

Just a few more metres.

Please.

Veiron changed back, the darkness leaving his skin as he shrank to his normal broad immense form. His eyes met hers and she smiled at him. He smiled right back at her.

And then stopped.

Erin didn't understand. Why would he stop?

He looked down.

Her gaze fell, her eyes widened, and she shook her head again. This wasn't happening.

"No," she screamed.

The bloodied golden tip of a blade protruded from his obsidian chest armour, right in the centre over his heart. Crimson spilled from beneath the armour, drenching his stomach and thighs. His scarlet eyebrows furrowed as he looked down at it and then up at her. Her eyes met his and she covered her mouth with one hand and still reached for him with the other.

He reached for her as his knees gave out, sending him hard to the ground.

Erin wrestled against the Devil, desperate to go to Veiron.

"I love you, Erin. Always will," he said and blood dripped from the corner of his mouth. Tears burned her eyes, spilling down her cheeks. This was not goodbye. She refused to believe it. He wasn't dying.

"Veiron," she said, desperate to tell him not to give up and that he would be fine. He smiled at her, that single look calming her and stealing away her pain, forcing her to accept what was happening. She nodded, knowing what he needed. Not her begging him to live and lying to him. Her throat closed, making it impossible to breathe, and she struggled to say the words without breaking down. "I love you too."

The angels descended on him. A bright white light exploded, blinding her. When it receded, they were gone, and so was Veiron.

"No!" Erin screamed, raw and hoarse. Pain blazed through her, turning her blood to liquid fire, and her skin itched. She scratched at it and the pain only grew worse, a thousand blades stabbing into her flesh. She looked down at her hands, past the curling ribbons of dark red flames that licked up her arms to the black claws that tipped her fingers.

She shrieked and broke free of the Devil's grasp but he caught her again, pinning her more firmly against his body, caging her in his arms.

The darkness shifted under her skin, pushing at it, until she felt it would tear her apart. Her shoulder blades caught fire, burning so fiercely she arched forwards and screamed.

"Do not fight it, Erin," he murmured close to her ear, containing her as she struggled against him, his voice soothing and soft. "It will be over soon and you will feel so much better."

How could she feel better? Nothing could make her feel better. She wanted to die.

The pain inside her increased until she couldn't breathe and it felt as though something was wrenching her heart from her chest.

Erin looked down and stared detachedly at the slick patch on her black t-shirt.

"You said you didn't want my soul," she whispered, watching the wet area grow, feeling the blood leaking from her, cold against her burning skin.

"I do not. It is broken and shattered by your loss. I had thought the death of Amelia may be your catalyst but this turn of events was not so unpleasant after all and it was certainly far easier than I had expected."

Erin swallowed and felt sick when a sharp metallic taste flooded her mouth. She tried to swallow again but couldn't hold back the tide of blood and choked on it. It spilled from her lips and down her chin. The pain in her heart grew, so fierce that it consumed her and she couldn't fight it. The darkness returned. The feel of claws scraping under her flesh, sharp pain lacerating her shoulders, and the grind of horns over her skull petrified her. Her bones ached and her body moved of its own accord, her joints cracking and limbs twisting into horrifying angles. Her teeth throbbed and sharpened, spilling more blood into her mouth, and her vision burned red.

There was a demon inside her trying to get out.

She wanted Veiron.

She needed him to hold her in his arms, close to him, and needed to hear him husk in his beautiful baritone that everything was going to be okay as her world fell apart.

Her gaze sought him but found only a dark pool of his blood.

She snarled, the unholy sound shredding the last of her nerves.

Her heart faltered, missing beat after beat. Was she going to die after all? Was the demon inside her going to destroy her?

"You said I didn't have to die. You lied." Erin found peace with that thought. Dying wasn't such a frightening experience after all. "Veiron cannot be dead... but if he is... then I will find him on the other side."

She touched the bleeding spot over her heart and felt him there, always within her, a part of her forever. The darkness inside her settled, as though her thoughts of Veiron calmed it too.

"I did not lie, Erin. You are not dying. You merely bleed because of your lost love. It will end soon, when you awaken."

Cold chased away the final remnants of her heat and her legs gave out, no longer strong enough to support her. The Devil held her, stopping her from collapsing, and lifted her. He cradled her gently in his arms and turned with her, carrying her to his black throne. He settled on it with her on his lap and stroked her hair. Horns shifted beneath her scalp again and she flung her head back and cried out.

179

The Devil cooed soft words and held her closer. He clumsily petted her head, as though he didn't know how to comfort. He probably didn't. She couldn't imagine the twisted bastard caring about anyone enough to worry about their welfare. He was incredibly gentle with her though. Could he sense that she was fragile and would break from the slightest touch? Erin grimaced and squeezed her eyes shut against the pain that tore through her, ripping down her arms like razor-sharp claws. The Devil cooed again.

He could coo all he damned well wanted but he would never ease the pain in her heart. He was the one who had done this to her and she had played right into his hands.

"What have you done to me?" Erin shivered, icy cold and fighting for air. "You've put something terrible inside me."

"No... Erin. I have put nothing inside you. I have done nothing to you." The Devil held her closer, wrapping her in his embrace, and wiped away her tears and the blood on her chin.

There was no comfort in his words and she didn't believe them anyway. He must have done something to her, placed some vile creature inside her, because she could feel it lurking in her heart and slithering through her veins. Pure darkness. Pure evil.

The only thing that gave her comfort was that she was dying. When the Devil had abducted her, she had feared that she would die in Hell, surrounded by fire and darkness. Now she feared nothing.

"Shh, Erin. I will not let you die. I will never let you die." He rocked with her and she frowned as her weakness began to leave her, strength returning slowly but not quickly enough to stop her from succumbing to the cold in her heart and the darkness conquering her mind.

Erin forced her eyes open and looked up at him. She croaked, "Because you need me alive to do your bidding?"

"No." He smiled, warm, cruel and evil all at the same time. "For the same reason that I have searched for you for most of your life, dearest Erin."

She shivered again, moaned and writhed as new pain tore through her, so hot this time that she felt as though her bones really would melt and her flesh would char. Darkness encroached and she fought it, afraid of what would happen if she succumbed to it.

She held the Devil's gaze, battling to keep her eyes open. "Why?"

Her eyes slipped shut and she didn't have the strength to open them again.

His voice drifted around her, soft and compassionate, strangely affectionate. "Because you are my daughter."

CHAPTER 27

A soft swishing sound was the first thing Erin grew aware of, shortly followed by heat on her skin that warmed her right down to her bones but did nothing to alleviate the ice in her veins and her heart. Other noises punctured the gentler one and shattered the numbing peace flowing through her, reawakening her pain and dragging her back up to consciousness.

"Erin!"

She frowned and tried to burrow into whatever was beneath her. It was hard and unyielding, but warm against her belly and breasts.

"Erin!"

Erin didn't want to wake. She wanted to stay in the darkness, wanted to drift through her remaining days unaware of the world that awaited her so she didn't have to feel the pain that came with it. It was hollow now and she wanted no part in it. She didn't belong there.

Warm liquid rushed over her feet and up to her knees and then rolled back again, leaving her legs wet. The air cooled them and it was bliss. She sighed, welcoming the relief from the heat on her skin.

"Erin, wake up."

Something shook her and the motion sent her spinning back to a time not so long ago when someone else had tried to rouse her like this. She hadn't wanted to wake then either, but that time it had been because she had discovered that the man she had been falling in love with was a Hell's angel.

Veiron.

Tears slipped down from the corner of her eyes and hissed as they hit whatever was beneath her.

She didn't want to wake because this time it was a female voice calling her and she couldn't face the questions and the pain, the heartache and the misery. It wasn't the person she desperately wanted to wake to and see.

The soft hands on her shoulders shook her again, drawing her into full consciousness, so she was laying face down pretending to be asleep. If she pretended for long enough, would they leave her alone? She wanted to be alone if she couldn't be with Veiron.

"Erin, please?"

How many times had she said that word to the Devil? It had no meaning now. She had struck it from her vocabulary and refused to respond to it. It was a powerless ineffectual word. Pathetic.

"Erin." It was a male voice this time, stern and hard, and not voicing a question. It was a command for her to give up her act and face the world. She had never realised until now how similar Veiron and Marcus sounded. It brought new tears to her eyes.

"Sweetie, what's wrong?" Amelia must have seen her tears. She laid her hand on Erin's shoulder. "You're burning up. Where's Veiron?"

Erin couldn't bear to hear his name. She covered her head with her arms and wished everyone would go away. She needed to be alone. She didn't know how to cope with everything. Not just what had happened to Veiron but what had happened to her too.

She felt different and it scared her, left her feeling weak and sick. She could feel the darkness flowing through her, just as the Devil had said she could, polluting her body. His evil in her veins. How was that even possible?

Unless.

Erin sucked in a steadying breath and pushed herself up. She was on the island but it wasn't sand beneath her. It was glass. Scorched patches dotted her black trousers and it felt as though the back of her t-shirt was missing completely. A thick crust of blood covered the material across her chest.

She raised her head and looked into Amelia's eyes, and then at her face, and then ran her gaze over all of her.

She had never noticed before now how different they were to each other. Amelia with her grey eyes, ample breasts and soft mouth that completed classical features. Erin had smaller breasts, was shorter, and had often been told she looked cheeky and like a bad fairy.

And she had amber eyes.

Like her father.

Her stomach turned and she swallowed against her desire to be sick.

"Where is Veiron?" Marcus said and she hated him for saying those words.

She couldn't look at Amelia, not now that she had realised that the Devil hadn't been lying to her, but Amelia had. There was no way the two of them could be siblings. Her entire life had been a lie.

She looked up at Marcus. He still wore his silver armour and blood had dried against his skin, flaking in places to reveal deep lacerations. He had his half-feather half-leather wings furled against his back and his twin curved silver blades hung at his hips.

"The angels took him... they... a sword... through his heart." It killed her to say those words and Marcus's pale blue eyes gradually widened with each one she spoke, until his expression turned to one of concern and then sorrow. No. Damn it. She wouldn't believe that look. "Christ, Marcus... tell me he's alive. He's immortal... they can't have killed him!"

He sighed, his broad chest heaving with it, shifting his silver breastplate. "I am sorry, Erin."

"No." Tears stung her eyes and her hands heated, skin so hot that her bones blistered. Claws scraped under her skin again and tiny horns shifted over her skull. Her fingernails ached and gums hurt. "I won't believe you. I won't!"

She looked to Amelia and found the same look of pity on her face, and then moved on, searching Einar's next and then Taylor's. Unshed tears lined Taylor's blue eyes. Curse the half-demon for believing Marcus. He was lying. Veiron wasn't dead.

Her strength fell away when she met the sombre blue eyes of Apollyon.

"I am afraid that even angels can die," he said, voice deep and cold, and she hated him for it.

She shook her head.

"He can't be dead."

And she couldn't be the Devil's daughter.

She pinched herself and when that didn't work, she clawed at her arm, desperate to wake up. It was just a vision. She would wake in Veiron's arms and tell him everything that she had seen and they would never go to Hell again. He would be safe and they would be happy together.

He wouldn't die.

He didn't want to die.

Marcus bent, carefully gathered her into his arms, and carried her up the white shore towards the villa he shared with Amelia.

"What happened to you, Erin?" Amelia whispered and Erin refused to look at her or acknowledge that question. She didn't want to tell anyone because doing so would be admitting she was the spawn of Satan and that was something she didn't want to believe, even when the evidence crawled beneath her flesh and flowed in her blood.

She tried to push out of Marcus's arms but he was too strong for her, his grip as unrelenting as the Devil's had been.

When he set her down on the deck, she immediately paced away from him and Amelia, needing the space. Her eyes kept shifting across to her own villa, the one she had shared with Veiron, and she fought back her tears. Was he really gone? Now, when she needed him so much? He was the only one who would understand what she was going through. He was the only one who could understand.

She couldn't breathe.

The thought that she might never see Veiron again cut at her, tearing through flesh and bone, cleaving her heart open.

Erin ignored everyone as they tried to comfort her. The only one who didn't was Apollyon. His gaze tracked her back and forth across the wooden deck and she could see in his eyes that he was wise to her. He knew that something wasn't right about her now and that it wasn't just grief over Veiron's death.

She wasn't the same as she had been before heading into Hell.

She kept her eyes downcast, a need to escape his knowing stare steadily building within her. The early morning sun was warm as it lit the ocean and a strip of the beach. She wanted to walk in that sun, feeling it soothing her and restoring her hope.

Marcus slid the door to the villa open and went inside. When he came out again, he was wearing his shorts, his wings hidden. Einar and Taylor stood off to one side, Einar comforting his lover, and Erin frowned at her. How could she give up hope so easily? There was no evidence to prove that Veiron was dead. He might have survived and they might only be questioning him in Heaven, detaining him.

Couldn't someone go to see if he was there, injured but alive?

She looked at Apollyon and then instantly looked away again when his gaze locked with hers. She couldn't ask him anyway. Heaven wanted him dead too. What had happened to her so-called guardian angel? Had he returned to Heaven? Could he tell her if Veiron still lived?

"We need to move," Amelia said, shattering the heavy silence.

Erin turned on her and then everyone else as they voiced their agreement.

"We can't leave." Erin's pulse spiked and black desires flooded her heart, urges that she refused to acknowledge. She didn't want to fight her friends. Violence wasn't her style. She was an artist, for God's sake. They were all lovers, not fighters. "I don't want to leave. If we leave then Veiron won't be able to find me."

Amelia gave her a look filled with pity. "That is exactly my reason for suggesting we leave this island."

"No. I refuse to leave. Veiron will come back. I know he will." Erin backed off a step when Amelia moved towards her, her hand outstretched as if to comfort her.

Amelia lowered her hand and sighed. "I know you're hurting, but we can't stay here. Please, Erin. We must all leave this place before something terrible happens."

Erin shook her head. "You can leave but I'm staying."

"I won't leave without you, and I wasn't giving you a choice. We're leaving. Marcus will carry Einar and I'll carry you, and Apollyon can carry Taylor."

Everyone nodded.

Erin didn't. She squared up to Amelia, staring deep into her grey eyes, challenging her. The darkness writhed frantically beneath her skin. Excited by the prospect of violence? That sickened her and she wouldn't give in to the urge. She wouldn't. She just needed to give Amelia a piece of her mind.

"Who made you the leader, anyway? What do you know about leading anything? Jack shit, that's what. So get the hell out of my face about leaving. Go if you want to, but I refuse to leave. I won't give up on him!"

Her heart pounded, blood thundering in her veins and heating to boiling point. Her fingers burned and she didn't need to look down to know that her power was leaking from her in deep crimson curls of flame. It caressed her fingertips and licked up her forearms, and for the first time, it felt comforting to feel it there, blazing within her, on her side.

She could protect herself. She didn't need Amelia to do it for her, or anyone here.

"Amelia, just give her some time," Einar said, always the voice of reason. She thanked him for it and for standing against Amelia with her. Would he be on her side if he knew the dirty truth about her though? She doubted it. If her secret got out, none of them would remain with her. They would want her gone and she would be alone.

Was this how Veiron felt when amongst those other than his own kind?

It was a cold, debilitating sort of feeling.

"We don't have time." Amelia went to grab her arm.

Erin slapped her hand away so hard that Amelia lost her balance and crashed onto the wooden deck. Was she stronger too now? Amelia looked up at her, disbelief shining in her grey eyes.

"Leave me the fuck alone." Erin towered over her, holding her gaze, unflinching. "And you can drop the big sister act already."

She stormed down the steps onto the beach, needing the space before she exploded and caused more harm. Her hands were hot, skin burning all over, itching with a need to unleash her power, and she feared she would lose it and succumb to the darkness inside her if she stayed around Amelia and the others.

Erin slowed when she passed the next villa. She kicked her boots off and removed her socks, leaving them on the shore, and headed further down the sand. When she reached the water, she straightened her course and followed the path she had taken with Veiron. Her heart ached but her tears no longer came. Anger burned in her, rage over what Amelia had said. She wanted them away from this island so Veiron couldn't find her. Amelia had never liked him, had always tried to prise them apart, and she had found an opportunity to do just that. She was trying to separate them and Erin hated her for it. Amelia wasn't doing it to protect her. She was doing it because it was what she had wanted from the moment she had seen Erin with Veiron.

The heat in Erin's veins slowly subsided, draining from her chest and then down her arms with each step she took, until it finally bled from her fingers, leaving her calm and then numb. She drifted along the shore, the warm water lapping over her bare feet, unsure where she was going and knowing that at some point she would run out of beach and have to turn back.

She wished she had wings like Amelia. If she did, she would fly up to Heaven and see for herself whether Veiron was dead or alive. Either way it would end the torment of not knowing. Apollyon had only said that angels could die. A fact she had already known. It was possible that Veiron had survived and needed her help.

As the sun rose higher, the villas on the island came to life, people opening the doors and heading out onto the decks and the beach. Erin walked to the strip of rocks that speared out into the ocean and sat on a large flat one, staring back along the shore towards the villa where the others awaited her and beyond it to the one she had shared with Veiron.

A couple came out onto the deck of the villa nearest her and glanced her way. Erin looked down at her chest and the dried blood there. If people saw her like this, they would ask questions. She removed her tattered black top to reveal her bikini and frowned. There was no blood on her chest, but there was a scar between her breasts, a single vertical line, as though the sword that had pierced Veiron's chest had pierced hers too.

Erin touched it, her thoughts with him and everything that had happened. It all seemed like a terrible nightmare when it had once been the sweetest dream. It was so hard to process the events and revelations of the past twenty-four hours. They threatened to overwhelm her whenever she tried, made her want to bury her face in her knees and hide there until the world no longer existed.

She wrapped her arms around her knees and hugged them to her chest. Her hair fluttered forwards in the cool morning breeze that blew against her back and she frowned and raised one hand, catching the strands that made up the coloured stripe down one side of her black bob. It was supposed to be lilac.

Now it was scarlet.

As red as Veiron's hair.

Had the Devil changed it during her awakening? Had he done so to torment her with what she had lost?

She hated him. She hated everyone right now and she wasn't sure if that feeling would pass. The darkness that flowed in her veins fed on her feelings, growing stronger whenever she felt something negative and making it difficult to let go of that emotion. She could feel it burning inside her, corrupting her, changing her. The Devil had called her compassionate and that it was a weakness and her sentimentality would be her failing. She felt as though the poison now flowing in her veins had already killed that side of her.

Families began to fill the beach, playing in the water and laughing with each other. Couples strolled along it, smiling and talking. All people who didn't deserve to get dragged into the fight she could feel was coming.

Perhaps her compassion wasn't dead after all, but merely numbed by everything that had happened and the changes to her that had taken place. Erin tried to shut out the darkness, the memories of the scrape of horns beneath her skin and the feeling that she held another form within her, just as Veiron did.

Veiron.

She needed to stay here and wait for him, regardless of the fact that she would place everyone in danger by doing so. The others could leave. She didn't want to see Amelia anyway. She hated her.

Erin sighed.

She didn't hate her.

She wanted to though. She wanted to be angry with her but she knew in her heart that she was only clinging to feelings that weren't really hers. She wanted to blame all her pain on Amelia when in reality it was all because of the Devil.

Why had he returned her to the island?

He had sent her back for a reason. Something told her that it was because he wanted her to suffer and be alone. He wanted everyone to find out what she was and leave her, so all her ties to this world were broken and she lost hope and every shred of positive emotions she possessed. He wanted to break her and rid her of her compassion and sentimentality.

He wanted her to embrace the darkness inside her and then return to him of her own accord, accepting him as her father.

It wasn't going to happen.

She would never do such a thing.

She would never be alone.

Erin touched the scar between her breasts and stared at it.

No matter what happened, Veiron would always be with her.

Erin sighed again. She was confused and hurt, and being alone was only worsening those feelings, allowing doubt to grow in her mind and fear to spread poisoned tendrils around her heart. She was already on her way to doing just what the Devil wanted. She couldn't let that happen.

She stood and brushed down her backside.

She had to leave with the others.

When Veiron returned, he would find her wherever she was. He would come for her and he would be fine, and she would feel like a fool for doubting him and believing that he had been killed. Together they would laugh about how silly she had been and what a close call it was, and they would tease everyone for leading her astray.

Erin sighed. He would. They would. She was sure of it.

She tipped her head back and looked up at the endless blue sky, hoping that everyone was wrong about Veiron and that he wasn't up there now, an angel again.

And that he hadn't forgotten her.

CHAPTER 28

Veiron beat his wings and couldn't contain the smile that curved his lips. Hot sun streamed down on him from high above, warming his skin, his armour and his feathers, relaxing every muscle in his body and imbuing him with a sense of peace. Endless sea stretched below him, glittering in the strong light, a beautiful reflection of the cobalt canvas above. The warm air teased his scarlet hair and flowed over his feathers, tickling them as he glided a short distance. He beat them again, a stronger flap this time, taking himself higher above the world.

It was so quiet.

He had never realised before leaving Heaven that it was noisy there. Wherever he went, there were fellow angels talking, discussing everything from their last mission to the latest inventions in the mortal realm. He didn't miss the constant background noise. He liked this silence. It soothed him as much as the gentle wind and the warm sun.

A bubble of excitement rose up in him and popped, birthing more bubbles that widened his smile.

A tiny green dot marred the sea ahead of him, embraced by turquoise waters.

His first mission.

Veiron looked down at the guardian angel below him. The pale-haired male's silvery-blue wings beat the air at a steady pace and his rich blue armour reflected the sun, the silver edging dazzling Veiron. Nevar had spoken barely a handful of words since their superiors had introduced them at the gates of Heaven and given them their mission.

Veiron couldn't believe that they had sent him out on his first mission so soon after his rebirth. He had only been back for a few months and had barely completed the first round of retraining. It was unusual for Heaven to send a newly reborn angel on such an important mission too, but his superiors had told him that he was perfectly capable of handling this and that they had every faith that the mission would be a success. Pride swelled his heart and he grinned. He would prove their faith in him was correct. He would see this mission through and it would be a success.

Veiron banked left and spun in the air, rolling down in an arc until he was flying next to the angel assisting him on the mission.

Nevar didn't even look at him. They weren't from the same division of guardians but Veiron had expected him to be civil at the very least. The angel seemed to detest him. Veiron had questioned him during their long flight but Nevar had shrugged and said he had no reason to hate him or anyone. Maybe he just wasn't talkative. Maybe it was because his superiors had reassigned him from another mission to this one with Veiron and he was angry about it. Either way, Veiron wasn't going to let it get him down. This was his chance to prove himself strong and capable, worthy of his superiors' belief in him.

"There is no sign of mortals on the island," Nevar said, deep voice battling the wind. "We are good to go."

Veiron nodded and swept lower, gaze scouring the white beaches skirting the small island. He spotted their target on the far side, in a curved shallow bay. She walked the shore, and she was alone.

Without a word to his companion, Veiron beat his wings and shot down. Wind buffeted him but he held his course, his wings pinned back to speed his descent. He landed hard in a crouch on the beach, sending white sand exploding upwards and shaking the island.

His target turned to face him, her short black hair swaying with the speed of her reaction. She stood before him dressed in only small black shorts and a tight t-shirt. Red flames licked over her hands. They stuttered and banked, and then died completely.

Veiron rose and straightened to his full height.

Her eyes widened, her shock rippling through him, and then tears filled them. She was afraid. Veiron smiled. This was going to be easier than he had thought.

Her hand covered her mouth.

"No... it can't be. No!" Her fingers shook and the tears in her eyes spilled onto her cheeks.

It wasn't fear that she felt after all. Veiron frowned, confused by the threads of emotion that he could sense in her. Her distress seemed genuine, as did her pain. It wasn't an act, and something wasn't right. He should only be able to sense hints of her feelings, detect them and pinpoint them. He could feel her pain. How?

It didn't matter how. He had a mission to complete.

Veiron held his hand out and called one of his curved silver swords to him. He grasped the blue and silver hilt and swept the blade downwards, slicing through the air. Her amber eyes widened further and she took a step back.

"Veiron?" she whispered and he faltered, pain tearing through his heart as though that word was a blade and she had cut him with it.

How did she know his name?

He hesitated and it cost him. The original angel came out of nowhere, her silver mutated wings beating fiercely, and crashed into him, sending him down with her on top of him. She smashed her fist into his face and her eyes flashed silver, as bright as her long hair.

Veiron growled and rolled with her, intent on pinning her beneath him and taking her life too. It would be a bonus and he was sure his master would be proud of him. She was gone before he could manoeuvre her, leaving him facing the sand, his back wide open to attack. She landed a hard kick on his spine between his blue chest armour and the strips that protected his hips, sending him face first into the sand.

"Amelia, no!" The target. Why was she stopping the original angel from fighting him? Did she fear for her comrade's life?

A wise woman. Veiron snarled, pressed his palms into the damp sand and shoved himself upwards, knocking the abomination off him.

He found his feet and turned on her. His blade clashed with that of the traitor, Marcus. Heaven had warned Veiron about him. Other voices called across the beach and Veiron silently thanked Nevar when he landed behind him, providing much-needed back up.

Veiron drew a deep breath and attacked Marcus and the original angel as Nevar fought the other traitors.

The sight of Marcus in armour so similar to his own disgusted Veiron. The man had no right to wear the armour of an angel. He was as much an abomination as his master. She didn't wear armour at all. A small pale cream dress was her only defence against his blade.

Veiron drove Marcus back and called his second blade, evening the odds. They clashed hard again, the dark-haired traitor wielding his twin blades with expertise that Veiron found difficult to match. He didn't have the battle experience of this former angel but he wouldn't be defeated here.

Veiron ducked to avoid one of Marcus's blades and launched his fist up, catching the man hard under his jaw. Marcus flew backwards and beat his wings to right himself in the air. Before he could attack again, Veiron turned on the one his target had called Amelia. She blocked his path to his target, a blade in her hand and a steely look in her eyes.

Why wasn't the target defending herself?

She stood a short distance away, eyes wide, frozen in time.

He could still feel her hurting. Perhaps it was a power of hers. She intended to weaken his resolve to capture her and present her to his superiors. That would never happen.

Veiron battled Amelia, driving her backwards, towards his target. When she realised what he was doing, she fought harder but she wasn't skilled enough with a blade to beat him. He slashed at her, keeping her occupied with defending herself. He could feel Nevar behind him, the angel now battling Marcus. The demon female lay injured on the beach, the fallen angel tending to her.

The tide was turning in his favour.

Veiron swung hard with both swords. Amelia leapt to dodge the blades, giving him the opening he had been waiting for. He sent one of his swords away, grabbed her leg, and spun with her. She screamed as he sent her flying and then hit the sand hard, sending a plume into the air as she tumbled across it.

Veiron turned to face his target.

The female lowered her hand to her side, swallowed, and looked him straight in the eye. A brave if foolish woman. Did she think she could intimidate him?

"You may come peacefully, Devil spawn, or you may fight me. Either way, I am taking you in." He called his second sword back to him and swept both blades through the air.

She tipped her chin up.

"I'll fight you. I don't want to… but I will. I will not let you hurt my friends."

He snorted. "Such evil cannot know true friendship. You have poisoned their minds with your darkness, just as your master poisons this realm."

Tears lined her lashes again. "How can you say such cruel things?"

"Cruel? Strange words from the lips of the antichrist. Do you intend to poison my mind too?" He cut through the air with his swords again and advanced on her. "I will not let you."

"And I will not fight you." She closed her eyes and held her head high. "So if you wish to claim my life to satisfy your new master, then do so."

New master? He halted again. Tears slipped from her lashes onto her cheeks and rolled down them and the sense of pain inside him increased. She swallowed and sniffed, but made no move to attack him or defend herself.

Why wasn't she fighting him?

He didn't have time to come up with an answer and what happened only left him with more questions. Pain blazed across his back and he roared, arching forwards away from the blade. He turned on the original angel and threw himself back into his fight with her, but not before he had caught the horror in his target's eyes and felt her fear.

She feared when he had been injured but not when he threatened to kill her?

His head ached as he battled Amelia, driving her towards Nevar and Marcus this time where they fought further along the beach. Marcus was winning. Veiron growled under his breath and struck at Amelia with each blade in quick succession, forcing her to defend. He needed to get to Nevar and assist him.

"Nevar, you know me!" Marcus said and Nevar looked as confused as Veiron felt. Nevar slashed at Marcus with his sword and shook his head.

"I do not know you, traitor."

"Marcus, he's the angel who tried to take me twice... my guardian," the target called from behind Veiron and Nevar froze.

Marcus saw his chance and took it. He twisted Nevar into his arms, pinned his wings with one arm and held his blade against his throat with the other. Nevar stilled. Veiron cursed.

"Is she right? You were her guardian and you tried to capture her for Heaven?" Marcus growled the words and Nevar's pale green eyes widened as the blade nicked his throat, spilling a thin line of blood.

"She lies. I have never seen her before today, nor you."

"She isn't lying, Marcus," the original angel said and swiped at Veiron. He was so caught up in what was happening with Nevar and Marcus that her blade cut across his arm. He hissed through gritted teeth and cursed at her this time. Her second attacked failed. He easily blocked it and pushed against her, sending her tripping backwards and gaining himself some space.

He raised one sword above his head and brought it down hard, intent on cutting her down before she could recover her footing. Bright blue light shone from her palms and the whole world exploded. Pain splintered his bones and his head spun, reeling as his ears rang and he tried to comprehend what had just happened. When his head cleared, he found himself sailing through the air and landing hard on the ground, close to his target. Victory.

Veiron went to launch onto his feet but his body didn't respond to the command. It blazed white-hot, every muscle burning with pain so intense he barely clung to consciousness. What had happened?

Had the abomination struck him with her power?

She appeared above him, her hands still glowing, and held her palms out towards him.

Veiron breathed shallowly, struggling against his pain, and stared up at her. He had failed. His superiors had been wrong. He was not capable of capturing the Devil's spawn.

Amelia glared at him. "Better luck next time."

"No," the target screamed and was suddenly between him and Amelia, her arms outstretched.

Protecting him?

"Don't hurt him!" she said and shook her head.

Amelia backed off a step. "He might look and sound like him, but he isn't him... remember that."

"I know... but I would sooner die than see Veiron suffer again." Those softly spoken words cut him deeper than any blade could and served to increase his confusion.

She had called him by his name twice now, refused to fight him or let him come to harm, and feared when he had been injured.

"Do I know you?" he said without thinking and pushed himself onto his elbows on the sand. His head spun but not as fiercely as it had before and the pain in his limbs had lessened to a dull throbbing. He lumbered onto his feet, spread his wings, and flapped them to align his feathers. They ached as much as the rest of him.

The target looked over her shoulder at him, pain in her amber eyes. The wind ruffled her short black hair, blowing it across her face, and she turned away and lowered her head. A look of sorrow crossed Amelia's face and Marcus sighed.

"The Veiron you knew died, Erin. He will not remember you," Marcus said and she nodded, and her pain increased again.

The Veiron she knew?

Was this all an elaborate lie to fool him and Nevar into lowering their guard? Why would he have known the Devil's daughter and these traitors?

"You are all traitors and liars," Veiron said and Erin turned to face him. Her eyes met his and the ache in his head worsened as he stared into them. He didn't know her. He couldn't remember his past life but he was sure that he would never have had a reason for knowing the spawn of Satan. "You lied about Nevar being your guardian. Why would such evil need the protection of an angel?"

She flinched and looked away, casting her gaze downwards.

"Erin?" Amelia whispered behind her and Erin closed her eyes. "Is he speaking the truth about you?"

Erin frowned and then nodded.

Amelia's silvery eyes widened and the same look of shock echoed on the faces of her comrades too. They hadn't known that Erin was the child of the Devil.

Was she playing them all for fools?

"Evil," he spat the word at her and she covered her face with her hands and hid there for long minutes.

"What do you know of myself and Amelia?" Marcus said and Veiron looked across at him. He still held Nevar against him, his sword poised to slit the guardian angel's throat.

"We have been told about you." Nevar spoke before he could. "You are traitors and must be captured or executed."

"You must know our accomplices then?"

Nevar nodded. "Apollyon, bringer of death, Lukas of the mediators and Einar of the hunters."

"And what of the Devil's men?"

"I do not know." Nevar grimaced when the blade nicked his throat again, sending a new rivulet of blood trailing down to his collarbone. "There was mention of a fallen angel."

Veiron took a step forwards to help him and stopped when Erin lifted her head and looked at him again. He stared into her eyes.

"That angel sacrificed himself recently when trying to save me... and his name was Veiron," she said and as much as he wanted to, he couldn't detect a lie in what she spoke.

"No." He shook his head, unwilling to believe it. She was tricking him. She was trying to confuse and weaken him. None of what she said, what any of them said, made any sense.

"Veiron," she whispered and he refused to look at her. He would not be deceived. "You died barely a week ago trying to protect me... and now you want to kill me? You must remember me. Don't you remember being with us in Hell and fighting the angels? You must remember!"

"You lie. I died months ago." He took a step back from her and glared into her eyes, anger rising like a tide within him. He flexed his fingers around the grips of his swords.

"You died no more than a week ago... and your last words in that lifetime were that you loved me."

Veiron stumbled backwards, head aching and spinning as he tried to process that. It had to be a lie. He had died months ago. He turned his glare on the sand and focused, trying to remember something about his past life so he could prove her wrong. The ache in his head sharpened into a deep stabbing pain and darkness loomed, threatening to render him unconscious.

"I do not know you," he said and looked up at her.

She had turned away from him and was now facing Marcus and Nevar.

"Don't you remember the rooftop in London around two weeks ago? You were there, talking to me, and Veiron fought you," she said to Nevar.

"Stop your trickery! It won't work on us." Veiron snarled and stalked towards her, intent on capturing her and putting an end to this farce.

She held her hand up and dark crimson flames curled from her fingers, chasing over her skin. He stopped. It seemed she had command of her power after all and had merely chosen not to use it during the fight.

"It is a lie, as I told you," Nevar said. "I have never met Veiron, the traitor, nor you before this day."

"You have met me twice. Once in London and once on an island where you fought Apollyon."

Nevar had fought Apollyon? Apollyon was the most powerful angel in existence. Had he killed Nevar and that was why the guardian angel didn't know the target? Veiron growled at himself this time. She was sucking him in with her web of lies and he was beginning to fall for it. They had to escape before she poisoned them as she had poisoned these traitors. He would not fall.

"It is no use," Marcus said in a solemn tone. "They have had their memories altered. Heaven has brainwashed them."

Veiron looked between her and Marcus and Nevar, unsure what to do. He didn't know her. He didn't know any of them. His head ached and throbbed, pain burning behind his eyes.

"Although I do not understand why they have changed Veiron's memories… unless he remembered something." Marcus's words swam in Veiron's pounding head, breaking past the pain and confusing him further.

"You are wrong," Veiron said.

"I can prove that Erin is not lying to you," Marcus countered and Veiron looked at her. She was so close to him, easily within reach. He could grab her and fly away with her, take her to Heaven and complete his mission. He could block out the lies and deliver her to his superiors as ordered.

So why did he feel a deep desire to remain here looking at her, listening to their poison, allowing them to lure him into their trap?

Her eyes shifted and met his, and a spark of warmth lit them. They entranced him and he found he couldn't look away. He didn't want to look away.

"There is a pool in Hell that records the happenings on Earth and in Hell. It will show you and Nevar." Marcus struggled to hold Nevar as he wrestled him.

"Lies," Nevar growled and beat his wings, trying to escape Marcus's grip. The sword cut deeper into his throat and he stilled again. Veiron shared his anger but something about Nevar said anger wasn't the only emotion his fellow angel was feeling. He was shocked too.

Veiron could understand that emotion. He wasn't sure what was truth and what was lie, and with each minute that passed, the line between them blurred and became less distinguished.

They had to get away.

"It is a trap." Veiron readied his swords. "You intend to lure us into Hell for your master."

His gaze flicked to Nevar's and met it. The angel gave a slight nod. He was ready too.

Veiron's eyes shifted back to the target. It would be too risky to grab her and try to free Nevar. He would rescue his comrade and then return to capture her. Her gaze rose to lock with his and the wind caught her black hair, blowing it to one side, away from her throat.

His eyes fell to the marks on the left side of it, visible above the neckline of her black t-shirt, and a jolt rocked him, heating his chest.

He shook his head to clear it, beat his wings, and shot past her and the original angel. Before Marcus could react, he had slammed into both him and Nevar. Nevar reacted immediately, shoving Marcus's blade away from his throat and tearing free of his grasp. They both beat their wings and took off, speeding high into the air.

Neither Marcus nor Amelia came after them.

Veiron looked down at them, watching them growing smaller and smaller as he sped towards Heaven.

He had failed.

Veiron hated that and the fact that he couldn't shake how the target had looked at him and how he had felt because of her gaze on him. The things she had said raced around his mind, leaving him with more questions than ever.

"We must report," Nevar said and wiped the blood from his throat.

Veiron nodded.

They would file a report on what had happened but Veiron knew it wouldn't give them what they both wanted.

It wouldn't give them answers.

Veiron needed those most of all.

And he wouldn't rest until he had them.

CHAPTER 29

The moment Veiron was lost from view, Erin collapsed to her knees on the beach, a wave of fatigue crashing over her. She hadn't grabbed much sleep in the past week, had been constantly thinking about Veiron and hoping that when he returned, everything would turn out all right.

Nightmares had haunted what little rest she had snatched, terrifying visions of Hell and of claws, fangs and horns that had left her shaken and cold to her marrow, filled with a sense of dread that she couldn't dispel. The visions were worse now than ever and they were scrambled too, flipping from one horrific scene to another and then back again, so fragmented that they didn't make any sense and offered her no clue as to what the future held unless it only held oblivion, fire and destruction.

Now that she had seen Veiron again and had seen with her own eyes that Amelia and the others had been right about him, she had nothing left to hold onto and the final shreds of her strength left her. She no longer cared if oblivion was all that lay ahead of her.

Veiron was gone.

Erin's ability to breathe had been lost to her when she had felt the quake and turned to see the cause. Veiron had stood before her, a changed man. His wings had no longer been a beautiful shade of crimson and his armour had lost its darkness. His long scarlet hair had been chopped short, but wild on top, and no trace of red had touched his eyes.

Even his personality had been startlingly different to the man she had fallen in love with.

She pressed her palms into the damp sand on either side of her thighs and scrunched it into her fingers, needing an anchor in the maelstrom of her emotions.

Her power had withered and died in his presence. She had told herself countless times that he had come to hurt her, to capture her for his new side, but it hadn't stopped her wanting to protect him, and it had been impossible to raise a hand to harm him.

She would never do such a thing.

She loved him too much.

A shadow washed over her and then Marcus crouched beside her, still wearing his silver armour. His wings were gone now though. She hated the pitying look in his pale blue eyes.

"Do not lose faith, Erin."

It was easy for him to say. The love of his life was still with him, could still remember him, and hadn't just come to kill him.

Marcus gently laid a hand on her shoulder. "I am convinced they have had their memories altered. The only reason they could have for changing Veiron's memories is that he remembered something. It is possible that he remembered you."

That wasn't a comfort at all. It only made her want to cry and give up all hope. What chance was there of saving Veiron from Heaven and this twisted game if Heaven could just change his memories and make him believe their lies? She had told him the truth and he had fought against it, voicing lies that his master had put into his head. He believed that he had died months ago. Even Nevar had forgotten about her and the two times their paths had crossed, and it wasn't because he had died. Apollyon had reported that Nevar had escaped their fight with only minor injuries.

Erin was beginning to believe the Devil. Both he and God were cruel and malevolent. They used their men to their advantage, uncaring of their feelings, shaping them into pawns that would do exactly as they ordered.

She wished she could free Veiron.

"Erin, we may be able to unlock his memories." That caught her attention and she raised her head and looked at Marcus.

It was a small comfort, a slender thread of hope that she clung to as though it was a lifeline. Even if they could restore whatever he had remembered, what future was there for an angel of Heaven and the Devil's daughter?

Veiron's words rang in her mind. Evil. She wanted nothing to do with Hell or her father, but Veiron still thought her evil. She clutched her chest and breathed deeply against the pain in her heart. Was this how Veiron had felt whenever she had said such terrible things about his kind and Hell? Had he hurt so deeply that it felt as though his life would end? He had wanted nothing to do with the Devil, had been against him just as she was, but she had reacted to him as though he was still aligned with that realm and that vicious man, and she had wounded him with her careless words. Evil. She wasn't evil, she believed that in her heart, but it still hurt to hear him call her such things.

Amelia came to sit on the sand beside her and Erin could hear Einar whispering to Taylor, comforting her as he healed her.

"Is it really true what he said?" Amelia's voice was low and cautious, and Erin nodded, knowing exactly what she was asking. "When did you find out?"

Erin sifted the sand through her fingers, focusing on the feel of it to distract her from the pain of her memories.

"When the Devil attacked us in Hell, I made a deal with him. He wanted me to awaken and promised I wouldn't have to die to do it. In exchange, he offered to call off his men." She closed her eyes and then opened them again and stared into the distance at the turquoise water that stretched into infinity. The sunlight twinkled on it and she felt the whole scene should have soothed her, but she felt nothing as she looked at it. "The angels attacked and I begged him to send you all away. He refused to save Veiron... he made me watch him die... and then I felt as though I was dying too."

Amelia touched her other shoulder but she shirked her grip.

"The Devil told me then that I was his daughter," Erin said and turned to face Amelia, locking eyes with her. "Which means I can't be your sister."

"Erin—"

"Am I your sister?"

"Yes." Amelia cast her gaze down at the sand. "But not by blood. You were adopted... but that doesn't mean you're not my sister."

"When were you going to tell me? Were you ever going to tell me, Amelia?" Erin's hands heated and she breathed slowly, trying to calm her rising anger. She had avoided talking about what had happened to her since Veiron had died and the Devil had returned her to the resort island. She hadn't wanted to face it because it meant admitting that she was the Devil's daughter, and therefore couldn't really be Amelia's sister. Now, the hurt that she had bottled up inside her heart broke free and flooded her, jumbling her feelings and leaving her afraid that everything she feared was about to happen.

She didn't want everyone to turn their backs on her.

She didn't want to be alone.

"I only found out when mum died and dad was so upset because they had both wanted to tell you, but they had never found the way to break it to you." Amelia reached out to her and then paused and lowered her hand into her lap instead. "We wanted to tell you... but then my life got turned upside down... and I was afraid of losing you."

Erin didn't know how to react to that. Amelia feared losing her? Erin realised what she meant. Amelia had never told Erin what had happened to her. She had been afraid that Erin would freak out on discovering that she was some kind of angel, just as Erin had feared Amelia would leave her on discovering that she was something straight out of Hell.

They weren't so different after all.

"Just because they aren't your biological parents... it doesn't mean that they're not your parents, Erin, or that I'm not your sister. Mum loved you as her own... and dad loves you. I love you."

There wasn't any comfort in those words. Her parents had never told her. All this time she had thought they were her real parents and Amelia was her real sister. It hurt to discover that it was all a lie, not just because she felt betrayed and that she had lost her family, but because it confirmed that the Devil wasn't leading her astray. He really was her father and her power had nothing to do with the power that Amelia commanded.

Erin couldn't breathe.

On the back of losing Veiron, it was too much for her to handle. She wasn't strong enough. She needed to get away and get some air, find some space, do something to make it all sink in so she didn't feel as though she was drowning.

"This hasn't changed anything, Erin. You're still my sister. I still love you. You have to believe that." Amelia touched her shoulder and Erin couldn't stand it.

She shot to her feet, pain erupting in her heart and scorching it. She wished it would incinerate it completely. She didn't want to feel anything anymore. Her whole life had been a lie. She had tried so hard to convince herself otherwise this past week—that it was the Devil who had lied so she would use her power to help him—but now she knew that he hadn't deceived her. She had deceived herself.

"I can't do this right now," she said and Amelia stood and blocked her path.

The love Amelia had claimed to feel for her shone in her grey eyes and Erin wanted to fall into her arms and hold onto her. She needed to feel Amelia's arms around her, comforting her just as she had done so many times in the past.

Another need overruled it though.

She needed to be alone. It was the only way she was going to find the quiet she needed in order to process everything that had happened today and in the past few weeks. She knew it was running away, but she didn't care. Her hands heated further, scorching her bones. She needed space or she was going to go nuclear.

"Erin, listen to me. You're my sister, by blood or not." Amelia caught her arm but Erin tore her hand off her, cast it aside, and shoved past her.

"Let her go. She needs some space, Amelia. It's been hard on her." Marcus again and she silently thanked him for his support. He had always been there for her since she had first met him, judging her needs better than Amelia had ever been able, and it seemed her new status as the Devil's daughter hadn't changed that about him. The relief that swept over her because of that almost overwhelmed her. He wasn't going to cast her out because of her father, and she knew Amelia wouldn't either. They wouldn't leave her alone to fend for herself.

Erin walked the beach, trying to get her head straight. Heaven had assigned Nevar to watch over her. Did that mean that they had known all along that she was the Devil's daughter? Had they placed her with Amelia's parents or had that been dumb luck? They had assigned Marcus to Amelia, so they must have known what she was. They must have placed her with that family on purpose.

With Heaven already guarding Amelia so closely, the Devil may not have noticed that they also guarded his daughter.

Or had her entry into that family been his doing? Had he hidden her there and the fact that Heaven had assigned a guardian to her been a coincidence?

Her head hurt.

Either way, she hated both realms and refused to work for them.

Erin sighed and wrapped her arms around herself. It felt as though these past few weeks had stripped her identity from her. Everything she had known had changed, leaving her unsure of herself and who she was. Was she still the same woman she had been before being captured and taken to Hell? She no longer felt the same. Heaven and Hell had beaten her carefree spirit out of her. They had destroyed her life, just as they had destroyed Amelia's, and Marcus's, and Veiron's, and everyone else they sucked into this vicious game.

She wanted them to pay for that.

She wanted to tear down Heaven and destroy Hell. She wanted them all to feel her wrath and end this game. They had no right to play with people's lives like this.

Veiron had never wanted the role they had given him, always forcing him to fall, to remember all the terrible things they had made him do in their names. They didn't care about who they hurt with their game. She and everyone else were just pawns to them, a means to an end, a player they discarded without regret.

The Devil had sacrificed one pawn to gain another.

His best man in exchange for his best woman.

Well, she wasn't going to play this sick game of his for him. She was going to stand against him and shake Heaven and Hell until they acknowledged her power and bowed at her feet. She would show them no mercy, just as they showed none to her and those she loved.

She would convince Veiron to listen to her and would reclaim her lost love and bring him back to her. Nothing would stand in her way. Not God or the Devil himself.

Veiron would come back for her. He would want to fulfil his mission and capture her, and when he returned, she would be ready for him. She would do all in her power to convince him that everything Heaven had told him was a lie and he loved her, and that they were meant to be together. He would listen to her. He would remember her.

A wave of sickness crashed through her and Erin clutched her stomach.

She could feel the Devil's blood coursing through her veins, a powerful darkness that had threatened to seize control of her more than once since he had awoken it within her. She had tried to master it, had spent the week hiding away from the others, practising with her power and learning to control it. It was too strong at times, ruled by her feelings. Whenever she remembered what had happened to Veiron, it spiralled out of control, burning at a thousand degrees, until she felt as though it would destroy her and the demon within would take over.

Erin slowly sat down on the sand and rubbed her stomach, trying to ease the churning ache there. She had thrown up several times when an attack like this happened and had quickly learned to rest and wait it out rather than trying to do anything.

Darkness swept through her, feeding on her fear and her pain, growing in strength until it began to feel good, drugging her with how strong she felt. The sickness that came with it as it writhed beneath her skin took the edge off how powerful she felt though and kept her grounded.

She forced her thoughts back to Veiron. Heaven would send him after her again. He was the perfect man for the task of capturing and eliminating her. She would never hurt him. The Devil wanted her too though. What if he came for her first?

Her power pushed again, heating her hands and causing her chest to burn. Her stomach turned and twisted, boiling and churning. She swallowed her need to throw up and clutched herself. Ribbons of crimson curled around her fingers and danced up her arms, gradually turning black.

It was as though something rotten festered inside her and it was going to kill her.

If Veiron didn't kill her first.

CHAPTER 30

Veiron could find no rest. He paced the small courtyard garden in the white fortress of Heaven, trying to find beauty in the towering white tree that speared upwards and spread silvery leaves to form a canopy above the square. Since returning to Heaven three days ago after his failed mission, his mind had been constantly on his target.

Erin.

She confused him.

The things she had said, the way she had looked at him, and the fact that she had protected him even though he had come to capture her, none of it made any sense. Neither did his reactions to her. He had felt her pain as though it was his own, and she had affected him in strange ways by merely looking into his eyes. A power of hers?

He had felt hot, flushed all over and burning inside.

Plagued by her, he had flown to the mortal realm, intent on seeing her again. They had moved, leaving the island barren of life and him with no trail to follow. Every instinct said to head down there again, to double check and ensure that she really was gone.

Was it desire to see if she was there driving him or a darker urge?

He had rested on the island. Tired from his flight, he had fallen asleep on the shore, warmed by the sun.

He had dreamed of her.

That dream still heated his blood to boiling point.

It had been everything wicked and darkly erotic, but it had felt familiar at the same time. He had seen himself biting her, sinking the sharp teeth of a demon into her throat in the very place where he had seen a mark. His wings had been crimson and had covered her, shielded her from the world as they had made love, keeping her to himself. Her moans had been breathless as she had ridden him, his cock sliding in and out of her hot sheath, his own groans as desperate and lost as hers. Each thrust had cranked his temperature up another ten degrees, but it had been the sight of her so lost in her passion, writhing and moaning, her bare body beautiful and covered in glistening moisture that had truly done him in.

That image of her stayed with him, was there whenever he closed his eyes, playing on repeat until he burned for her.

Had she been telling the truth and they had once been lovers?

Or was the dream merely that, a dream, a figment of his overwrought mind brought about by the things she had said?

She had planted the seeds into his imagination and it had grown them, turning them into something sensual and erotic, into something that had never happened.

Veiron pinched the bridge of his nose and closed his eyes.

He needed to speak with someone about it and the things that she had said, but he didn't want to go to his superiors and Nevar had disappeared shortly after they had given their report.

His superiors wanted him to return to the mortal realm and continue his mission. He had tried to question them about his past life but they had refused to answer, stating that it was not of consequence and that he would do best to focus on his mission. He didn't want to focus on his mission. He wanted to know how the Devil's daughter had known his name and whether everything she had told him was the truth.

He sighed and stalked out of the courtyard, drifting through the white corridors, heading towards the main entrance of the fortress. Perhaps another flight would clear his mind and give him the peace he needed. He would fly a while and then return to look for Nevar.

Veiron pushed the double doors of the fortress open and squinted at the brightness that assaulted him. He waited for his eyes to stop stinging and then opened them.

Instead of the pristine white grass and beautiful gardens of Heaven, he stood amidst lakes of boiling lava and spires of black rock.

Panic washed over him quickly followed by calm as he called his swords to him, grasping one in each hand. How was it possible that he had gone from Heaven to Hell in the space of a heartbeat?

"Veiron?" a soft female voice called to him, a voice that he recognised, and he wheeled to face the owner of it.

Erin stood before him, her smile dazzling and amber eyes bright and entrancing. She wore nothing more than a tiny black tank and shorts. Something was different about her.

The strip of colour in her black hair. It was lilac now. It had been red before. Had she changed it?

He palmed his swords and realised he was missing one. He looked down and frowned at the broadsword in his right hand, causing something to jingle as he did so. He raised his free hand and touched the back of his head and tensed. His hair was long, tied with some sort of leather thong that had bells on it.

He looked himself over. Rather than his blue armour, he wore black jeans and heavy boots, and no top.

"We should keep moving," Erin said and hobbled past him. His gaze slid down her slender bare legs to her feet. They were swathed in black.

His t-shirt.

He had bound her feet with it and she had touched his back.

He flinched against the pain that stabbed his skull and clutched his head with one hand, squeezing his eyes shut.

When he opened them again, the scene was different and Erin was gone. He sat before a fire in the middle of a jungle and he wasn't alone. The abomination and the traitor were with him.

Tears shone in her grey eyes as she stared across the fire at him.

"I can't leave her there, Veiron," Amelia whispered. "Marcus won't let me go and I'm afraid that if he goes alone, he won't come back... or he won't be able to find Erin. Please... I know I'm asking a lot of you but I need someone strong who knows Hell and won't rouse suspicion. I need her back."

Veiron's mind reeled and the ache in his head worsened. She was asking him to go to Hell because he knew it and wouldn't rouse suspicion? She wanted him to find Erin for her?

He reached around and ran a hand down his long ponytail, and then flicked a glance down at the broadsword resting beside him. What was happening? It all felt so familiar, as though he had lived these moments before.

Like a memory.

He roared against the pain that exploded behind his eyes and clutched his head with both hands, gritting his teeth.

The sound of battle erupted around him and he found himself running, pushing forwards. He flicked his eyes open and quickly took in his new surroundings. Hell again and the midst of a battle involving angels from the division of death. Their glossy black wings and the gold edging around their obsidian armour reflected the fiery pools of lava in the cracked basalt ground.

Veiron flexed his fingers and found a black rod in it, tipped at both ends with a crimson blade. He glanced at his black and scarlet armour, and then at the angels. They were coming for him. They weren't on his side. He ran forwards and turned his head in that direction.

Erin was there, held with her back against the Devil's chest, his arm across her front, restraining her.

She was reaching for him.

Veiron instinctively reached for her.

Sharp pain lanced his chest and he looked down to see the tip of a golden blade protruding from his breastplate and blood spilling down his bare stomach.

He looked back at Erin and collapsed to his knees.

She still reached for him.

His mouth moved but his ears rang, the noise so loud that he didn't hear what he said. She spoke too, her expression soft, full of love and affection.

Love that she had mentioned.

She had said that his final words had been to tell her that he loved her.

The buzzing in his skull increased, the pain so intense that his vision wavered. Darkness loomed up and then closed in on him, and Veiron fought it. A desperate urge to reach Erin consumed him and he tried to stand.

Angels descended on him and a bright light engulfed them all.

When the light receded, he found himself standing in the middle of the garden between the white fortress and the holding cells in Heaven. His head ached, throbbing madly.

How had he got here?

He looked around him, gaze tracking some of the angels that passed him, and tried to remember. The last thing he recalled was exiting the fortress. The ache in his head worsened. He closed his eyes and images flickered through his mind, disjointed fragments of moments that felt so familiar. Each time he remembered one, it disappeared. What was wrong with him? Was he sick?

He spun around, feeling disorientated as the beautiful pale gardens of Heaven switched to the harsh black landscape of Hell and back again.

What was happening to him?

He caught a snippet of something that stayed with him—an image of Erin reaching for him and he for her.

That image evoked an intense need to see her again and he couldn't ignore it.

She had infected his mind somehow and he wouldn't be well again until he had completed his mission.

Veiron beat his silver-blue wings and flew over the huge white wall that protected the realm of Heaven. He twisted in the air and shot downwards, the wind buffeting him and the clouds leaving a fine layer of moisture on his bare skin and his blue armour.

He would find his target and he would capture her.

He would succeed this time.

Veiron folded his wings back and picked up speed, zooming down through the clouds, back towards the island. His gut said that he would find her there this time and it wasn't wrong. As the small green island came into view below him, surrounded by clear jewel-like blue waters, he felt her presence on it. She wasn't alone. Others were on the island with her but there was a chance that they wouldn't be close to her when he arrived.

Could he swoop down, snatch her and make off with her before anyone noticed? He doubted it. She would fight him if he tried to take her. She hadn't wanted to fight him before but every instinct he had said that she would fight him if he tried to separate her from her friends.

Veiron spread his wings to slow his descent and scoured the island. He found what he was looking for sitting on a small spit of rock on the opposite side of the island to everyone else. When he drew close to her, she looked up and showed no sign of moving.

He landed near her on the beach and strolled along it, curious now, wanting to see what she would do. Would she attack when he was close enough or run away? Would she call for her friends or fight him alone?

He stepped up onto the rocks and she did none of those things.

She got to her feet and faced him, her short black dress fluttering in the warm afternoon breeze. Her skin had lost its colour, far paler now than it had been before, and there were dark circles beneath her haunted amber eyes. Was she sick?

"You took longer than I expected," she said, soft voice calm and not a trace of fear touching it. If anything, he would have said she was angry with him for not coming for her sooner, but her expression remained emotionless. "Have you thought about what I said?"

Veiron stopped, one foot on the higher rock in front of him, and frowned at her. She had been waiting for him.

"We had to go away. Amelia wanted to speak to Apollyon and Lukas about everything. I wanted to stay but Marcus insisted I go too. Did I miss you while I was gone?" She didn't wait for his reply. "I suppose I must have. I was sure you would come back for me. Have you remembered anything?"

His frown hardened. Had she known he would see things while in Heaven? Had she orchestrated the whole thing, placing those seeds in his head just as he had feared? Her amber eyes probed his and she sighed.

"I take it that's a no. I wish you would say something."

"I have come to capture you and complete my mission. You will not fight me and stop this from happening?" He studied her expression, watching for a sign that she was lying or was out to trick him.

She shook her head and only honesty touched her voice. "I would never fight you, Veiron. You can take me in."

She held her hands out to him, wrists together, and smiled.

He frowned at her odd gesture. Perhaps it was a human one that he wasn't familiar with. He stepped up onto the rock and grabbed both of her slender wrists in one hand. Fire flashed across his skin and pierced his skull. He flinched and released her, images of her flickering through his mind so quickly that he felt sick.

"Veiron, what's wrong?" She touched his face, her palms gently cupping his cheeks, warming his skin.

The pain faded as though her caress had soothed it away and he slowly opened his eyes and looked down into hers. Concern blazed in them, the emotion so intense that it stole his breath. There was love in her eyes too and the sight of it evoked images of him in Hell, desperate to save her but unable to because he was dying.

Veiron growled in frustration, swept her into his arms so fiercely that her head knocked against his breastplate, and beat his wings. He flew upwards hard and fast, determined to feel the wind on his face, feel it flowing over his silver-blue feathers, smoothing out his jumbled feelings.

"Veiron?" she whispered and he ignored her. He had captured his target and he would take her to Heaven, and he would be done with her and her trickery. "Why don't you remember me?"

There was such hurt in those words. He couldn't stop himself from looking down at her. No tears lined her eyes this time but her pain shone in them. Not a lie.

"Why can't you remember what we shared?"

"Because I had never met you before the other day and none of what you say is real."

Her pain increased and she looked away from him. Her hair fluttered and danced in the wind, obscuring her face so he couldn't read her expression. She curled closer to him and shivered. The air was growing colder. A shocking desire to pull her nearer to him and share his body heat with her drove through him. He pushed it away.

"I love you." She didn't look at him and the wind made her voice quiet, but he still heard her. A strange spark heated his chest, a mixture of warm feelings and terrible pain. She faced him again. "You were the only one who ever understood me and what I was going through."

He stopped dead and beat his silver-blue wings to keep himself stationary, staring at her all the while. It didn't seem like an act to make him lower his guard.

"You can't believe what Heaven told you, Veiron. They're playing you. It's all a stupid game to them and to Hell. We're just pawns." She looked up into his eyes, seized his shoulders, gripping them tightly, and pulled herself closer to him. "Don't trust them. They've done something to you. Heaven is just going to use you to capture me and then it will let you fall again, just as it always does."

Veiron glared at her. Heaven would do no such thing. Angels fell of their own accord, not because their master decided it. He wished he could push her away but he couldn't without dropping her. He could ignore her and shut out her lies though. As soon as he was in Heaven, he would be safe again, rid of her toxic words that cast a veil of doubt over everything that he knew.

He beat his wings and flew upwards again, intent on reaching Heaven and blocking her out.

She wriggled in his arms and looped hers around his neck, pulling herself up so she was eye level with him.

"Curse you," she said and then slanted her head and meshed her lips with his.

Veiron halted and tried to evade her but she held him firm, kissing him. A spark of recognition and a sense of familiarity shot through him followed by a flood of images. He saw them together on a beach, walking hand in hand under the moonlight, and then she was standing on a bed, smiling and holding her arms out to him.

Veiron managed to break away from her and breathed hard, head splitting in two as he tried to make sense of the fragmented images. He licked his lips and tasted blood. Had she bitten him?

His gaze fell to her mouth. A red streak marred her lower lip and the temptingly soft pink flesh around it was swollen. It must have split when he had grabbed her on the beach and she had banged her face on his armour.

The taste of her was so familiar.

Veiron's eyes dropped to her neck. Teeth marks. He had seen himself biting her in the throes of passion, lost in her and in love with her. The pain splitting his skull open burned more fiercely and he almost clutched it. Erin's grip on him tightening brought him back to his senses and he kept hold of her instead. He breathed hard, battling the encroaching darkness, barely holding on to consciousness. Why did he almost pass out whenever images of her flooded his mind? Why did they disappear as quickly as they had come, but didn't disappear completely? He felt he had lost some but could still remember others.

"I cannot take this," he whispered and stared down into her eyes. "I do not want to remember things that are not true."

She softly stroked his cheek and the pain in his head eased again, as though her touch was magic. "They are true."

She caressed the marks on her throat.

"You bit me while we were making love, Veiron... you saved me from Hell... you saved me so many times... but I failed to save you. You died and it was all my fault." Her voice hitched on the last few words and he wanted to tell her that whatever had happened to him it wasn't her fault. If he had died as he had seen in those images and as she had said he had, then he had died for her. It had been his choice, because he had wanted to save her and had been willing to sacrifice himself to do so.

He lowered his gaze to her throat again and the marks on it. Desire pulsed through him whenever his eyes found them or whenever they met hers, and he was beginning to believe that desire was his true feelings and not a spell she had cast on him. It came from deep within him, heated his blood like an inferno and set his heart pounding. He had never felt anything like it and he feared he never would again if he let this woman out of his arms.

"Veiron?" She brushed her soft fingers across his cheek and then swept them into his short red hair, and his eyes rose to meet hers. She smiled at him, worry reflected in her eyes and in her touch. "Are you feeling okay?"

"I see things," he said and then told himself to be quiet. She didn't need to know about them. It would only strengthen her hold over him. She would seek to soothe him, to take away his pain, and he would fall right into her hands.

"Tell me," she whispered. Exactly as he had predicted. She sought to use his weakness against him. He would not fall for her ploy.

"They give me headaches." He frowned when she lifted her fingers to his left temple and ran their tips in soothing circles over his skin. He would tell her no more. That had just been a slip.

"What do you see?"

"You... me... the traitor and the abomination. Hell. It is a trick. You have cast some sort of spell on my mind."

She shook her head and continued caressing his temple. "Not me. You do remember me then?"

She looked pleased by that. Veiron said nothing. He wasn't sure whether he had remembered her or whether the lies she had planted in his head had merely borne fruit.

"Do you still remember things about us?" she said.

"They are all lies. My mind rejects your trickery. When the images cease, my head hurts and the false memories disappear."

"Or your false memories take over again."

Why was she insisting that what he saw with her was the truth and that Heaven had changed his memories?

"Speak with Marcus and you will see that I'm telling the truth, Veiron." She lowered her hand to his chest and he almost missed the feel of it on his skin, smoothing out his troubles, leaving him feeling compliant and all too willing to do whatever she asked of him. "We can show you the truth. There's a pool in Hell that can show it to you."

Veiron growled at the mention of Hell and beat his wings harder, carrying them more quickly towards Heaven. His chest hurt, a dull throbbing that spread through him, leaving a bitter taste in his mouth.

"I knew you were tricking me. This is all some power of yours... some evil you have cast upon me!" He doubled his efforts, desperate to reach Heaven and get away from her. He couldn't take it. He could no longer tell truth from lie. She poisoned his heart and his mind, all in some attempt to turn him against his master. "Oh, you are evil indeed. Your father's progeny without a doubt. How you trick and tempt an angel. He would be so proud of you!"

She gasped and tears filled her eyes. "How can you say that to me? How can you be so cruel after everything we've shared?"

"Desist! I will listen to no more of your foul lies. You seek to make me fall."

"No," she barked and grabbed his armour over his shoulders. "I would never do that to you. I tried to make him stop... I tried to make him save you too... he refused. You didn't want to die. You didn't want to become an angel again, forgetting everything the Devil and God had put you through... you have to believe me, Veiron."

"I believe nothing that comes out of your mouth." He turned his focus away from her, trying to block her out, but she pulled herself up. The shift in her weight in his arms caught him off guard and he tipped forwards, almost losing his grip on her as they plunged downwards. She shrieked and clung to him and he resisted the urge to tighten his grip on her as he righted himself and continued upwards.

"You died barely a week ago, Veiron. I saw you die with my own eyes. Whatever you remember, it happened. You died trying to reach me and save me from the Devil."

He halted again and stared into her eyes. Why had that shocked him? Of course she would know what he had seen. She had been the one to plant those images in his head somehow. She had constructed the false memories that plagued him.

"Why would you need to be saved from your father and why would I be the one doing it?" he said and she lowered her gaze to her lap.

"Because my father... if you can call him that... is a vicious, evil bastard. He tricked me and you died because of it... and you tried to save me because you love me." She slowly raised her head, her eyes drifting up over his chest and then his neck before they finally tentatively met his.

"I do not love you." He steeled himself against the tears that lined her dark lashes and the pain that radiated through him. "I feel nothing for you. You will come with me to Heaven where you will be contained and questioned."

Her expression turned solemn and her voice lost its warmth, gaining a note of resignation that he discovered he didn't like. "No, Veiron, I won't be contained and questioned. I will be killed. Let's not pretend anything different will happen."

She had known her fate all along yet she had still allowed him to take her, had refused to fight him and had accepted the death sentence that awaited her in Heaven. What strange sort of creature was she? She confused him at every turn, entranced him whenever she smiled and it showed in her eyes, and bewitched him with only the sound of her voice breathing his name.

"I will prove that you know me, and that you care about me, and that you just don't remember that you do because Heaven has tampered with your mind."

He frowned at her. "What do you mean, prove that I know you? I will not allow you to lure me down to Hell for your master... so how will you do such a thing?"

Erin smiled and briefly pressed her lips against his.

Nothing happened other than a momentary hunger to return the kiss.

"You tried that before. It did not make me recall whether I loved you or not. It did not prove anything."

She nodded and stroked his cheek, her amber eyes darting between his. "I really hope this will."

Erin pushed out of his arms.

He tried to grab her but he was too slow. She fell, tumbling head over heels through the air, hurtling towards the ocean several thousand feet below.

Veiron twisted in the air and beat his wings, shooting down towards her, his heart thundering against his chest, commanding him to save her.

What was he doing?

She was immortal but she would still die by hitting the ocean from this height. His mission would be over.

Something deep within him hurt at the thought of her dying and said he couldn't allow it to happen. He had to save her.

He pinned his silver-blue wings back and shot towards her, the air warming as they drew closer to the ocean's surface. She flipped onto her back, her arms and legs flailing upwards, and her terror flooded him. She didn't want to die. She didn't have to fear. He would never let that happen.

Nothing would ever hurt her.

Nothing.

Veiron growled and doubled his effort, giving one huge flap of his wings to help speed him downwards. She reached for him as he closed in. Veiron stretched his arms out to her. The second their fingers touched, relief swamped him, instantly lightening his insides and driving out the fear. He clutched her hands, pulled her into his arms and spread his wings to stop their descent, and his relief became something more, something astounding.

She felt so right in his arms, as though she had been made for him to hold like this, to protect from the world and care for.

"Oh, Veiron," she whispered and threw her arms around his neck, burying her face against his throat.

She trembled, freezing against him, and he clutched her to him, beating his wings to keep steady in the warmer air. The feel of her tears on his skin called to him, making him tighten his hold on her and stroke her back to soothe her. Her heart thundered close to his, echoing its beat. He had never felt such deep fear and such monumental joy so close together. It consumed him and he clung to her, needing to feel her in his arms and know that she was safe.

"I was so scared you wouldn't catch me," she whispered against his neck.

"I would never let you come to harm," he said without thinking and then paused. He had felt that while trying to rescue her too. This crazy, dangerous yet beautiful female meant something to him.

"Will you come with me now?" She shifted closer to him, nuzzling his neck and sighing. "I swore I would never say this again, but... please?"

His heart said to go with her to meet Marcus again and see what the traitor had to say.

His head ached, the pain debilitating and causing his thoughts to swim. What was it he had wanted to do again? He looked down at the slender woman in his arms and his head instantly cleared.

He wanted to go with Erin.

He had to because he was beginning to suspect that she wasn't lying and that he did know and die for her.

CHAPTER 31

"What is he doing here?" The abomination greeted Veiron at sword-point, waving it in his face, as though such a paltry weapon could intimidate him. Her appearance wasn't helping matters. She wore a pale blue short dress, had her long silver hair twirled into a knot, and the arm that held the sword had spots of something white along it. Some sort of cream.

The yellow bottle held in the traitor's hand where he stood a few metres behind the abomination next to a towel spread over the sand and a sun parasol looked like it might have contained whatever cream now spotted her.

Marcus tossed the bottle onto the towel and stalked towards them. At the same time, Erin slipped down from Veiron's arms and casually pushed Amelia's sword aside.

"The boy is here to discover the truth," a deep voice rang out and Veiron's gaze shifted to the owner of it.

Apollyon. The great destroyer. The angel of death. Heaven's most powerful angel, and another traitor.

He too failed to intimidate Veiron in his current outfit of black knee-length shorts and nothing else. The warm breeze tangled the long black ponytail tied at the nape of his neck and Veiron stared at it, vaguely recalling having hair that long once. His head hurt again and he pressed his right hand against his forehead and cursed.

"Heaven does not want you to remember," Apollyon said and Veiron cracked his eyes open, fixing them on him. "It is trying to make you forget."

"Is it a curse?" Marcus this time and Veiron's gaze snapped to the dark-haired male. Black shorts seemed to be the male uniform on the island but Marcus's were looser and shorter, ending mid-thigh. They were wet too.

"It may be." Apollyon approached him, exuding confidence and power that had Veiron instantly backing away. The desire to call his weapons to him was strong but he ignored it. Calling them and arming himself would give Amelia reason to launch an attack. He couldn't do such a thing. His gaze slid to Erin. Not when it would place her in harm's way.

His head ached again. Veiron grunted and clutched it, battling a wave of nausea that felt as though it might render him unconscious. He couldn't allow that to happen. It would leave him vulnerable.

A soft hand against his cheek made him open his eyes. He stared into Erin's amber irises. She stroked his cheek and then tiptoed and ran her fingers in circles around his temples, easing his pain.

"Move away from him, Erin. I don't want you anywhere near him," Amelia snapped and extended her sword towards him again.

Erin didn't move. "I'm sick of hearing that. You never wanted me anywhere near him. What about what I want? Isn't that important too? Besides, he won't hurt me."

"How do you know this isn't all a trap? He's probably using this as a chance to get you to lower your defences so he can capture you."

Erin smiled up at him. "He already captured me… but he brought me back."

"What?" Amelia stalked forwards and Marcus caught her arm, holding her back.

Erin slowly set back on her heels and turned to face them. "I let him capture me and we talked, and he wants to speak to Marcus about what he said. He wants to know his past, and the truth. It's his choice."

Veiron noted that she failed to expand on how she had convinced him to return with her. Would Amelia be angry with her if she knew that Erin had chosen to freefall towards Earth and her possible death in order to prove to him that he felt something for her?

His superiors had informed him that they had grown up together despite being born to different parents. Heaven had placed Erin with Amelia's family so they could keep an eye on her and were aware of her location at all times, and so the Devil wouldn't find her. It had been decided that the Devil would find Amelia and would be so consumed by his success in hunting her down that he would overlook Erin, not realising that she was his daughter.

"Please, Erin… think about it for a moment. What better way to gain your trust than to pretend to do as you asked? He might be planning to wait until we're all asleep before capturing us all."

"Then we won't all sleep at the same time. Is it too much to ask that you show a little faith in me for once and stop trying to control my life?" Erin tipped her chin up. "Veiron stays or I go, it's as simple as that. You're not the boss here, Amelia. In the immortal words of the man behind me, get off the power trip before I knock you off it."

He had said that? It didn't sound like the sort of thing he would say but Amelia had been starting to annoy him and he had considered saying something about her attitude towards the woman who had grown up with her as her sister.

"Maybe we should go." Erin turned to him and he shook his head. He could see that she was hurting, could feel it, but he couldn't let her run away from those seeking to control her.

"I have come here for answers and I will have them." He raised a hand to sweep his knuckles across her soft tanned cheek but Amelia's sword pressed against his throat.

"Don't touch her," Amelia growled, her grey eyes burning silver.

"Will you drop it already?" Erin grabbed Amelia's hand and twisted her arm, forcing her to drop her sword. The moment the sword hit the sand, Erin released her and Amelia rubbed her wrist. "Stop trying to drive the only man who has ever truly given a damn about me out of my life!"

A huge blast of orange light exploded from Erin's hands, hit Amelia square in the chest and sent her flying into the air. Amelia's silvery wings erupted from her back and she spread them, righting herself and stopping herself from hitting the sand.

"Erin," Marcus barked and Erin breathed hard, staring at her hands with wide eyes.

"I didn't mean it," she whispered and looked at him, shaking her head, and then at Amelia.

Amelia glided to the ground and folded her wings back. "I know. I'm sorry. I shouldn't have pushed you. It was wrong of me."

Erin's hands fell to her sides and she glanced over her shoulder at him. "Is it possible that Veiron is cursed?"

"Anything is possible." Marcus looked him over and Veiron didn't like the hard edge to his pale blue eyes. "He cursed me once after all."

He had?

"Do you have any tattoos?"

Veiron shook his head. "None that I know of."

Marcus turned his back to him. Elaborate blue-grey wings covered his shoulder blades.

"You placed this curse on me. It no longer works. You removed it for me too… you have nothing on your back like this?" The man turned back around to face him. "We should check you over to be sure. It could be small and you might not have noticed it."

Veiron nodded and focused so his silver-blue wings disappeared and he could remove his armour. He didn't want to send it away using his powers. He wanted it on hand in case something happened to him.

Erin stood close to him, her amber eyes locked on his wings as they shrank into his back. If he had known her before his death and had been a demonic angel working for her father, then his wings had been crimson once, as they had been in his dream of her making love with him.

A scowl knitted her dark eyebrows. Did she not like his wings as they were now? Or his hair?

"You had tattoos," she said when his wings were gone and stepped closer to him.

She ran her small hands over his blue armour and a fierce ache to feel them on his bare chest bolted through him. He stared down into her eyes, losing awareness of the others as her pupils dilated, desire heating her amber irises until they resembled molten lava. She swept her hands over his shoulders, fingers brushing bare skin, and he sucked in a sharp breath to steady himself. Her touch was electric, scorching him at a thousand degrees, making him burn for her.

Veiron stepped into her, driven by a desire to have her closer to him, to capture her waist and drag her soft body into the hard length of his. He wanted to possess her.

"I liked your ink." She grazed her short nails over his biceps and held his gaze. "It was sexy."

"Yours is sexy too." He paused and frowned, echoing the shock rippling across Erin's features.

"You remember my tattoo?"

He ignored the ache building behind his eyes and didn't think about anything, just let it flow out of him. When he wasn't trying to remember, things came to him painlessly.

He could picture her tattoo in his mind, could remember tracing it with his tongue and his fingertips, eliciting soft breathless moans from her.

"A dragon, curled around your spine… like your painting."

Her eyes shot wide. "You remember the painting too?"

Pain erupted when an image of it flashed in front of his eyes and he clutched his head in both hands and doubled over, growling and gritting his teeth. Darkness swam at the edges of his mind and he swayed, fighting it and the waves trying to pull him under.

"Veiron. It's okay. I've got you," Erin whispered, hands stroking now, caressing his arms and then his hands, covering them and easing them away from his head. She replaced them with hers, burying her fingers into his short scarlet hair and running the pads of her thumbs around his temples, easing the pain away again.

A fresh wave of darkness surged through him and he didn't have the strength to fight this one. He fell into Erin's arms, feeling them wrap around him and her easing him to the warm sand, and then darkness took him.

He wasn't alone.

Someone was watching him and it wasn't Erin.

Veiron screwed his eyes up and clawed his way out of the darkness, struggling towards the light. He moaned, his head thumping. Where was he? Still on the beach where he had passed out?

He clumsily groped at his surroundings.

"You have been out cold for several hours. We moved you to a more comfortable location." That deep voice belonged to Apollyon.

Veiron swallowed and forced his eyes open. It was night. Torches burned outside, staked into the sand. Apollyon stood in the doorway of the shelter, arms folded across his broad bare chest, blue eyes fixed on Veiron.

"Erin tended to you until I made her leave. She needed to eat and rest. She will come back soon."

"Until then, I am your prisoner?" Veiron met his gaze.

Apollyon smiled and nodded. "Erin gives you too much free rein because of her feelings for you. I do not trust you… but I do not need to. It is not my trust you should be winning but hers. You have done nothing to earn what she has given you. Erin is the reason you're still alive in your current form, not dead again and sent back to Heaven."

He knew that. Everyone else on the island would have killed him when he had come down with Nevar had it not been for Erin's intervention and wishes. He had done nothing to earn her protection. He had tried to kill her.

"Here." Apollyon held his hand out to Veiron.

Veiron slowly pushed himself up into a sitting position, afraid that if he moved quickly he would suffer another attack and pass out again. He peered at Apollyon's palm. Two small white discs sat on it.

"I contacted Lukas and he believes that pills of this sort work for us as they do for humans." Apollyon leaned over him and Veiron took the pills, holding them in his palm and eyeing them closely.

"What will they do?" He looked up at Apollyon, who had resumed his position as sentinel at the door of the small ramshackle shelter.

"Take away the pain in your head. Lukas once imbibed a large quantity of alcohol and suffered what humans call a hangover. He took human medicine and it helped ease his pain. It may do the same for whatever pain attacks you when you try to remember something."

"Do you know why I experience pain when I try?" Veiron closed his fingers over the small white pills.

Apollyon lifted his shoulders. "No… perhaps it is a curse as Marcus believes, but we did not find any marks on you."

Veiron looked down and quirked his right eyebrow. It appeared he was naked. They hadn't even left him the modest protection of his loincloth. A blanket lay over his legs but he knew that beneath it he was as nude as the day he had been reborn.

"Did Erin assist you in this?" His cheeks heated at that thought.

"No." Apollyon shook his head and then jerked it towards Veiron. "Take the pills."

Veiron didn't trust them or Apollyon, but he did as instructed, tossing the two pills into his mouth and swallowing them. They were hard to get down and stuck in his throat.

"How's the patient?" Erin's soft voice drifted through the open end of the shelter and she appeared in view behind Apollyon, carrying a round brown object with a flat top.

"Having difficulty swallowing," Apollyon said and she frowned up at him.

"I thought I said to give him the pills with liquid?" She clucked her tongue in reprimand and Apollyon's expression remained unapologetic.

Erin stepped into the shelter and knelt beside Veiron. He grabbed the blanket over his legs, holding it to him so he didn't accidentally flash her, and then remembered that they had apparently been lovers. That certainly would have entailed her seeing him naked.

A brief image of her riding him flashed across his eyes and fire swept through his blood, shooting it all in one direction. His groin.

Veiron pooled some of the blanket over his crotch so she wouldn't see the change happening to his body. She didn't seem to notice. She held the brown round object out to him.

"Drink this," she said and he took it in one hand, keeping the other firmly over himself, and looked into the hole in the top.

"What is it?" He sniffed. It smelled strange.

"Coconut. They grow on the island. I knocked it off a tree."

"How?" Veiron lifted it to his lips and drank the liquid. It tasted better than it smelled, and it dislodged the pills that had stuck in his throat.

"With my power. I'm trying to learn how to control it. When I can control it, I'm going to kill my father and then I'm going to kill your boss and this whole stupid game will end."

Veiron choked on the coconut liquid. Erin quickly took it from him and patted him on the back. Her patting gradually slowed until she was resting her hand on his flesh. His bare flesh. He pulled more covers over his crotch.

"Should I leave you two alone?" Apollyon's grin was nothing short of salacious. "It seems Veiron would like to refresh some of his memories."

Erin raised her eyebrows so they disappeared under her fringe. "I don't get it."

Apollyon's blue gaze flicked down to Veiron's hand and Veiron cursed him for drawing her attention there. Her eyes drifted to the blanket pooled over his lap. They widened. Her cheeks darkened. Her gaze shot to the coconut balanced on her lap.

The dark angel chuckled, turned and walked away, leaving him alone with Erin.

She continued to stare at the coconut. "At least part of you remembers me."

The stain colouring her cheeks darkened. His face heated too. As a newly reborn angel, he had no knowledge of carnal matters, although if Erin was to be believed, he might know more than he remembered.

His gaze settled on her mouth, his breathing accelerated, and he found himself desiring to lean towards her and capture those soft pink lips with his own. He wanted to kiss her.

He couldn't. He was here for answers. The truth.

His becoming intimate with her could be exactly what she had planned. She may have lured him here with a false promise of answers so she could work another spell on him, bringing him under her command and turning him against Heaven.

Her eyes shifted to meet his and then dropped to her lap again. The dark circles beneath them were worse now and her skin seemed even paler in the low light.

"Are you unwell?" he said without thinking and she shook her head once and then sighed.

"I'm not sick... I just haven't slept well since..." Tears lined her lashes and she bit her lower lip. It trembled.

Perhaps not a sickness of body but a sickness of the mind affected her. She was born of the Devil's seed and he was a being who couldn't contract illnesses. It would make sense that she was not physically sick.

"Why have you not slept well?" He dipped his head so he could see her face more clearly.

Her eyes darted to his and the pain in them spoke to his soul. "My visions are back... my nightmares. The only time they stay away is when I sleep in your arms and since you... since you... well, they're worse now. I see terrible things but none of it makes sense. I feel worse if I sleep than I do if I force myself to remain awake."

An overwhelming desire to smooth his palm across her cheek, lure her into his arms and tell her to sleep bolted through him but he tamped it down. It could be another trick. He stared into her eyes and felt the pain that glimmered there in his heart. It wasn't a trick. She looked close to collapse now and had seemed so haunted earlier on the beach.

A scared, tired woman.

Not the evil destroyer that Heaven had painted her. Just a frightened and hurt female. She didn't seem like a threat to him. He felt sorry for her. If she could not sleep, she would continue to weaken, and she would have no hope of surviving an assault by Heaven.

He recalled what she had said.

"You seek to destroy your father?" He studied her face for a reaction to that question. Her eyes locked with his, the softness in them hardening to ice. That look of sheer determination and seething hatred answered his question. "Why?"

"Because he took you from me. He used your death to awaken my powers... and I don't think it's because he wants me to be a happy independent woman. He wants those powers, or at least he wants me to use them for him somehow."

"So you intend to kill the Devil?"

"It sounds ridiculous when you say it like that." She set the coconut down, picked at the white flesh inside it, and popped a piece into her mouth and chewed it thoughtfully. "Do you think it's possible to kill the Devil?"

"No." It wasn't. Not at all. Killing the Devil would be as easy as killing God. It wasn't something that could happen. They had fought each other since time immemorial and neither of them had succeeded in destroying the other. Erin stood no chance.

That thought made him want to gather her into his arms, call his wings and wrap them around her. He wanted to tell her to forget her desire for revenge and not get herself killed for his sake. She was insane to think she could defeat them.

Veiron's head ached again. What was he thinking? She was his enemy, his mission target. He was supposed to take her into custody and up to Heaven, not protect her from his realm and her father's.

"You thought it was possible once," she said and he frowned at her. "When I first met you, you were bent on killing the Devil and God because of what they had done to you."

That shocked him. If he really had known her in the past, then he had once believed he was capable of destroying the two most powerful beings in existence.

"It is not possible. God and the Devil maintain the balance in this realm. It cannot exist without both of them." It was something fundamental that all angels learned during their first few days of life. Their duty was to maintain that balance. Had he truly desired to kill them in his previous life? Attempting such a thing was suicide.

"I miss you," she whispered and stood. She didn't look at him. She swept out of the shelter, leaving him alone.

He frowned. She missed him. Not she had missed him. She didn't consider him as being back then. Would she continue to miss him until his memories had been restored?

Veiron growled at himself. He was letting everything sweep him along when he was supposed to be getting answers. Once he had seen whatever it was that Marcus had wanted to show to him, he would know the truth. He would know whether everything Erin had said was a lie or not.

But what good would that do him?

He still wouldn't remember her.

He needed to see it though.

He focused through the dull ache in his head and scanned his surroundings. No sign of his armour. What had they done with it? It didn't matter. He closed his eyes, focused on his power and called his armour to him. His loincloth appeared first and he stood, making it easier for the pieces of his armour to appear too. His blue and silver greaves and boots covered his shins and feet. His vambraces encased his forearms, and the slats of armour appeared around his hips. His breastplate materialised followed by his back one, the two locking together over his shoulders and his ribs.

Veiron didn't call his wings. He raked his fingers through his hair and walked out onto the moonlit beach. The torches cast a warm glow on the sand around them and there was a fire to his left, circled by other shelters beneath the palm trees. Amelia sat there with Apollyon, the two of them deep in conversation. Veiron cast his gaze around, noting that he had seen neither the fallen angel nor his half-demon mistress since returning. Had they gone back to wherever they lived?

He looked up at the starry sky and wondered if he would ever be able to do such a thing. If Marcus was right and Erin was telling the truth, he would never be able to return to Heaven. He wouldn't know what to do. He searched the shore for Marcus and found Erin instead.

She stood near the water with her back to him, the waves lapping at her bare feet and her arms wrapped around herself. The moon shone down on her, silhouetting her slender body and shining through the dark material of her dress, revealing her thighs. His body responded to the sight of her and he drew slow deep breaths to calm his raging desire.

She turned at the waist and looked over her shoulder at him. He could feel her sorrow and her pain, could sense it eating away at her. There was a weight on her shoulders and it was taking its toll on her. If she did speak the truth about him, about them, and everything that had happened, then he felt sorry for her. She had been through so much but she still stood firm, resolved to face her future no matter how bleak it looked.

He admired her for that.

He walked towards her and her expression softened, her eyes sparkling with affection that he didn't deserve to have directed at him. He had come here to capture her and take her to Heaven, and she had been right, he had known that Heaven would ultimately kill her.

He no longer believed that Heaven wanted to eradicate her because she was the antichrist and in league with the Devil.

It wanted her dead because she posed a threat to it.

But she also posed a threat to the Devil.

Would her father be coming after her too or had her awakening only been part of a grander plan for her?

Her cropped black hair fluttered in the breeze, revealing the scar on her throat. Marks he had apparently placed there. He didn't remember having teeth sharp enough to leave marks like that but he had in his dream and they felt so familiar to him.

Her eyes met his and he was lost in them again, warm from head to toe, drifting towards her without realising it.

A firm hand caught his shoulder.

"Are you feeling better?" Marcus said and Veiron nodded. Marcus released his shoulder. "Then we should get going."

To Hell.

Veiron's heart pounded. He stared into Erin's eyes, hoping that she hadn't been playing him and this wasn't a trap, because he didn't think that he could bear it. Somewhere along the line, he had begun to believe her and hope that what she had told him was the truth. He wanted to be the one this willowy female loved and had shared herself with.

He wanted to remember her.

CHAPTER 32

Marcus had deemed it too dangerous for all of them to venture into Hell, so Veiron went with Apollyon. It turned out that the ruler of the bottomless pit could create a gateway to Hell and easily enter and leave it at will. Veiron knew of the area where they were heading. It was protected by angels of Apollyon's division, the only place in Hell where Heaven dared to keep a small force on standby at all times and none of the locals bothered them.

Veiron glided down on the hot air that rose from the realm far below him, his focus on the glowing orange line that marked their destination, pinned there to stop his mind from wandering back to the woman he had left on the beach above.

She would be safe with Marcus and Amelia there, but he couldn't shake the desire to return to her and see with his own eyes that she was all right.

"Not much further," Apollyon said, gruff tone conveying his dislike for the realm below them. Dislike that Veiron shared.

Hell was a dangerous place to enter, especially for an angel in his condition. Doubts filled every corner of his mind and the Devil would feed on those, using them against him, trying to sway him into falling. He would do no such thing. Erin and her comrades believed that he was destined to fall even if he devoted himself to Heaven. He had no choice in the matter. That didn't sit well with him. If it was true, he wasn't sure how he would feel. He wasn't sure how he felt about any of it.

"You are not the only angel who has had their memories tampered with by Heaven."

Veiron glanced across at his dark companion, the action causing his path to waver so his pale wings almost collided with Apollyon's black ones. He straightened his course, fixing his gaze below him again.

"What do you mean?" he said and resisted his desire to look at Apollyon when he answered.

"Heaven changed some of my memories too. It is no lie. There is an eternal game between Heaven and Hell, and Amelia is at the centre of it. Marcus is Heaven's pawn and he came close to killing Amelia, controlled by Heaven against his will. You were the Devil's player, and will always fall and pledge yourself to him. I was the one tasked with awakening Amelia from her mortal form into her angelic one." Apollyon huffed. "They forced me to kill her... shortly afterwards we realised that they had played with our memories."

Veiron's stomach twisted. He wished people would stop saying that he would fall and pledge himself in service of the Devil. It wasn't something he would ever do.

Apollyon hadn't wanted to kill Amelia either but Heaven had made him do that, if the dark angel was to be believed.

Meaning, Veiron had no choice in the matter. If Heaven and Hell decided he would fall, then he would fall. It didn't matter what he wanted or what he did.

"When we land, let me do the talking," Apollyon said and they broke out into an enormous cavern. Endless black surrounded him, broken only by boiling pits and rivers of lava. The landscape of Hell was as inhospitable and harsh as he had seen in the images of Erin.

"Perhaps I should do the talking." If Apollyon was saying that they would need to convince the contingent of angels down here to let them pass or give them access to the pool everyone was talking about then it made more sense for him to be the one to do it. After all, he wasn't on Heaven's list of wanted angels. "Just lead the way."

Veiron landed on the basalt plateau and quickly scanned his surroundings, searching for any sign of trouble. A young angel from the division of death came around a tall set of rocks directly ahead of him, a good distance away from the glowing edge of the plateau. The bottomless pit was down there. Was the Devil there now, waiting for Erin or planning something?

An urge to turn back and fly directly to Heaven shot through him and he fought it, focusing on why he was here. It wasn't the first time he had felt a strong desire to do something that didn't feel right to him, that felt as though it went against everything he wanted. It had happened several times since his failed attempt to capture Erin with Nevar.

"If you feel any weird desires, do your best to ignore them," Apollyon said, as though he had read his mind, or had he seen the struggle crossing his face? "It is not the Devil that toys with you. It is Heaven. They will have realised by now that you are missing and will seek to control you."

Control him? Just as they had controlled Marcus and Apollyon, forcing them to do things against their will? What if he discovered that Erin had been telling him the truth about everything and returned to her only for Heaven to seize command of his body and make him carry out his mission?

Would he be strong enough to fight his orders as Marcus had to protect Amelia or would he succumb to them as Apollyon had?

Veiron didn't want to find out the answer to that question. He drew a slow deep breath, held it and then expelled it and repeated the process until the urge had passed.

"It will be more difficult for them to control you when you're down here. I had expected them to exercise some manner of control over you before now. Perhaps the reason they needed to change your memories also lessens their ability to command you." Apollyon's words offered no comfort or relief. If it was Heaven commanding him to do as they bid, then they still had some power over him, enough that he might not be able to ignore his orders.

He didn't want to hurt Erin.

He scrubbed a hand down his face and furled his wings against his back. He needed to get a grip. For all he knew, Erin and everyone may have lied about everything. He couldn't believe what they had told him until he had seen it for himself.

"Where is this pool?" Veiron said, more determined than ever to see his past life and see if Erin had spoken the truth.

"This way." Apollyon pointed towards the rocks and the angel waiting there.

Veiron grabbed Apollyon's arm. The dark angel shot him a vicious glare that Veiron chose to ignore and dragged him towards the angel.

"I must see the pool. I wish to show this traitor the things he has done before taking him up to Heaven for trial." Veiron pushed past the fair-haired angel before he could respond and maintained his grip on Apollyon's arm, keeping him in front so it looked as though he was guiding him when in reality Veiron was following.

Apollyon waited until they had moved out of sight of the angel before speaking.

"You have some cheek, Rookie." He twisted his arm free of Veiron's grasp and pointed directly ahead, towards an area where pale flickering light lit the black jagged rocks. "There. Go to it and think about your past life and whatever you remember of it and it will reveal all to you."

"It cannot lie?" Veiron was sure that Apollyon wouldn't tell him if it could be rigged to lie but he had to ask.

"It belongs to Heaven but they have no control over it, not as they do the pools in Heaven that record what happens in the mortal realm and only this pool records events in Hell. Go. I will keep watch."

Veiron nodded and swallowed, his mouth dry and not from the heat of Hell. He took a deep breath to steady his nerves and choked on the acrid foul air. How in the three realms had he been able to live in this place if he had been a Hell's angel? It was horrific. He had been here mere minutes and he already longed for the cool clean air of the mortal realm or the sweeter air of Heaven.

He flexed his fingers and slowly approached the glowing pool. It wasn't large, more like a pond really. Images flickered on its still surface, the scene switching rapidly. It could show him anything he wanted to see?

He crouched beside it, his left knee on the black ground, and leaned his right elbow on his thigh. He held his left hand over the surface, palm down, feeling the temperature rising off the water shifting with the images. The speed of the change in images began to slow until they focused on one, playing it out before him as though it was what mortals referred to as television.

Erin.

She walked the moonlit shore of the island, gaze cast downwards and arms wrapped around her slender body.

He wanted to remember her.

The scene shifted, whirling back through images that he couldn't make out and then slowing to reveal Hell. Erin was alone again, sitting with her back against a black wall. The image zoomed outwards to reveal a cell with only three walls, the fourth being created by an opening that gave the prisoner the option of a long fall to their death.

He watched, curious to see what would happen to her and why she was being held. All angels suffered from severe curiosity, especially about things that were or had previously been forbidden to them. It was part of the reason he was here now, studying the past in a pool. The other part of his reason twirled when the door to her cell opened and almost fell over the edge. A man saved her. A man Veiron and all angels could recognise. The Devil.

The scene sped forwards and his gaze followed Erin throughout it and then the following ones, until the images slowed again and he saw himself standing in the doorway of her cell, a broadsword in hand, his scarlet hair long and tied back in a ponytail.

Erin hadn't lied.

He had once been a different man, but there was no proof yet that he had been a demonic angel or they had been involved with each other.

He focused and forced the scenes to leap forward, impatient to see the rest of his past life. He believed now that he had died but he needed to see that he had been with Erin and had loved her, and that she had loved him.

They disappeared from Hell in a fashion only a demonic angel could use and the images careened onwards through time, giving him a brief glimpse of himself and Erin in a mortal nightclub and then a fight with Hell's angels.

Icy claws punctured his heart.

Erin lay bleeding, cut to ribbons by a demonic angel. He had failed to protect her.

Tears blurred his vision and he blinked them away, his rage burning them up. A desire to kill and have revenge blazed through his blood but he tamped it down, watching himself act out that vengeance in the pool.

Erin hadn't lied.

He had crimson wings and the form of a demonic angel.

Yet she still looked at him with love in her eyes.

She stood on a bed in a pale-coloured room, her arms open to him, and accepted him with a kiss.

The rush of images of them together that followed it both transfixed and angered him, saddening and warming him at the same time. It was strange to see himself looking so different to his current appearance, and to see himself fighting so fiercely to protect the petite woman who looked at him with so much love and devotion even though he was demonic.

Veiron knew deep in his heart that her desire for him then hadn't been born of her link to Hell, to the realm surrounding him now. She hadn't known that she had the Devil in her blood.

He saw her pain and confusion as her visions revealed her unknown power, and she unleashed them on the angel he knew as Nevar. She hadn't lied about that either. They had fought on a rooftop in a city because Nevar had sought to take her to Heaven, to take her from him. She had attacked the angel with her power, protecting Veiron and forcing the angel to retreat.

Nevar couldn't remember it, so Heaven must have tampered with his memories too.

Veiron's anger spiked back up but faded again when the scene shifted and he saw himself with Erin, walking a moonlit shore hand in hand. She was beautiful as she looked at him with so much love shining in her eyes. He ached for her to look at him that way again, for her to realise that he was still the man she had loved back then, even if he couldn't remember her. He still wanted to protect her, and he was coming to care for her again.

Hell filled the pool and he witnessed the fight she had mentioned with the angels, the one he remembered in part, and forced himself to watch as he died, killed by an angel and taken back to Heaven. He didn't follow himself there though.

Veiron stayed with Erin, captivated by her and how distraught she was. Her pain beat in his heart as she suffered, held by the Devil, devastated by his death and scared by what was happening to her. Veiron frowned and held his hand closer to the pool, aching for her as she awakened, listening to everything she said to her father in that moment and wishing her faith in him had been proven true.

Her fear clawed at him as she struggled against the change and another form shifted beneath her skin, turning it dark wherever it pushed hardest.

But her suffering as she awakened was nothing compared with what came afterwards when the Devil returned her to the island and she struggled to cope with what had happened to her and Veiron's death. It tore at him and he longed to see her, wanted to reach into the pool to her and offer her comfort, needed to wrap her in his arms and protect her from all the cruelty and pain in the world.

She had suffered enough but Heaven had used him against her. They had sought to hurt her further and weaken her by sending him to capture her. They had known that she wouldn't be able to use her powers on him because she loved him.

The knowledge that they had burned away his trust in Heaven, leaving him cold to the bone and unsure of everything. He had been so certain that Erin and the others had lied, that this had all been a trap, and that Heaven was good and pure and intended only to protect the world from the danger Erin represented.

Now he was only certain that Heaven wanted her dead in order to protect itself, and it had used him and Nevar, tampering with their memories as they had tampered with others.

He felt sick.

Veiron stood on unsteady legs and let the pool switch back to showing the present Erin where she stood on a beach staring at the moon.

He needed to see her.

He turned away from the pool and walked over to Apollyon where he waited a few metres away, his back to him. When he touched the dark angel's shoulder, he turned and his blue eyes were full of compassion and understanding. He had suffered because of Heaven too.

"Have you seen enough?" Apollyon said and Veiron nodded. "Then we should leave."

It was what he wanted most.

Veiron followed him in silence, lost in his thoughts as Apollyon opened the path to the mortal realm and they flew upwards. He ached to see Erin and tell her that he knew the truth now, but he feared being around her at the same time. He wasn't sure what he would do if Heaven tried to control him and make him hurt her. He hoped he could overrule their commands and stop himself from going through with it.

The flight to the mortal realm seemed to take forever, the darkness ahead of him never ending. A cool salty breeze blew down the crevasse and Veiron breathed deep of it, using it to rid his lungs of the toxic air of Hell and soothe his pain.

Finally, he broke free of the earth and spread his pale wings to slow his ascent. The ground beneath them began to close, the sand shifting to repair the crack Apollyon had created.

Amelia and Marcus were instantly on their feet and approaching them. Apollyon landed first and Veiron was grateful when he herded them away, giving him space. Veiron landed and his gaze sought Erin. She sat at the far end of the palm-fringed beach, holding her knees to her chest, her head tipped upwards towards the starry sky.

Veiron walked the shore towards her, footsteps silent on the white sand, and focused so his wings disappeared. He sent his armour away too, replacing it with shorts similar to Apollyon's, mortal clothing. He didn't want to see his armour tonight. It was a painful reminder of what he was and what he had just witnessed.

Erin didn't look at him when he reached her.

Veiron sat on the sand beside her, unsure how to proceed. He wanted to break the silence but he couldn't find his voice. He stared at the water, watching the moonlight ripple across its black surface, and then tilted his head towards Erin.

She was beautiful, the soft silvery light of the moon turning her eyes dark and skin milky. His gaze traced her profile. Too beautiful to be born of sin and brimstone like her father. The sight of her caught his breath, stole his heart, and left him speechless. He wished he could speak to her. There were a thousand things he wanted to tell her, things that might lessen her suffering and some that would probably only worsen it. But most of all he wanted to tell her that whatever he had felt for her before his death and rebirth, he was beginning to feel for her again now.

It wasn't enough for him though. He didn't only want to feel for her, he wanted to remember her too. He wanted to remember his old feelings for her not discover new ones. They weren't the same thing. He wanted to recall everything so she wouldn't spend forever feeling as though he was no longer the man she had once loved and so she could let go of her desire for revenge.

"Did you see everything?" she whispered, never taking her eyes off the moon.

Veiron nodded. "I saw it all. I know you were telling the truth, and I am sorry for how I treated you."

"It wasn't your fault. They made you do it." She paused and sighed. "Do you know what Heaven did to you now?"

"No."

Her gaze fell to his and she frowned. "You didn't see your rebirth and what happened?"

He shook his head, took a deep breath to find his courage, and lifted his hand and gently brushed his fingers across her pale moon-kissed cheek, holding her gaze.

"I stayed with you," he said and her eyes widened. "I stayed so I could see what happened to you. I had to see it. I am so sorry."

Pain filled her eyes and her jaw trembled. He stroked her cheek, enjoying the softness of her skin beneath his fingers and calling himself cruel for using her suffering as an excuse to touch her. He couldn't help himself. He needed to touch her like this, had desired it for so long now.

"It's not your fault." She lowered her head and turned her face away from him, so his hand slipped from her cheek. His fingers instantly cooled, missing her heat. "It's their fault."

Her tone had hardened again and her anger flowed through him.

"Fighting them is not the answer." No matter how much he desired it was. He wanted to destroy both realms for what they had done to him and to Erin, and to everyone on this island.

"Yes, it is," Erin said, grim determination darkening her usually soft voice. "It is because they brought this upon themselves. They hurt Amelia and Marcus, and Apollyon. They hurt me... and they hurt you. They took you from me and I won't let them get away with that. I'm going to fight them, whether you like it or not."

She glanced across at him, eyes steely and bright.

"Will you fight with me?"

Veiron was beginning to see why he had fallen in love with Erin. She faced everything head on without flinching and was willing to take on the two most powerful beings in the world because they had hurt those she loved and wronged her. She was brave, and beautiful.

"Always." He nodded and his heart thumped harder when she smiled right into his eyes.

"You're starting to sound like your old self." Her bright tone tailed off at the end, turning sombre.

Veiron sighed and she looked away from him, raising her eyes back to the moon.

"I wish I remembered you for myself... not just saw myself with you in some pool," he whispered and she bit her lip. It trembled regardless of her attempt to stop it and he cursed himself when tears lined her eyes, sparkling like diamonds. He hadn't meant to hurt her with his words. He had wanted to be honest with her and let her know that he was here with her now, and that he wanted to be with her again. "I want to remember you, Erin."

She closed her eyes and gave an almost imperceptible nod as she swallowed.

Veiron turned his gaze to the moon and the stars, absorbing how peaceful it felt to sit with Erin. How right it felt. Would he ever regain his memories of her? Would she love him even if he couldn't? They could make new memories together but he knew she would be haunted by the ones he had lost and the past he couldn't remember.

Her fingers brushed his where they rested on the sand and he stilled as she slipped her hand into his. Veiron shifted his hand and she tensed, clutching it.

"Just let me... for a little while?" she said, voice so low that it might have been the breeze blowing in off the sea and his imagination that formed those words.

He finished moving his hand as he had intended, linking their fingers together, and glanced at her out of the corner of his eye to find her smiling at the stars.

What future could an angel and the Devil's daughter have?

Whatever that future was, whatever it entailed, he wanted it and he was willing to do anything to achieve it.

CHAPTER 33

It had been three days since Veiron had visited Hell and returned to her, aware that she had told him nothing but the truth. Those three days had been sheer torture. Erin hadn't known what to expect when Veiron finally believed her and saw his past life and his time with her, but she hadn't anticipated him coming to her and telling her that he wanted to remember her.

She hadn't expected him to hold her hand like that and sit with her in silence that had felt too comfortable.

She hadn't expected to end up resting her head on his shoulder and falling asleep on him, only to wake in her makeshift home with him lying beside her on top of the covers and still holding her hand, watching her. She had slept for fourteen hours straight and he hadn't left her side once. She had dreamed of him and those sweet dreams had torn at her more viciously than her nightmares, leaving her feeling weaker than ever. When she had looked into his eyes, he had told her that he would sleep like it again if she desired it, so she might find rest and regain her strength.

It had confused her feelings and muddled her heart, and now she wasn't sure what she was doing. The Veiron she had loved was dead and gone, but he was alive too. She couldn't deny that he was different now. The cocksure arrogant side of him seemed to have died with his demonic past and while there were glimmers of it sometimes as he spoke with the others and planned what they would do next, she still felt as though she was looking at a different person.

And then he would look at her across the group and fall silent, staring into her eyes, his dark ones so beautiful as they softened and glittered with something she could easily fool herself into believing was affection.

It killed her when he did that.

She wanted Veiron back, the one he had been before he had died and Heaven had fiddled with his mind. She had hoped he would come back from Hell and tell her that he had seen Heaven tampering with his memories and that he would be his old self if he could only get them back.

Was that too much to ask?

Erin scuffed the sand with her bare foot and basked in the sunlight, letting it wash over her in the hope it would soothe away her confusion and make everything clear to her.

Veiron wanted to remember her.

She wanted him to remember her too.

Sometimes she felt that if she just gave him a chance, she could come to love his reborn self as she had loved him before his death. It only lasted a short while though. He would do something that would remind her of how he had been before and that he would never be that man again, and it would hurt so much that she would have to leave and find some air.

That was the reason she was standing alone on the other side of the island, as far away from everyone as she could get.

Heaven and Hell had taken everything from her that day.

It had taken Veiron and replaced him with a man who left her confused and vulnerable.

It had taken her sister and her family from her. Her past.

It had left her bereft and cold inside. Dark inside. That terrified her. There were times when that darker side of her pushed and a change came over her. She fought it whenever it happened, afraid that someone would see.

Afraid that Veiron would see.

She couldn't let him witness that side of her. He was an angel again, a man of Heaven. Good. And she was evil. The old Veiron would have understood and comforted her. She could have told him all about it, even let him see it, and he wouldn't have judged her. He would have supported her. The new Veiron would want to kill her.

Erin cursed herself and scrubbed her eyes with the heels of her hands. She pulled in a deep breath and slowly exhaled. She was stronger than this. They hadn't beaten her yet. They had shaken her world and turned it all upside down, but she wasn't defeated. She could rise above this and come out of it stronger than ever.

She had come so far with her powers now that she was close to feeling ready to return to Hell for the showdown with her father that her heart demanded. If he had left her alone, she never would have gone through all this pain and suffered so much. She would have had her family still.

But she wouldn't have had Veiron.

Her heart ached at the thought of how life would have been had she not been captured and taken to Hell. She hated both Heaven and Hell for their part in what happened to her but she could never regret it because it had brought her together with Veiron and she had known true happiness.

Now she knew true pain.

Erin picked up a piece of driftwood and scribbled in the white sand with it, keeping her hands occupied while she thought about how far she had come and where life would take her next.

A storm was brewing.

Everyone on the island could sense it.

It wouldn't be long now before Heaven or Hell, or her group, made a move.

Would Veiron fight by her side when that happened?

Could she bear that?

If she saw him fight, it would only cement her feeling that he was a different person now, and that would only confuse her further and distract her, leaving her open to attack. Would Veiron protect her if that happened? She wasn't sure how she would feel if he did, or whether she wanted him to do such a thing. She wanted to scream whenever he did something that reminded her of his old self and protecting her was something he had done so often in his previous life.

"It is not safe for you to be alone."

That deep voice sent a shiver of heat over her skin and she glanced over her shoulder at Veiron, meeting his dark eyes. He stood in the shadows of the palm trees wearing only a pair of long black shorts, the gentle breeze ruffling the longer strands of his short scarlet hair. If it weren't for his hair and his lack of tattoos, she might have been able to fool herself into believing that her Veiron stood before her.

Erin looked away from him and prodded the sand with her stick.

Veiron sighed and she stilled as he approached and rounded her, coming to stand before her. She lifted her eyes to his again and caught the look in them, the one she hated most of all. He knew that she hurt whenever she saw him and his dark eyes offered a silent apology for it.

He felt sorry for her.

Erin had preferred it when he had been trying to kill her.

At least then he hadn't made her feel like some sappy girl clinging to a dead love.

"I brought you something." He held out a green coconut to her.

"I'm not thirsty," she said and looked away from it.

"Oh." He lowered it and held it in both hands in front of his stomach.

Erin refused to look at it. She could understand why he had chosen to ditch his Heavenly armour but she wished he had chosen to put on a few more clothes. His body was a distraction. Whenever she set eyes on it, she wanted to lick every ridge of muscle and nibble him in a few choice places.

"Erin, I…"

"I'm sorry, that was rude of me. It's a very nice gesture. Thank you, Veiron." Erin hastily took the coconut and didn't have the heart to tell him that she had no way of opening it and wasn't even sure it would taste any good if she did. She had only had coconuts that were darker in colour, browner on the outside.

He had brought her a peace offering though, and she had to take it, even though it only pointed out the vast differences between how he was now and how he had been.

The old Veiron wouldn't have given her such an offering. He probably would have thrown her over his shoulder, walked into the shallows and tossed her in the sea to kill her sombre mood.

No. That wasn't true. She frowned and stared down at the coconut. It began to swim in her vision as tears filled her eyes. Veiron had done something similar back in London. He had brought her fruit as an olive branch, and shortly afterwards, they had shared their first kiss.

Erin blinked away her tears. Perhaps he was more like his old self than she had given him credit for, but it didn't change how she felt about him.

"You do not want it." Veiron snatched the coconut back. "You do not need to pretend that you do."

Before she could grab it and say that she did want it really, it disappeared from his hands.

That was cheating.

He turned away from her and walked into the turquoise water, stopping when it lapped at his shins.

Was he in a mood with her now?

He huffed.

Erin growled in frustration. What did he have to be moody about? She raised her stick with the intent of throwing it at his back, and then lowered it again when it dawned on her.

Everything he knew was a lie too.

He had trusted Heaven and they had done terrible things to him. He had lost his past, just as she had.

Now, he was alone in the world and, if what Apollyon had warned her about was anything to go by, was in danger of being used against his will to harm her. She couldn't imagine how he felt but she could sympathise. She wasn't sure how to feel, and he probably wasn't either. He had seen himself with her, in love with her, a woman he had been sent to capture and probably kill. He remembered snippets of his past life but at great cost. The headaches he experienced whenever he caught hold of one of his true memories had rendered him unconscious several times in the past three days but he hadn't stopped trying to remember.

She wasn't the only one suffering because of Heaven and Hell. They were still playing with Veiron, hurting him and controlling his life.

Erin dropped her stick on the white sand, padded down the shore to him and into the shallows. The water reached her bare knees but she didn't care. She stood beside him, staring into the distance with her focus fixed on him, so he wasn't alone.

He sighed again.

Erin playfully shoved his arm.

Veiron frowned down at her.

She shoved him again.

His crimson eyebrows knitted tightly above his dark eyes as they narrowed on her. "Stop that."

Erin shook her head and pushed him harder. He must have been off balance because he lost his footing and fell in the shallow water, splashing it all up her short black dress and in her face. Saltwater burned her eyes.

She rubbed and then opened them and peered down at Veiron, afraid to see the expression on his face.

He scowled up at her, the water washing over his legs and stomach. "What was that for?"

"Sorry… it was just meant to be a nudge to make you smile. I didn't mean to push you over." She held her hand out to him. He glared at it. Erin tried to contain her smile.

"You desire to make me smile, yet by soaking me and making me look like a fool, it is you who have found your smile."

She supposed it was. Erin opened her mouth to speak and he grabbed her right ankle, yanked it up, and sent her crashing into the water. She came up spluttering, arms slapping around as small waves rolled over her.

Veiron laughed.

"Bastard," Erin muttered and sat up in the water. The waves shifted the sand and she grimaced as it found its way into her knickers. She was going to be picking sand out of naughty places for the next week, but at least Veiron was smiling again.

"Can I swim?" he said and she shrugged.

"You can snorkel, so you can swim... but I'm not sure how strong a swimmer you are. It was a house reef so it was pretty safe."

"I am going to find out." He stood and then dived into the deeper water.

When he didn't immediately come up for air, sharp needles pricked down Erin's spine. She waded out into the water, scouring it for a sign of him.

"Veiron!" She couldn't see him anywhere. Could angels hold their breath longer than mortals? Was he drowning? She hadn't swum on this side of the island before because Apollyon had warned her that the current was stronger here and had dragged him towards the edge of the reef and open sea. Her heart beat wildly against her chest and her stomach twisted. Was Veiron caught in that current? "God, Veiron... I'm coming."

She dove into the water and opened her eyes in time to see something dark right in front of her. She collided with it and it moved, and her panic spiked. Her mouth opened to let out a scream and water rushed into her lungs.

Every instinct she had said to breathe to get the water out but it only let in more. She choked on it and struggled to reach the surface, pulse racing and mind spinning and growing darker. She wasn't sure which way was up and which was down. She flailed her arms and kicked her legs, and hit something again.

Cool air assaulted her back and Erin retched, the water burning up her throat and setting her lungs aflame.

"Erin!" Strong hands lifted her higher, away from the small waves, and gently turned her face up. The sun kissed her wet skin and she continued to cough, heart thundering as adrenaline sped through her, leaving her trembling and weak. "Erin?"

She cracked her eyes open and sucked in a long wheezing breath. Veiron towered over her, scarlet hair slicked back and dark eyes wide.

"Erin," he whispered and gathered her closer to him. "I will get you to shore... keep breathing slowly. Not too much at a time."

She nodded. She could do that. In fact, it was all she could do as he carried her and carefully laid her down on the warm sand. His right arm supported her back as he knelt beside her.

"You... scared... me." She managed to get the words out and his expression softened.

"I did not mean to get in your way when you were coming to swim too." He picked damp strands of her black hair from her face and she shook her head.

Her throat blazed, as rough as sandpaper, and she cursed it. He didn't understand but it was a relief to know that she had collided with him, not something with fins and large sharp teeth.

"You..." she wheezed.

He shook his head and stroked her cheek. "You shouldn't speak. Wait."

He held his hand in front of her throat and stared hard at it. What was he doing? Her eyes widened. Warmth seeped over her neck, going deep into her flesh, and the pain eased. She looked down at his hand. Pale beams of light shone from his palm. Erin's gaze snapped up to his.

"You can heal now?" she said and her eyebrows rose at how normal she sounded and how painless speaking had been.

Veiron froze, his hand hovering above her chest, the light warming her skin and soothing her aching lungs.

"I could not before?"

Erin shook her head.

He drew his hand away and settled it in his lap. His smile was false and she could see straight through it to the pain it masked. "It seems they have made a few improvements."

Erin settled her hand over his. "They're only powers. It doesn't change who you are. My powers didn't change who I was... and Amelia's powers didn't change who she was."

"So you are still Erin... and she is still Amelia," he whispered and stared at their joined hands. "But am I still Veiron?"

Erin took her hand away and avoided his gaze. She didn't have the answer to that question and he knew it.

"Am I still Veiron to you?"

Erin closed her eyes. Her heart wanted her to say that he was still Veiron, the man that she loved, but her head said that he wasn't. She wanted to believe that he hadn't changed but the proof was right in front of her. He was different now.

But he was still the same too.

"I wish to be Veiron to you," he murmured and touched her cheek.

Erin jerked away and instantly regretted it. She opened her eyes in time to see him standing and grabbed his hand, keeping him in place.

"I'm sorry," she said and looked up at him, catching the hurt in his dark eyes. "This is still so... confusing. I know it must be confusing for you too."

He turned his face away from her, towards the sea. "Marcus says there may be a way to free my memories."

"And that's something you want?"

He looked down at her and drops of water rolled down from his hair, cutting over his cheek before dripping onto his bare chest. "More than anything, Erin. I want to be whole again... me again. I need to remember everything that Heaven erased from my mind."

How much had Marcus told him about the game? Erin hoped that he hadn't told Veiron the one sure way of regaining his memories of her and his past life. It had been Marcus who had told her how much Veiron hated that he was destined to remember everything when he fell into the Devil's service. Surely Marcus wouldn't place such an idea into Veiron's head? She wanted him back but she wouldn't put him through that and she didn't want him to choose to go through it either. He despised working for her father.

"What is it?" he said and frowned. "You know something. What is it that you know?"

"Nothing." She hated lying to him but she had to because the only alternative was telling him the truth and she couldn't let him fall again.

Not for her sake.

"Do not lie to me." He caught her wrist and pulled her up to him. Her front collided with his but he held her arm high above her head so she couldn't place any distance between them. The feel of his hard body pressing into hers with each breath stirred desire that heated her blood. Her lips parted and his gaze fell to them, burning into them with intent. She wanted that kiss that his dark eyes promised but feared it at the same time.

She couldn't do this.

Her hands heated and heart thumped, darkness obliterating the passion in her veins. Veiron's frown hardened and his gaze shifted to her hand. It began to burn. He released it and she distanced herself, partly to stop herself from giving in to her desire to kiss him but mostly because she feared her power would hurt him.

She didn't want to hurt him.

"Please, Erin. If you know of a way for me to regain my memories, then tell me how. I need to have them back... I need to remember." He reached for her but she backed away, placing more sand between them.

She ached for him.

He wanted to remember her and there had to be a way to make that happen without him falling.

Could she go to Heaven and make them give Veiron his memories back?

She almost laughed at herself. Heaven wouldn't do such a thing. It would use an entire legion of angels to weaken and capture her. It would kill her.

What about her father?

Erin's hands burned hotter and the fire spread to her chest. She clasped her hands over the spot above her heart and stared at Veiron.

The heat in her grew fiercer, blazing in her blood, and flames broke from her skin, flickering over her hands.

Her father could do something. She could go to him and offer him something, and he might give Veiron back to her.

He might grant both of their wishes.

A dark voice curled through her mind, seductive and sensual, tempting her. *Daughter.*

Erin tensed. What the hell? Either she was going crazy at last or her father had just spoken to her. If she could hear him, did that mean he could hear her? Could she talk to him about striking another deal? Did she want to do such a thing after what had happened last time?

God, what was she doing?

An unholy roar echoed around her mind. That sounded like her father all right.

Have you still not learned your lesson about that foul creature after everything you have been through? The Devil snarled in her head and she felt like telling him that she wasn't about to trust either him or the other one. *I believe you were making a deal. Something in exchange for this disgusting creature's memories.*

She nodded, still struggling to comprehend what was happening. *Do you know what Heaven has done to him?*

"Erin?" Veiron said and she didn't retreat this time. She let him close the gap between them, needing to feel him nearby.

Her father's voice echoed in her head. *Something caused him to remember you. Heaven sealed those memories to stop their pawn from disobeying. It doesn't seem to have worked. I must say, I find this turn of events most amusing. An angel longing for something born of Hell.*

Erin ignored that comment. She wasn't born of Hell. She was only born to the ruler of that realm. As far as she was concerned, she belonged in this realm, in the mortal world, and nothing would ever change that.

Can you break the seal? Her heart fluttered at the thought that he might have that power.

He snorted. *Of course.*

Then I want to make a deal.

Laughter rang in her mind. *I thought you wished me dead?*

Nothing will change that... but I might be willing to compromise if we can come to some agreement that benefits us both. I want to make a deal.

Very well. I will hear you out. Two of my finest are on their way to collect you.

Two of his finest? Hell's angels.

She hadn't meant that she wanted to go to Hell to see the Devil and do a deal in person. She wanted to do it all via the weird connection they shared. She didn't want to leave the island.

What was she doing? The Devil wasn't going to help her. He was going to get what he wanted and betray her again, just as he had before. Was it too late to change her mind?

Father?

No response. Typical. He had what he wanted and now he was going back to ignoring her. She had to think of a way out of this, because she knew in her heart that it wouldn't end well. There were Hell's angels en route to take her down to him and she didn't think they would listen to her if she said she had changed her mind and didn't want to see her father after all.

How would Veiron react when they came?

Veiron's hands brushing hers brought her back to the world and she stared up at him, mind racing as she tried to come to terms with the gravity of what she had just done. She hated the man who called himself her father and wanted to kill him, but only he had the power to restore Veiron's memories and give him what he wanted. If she had that power, she would grant his wish in a heartbeat, but she didn't. All she could do was make a deal with the Devil and pray that he didn't betray her this time.

Her chest ached, a deep throbbing that reached right down into her bones. She stared up at Veiron, afraid that this would be the last time that she saw him. The Devil would set a high price when she stood before him and pleaded him to give Veiron back that which Heaven had taken from him. She didn't want this to be their last moment together, and she would bargain as hard as she could, but she knew in the end that she would do whatever the Devil asked of her. Veiron had been through so much because of her. She had failed to save him but she could do this for him.

She could make him whole again.

"What is wrong?" Veiron whispered and moved one of his hands up to her face, holding her cheek in it. His hands were so warm, even hotter than her skin, and she closed her eyes and leaned into his touch, memorising how it felt and how it made her feel. There was love in his caress, love that she had ached to feel again since the day she had lost him, and now she was leaving him.

She wasn't sure how to answer his question. He would try to stop her if he knew what was going to happen and she couldn't allow that. She was doing this for his sake, for everyone's sake. She wouldn't just ask for Veiron's memories back. She would make everything right.

"I'll be fine soon," she said and smiled, hoping to hide the burning ache in her chest behind it.

The ground trembled and then stilled.

Veiron frowned.

The clock ticking in Erin's head sped up. This could be her last moment with Veiron. He wasn't the same man she had fallen in love with but that hadn't altered her feelings for him. She still loved him with all of her heart and nothing would ever change that, not his lack of memories or him regaining them.

She cursed fate. Why give her clarity now when she was about to leave?

The ground shook again.

It was too late now to back out.

She had to go to her father and make him do as she asked, and then she would betray him just as he had betrayed her. She would kill him.

Erin stepped into Veiron, tiptoed and captured his cheeks in her palms. She meshed their lips together, keeping the kiss soft and light, hoping that he would feel the love in it.

Veiron slid his hands over her waist and she thought he would push her away but he pulled her closer and slanted his head, returning the kiss. It was tender and sweet, and everything she couldn't take.

Erin broke away from him and ran along the sand, struggling for breath as the weight of what she had done sank down on her shoulders.

She stopped by the rocks that sheltered one side of the curved bay and turned back to face him. Veiron stood in the spot she had left him, confusion written in every feature, his hands still held out in front of him, level with where her hips had been.

Erin drew in a deep breath. The sand trembled and smaller rocks fell down the boulders behind her, clacking as they bounced down to the beach.

"Erin?" Veiron said and pain lashed at her heart.

What the hell was she doing? Was she making a terrible mistake? The Devil was partly responsible for Veiron's death and it was insane of her to think that she could strike a deal with him that would end well, with everyone getting what they wanted. Look how well her first deal had ended.

She could only think of one reason the Devil wanted her to meet him in person to discuss the terms of the deal too, and she didn't want to end up parted from Veiron and everyone. The Devil knew what Veiron meant to her and he would demand a high price for his memories. He would exploit her love for him.

What if he asked her to remain in Hell?

She couldn't let that happen, no matter what. It would hurt Veiron if he could remember her and she was no longer with him, and as an angel of Heaven, he couldn't spend his life with her in Hell. It wasn't what he wanted, and it wasn't what she wanted either. It would kill her.

She wouldn't let it happen.

The ground trembled again, stronger this time, so violently she almost lost her balance.

"I have to go now," she said and Veiron frowned and lowered his hands. Her throat tightened, chest constricting as she struggled with what she wanted to say. "Tell Amelia that I love her and that I'm glad she found Marcus, and to stay safe."

Tears lined her eyes and heat caressed her calves, hot air blowing up the skirt of her black dress. The ground bucked and shook. The stench of sulphur hit her. She could do this. She would strike a deal with her father and as soon as she knew he had upheld his part of the bargain, she would make her move. She was ready to face him and this way Amelia and the others wouldn't be in danger.

She sucked down another breath and stared deep into Veiron's eyes.

"Remember me... because I will always remember you. I love you."

Heat scorched her back and she almost fell as the ground opened behind her. Two immense Hell's angels rose out of a burning crevasse, spread their leathery wings and clamped huge black hands down on her arms. Erin panicked.

"Veiron!" She reached for him but it was too late.

The last glimpse she caught of him he was running towards her, arms outstretched, reaching for her.

Darkness swallowed her.

Erin clung to hope.

She was strong enough to do this.

She would set everything right and would strike the first blow for her side by killing her father, and when it was all over, she would see Veiron again.

She would.

CHAPTER 34

The darkness around Erin receded to reveal the place of her nightmares. A huge semi-circle of sharp black spires enclosed the paved courtyard she had seen in her visions and an obsidian fortress rose before her, reaching so high into the darkness that it blended with the black ceiling of Hell. Hot air filled her still aching lungs, making it difficult to breathe when combined with the lingering trace of her panic. She could do this. It rang in her head like a mantra, repeating over and over, giving her strength and courage.

A creak cut the silence and shredded her nerves. Erin whipped around to face the towering black doors of the fortress. They cracked open down the centre, revealing a chink of orange light that brightened as they swung apart. A break in that light caught her eye, a black shape that wavered in the heat haze and looked so small compared to the massive twin doors.

Her father.

He strode towards her and the shadows clinging to him dissipated, revealing him in all his grim glory. A smile tugged at one corner of his mouth when he spotted her, his amber eyes brightening to match the rivers of Hell and the inferno at his back.

"Daughter," he said, voice low and teasing, designed to soothe and tempt.

Everything about this man made him look as though he had been created purely for seducing mortals and leading them to their downfall, from his glossy black hair to his perfect classical features, to his sharp black suit. Whoever her mother had been, she probably hadn't stood a chance against him when he had turned on the charm.

"The one and only... or one of many?" she said, sure that there were others like her out there, the product of a seduction by the man now standing only thirty feet from her on the wide black steps that curved across the courtyard.

A flash of Veiron tumbling down those steps filled her mind but she steeled herself and refused to give in to her fears. Veiron was up on the island, away from Hell, just where she wanted him to be. She would cut her deal and do what she had come here to do and then she would return to him. Everything would be right again. She would give him back his memories.

She would save him for a change.

In a manner of speaking.

"The only one." The Devil preened his hair back and flashed a smile. "Although, it is not for lack of trying."

"I thought you couldn't leave Hell... so how did you meet my mother?"

His smile widened. "It is true that I am trapped in this realm for the time being, but that does not mean I am without a way of satisfying my needs. My men often journey to the surface to select suitable females for my entertainment."

"You're telling me you have your angels kidnap women so you can seduce them here, in Hell? Do you even give them a choice?"

"They are willing, Erin. The pleasure they experience is payment enough for what they go through afterwards."

Erin frowned. "Afterwards... as in when you send them back to Earth pregnant with your spawn?"

"I will admit that I am trying to ensure my future by fathering a child with all women who spend time in my company, but most mortals are not strong enough to carry my seed. The foetus tends to destroy them from the inside."

"You sicken me," she growled. "How can you have your lackies bring women down here for you to seduce?"

Darkness crossed his face, his amber eyes brightening to gold, and then it faded back into a fixed smile. "Whenever I am able to leave Hell, I do so and find women in the mortal realm to seduce and pleasure. Does that make it alright to you?"

"No... it's still disgusting and despicable... thank you for this whole lot of TMI." Erin frowned, repulsed by the thought of this man kidnapping and having his way with as many women as he could and the consequences of his one night stands. How many innocent women had died because of him? Her mother had survived. Had she been special somehow, able to bear this man's child without suffering the same fate as those before her? Erin trembled, afraid to ask but needing to know. She had loved the woman she had called mother, but someone else had given birth to her and she wanted to know if that woman still lived. "What about my mother?"

His smile widened. "You desire to know who she was... family ties are very important to you?"

She nodded. They were. It was the reason she hadn't been able to hold onto her anger towards Amelia and the people she had known as her parents. She still loved the woman she saw as her sister and she didn't blame her for keeping the truth from her.

He inspected his nails. "I do not know who your mother was, dearest Erin."

"Could she have survived my birth?" This wasn't why she had come. It didn't matter how many times she told herself that. She couldn't stop the questions from flowing. He shook his head, confirming her suspicions. "I killed her, didn't I?"

He nodded again. "You were destined to destroy her, whether it was during her pregnancy or during your birth. You cannot have ties to the mortal world."

"But I'm part mortal!"

He descended the first of the five steps that led down to her and shook his head again. "You are not mortal at all. Nothing was taken from your mother. No DNA... no genes whatsoever."

Erin's throat closed. "What are you saying? How is that possible? A baby shares genes with both parents."

"Under normal circumstances. You are not normal, dearest Erin. You are extraordinary. Your DNA is a perfect match for mine."

A chill skated down her spine and froze her limbs. He smiled at her, as though he was pleased she had figured it out for herself.

"I'm a vessel." God, that couldn't be right. He had wanted to take care of her, had been proud when she had exhibited powers, and had wanted her to awaken to her full potential. He had talked about changing her and doing away with her softer and more compassionate side.

Erin felt sick. She clutched her stomach and doubled over, dry heaving. Sweat broke out across her brow and she retched again, hands shaking against her belly. She clutched the damp black material of her dress and breathed slowly. It was just the saltwater that she had swallowed. She wasn't going to let this revelation stop her. She wasn't just a vessel for the Devil.

She straightened and faced him again, and caught the brief flicker of concern in his amber eyes.

"Worried your vessel is going to die?" she snapped and he raised a single black eyebrow.

"Not at all. Things are progressing faster than I had anticipated. That is all. It requires a change in my plans."

His plans? Was he going to inhabit her body and escape Hell, wreaking havoc on the world she loved, and Heaven too? Would she survive his possession?

She would never see Veiron again.

Erin bent over and threw up.

The Devil sighed. "Such a weak constitution. We shall have to do something about that."

He descended the remaining steps and his shiny black leather shoes appeared in view at the edge of her vision. She had half a mind to aim her next bout of vomiting towards them.

His hand came to rest on her shoulder, her skin instantly heating beneath it. That heat flowed into her flesh and along her limbs, coursing through her blood. The sickness wracking her faded, strength replacing it, making her feel more alive and healthier than she had in weeks.

"That is better. We need you strong, Erin. You have a responsibility to take care of your health now."

A responsibility? Erin eased herself up and wiped the back of her hand across her mouth. She didn't want to be his vessel. Was there nothing else she could do for him instead?

"Now, let us flesh out the terms of this deal," he said, his smile wicked.

He thought to betray her again by finding some loophole. She wasn't going to make the same mistakes twice. She wasn't a fool.

"You will restore Veiron's memories to him and undo whatever Heaven has done to him, and you will leave him, Amelia, Marcus, Apollyon, Einar, Taylor, Lukas and everyone they love alone. You will not raise a hand to harm them, will not command your army or anyone to do any such thing, and you will not use me against them." Erin held his gaze, unwavering, strong, showing him that she had grown up a lot since the last deal she had made with him and she was wise to his tricks now. "In exchange, I will join your side and pledge myself to you... but only if I see they are safe and well, and are unharmed. If anyone goes after them or harms them, then this deal is void."

He grinned. "Erin, you speak as though you do not trust your own father. You do not get to set all the terms. I swear to do all that you ask... but are you prepared to do all that I ask?"

She was, but she wasn't really going to go through with it. She would wait to see if he kept his end of the deal and then she would find a way to go back on the whole thing and kill him.

"In exchange for the safety of those you have mentioned and those they love and those you love, you will provide me with a vessel in the mortal and angelic realms," he said and she nodded, her heart thumping against her ribs. She had no intention of doing any such thing. "In exchange for Veiron's memories, you will surrender yours."

Erin froze. Her heart stopped. Hands shook. Skin prickled with ice.

What?

He wanted to take her memories from her. He had seen through her. If he took her memories in exchange for restoring Veiron's, she would forget everything. She wouldn't remember him and her friends. She wouldn't remember this deal. She wouldn't remember her plan to destroy the Devil.

She couldn't agree to that.

She didn't want her friends to suffer anymore or Veiron to live life feeling he wasn't a whole person, but she couldn't sacrifice herself to achieve those things.

Could she?

"What if I say no?" she whispered, knowing she was showing her weaker side by asking such a question.

The Devil shifted his hand to her face. "I will kill your friends one by one until you agree."

She swallowed. She couldn't stand by and let her friends die because she was afraid. The Devil wanted her alive, as his vessel in the mortal and angelic realms. That meant that in Hell she would be herself, didn't it?

"That isn't fair. I need more details," she said and he huffed.

"Fine. What do you want to know?" He waved his hand and his obsidian throne appeared. He arranged himself on the seat, crossed his legs at the knee and stared at her.

What did she want to know? She needed specifics. This wasn't the sort of decision she could just leap into. If she did, she was likely to end up as a soulless carcass that couldn't think or feel. She was striking a deal and it was time to negotiate.

"Will I forget everything?" she said and he nodded. "Unacceptable. I refuse to agree to that. I want to remember everything whenever you're not in my body."

"Unacceptable," he countered. "A compromise is necessary. What you ask for cannot be done. I must have something in exchange for Veiron's memories."

As far as she could see, he was getting something in exchange. He was getting her body as a vessel. What else did he want from her?

"Why take my memories?" She couldn't get past that. What advantage did he gain from taking her memories other than stopping her from attacking him and backing out of their deal? That was reason enough, she supposed. "What if I offer something else in exchange? There has to be something else you want."

"Veiron's head on a spike?" He smiled and she wanted to punch him for finding the image of Veiron's head separated from his body amusing.

"I will attack Heaven for you and then if you still want to use me as a vessel, I will go along with that too."

His eyebrow quirked again. "An interesting proposition. Go on."

"I will stand at the head of your army and take on your greatest foe. You said it yourself. I'm basically a clone of you. So I can use the same powers as you, right? So there's no need for you to go to Heaven in my body and risk yourself. I can attack it tomorrow and voila, it's game over and score one for Hell."

The Devil eased onto his feet and stared at her. "Tomorrow? You are inexperienced in battle but attacking them now does give us an advantage. They will not be expecting it. I will accept but on these terms. In exchange for Veiron's memories, you will lead my army on a direct assault on Heaven with the aid of him, Marcus, Amelia and Apollyon. If you succeed, they will gain their freedom. I will no longer pursue them."

Erin exhaled slowly. That was a little more than she had bargained for. She couldn't speak for everyone like that.

"All of them will be protected by Hell from Heaven? If any of them are hurt or die, the deal is over, busted, totally dead." She held his amber gaze, hoping he couldn't see straight through her façade to the fear in her heart.

He studied her in silence and then sighed. "Fine. I will assign my men to flank them at all times and will remove them from the battle if they are in danger of dying. I have one more caveat."

His expression gave nothing away and she feared what his request would be. She was already giving him so much. Now the bargain had become one just for Veiron's memories. The safety of those she loved was no longer guaranteed. She hated him for playing her again. He was doing it on purpose. He knew that she would do whatever he asked to free Veiron's memories and he was bleeding her dry. What else could he possibly need from her? He already had her as a vessel and she and her friends attacking Heaven.

"You will not turn your power on me." Those words were dark, spoken on a low growl, and his amber eyes burned like fire, scorching hers as they held them.

Bugger.

Erin swallowed and then started pacing across the black basalt slabs. There was no way she could keep still, not when she was bargaining with everyone's lives without their permission. She sucked in a deep breath and exhaled it, trying to find some balance. It was too much. He wanted too much. The others would never agree to it and if they didn't help her, then the Devil would see the deal as broken and would take Veiron's memories again, or worse.

"It's too much. I can't." She stopped and turned to face him. He scowled at her. "I'm sorry. I can't speak for them. There has to be something else... another way to make this deal work."

He stared at her in silence, eyes bright and focused on her. She had to think of another way because she couldn't put everyone at risk without their permission.

"How about this? You don't lay a finger on the people I mentioned, those they love and those I love, and you restore Veiron's memories. I'll be your vessel, but I will keep my memories, and I will serve you. I won't attack you and will remain in

Hell for half the year. The other half I can spend in my realm, with Veiron and my friends. I will also speak to the others about attacking Heaven for you."

He sighed. "This does not sound like a good deal to me, Erin. I will give you two choices and then you must decide. If you do not choose one, then I will send my men to kill the first of your friends."

Erin swallowed. The look in his eyes said that he was serious. He was going to get what he wanted, even if he had to bully her into it.

"Your first choice is this. You, Veiron, Apollyon, Amelia and Marcus attack Heaven with my army. I offer them no protection during the battle. If you succeed and they survive, they are free and I will not pursue them, and will restore Veiron's memories. If I have need of you in the future, you will all fight for me again, without question. If I have need of a vessel, you will provide me with one."

That deal sounded far worse than the one he had offered her before and she had the terrible feeling that his offers would continue to grow worse until she gave up and just agreed to anything he demanded.

"But I don't have to remain here when you don't need me?" she said and he nodded. "And my second choice?"

"I will restore Veiron's memories and will not seek to harm those you mentioned, those you love and those they love. In exchange, you will provide me with a vessel and remain here in Hell with me, in my fortress, under lock and key. You will remember everything but you will not be able to attack me. You will serve me and obey my every order, as a doting daughter should. You will never see those you love or your friends again."

Erin thought it over. Door number one meant putting everyone's lives at risk without their permission, and not just once but whenever the Devil demanded it, but it did mean she would be able to live with Veiron and everyone in the mortal realm. Door number two meant everyone would be safe, Veiron would be whole again, but she would be stuck in Hell. In the Devil's fortress no less. Plus, it sounded a lot like he was planning on using the obey clause to make her do everything he commanded. What if he commanded her to do things she didn't like? What if he ordered her to forget?

God and the Devil could make their angels do things against their will, and they remembered what they did, and hated themselves for it.

And there was that vessel issue too. Something told her that when the Devil occupied her body, she would be in there with him, witnessing every horrific act he carried out, feeling endless darkness and evil flowing through her. Could she experience such a thing and not lose a piece of herself in the process? Would exposure to all that horror eventually destroy her?

She closed her eyes and hung her head.

She had never wanted to hurt anyone, had never thought her normal life would turn into this and she would become the antichrist. She had never thought she would meet a man like Veiron.

"I am waiting, Erin. I have given you choices, something I have never done for another, and now you must make your decision. The fates of your friends are in your hands."

She clenched her fists. She couldn't bear the thought of forcing everyone she loved and her friends to fight on the Devil's side against Heaven, but her only other choice was to become the Devil's slave and live in his fortress, and she would never see them again. There was no way Veiron would be able to reach her, and Marcus would never allow Amelia to try either. The Devil would find a way to attack them should they try. She knew it in her heart.

She didn't know what to do.

But she had to do something.

She had the power to save everyone, to protect them all from whatever terrible future fate had in store for them.

Erin raised her head, opened her eyes and held his gaze.

She could do this.

She could sacrifice herself for the greater good.

CHAPTER 35

Veiron skidded to a halt on the hot sand, his eyes wide and arms still outstretched. Heat curled up from the glowing crack in the ground and he stared at the place Erin had been, replaying how she had reached for him and called his name. He had reacted on instinct, his desire to protect her seizing him so fiercely that he had obeyed in an instant, running for her, determined to save her from the two demonic angels that had come for her.

He breathed hard, bare chest heaving, and lowered his gaze to the glass fault line in the sand.

Erin had known they were coming.

Why hadn't she told him?

He unleashed a growl of frustration and called his weapons to him.

He frowned at the black and red double-ended spear in his grasp.

This was not his weapon.

Or was it?

With another growl, he threw it into the sand, so hard that the blade at one end disappeared completely. The white sand around it fizzled and melted.

What the fuck was going on here?

Veiron reeled at his use of the profanity. That wasn't like him.

His head split and he dropped to his knees, doubled over and clutched it in both hands. He gritted his teeth and growled again. The pain eased but he stayed where he was, curled up and staring at his knees, trying to make sense of everything.

Why hadn't Erin told him that they were coming for her? He could have protected her. He would have fought the two Hell's angels for her and stopped them from taking her down to her father. Her father. He frowned and then screwed his eyes shut. She hadn't.

She couldn't have.

He wouldn't let her.

Voices broke the steady sound of his breathing and the gentle waves caressing the shore to his left.

The others were coming.

Veiron picked himself up off the sand, dusted it off his knees and pulled the spear from the sand. He would need his armour and would need Apollyon to open a gate for him. First, he had to deliver Erin's message.

Amelia and Marcus ran towards him, their fear evident in their expressions and the panicked edge to their eyes as they darted around, searching the area. When Amelia's gaze came to rest on him, she stopped dead and Marcus almost slammed into her.

"Where did you get that?" Amelia's voice was hoarse and she stared wide-eyed at the weapon in his hand. "Oh my God... where's Erin?"

Tears lined her grey eyes and she stormed towards him.

"Did they take her? Why didn't you stop them? Did you let them take her, you bastard? I knew no good would come of trusting you!" She punched him hard on the jaw and he stumbled to his right, put his foot out to stop himself and straightened.

He turned on her, fury boiling in his veins, burning from her accusations and her attack on him.

"She knew they were coming," he snapped and pushed her away from him. "She didn't tell me. She distanced herself so I couldn't reach her in time to stop them."

"It's still your fault!"

Veiron snarled. "Why don't you just back the fuck off?"

Her eyes shot wide again. "What did you just say?"

"I said back the fuck off. I have this. Apollyon can open a gate and I am going down there to kick the snide little fucker's arse and get her back."

Everyone stared at him now.

"What?" he bit out and they all jumped, even Apollyon.

"Are you feeling alright?" Marcus said and eyed him closely.

Veiron's shoulders itched but he ignored his wings. They would have their freedom soon enough. Right now, he needed to focus on getting a gate to Hell open.

A blast of heat hit his back, sending him tripping forwards. Marcus caught him and Veiron straightened, intending to thank him for the catch, but found Marcus staring beyond him, sheer disbelief in his pale blue eyes.

He turned to see what all the fuss was about.

A white portal blazed above the spot where Erin had disappeared.

"Did you do that?" Marcus said, tone low and filled with caution and curiosity.

"I do not think so." Veiron walked towards the portal and reached his free hand out towards it. It radiated heat at such a temperature that he was sure it would burn him if he moved any closer than a metre.

"Where did you get the weapon?" Marcus's voice hadn't grown any less curious.

Veiron looked down at the double-ended spear in his right hand. "I think it's mine."

"What the hell?" Amelia said and he glanced over his shoulder at her. The moment his eyes met hers, her anger and confusion melted into fear that stabbed him in the heart. "You don't think…"

He nodded. "I think Erin has cut a deal."

Amelia shook her head. "She wouldn't. Not after what happened last time."

"You are right. This is my fault. I talked to her about how I wanted my memories back and she went to see her father." Veiron stared at the spear, not wanting to see the hurt and fear in Amelia's eyes. "I will fix this."

"I do not think this is a case of her merely getting your memories back. Can you remember anything?" Apollyon approached him, his height and breadth giving him a formidable appearance despite his casual attire. Veiron shook his head. He couldn't remember anything more than he already did. "You died. Up until now I thought that Heaven had simply changed your memories but something else is at work here."

Marcus stepped forwards. "Apollyon is right. You shouldn't be able to wield a demonic weapon and create a portal."

Veiron looked back at the portal in question and then down at the spear. They were both right. They had thought Heaven had changed his memories because he had remembered something about Erin but that couldn't be the case, or it wasn't the only thing they had done to him. He had the power to create a portal to Hell as he had seen himself do in the memories the pool had shown him and had the same weapon as he'd wielded as a demonic angel.

"I need to see what happened after my death," Veiron said and leapt into the portal.

He landed hard on the black basalt ground of Hell and rolled onto his feet. The portal behind him didn't close. It burned hotter and brighter, and Amelia, Marcus and Apollyon tumbled through it. Apollyon landed on his feet as though he had jumped through portals a thousand times. Amelia landed in a heap and Marcus hit the ground beside her. He was first onto his feet and helped her up.

"You were not supposed to follow me." Veiron huffed and scoured the area. They were on the plateau near the bottomless pit. It made sense that his portal would bring him here. It was the place he had been thinking about when he had leapt into it. It was the only place in Hell he knew.

Or at least could remember.

"Well, we're here now, so live with it." Amelia pressed her hands into the small of her back and arched forwards. She sighed as though whatever had been bothering her had cracked back into place. "I need a new outfit… one suitable for kicking butt."

Her summer dress disappeared, replaced by a flowing white garment that wrapped around her body and faded to blue at the hem midway down her thighs. Silver armour edged with blue appeared over her chest, moulded to the shape of her breasts, and encased her back. Strips of armour melted into existence over her hips and then white boots appeared, followed by greaves to protect her shins. The last pieces of armour to appear were her vambraces, wrapping around her forearms. She unfurled her silvery half-feather half-leather wings and flapped them.

Marcus had changed into his armour too and his eyes swirled silver-blue as he scanned the area, remaining close to his love.

Apollyon switched his clothes in the manner of someone who had long ago tired of the theatrics and found it boring and tedious now. One moment he was wearing jean shorts, and the next he was in his gold-edged black armour. His black wings erupted from his back, their span more impressive than Amelia's smaller wings, and even Marcus's.

Veiron couldn't compete either and he didn't need his wings yet so he held them at bay. He focused and switched from his casual mortal attire into his blue armour.

It was darker than before, closer to midnight blue rather than royal blue.

Something definitely wasn't right and he was going to find out what the fuck it was. He growled and sheathed his spear at his waist.

"Now, there is anger in its purest, most undiluted, and beautiful form."

Veiron snapped around to face the owner of the voice and found himself staring at Apollyon. He sat on one of the tall domed black rocks that surrounded the pool, one leg bent at the knee and one trailing down his makeshift throne. Only something was off about him.

Veiron had watched his armour materialise on him not a minute ago but now he only wore his loincloth and the strips of metal that covered it were tattered and old, and his black greaves and boots. His hair was shorter and wild, and his eyes were golden.

Not Apollyon.

He grinned at Veiron and tugged on a thick black chain. Someone groaned. Veiron's gaze shot down and widened.

"Nevar!" he said and tried to race forwards to help the guardian angel but the real Apollyon caught his right arm and held him back.

Veiron tried to shake him, intent on freeing the guardian angel from the chain that wrapped around his bare bloodied chest, circled his neck, snaked up his injured arms and bound his wrists above his head. A short length of chain ran up the rock and ended in a huge black metal ring driven into the top of it near the man who looked like Apollyon. Nevar's feet dangled a few inches from the ground. How long had he been chained, suspended against the rock? Half of his armour was missing, only the pieces around his hips remaining and one of his greaves. The other was gone, leaving his right shin exposed, and his boots were gone too, as were his wings. Veiron hoped Nevar had merely hidden them to stop his foe from harming them. Lacerations, blood and bruises marred every inch of his body. Veiron growled, his anger spiking at the sight of an angel in so much pain and distress.

The man holding him grinned and yanked the chain again, tearing another pained moan from Nevar.

"You know this wretch?" The man's smile held and Veiron had never seen such pure evil. It shone in his golden eyes as he turned them on Nevar, grinning down at him. Pride fluttered across his face and he reached down and stroked Nevar's bruised and swollen cheek. The white-haired angel tried to move out of reach of the man's caress but the chain bit into his neck, choking him.

"Let him go." Apollyon's voice boomed around the black cavern.

Nevar's green eyes slowly opened and settled on Veiron. He swallowed and his hands twitched, and then he tried to catch the chain. The man holding him pulled on the chain again, stretching Nevar's arms, and he cried out, his scream echoing for long seconds after he had bitten his tongue to silence himself.

"Let him go." Veiron drew his spear. "Or I swear I will butcher you."

The man laughed and kicked Nevar in the head, ripping another cry from him. "No… I do not want to release him."

He turned his focus on Apollyon.

"Brother," he said and Veiron looked at Apollyon out of the corner of his eye. The dark angel glared at the man.

"Never call me that." Apollyon drew one of his golden swords out of the air.

The man shrugged, shifting his black wings. "Perhaps you are more like a father."

Apollyon growled and the air around him thickened, flooding Veiron with a sense of his immense power. "Definitely never call me that. Release the angel, Asmodeus."

"No." Apollyon's doppelganger shook his head. "I like him where he is. The angel was prying, seeing things that he did not like. I will make him forget."

Nevar bucked and pulled at the chain, pushing himself up the rock with his bare feet. "No. I don't want to forget... not as Veiron has."

"Be quiet." Asmodeus pulled the chain again and it tightened around Nevar's throat. He looked down at the guardian angel.

Apollyon roared a battle cry and attacked. The doppelganger snarled, released Nevar's chain and a sword materialised in each of his hands. He launched himself from the rock and crashed into Apollyon. Apollyon rolled with him, avoiding his blades, and came out on top. He kicked off, spread his huge black wings and beat them, flying towards the edge of the plateau.

Asmodeus followed him.

Marcus and Veiron stared after them.

"I'll explain about him later," Amelia said and rushed over to Nevar. She drew a silver sword out of the air and brought it down hard, smashing the chain. Nevar fell to the ground in a heap, wheezing as he fumbled with the chain.

Veiron carefully removed it from his bloodied wrists, his arms and bruised neck. Marcus stood with his back to them and his two curved silver blades in his hands, watching the fight between Apollyon and his twin, guarding them all, and Veiron was grateful. Time was of the essence. He needed to make sure that Nevar was going to be all right and then he had to see what Heaven had done to him. Once armed with that knowledge, he would go after Erin. He needed to see it first though, was sure that it was crucial he know now what had happened to him because he shared Apollyon's suspicion that Heaven hadn't changed only his memories.

"What happened?" Veiron said as he finished removing the chain and cast it aside.

"I saw it all," Nevar whispered, voice hoarse. He struggled to breathe without coughing and sat back, leaning against the rock. He closed his eyes and sighed. "I needed to know the truth. I came here and found the pool. I saw, Veiron. They made you forget."

"I know." Veiron laid his hand on Nevar's bare shoulder and wished there was something he could do to ease the angel's pain. He glanced at his hand. He could heal him.

He drew a deep breath and focused on his hand. The wounds beneath it healed and he moved his hand, sweeping it over only the deepest cuts and then the black bruising around Nevar's neck, until they began to heal and fade.

"I wish I could do more," Veiron said and curled his fingers into a fist. "I cannot spare the strength though. I must find Erin."

"You knew her." Nevar slowly lifted his hand and rubbed his throat. "When you were reborn. You remembered her and everything about your past life. You weren't reborn as you should have been. Something interfered with it."

"What?" Veiron frowned at him and Nevar waved to his left, towards the pool. "I think I know. I will show you."

He knew? Veiron helped him stand with Amelia's assistance and carefully placed his arm around Nevar's waist. He guided him around the corner and halted.

"He killed them before turning on me," Nevar whispered and Veiron looked away from the three dead angels strewn across the rough basalt ground. "He does something that stops them from being reborn."

Veiron nodded and helped Nevar towards the pool. Apollyon had defected but Veiron was sure that he would destroy whatever evil he was fighting if he saw the dead angels. The man still felt some allegiance to Heaven and his kind, and no angel wanted to face true death. These angels would have fought the monster that looked like Apollyon because they believed they would be reborn if they died. It would have given them courage. Now, God only knew where they were. Were they dead, their souls caught in limbo forevermore? He shuddered at the thought of suffering such a fate.

Nevar collapsed in front of the pool and held a trembling hand out over it. The images rippling across its surface shifted to reveal the same moment that Veiron had witnessed. He was walking a moonlit shore with Erin, holding her hand.

The scene continued past what he had seen in the pool before and he watched it playing out.

Nevar pulled his hand away from the pool and the image froze on one of Veiron kissing Erin.

"How did this interfere with my rebirth?" Veiron frowned at the image and what he had seen. "I can't see how it could have."

"Neither did Heaven." Nevar slumped backwards, sitting on his feet. "You bound yourself to a power, one independent of Heaven and Hell. Heaven didn't realise it. It is a weak contract as it is though. She did not have enough power at the time to bind you to her in a lasting way. Each day sees the contract weaken."

Veiron wasn't quite following. He stared at the image of them kissing, the words they had spoken to each other playing on repeat in his mind. They had pledged themselves to each other for eternity. "Are you saying I wasn't reborn as an angel of Heaven?"

Nevar nodded.

"But my appearance?" Veiron looked down at his armour and then at the spear.

"The work of Heaven. See for yourself." Nevar motioned towards the pool.

Veiron leaned over it and held his hand out above the surface. He needed to see his death again and follow himself this time. He had to see what Heaven had done to him.

The images swept forwards and he didn't slow when he saw himself fighting the angels and then his death. Heaven burst into view and he watched in horror as he was reborn in the same form he'd had before death and the angels killed him again.

It didn't affect anything.

He came back as he had been before, only his eyes were no longer crimson. They were golden with scarlet flecks running through them.

Heaven killed him again.

And again.

Veiron's stomach twisted and turned, and he bit back his fury and his need to destroy Heaven for what they had done to him. After his fifth death, when he lay drenched in blood and weakened, they stripped him of his armour, broke his scarlet wings and tore them from his back, and chained him. He growled the whole time he watched them changing him, sending angel after angel to use their talents on him, erasing his memories and altering his appearance.

He didn't want to see any more.

He turned away and Amelia was there, her grey eyes soft with compassion.

"Veiron," she whispered and he shook his head and stood.

Now wasn't the time for this. Erin was in danger and he had to find her and save her. He had to stop her from giving the Devil what he wanted. She was his to protect.

Mine.

She was his master.

Apollyon rounded the corner, one arm braced across the throat of his twin, the other clutching the end of the chain that now restrained him, wrapped tightly around his broad chest and pinning his arms to his sides. Asmodeus snarled and writhed, cursed them all in a black tongue that Veiron understood. The language of Hell.

"What were you doing here?" Apollyon said and his twin laughed. He tightened his arm across his throat, cutting off the evil angel's air supply, and then loosened it again. "Tell me."

"My master told me to guard the pool, so I guard the pool." Asmodeus struggled again and then relented when Amelia drew her sword and aimed the tip of it at his stomach. "He desires all angels are kept occupied while he tends to a certain delicate matter with his daughter."

"Where is Erin!" Veiron burst forwards and grabbed the chain around the man's chest. He dragged him from Apollyon's grip, getting in his face, and growled. "Tell me where she is."

The man smiled cruelly. "I would not disturb them. My master would not be pleased. It takes a lot of focus to inhabit the body of another, even if it is your own flesh and blood."

Veiron raised his spear.

Apollyon's twin ducked to evade his strike and twisted. The chains binding him blazed red-hot and Veiron cried out as they burned his hand and released them. A gust of wind hit him and he raised his head in time to see the man lifting into the air. Veiron growled. He would pay for that.

"Leave him," Apollyon said, deep voice deceptively calm. "You are no match for him and time is of the essence. You must reach Erin in the pit before she does something we shall all regret and the Devil gains control of her."

Veiron toyed with telling him to go to Hell and then thought the better of it. He needed to reach Erin. His male pride would have to wait. She was more important than proving Apollyon wrong about his strength by defeating his doppelganger. He snarled, turned away from the dark angel and unfurled his wings.

They weren't completely silver-blue. Some of the feathers were lilac, as though his original crimson wings were trying to break through.

If he had contracted with Erin and had been reborn as her servant upon death, then he would have expected his appearance to change, as Marcus's had when he had contracted with Amelia. Marcus had explained that he had been a guardian angel once and Amelia had become his master. That was why Marcus had wings like her. Had Erin truly liked his demonic appearance and hadn't wanted to change it, not even subconsciously? He smiled at that. It was just like her to accept everything about him and not want to alter him. He beat his wings and took off, heading towards the edge of the plateau.

Amelia and Marcus followed him. Apollyon shouted something foul in the language of Hell and went after his doppelganger.

Veiron kept low to the ground, beating his wings as quickly as he could, determined to reach Erin before she allowed the Devil to inhabit her body. The edge of the plateau zoomed towards him, the abyss beyond it glowing fiercely. Heat washed over him and the air thickened, the humidity making it difficult to breathe when combined with the stench of sulphur. He shot over the edge, spun in the air and dove. The hot air buffeted him and he wove around the strongest currents, spinning and twirling, his wings pinned back to maximise his velocity. The ground hundreds of feet below came up fast.

He spun in midair just twenty feet above a black and orange river of lava and flapped his wings. Fire broke from the surface, barely missing his legs, and he stretched his wings wide, catching the thermals and using them to his advantage. He sped over the cragged black landscape of Hell, over the heads of demons that clawed the air in an attempt to grab him and spat black words when they missed, his eyes pinned on the distance and the immense black fortress that rose up to pierce the cavern of Hell.

Erin.

He was coming for her.

"Veiron, slow down," Amelia called after him but he didn't relent. He flapped his wings again and again, picking up speed, intent on reaching Erin before it was too late. He didn't care if he had to go one on one with the Devil. He had to reach her.

He rolled in the air to avoid a spire of black rock and shot upwards, over the huge spikes of obsidian that surrounded the fortress.

His gaze sought Erin.

She stood in the middle of the courtyard, facing the Devil.

They were still separate.

"Erin!"

She whirled to face him and he shot downwards, landing so hard behind her that he shattered the black slabs that paved the courtyard. He rose to his feet and drew his spear.

"Erin," he said and her amber eyes met his.

A huge blast of black energy struck him in the chest, sending him careening into the wall of rock encircling the area. He grunted on impact and again when he smashed into the ground. Veiron pushed himself up onto his knees and then stood, unfurled his wings and beat them. He shot towards Erin and she reached for him. Another blast slammed into him and he crashed into the wall again, hard enough this time that the spire of black rock shattered and rained down on him, burying him.

Every bone burned in agony and fire filled his veins, stealing his strength. He pressed his hand against his chest and focused, using his ability to heal to dull the pain, and then pushed the rocks off him and wobbled to his feet.

"I will not let you stop me," Veiron snarled and skidded down the black rocks to the courtyard. He stalked towards Erin.

The Devil growled. "You always were a stubborn maggot."

"Erin." Veiron ignored him and reached his left hand out to her, clutching his black and red spear in his right. "Come back to me. Forget all this. I know what happened to me now, Erin. I saw what Heaven did to me."

"I can't," she whispered and wrapped her arms around herself. "I made a deal."

Veiron halted. "No."

The Devil smiled. "Yes. You are too late. She has already agreed to my terms. You should be happy. She does this for your sake."

Veiron growled at him and swept his right hand out, causing the black rod of his double-ended spear to extend. The twin blades glowed crimson.

Erin stared at it and then at his armour. "I don't understand."

"Heaven did not only change my memories, Erin. It changed my appearance too... but the more time I spend with you, the weaker their hold on me becomes... but your hold on me is weakening too."

She shook her head, her black eyebrows furrowing so they disappeared beneath her fringe. "I still don't understand."

The Devil laughed, disappeared and reappeared right behind Erin. He reached around her and stroked her cheek, and she swallowed, fear brightening her eyes.

"This is somewhat annoying and unexpected, but it does not matter now. She is mine. There is nothing you can do about it." The Devil ran the backs of his fingers down her cheek again and Veiron's blood boiled.

"Let her go." He stormed towards them and the Devil held his left hand up.

Black flames danced across his fingers and wrapped around his palm like ribbons. Veiron halted again. One more blast of the Devil's power, and he would probably end up back in Heaven. Using his healing ability to stifle his pain drained him of strength. He couldn't afford to attempt to heal himself again.

Veiron lowered his spear. "Use me instead. Let Erin go and I will take her place."

"No, Veiron." She struggled against the Devil and managed to escape his grasp, only to be caught and pulled back against him. "You hate what they do to you. When you fall, you remember everything, and you hate the game they play with you and the fact that you are always destined to fall even when you love Heaven so much. I don't want you to go through that again."

He smiled at her, silently thanking her for caring about him enough to be here trying to regain his memories for him so he didn't have to fall. He wished she had told him this earlier though, back on the beach before she had contacted her father. He might have done then what he would do now, and could have spared Erin the torment of dealing with her father. If he would remember everything by falling, then he would do just that. His contract with Erin would keep him from truly being the Devil's servant and they could escape this place and cement their bond. He could trick the Devil into giving him back his memories.

"It is my choice this time, Erin." Veiron focused and shortened his spear, and sheathed it at his waist. He held his empty hands out. "I will pledge myself in service of you, Devil. Forget this deal and accept me as your servant."

"No," Erin shouted and struggled again. "Don't listen to him, please. You don't want to fall, Veiron. Don't do this."

Veiron stared into her eyes. "I do want to fall, Erin. I want to remember you. I want to remember everything for once. I have the power to regain my own memories. You do not have to sacrifice yourself for my sake."

"Veiron," she whispered and shook her head. "Please, don't."

"I want to remember our love and the reason I cannot take my eyes off you... the reason you make me feel alive. I know it would become more than a distant glimmer of a feeling if I had my memories back and everything that has been done to me is undone. It is my choice this time and I am going to fall, Erin... I need to. I need to remember you and our love."

The Devil sighed. "All very touching... only I have no intention of accepting your offer."

Erin tensed when he pulled her closer to him and cupped her cheek with his right hand, running black claws over her sun-kissed skin.

"Heaven chose a clever place to hide her but they should have known I would find her one day. A daughter," the Devil said and slid his amber gaze towards her. "She is everything I had hoped for too. So noble and willing to do whatever it takes to save those she loves. So pure and virtuous."

It didn't seem like the sort of thing the Devil would want in a child. Veiron glanced back up at the plateau to see Apollyon locked in battle with his twin. That creature was everything Veiron thought the Devil would want in his offspring. Pure evil.

"I admit... I was not pleased when I first discovered my only progeny was female... but she has turned out so much better than I had thought possible. Her virtuousness, her ability to love, her capacity for great kindness was something I thought to wheedle out of her but I see strength in it now, and a means of gaining that which I desire most." The Devil stroked her cheek with his claws and smiled over her shoulder at Veiron. "She will provide me with a vessel that will grant me all the power I need to tear Heaven asunder and free myself from the pit. Both the mortal and angelic realms will quake in fear."

Veiron drew his spear again. "I will not allow you to inhabit her body. I will kill you first."

"Who said I desired to inhabit her body?"

Erin's eyes widened. "You said you did."

"I said you would provide me with a vessel. You would fight me. It is in your nature. I need a vessel that is both powerful and compliant, one raised to allow me to enter it at will and one happy to carry out my commands and stand at the head of my army when I do not occupy it." The Devil grinned, his eyes flashing bright gold, and slid his hand down her body and laid it over her stomach. "When the fruit you bear ripens, I will have the vessel I desire. I will be invincible."

CHAPTER 36

The shock in Erin's enormous eyes echoed within Veiron. She hadn't known but that didn't stop anger from rising up and obliterating his surprise. The force of it shocked him.

"Whose child is it?" Veiron spat the question at her and she frowned at him.

"You said you were damn well sterile... clearly you're not as sterile as you bloody thought!" Her amber eyes narrowed and brightened, just as the Devil's had done, and Veiron could sense her anger rising, coming to match the strength of his. "It's yours."

"Impossible," Veiron said and ignored the Devil when he laughed. "I did not lie to you... if I did say that... angels cannot procreate. Who else have you slept with?"

"No one, Veiron, I swear. It is yours." The fury in her eyes faded and she settled her hands over her stomach. "It explains the bouts of sickness I've been experiencing. I thought it was my power... Christ."

The Devil roared in her ear and she flinched. Veiron snarled at him and drew his spear, his instinct to protect her kicking into overdrive. Her eyes opened again and tentatively met Veiron's.

"I don't know how it happened... but whatever grows inside of me, you are the father." Her hands trembled against her stomach, as bleached of colour as her beautiful face. He felt her shock in his own blood, felt her fear and trepidation as though it was his own. Perhaps it was. Fathering a child was not something he had ever considered because it was impossible. The muddled emotions he felt in Erin said parenthood wasn't something she had ever considered either.

"Are you sure?" he said and she nodded.

"You're the only man I've slept with in the past year so it can't be anyone else's child now, can it?" she snapped, her words a low growl that conveyed every ounce of her anger as it reached a rolling boil again.

Veiron stared at her. A flash of her in the tub, hands hot against his body, burning up as she rode him, sent his temperature soaring but chilled him at the same time. Her gaze held his and he knew she was telling the truth. If she carried life in her womb, it was his seed that her body quickened and used to create it.

"How?" he whispered.

It was the Devil who answered. "Erin is of my flesh, and I am able to mate with all. You are correct, Maggot. You are sterile... but this is not a problem for my daughter. She took your dead seed and gave it life, just as I can take a barren womb and give it new life."

The Devil placed his hand over Erin's on her stomach.

The surprise and fury in her beautiful eyes faded and fear rose and took their place, obliterating them. She clutched her stomach and her lips parted.

Veiron felt her fear in his blood, knew why her demeanour had changed so abruptly. It wasn't only fear born of the Devil wanting their child. It was fear of being a mother. He had witnessed her terror when her other form had shifted beneath her skin and could see in her eyes that she was imagining what the child of the Devil's daughter and a demonic angel would look like. He wanted to tell her that it didn't matter, that no matter what their baby looked like, it would be theirs and it would be loved, and they wouldn't let it come to harm.

He was damned if he was going to let the Devil have their child as his vessel. He would protect both Erin and their unborn baby.

He clutched his spear and met the Devil's gaze. The man smiled at him, radiating confidence with a cruel edge, one that challenged Veiron.

"What do you intend to do?" the Devil said, his smile growing wider. "You are powerless against me. You have both been doing exactly as I had planned the whole time."

He caressed Erin's cheek and she shifted away from his touch. Veiron growled. The Devil lifted his hand away from her stomach, black flames licking over his fingers and up the arm of his suit.

"No sudden moves," he chided and Veiron stilled.

Amelia and Marcus landed a short distance off to Veiron's right.

"The warning extends to everyone." The Devil flicked a glance at Amelia. "You would not want her harmed now."

"You wouldn't," Veiron said and took a step towards them. One way or another he would free Erin from her father's grasp. Once she was out of his reach, they could fight him and find a way to undo the deal she had made. If she had bargained for Veiron's memories, then the Devil hadn't fulfilled his side of the deal yet. Veiron still couldn't remember her or his past life.

"You are probably right. She is more valuable to me alive." The Devil's smile faded and darkness shifted across his expression. "For now at least. I was so disappointed when I discovered my only offspring was female but this turn of events isn't so unpleasant... or unexpected. In fact, the whole affair turned out rather well."

Veiron frowned and his anger spiked back up, burning hotter than ever. "You let me rescue her."

The dark-haired male's grin said it all. "Of course I allowed you to save her. Why else would you manage to escape so easily? I saw an opportunity to improve a bad situation and get what I wanted. Everything since then has gone according to my plan. You both played your roles so perfectly."

"You used us." Erin's eyes widened and fixed on Veiron.

"No need to make it sound so crass. I had seen that you were destined to end up with this disgusting creature and decided to... give you a nudge towards each other."

"A nudge?" Erin struggled against the Devil and he tightened his grip on her. "Did you make us do things?"

He laughed. "No. Always so concerned about the things you care about, aren't you, Daughter? I did not make you love Veiron, and did not make Veiron love you. That sickening emotion was destined to bloom between you. I merely gave you both a helping hand. I admit that sending my men after you to keep you together was not my finest hour, and neither was allowing one of them to harm you, but it was necessary. I needed your feelings to develop more quickly."

Veiron glared at him. "You were impatient. You had a daughter but you wanted a son, so you forced us to remain together. You put your own daughter at risk. What sort of sick—"

The Devil held up his hand and Veiron bit his tongue. He was regaining his strength but hadn't healed enough to withstand another blast of the Devil's power.

"I was impatient," the Devil said and stroked Erin's bare arm. "I realised I had gone too far that night and backed off to allow things to progress naturally. They did. Erin entered the right stage of her cycle on the island and you sired a child with her."

Erin's cheeks paled again and she covered her mouth with her hand. Amelia gasped.

"Erin?" Veiron whispered and she looked at him, her amber eyes swimming with tears. "I will get you out of here. I swear it."

"And how will you do that, Maggot?" The Devil grinned over her shoulder at him. "You failed last time... and witnessing your death was just the catalyst Erin needed to awaken. Not only that, but I removed you from the equation, leaving Erin desperate enough to turn to me... but there seems to have been a complication."

"You bastard," Erin screamed and stamped on the Devil's foot, elbowed him in the chest, and then flicked her hand over her shoulder and cracked his nose. He snarled and released her and she stumbled forwards.

Veiron reached for her but she didn't come to him.

She turned on her father, bright orange flames caressing her hands and dancing over her bare arms.

Black blood poured over the Devil's lip and he rubbed the back of his hand over it, smudging it across his face. The blood instantly stopped flowing and disappeared, leaving his appearance perfect again.

"Where was that spirit when I held you captive?" He flicked the blood off his hand. "If you had displayed the rage and hunger for violence you have shown at times in these past few weeks perhaps I would not have needed to go through so much trouble. I could have used you as my vessel after all."

"I will never be your vessel and neither will my child!" She threw her hands forwards and unleashed a crackling orb of golden energy. The Devil held his hand up and the blast exploded against an invisible barrier surrounding him. "This wasn't part of our deal. It's off."

She released another bolt of golden fire and the Devil disappeared.

Veiron's neck prickled and two strong hands grasped his shoulders. He cried out as sharp claws dug into his flesh and burned him, eating into him like acid.

Erin spun on her heel to face them.

The Devil stepped up behind Veiron and he twisted at the waist and beat his wings, trying to free himself. The man pressed his fingers deeper into Veiron's flesh and he burned hotter, the heat stealing his strength, rendering his arms immobile.

"Don't," Erin said and shook her head.

"Obey me, or I will destroy the man you love," the Devil hissed over Veiron's shoulder and Veiron snarled and tried to dislodge him again. He couldn't move. The acid burning through his veins had spread to his flesh, scalding every inch of him. He gritted his teeth against the pain and held Erin's gaze, silently trying to tell her to leave while she had the chance. It didn't matter if he died again. He would be reborn as he was now and he would come back for her. They would finish this somehow.

She couldn't risk her life or that of their child for his sake.

"Don't, please." Erin lowered her hands.

Veiron swallowed several times and mustered all of his strength. He had to convince her to go.

"Do not, Erin," he whispered and swallowed again to wet his dry throat. "Leave while you can. Do not do this for me."

Her eyes flickered between his and the man's behind him, her expression turning uncertain.

"We could amend the deal," the Devil said and Veiron shook his head, silently cursing him for tempting her, his own daughter. "In exchange for your son, I will revive Veiron's memories by accepting him as my servant. I will not inhabit your child or you, but he and you will stand at the head of my army and the child will serve as my destroyer. A small price to pay in exchange for your lover. You could be together again. A happy family. It is what you desire most, is it not?"

Veiron snarled and focused so his wings disappeared. He unleashed them again, so fast that they smashed into the Devil and caught him by surprise. His claws tore out of Veiron's shoulders and Veiron propelled himself forwards and hit the black ground a few metres from Erin.

She looked down at him and then beyond him to her father.

"Come, Daughter. Make your decision."

CHAPTER 37

Erin's gaze danced between Veiron where he knelt on the ground, covered in blood and black dust, and the man who called himself her father. She placed her hand over her stomach, torn between accepting his offer and fighting him.

She had thought her sickness had been due to the increase in her power caused by her awakening and her grief over losing Veiron. What if she was pregnant though?

Her skin prickled, coldest across the back of her neck and down her spine, and her stomach somersaulted. When she had awoken, and times after that, she had seen her claws and had felt the shift of horns beneath her flesh. Would her baby be like that and like Veiron had been during the time they had conceived it? Would it come out with fangs and claws, and black skin, with glowing red eyes? Her insides flipped again. There was no point in asking whether it would. She knew in her heart that it would be like her and Veiron, and it frightened her. She only hoped that like them it would appear human most of the time too. She didn't fear the baby and she wouldn't fear its demonic appearance if it had one. She was frightened that it would never be able to lead a normal life in the mortal world and that would drive it to become evil, like her father.

Her eyes flicked to Veiron and he pushed himself up onto unsteady legs.

"Come to me, Erin." Veiron held his hand out to her and she wanted to go to him more than anything but she feared that if she took a single step towards him that the Devil would attack him. She had to find a solution, one that didn't involve making deals with her father and placing those she loved at risk.

Veiron wanted to remember her and had been willing to fall to achieve that but she wasn't willing to let him go down that route. In the time she had known Veiron, she had discovered the depth of the hatred he felt towards the game that Hell and Heaven played with him and the two beings that used him as their pawn. She wouldn't let him go through that again.

She looked over her shoulder at Amelia. The look in her grey eyes gave Erin strength. Whatever happened, her sister would be there for her. They weren't sisters by blood but that didn't matter. Amelia was her family. They had grown up together and had always been each other's best friend. She would do anything for Amelia and she knew that Amelia felt the same way.

"If you're scared that Veiron will fall foul of Heaven's commands, then let him contract with me. Let him become like Marcus and be free, not a servant of the Devil," Amelia said and while Erin was grateful for the offer, she could never accept it and Veiron would never accept it either.

He wanted his memories back.

The Devil could give that to him.

If he fell, he would remember everything, but it would pull him back into the game again. If he pledged himself to Amelia, he would be free of it, but Heaven and Hell would seek to kill him in order to reset the game, just as they desired to kill Amelia and Marcus.

"I don't want anyone to come to harm," Erin said to no one in particular and looked back at Veiron. He shook his head and she glanced down at her feet. She couldn't make a decision while everyone was looking at her, waiting to hear what she would do. She needed time to think about it but the Devil wasn't going to give it to her. He had been pressuring her to agree to a deal since she had appeared before him and she had a feeling that this would be the last time he changed the one he was offering.

She frowned.

He did keep changing it.

Whenever she looked as though she would bolt and leave, or fight him, he sweetened the deal. He wanted her to agree to it. He needed her child.

Did that mean that if she chose to leave right now, he wouldn't harm her?

Her gaze shifted to Veiron again. He wouldn't harm her but he would hurt Veiron and those she cared about in order to force her to agree.

"Erin," Amelia said and she closed her eyes. "I swear I will keep us safe. I will protect us all. We can do it together. You can learn about your power and discover everything there is to know about it and we can do this together. Please, Erin."

"Do not listen to your sister or the Devil, Erin." Veiron's deep voice forced her eyes open and she looked into his. They pleaded with her, their dark depths full of affection and despair. "I know what happened to me now. I have seen everything. I saw what happened that night between us. I remember it. You must too. You promised me forever."

A chill slid down her spine and arms.

"Silence!" the Devil shouted and Veiron's mouth moved but no sound came out. He glared at the Devil.

"Erin, that's the—" Amelia's voice cut off and Erin looked over her shoulder. Her sister and Marcus were gone. She faced the Devil.

"I am growing bored of these interferences. It's all so touching, so sweet, so sickening. Make your decision. The fate of this disgusting creature is in your hands."

Erin glared at her father, searching his eyes. They showed no hint of fear but she could feel it in him. He had silenced Veiron, and had sent Amelia and Marcus away because they had tried to tell her something vital.

"Decide, Erin." The Devil disappeared and reappeared right in front of her.

She stared at him, letting the jumbled panicked thoughts flooding her mind unravel and sort themselves out into order.

Her DNA was a perfect match for the man's in front of her.

Meaning, she had all the same powers that he possessed.

She had the Devil's dark power in her veins. His blood flowing through her.

In the eyes of God, was she the same as the Devil?

If an angel fell and pledged himself to her, would it be the same as pledging himself to the Devil?

Her heart accelerated.

Could she accept Veiron as her servant?

Her eyes widened.

That was what he had been telling her. She had promised him forever.

Erin kept her eyes locked with her father's.

"I want that forever that I promised you," she said and saw Veiron smile out of the corner of her eye. "And I will do anything to achieve it."

The Devil's eyes narrowed. "Have you made your decision?"

Erin nodded. She focused and recalled everything she had seen the Devil do. He stepped towards her and Erin threw her hands forwards, unleashing a blast of fire. He blocked it as he had before and she willed herself to disappear. Fiery darkness engulfed her and when it disappeared, she was standing next to Veiron. He jumped and opened his mouth, but still no words came out. She grabbed his hand and focused on making them both disappear.

The darkness swept over her once more and receded to reveal the plateau they had landed on when Apollyon had helped them come to Hell to save Veiron, Marcus and Einar.

Apollyon was sitting on a rock a few metres away, bloodied and beaten.

He raised a hand in greeting and sighed. "Not my finest hour. I had hoped no one would see this."

Veiron mouthed something.

Erin frowned and hoped it would work. "Speak."

"He got away?" Veiron said, his voice hoarse, and then rubbed his throat.

"Who got away?" Erin frowned at both of them and a black voice boomed out of the glowing landscape hundreds of feet below. "It'll have to wait."

She turned to Veiron. "I can contract with you, can't I?"

"Not contract, no. Your power is that of the Devil. We formed a bond because I chose to pledge myself to you and you accepted it. It is the reason I was not reborn as I should have been. This appearance is false. Heaven killed me five times over in an attempt to undo what you had done, but it did not work. They couldn't break the bond between us. It is waiting to be sealed. You are powerful enough now." He caught her hands and held them together in both of his.

A shiver raced over her. "How do I seal it?"

"We exchanged a vow, Erin." He squeezed her hands and stared down into her eyes, threads of crimson and gold shining in his. "We must exchange it again."

She nodded and then froze. "Wait... you mean you're going to fall?"

"I already am fallen. I was never reborn as an angel of Heaven. I remained as I was, your servant in part." Veiron released her hands, drew his spear and knelt before her. He rested his spear across both of his upturned palms and bowed his head, and raised the weapon towards her. "I swear fealty to you, Erin. I am yours and only yours to command until the end of time."

Erin hesitated, unsure what to do. She glanced across the bumpy black ground to Apollyon. He motioned for her to touch the spear. She smiled her thanks and laid her hands on the black rod.

"I accept you as my knight and as mine, and I swear to you that I am yours and only yours, now and forever, until the end of time." Erin almost laughed at how silly she sounded, and then shrugged and decided to go all the way. "I accept you as my servant, Veiron. Do you accept me as your master?"

"I do."

Red light blazed from the engravings along the black rod of the spear and shone across the twin crimson blades. It swept down Veiron's arms and the colour of his armour changed as it passed over it, darkening to black with metallic red edging. The light raced up his arms and his tattoos appeared, curling around his biceps. His chest armour switched colour and she gasped as the light shot over his wings and the feathers bled from pale silvery-blue and lilac to darkest crimson.

She wrinkled her nose up when the magic light failed to change one aspect of him.

Veiron rose to his feet, immense and imposing, a grin tugging at his sexy mouth. He rolled his shoulders, flexed his fingers and then lunged for her. She shrieked as he swept her up into his arms and he silenced her with a deep kiss that melted her right down to her core and brought out her own smile.

The black voice curled from the pit again and the ground shook.

Veiron released her mouth and drew back, still grinning.

"Remember me now?" she said with a smile of her own.

"You bet your arse, Sweetheart." He wrapped his wings around her and kissed her breathless again. Erin melted into him, moaning as she returned his kiss, battling his tongue with her own and losing herself in him. She had missed this so much.

There was one thing she still missed though.

She braced her hands against his black armour and broke free of his kiss.

Her nose wrinkled again. "Your hair is still short."

Veiron scrubbed a hand over the longer lengths on top, easily holding her up with just one thick muscular arm. "It'll grow back. You can't have everything, you know."

The ground trembled again.

"I think you pissed dear old daddy off." Veiron set her down on the ground and she wanted to burrow back into his arms and order him not to say what she could feel coming.

Instead, she tipped her chin up and faced the edge of the plateau, waiting.

"What do you think you're doing?" Veiron moved in front of her, shielding her with his glossy red wings.

"Getting ready to fight." Admittedly, she had never fought a battle before. She didn't count the last time they were in Hell because no one had wanted to fight her then. She didn't think the Devil would be so kind this time.

"I don't bloody think so."

"You're my servant. Do as you're ordered." Erin grinned when he cast a dirty look over his shoulder at her. Yes, she was going to play that card often so he might as well get used to hearing it. "We're in this together, Veiron."

"You need to take care of yourself," he whispered and looked so beautifully concerned that she wanted to kiss him.

"This is me taking care of myself. You can't fight him alone. If we're going to stand a chance of getting out of here, we need to work together. Besides... I'm the Devil's daughter and you're the father."

His look softened and then he shrugged his broad shoulders. "I guess you're right. It's going to take more than a scrap with his granddaddy to hurt him... but I want you to fall back if you're in any danger. Understood?"

Erin nodded, stepped up beside him and slipped her hand into his.

The Devil appeared in a flash of black smoke.

He ran his gaze over Veiron and curled his lip, and then looked beyond them. His eyes narrowed. "Great Destroyer."

"Pain in my backside," Apollyon said, so close to Erin that she jumped. She hadn't noticed him move.

He stopped beside her and stared at the Devil.

"It is still many years until our next battle." The Devil dismissed him with a regal wave of his hand. "Do not interfere."

"You left the pit."

The Devil glared at him.

"Hardly." He swept his hand out, motioning to the edge of the plateau directly behind him. "Mere inches. I have obeyed the rules of my confinement."

"I was not talking about now. You have left it in the past. I have it on good authority that you visited Erin in the prison. That is not mere inches from your fortress." Apollyon held his hands out in front of him and called his twin golden blades. "You know I cannot let that pass unpunished."

The Devil laughed, his amber eyes flashing gold. "You are in no condition to fight me. If you battle me now, you will lose and I will be free."

"Is that true?" Erin looked across at Apollyon. He frowned, his rich blue eyes darkening with it, and then slowly nodded. Erin laid her hand on his bloodied shoulder. "Then I cannot let you fight. This is not your battle."

He turned his frown on her and disappeared. Erin lowered her hand and hoped that the dark angel wouldn't be angry with her for sending him away to Earth. He was too weak to fight her father right now and she couldn't let him escape his prison.

Erin glanced at Veiron.

"Don't even think about it, Erin." He didn't take his eyes off the Devil. "I've been waiting for this moment for centuries."

She knew that and it was the only reason she wasn't giving in to her desire to transport both of them out of Hell. They had to do this or her father would never leave them alone. He needed to see that together they were undefeatable and that they wouldn't give in to his demands or let him control their lives, and that they would easily destroy any army that he sent after them in the mortal world.

This fight wouldn't just be a warning to the Devil though.

It was a warning to Heaven too.

"I do not wish to fight you, Daughter." The Devil held his hand out to her.

"Too bad, because I really want to fight you, and Veiron has been itching to kick your arse for a long time." Erin focused on her hands and her power, channelling it towards her palms. "Personally, I think I like the look of your throne. I made you bleed earlier. Veiron doesn't think you can be killed... something about balance between the realms... but your blood flows in my veins, doesn't it. Does that mean I can kill you and take your place as ruler of this realm?"

Veiron flicked his right hand out, extending his spear. "I think you might be right."

Erin grinned at her father, revelling in the flicker of fear in his amber eyes.

"Let's see if I can kill you, Daddy dearest."

She threw her hands forwards and unleashed twin orbs of fire.

CHAPTER 38

The Devil held his hand up and the orbs of energy hit an invisible shield, exploding on impact and blinding Erin. She hurled another two and hoped for the best. Her vision came back and her fireballs were hurtling into the distance. The Devil was gone.

A grunt drew her attention to her right. Veiron slashed at the Devil with his spear, sweeping it in a wide arc that forced the Devil to withdraw and arch backwards to avoid the red blade. Veiron swept it back again, jabbing it forwards at the same time, and the Devil disappeared as the blade was about to stab him. Erin considered that cheating, and two could play at that game.

She waited for him to reappear and then teleported to the spot directly behind him, pressed her hands against his back and growled as she released another blast of power. At this distance, he couldn't shield himself. The fiery bolt propelled him forwards, back towards a waiting Veiron. Veiron roared and swung his spear, slamming the thick black rod of it into the Devil's side.

The Devil doubled over from the impact, grabbed the rod, and pulled Veiron towards him. He shoved his hand against Veiron's chest, sending him flying through the air. Erin flinched as he landed hard, sending a plume of black dust and rubble up into the air, and didn't wait to see if he was all right. She teleported again and appeared between him and the Devil. She yelled and threw her left hand forwards, unleashing another blast of her power, and then her right. The first orb shot towards his head and the second towards his shins. He deflected the one aimed at his head and chest and leapt over the second. It hit the ground and exploded, showering the whole area with shards of basalt and leaving a crater behind.

Veiron shot past her, nothing but a blur, his spear held in both hands at his side. He beat his crimson wings and jabbed his spear towards the Devil, who instantly blocked it. Veiron pulled the spear back, flapped his wings, flipped over his enemy and roared as he brought the blade down hard towards his head from behind. The Devil turned and held his hand up, freezing Veiron in midair.

Giving Erin his back.

She smiled. Her man was clever. While he was far less likely than she was to deal damage to the Devil, he could distract him so Erin could.

She teleported behind the Devil and slammed her fist into his lower back. Her power increased the force of her blow and fired from her as it struck him, a double whammy. He stumbled forwards and turned on her with a snarl, his eyes glowing crimson and white teeth sharp.

Veiron unfroze and grinned as he brought the blade of his spear down. It sliced down the Devil's back and he cried out, fury brightening his eyes. He snarled and launched himself at her. Veiron was there before he could reach her, his arms and wings wrapped around her and his back taking the brunt of the Devil's blow. He grunted and growled, and Erin panicked.

"Veiron?" she said and broke free of his grasp. He grabbed her shoulders and she caught his arms to hold him upright, and searched his eyes. "You okay?"

He nodded. A bright red glow lit him from behind and Erin focused. She teleported Veiron before the blast could hit him and landed hard on top of him a short distance away. He growled.

"Sorry." She grimaced and another blaze of red shot towards them. "I'm still getting the hang of all this."

She focused and shifted them again, the darkness enveloping them for longer this time before it faded and she found herself right at the edge of the plateau. At least they were standing.

A blast of black energy hit her square in the chest and sent her flying. Erin screamed and pushed all of her power to her hands and unleashed everything she had. The world spun around her, flickering black and gold, and then red as her blast hit something. It exploded with such force that a shockwave hit her and flipped her head over heels. She twirled violently, trying to focus so she could teleport. She couldn't tell which way was up and which was down but she knew which way she was heading, and fast.

Something slammed into her waist and yanked her so hard from behind that she threw up.

"Sorry," Veiron grumbled, twisted her in his arms and nestled her close to his body, one arm against her back and one under her knees.

Erin swallowed and shook her head. The embarrassment of vomiting in front of the man she loved was a small price to pay for being saved from a horrible fall to an excruciating death. Besides, it probably wasn't going to be the only time she threw up in his presence over the coming months.

Veiron gathered her closer and spread his crimson wings. They glided down towards the fortress and landed in the courtyard. Veiron furled his wings against his back and went to set her down but she locked her hands around his neck. She tried to teleport them but nothing happened. Erin focused her power on her hands but they remained cold, as icy as her blood. She had suffered this cold before when she had been training and had tried to do something big. Had she expended too much of her power at once?

"Take me somewhere else. Quickly." She still couldn't shake the vision she'd had of Veiron in this place and she didn't want to fight the Devil here.

Veiron's red eyes met hers and offered a silent apology. He nodded, opened his wings and beat them.

The Devil appeared before them, no trace of blood on him and his suit immaculate again, as though the blows they had managed to land had never happened. He picked fragments of basalt from his black hair and casually flicked them to the ground. Each fragment hit the pavement with such force that they left spots of lava behind.

He straightened his shirt cuffs and tossed a bored look her way. "You will have to try harder than that, Daughter."

His smile unnerved her.

He cocked his head to one side. "I see you have discovered the limit of your power. It was an impressive display but in your current condition, you are no match for me."

Erin looked down at her stomach.

Was he saying that she had no hope of defeating him while she was pregnant? She focused on her belly and felt the warm glow there. It was the only place she felt warm, and it was a place that was constantly at the back of her mind, her will focused on protecting the baby inside her. Her power was split between fighting and protecting, but she couldn't place her baby at risk by changing that and using all of her strength to fight her father.

Erin looked up into Veiron's beautiful eyes. Flecks of brightest crimson shifted in liquid gold. She had thought his red eyes were the most amazing thing she had seen but they didn't compare to the breathtaking beauty of his golden ones. This was a change she didn't regret, because it was a reminder that they were joined now, together forever, and no one could take that from them. Not Heaven, and certainly not Hell.

She turned her head and looked across at her father. "You're wrong. If I were alone, I might not be a match for you... but I'm not alone. Together, we can defeat you."

Brave words that she didn't fully believe but she'd had to say something to catch the Devil off guard and make him doubt himself and his powers. She wanted him to fear that she might be right and could defeat him. It would play on his mind and might give her the opening she needed to make her threat come true.

She focused hard and mustered enough energy to disappear from Veiron's arms. She reappeared on the steps behind the Devil and swayed, her head spinning and heart pumping hard. Her hands shook, numb with cold now. Erin rubbed them. There had to be a way to recover full use of her powers and help Veiron. She wasn't going to sit on the sidelines while he fought her father.

Veiron launched himself at the Devil and her father held his hand out and drew a black and red flaming blade out of the air. He blocked Veiron's spear with it and the back of his suit jacket shredded.

Huge black wings made of shadows burst from his back, shifting like smoke in the stifling air.

Damn.

Maybe she could fly after all.

Erin breathed on her hands, trying to warm them up. They were like ice. She could only stand and watch as Veiron flew upwards, luring the Devil with him, and they clashed in the air. She rubbed her hands together and willed her power to come back. Her limbs shook, bones frozen and blood like icy sludge in her veins. Veiron growled and attacked the Devil again, only to be knocked back and sent flying through the air. The Devil went after him, his flaming blade a bright arc in the darkness. It cut across Veiron's left wing and he cried out.

Come on. Erin rubbed her hands harder. She wasn't going to stand here like a useless little girl and watch the man she loved die. Not again. Heat swelled in her stomach. Erin flinched as Veiron barely dodged the Devil's next attack but wasn't quick enough to evade the blast of power he unleashed after it. It hit Veiron and sent him tumbling through the air.

Veiron spread his crimson wings to right himself and dived downwards, gaining some space.

Erin focused on the heat inside her. She was stronger than this. She wasn't going to let her power boss her around. A small red flame broke out of her thumb, flickered and died. It was a start.

The tiny patch of heat on her thumb slowly spread along the length of it and then crept over her hand.

Veiron clashed with the Devil again and her father laughed, disappeared and reappeared right next to him. He grabbed Veiron by the throat, beat his shadowy wings, and shot downwards.

"Veiron!" Erin ran forwards, her eyes glued to him, heart racing. He struggled against the Devil's grip but didn't escape it in time.

He smashed into the ground and a huge shockwave shot out and knocked Erin flying. She tumbled through the air. She'd had just about enough of this. She had wings and it was about time they damn well came out.

A hot blast swept across her shoulders and caressed her arms and she stopped short of hitting the wall of the fortress. Erin slowly looked behind her. Black shadows fluttered from her back, flowing out of her and forming wings.

They disappeared and she dropped to the ground, landing in a crouch.

Erin ran down the steps to the paved area of the courtyard and towards the huge ball of dust lingering in the air where Veiron and the Devil had hit. Veiron. He had to be all right. Would she know if he wasn't? He was her servant after all.

She sprinted into the dust cloud and waved her hand in front of her face to clear it. She couldn't see a thing. She choked and covered her mouth and nose with her hands, trying to stop the dust from getting into her lungs.

"Veiron?"

Something growled and a huge dark shape loomed out of the dust cloud. Erin halted and then backed off a step, straight into something else.

Hot hands settled on her shoulders.

The dust swirled and cleared, revealing Veiron before her in his demonic form. His eyes blazed gold as they settled on her and then the man behind her. Blood soaked his left arm and part of his left dragon-like wing hung limp, the bone snapped midway down the outside. He growled again, bearing red sharp teeth.

"Release her, coward," he snarled and the Devil laughed from behind her.

"Why would I do that?"

Erin smelled blood. She looked down to see a trail of black running down her chest and panicked. Was she injured? No. She had cut herself before and her blood was red. She glanced at the Devil's hand. Black blood covered it. He had injured Veiron but had harmed himself in the process, or had Veiron hurt him?

Veiron growled, the dark sound echoing around the spires surrounding the courtyard.

"Release her." He lumbered towards them, immense and lethal, his heavy steps shaking the ground.

The red blades on his spear gleamed wickedly, one of them drenched in black.

He had cut the Devil.

An idea struck her.

Erin met Veiron's golden gaze and held it, silently conveying her plan. He frowned, his black brow crinkling, and shook his head. She widened her eyes at him in a way she hoped conveyed it was an order and he had better do it. She was seventy percent certain that she would be able to manage her part in the plan.

He grunted and then growled, flashing twin rows of vicious sharp red teeth. Erin took that as an agreement to go along with her insane idea and also a warning that he was already growing tired of her pulling rank. He could assert his authority over her later, in bed, when all this was over. Right now, she needed him to do exactly what she asked.

Veiron twirled his spear, pointed it at the Devil, and then clutched it in both hands and drew it back towards him beside his head.

Erin's stomach fluttered.

She hoped she had enough power to pull this off. She grabbed the Devil's hands where they clutched her shoulders and focused on holding him there, her mind on using her power to stop him from teleporting.

Veiron charged at her, hunkering down and shaking the black ground with each step.

The Devil struggled behind her and she tried not to panic. So a huge black demonic angel was thundering towards her with a spear aimed at her chest. She trusted him, and she had wanted him to put everything into this attack and come at her full speed. She just hadn't expected him to look so frightening. Her hands chilled.

Oh, now was not the time for her power to flake out on her.

"Release me," the Devil hissed into her ear and she felt hazy from head to toe. Releasing him sounded good.

No, it sounded bad. Completely against her plan.

She held him tighter and her hands chilled another ten degrees. Veiron closed in. She caught the flicker of hesitation crossing his face and she nodded, trying to convince him to continue.

"Release me!"

It did sound good, and with a several-hundred-pound demon charging her, she was inclined to do just that and get the hell out of his way.

Veiron's blade touched her chest.

Fiery darkness engulfed her.

A black roar deafened her and she reappeared before she had intended, hitting the ground hard. The earth bucked and shook beneath her, cracking in places to reveal boiling lava. She pushed onto her feet and leapt as the slab beneath her slid down at one end and tipped up at the other. It sank into the lava and Erin ran, ducking to avoid the shards of rock breaking off the spires of black above her and leaping over the bubbling pools of fire erupting from beneath the broken paving.

Had Veiron done it?

Erin chanced a glance towards where she had left him and her heart stopped.

The Devil stood with the blade of Veiron's spear sticking into his black-blood-soaked chest, holding the shaft of it in his left hand and Veiron by his neck in his right. He roared again and threw Veiron down the steps in front of him. Veiron tumbled down them, changing back into his mortal appearance as he did so, his wings twisting beneath him and then disappearing. Erin shook her head. This was not happening. She wouldn't let her vision come true.

Her black shadowy wings erupted from her back and she shakily beat them, almost flying across the courtyard. It was more like hopping and flying and hopping again but she didn't quite trust her wings yet. They had disappeared on her once already and she didn't want to fly too high and end up plummeting into one of the lava pools now dotting the courtyard.

The Devil pulled Veiron's spear from his chest, held it in both hands and aimed it at Veiron's back. Veiron didn't move. He remained face down on the ground, his eyes closed.

Erin hopped, flew, hopped and focused her power on her hands again. Her wings disappeared mid-flight and she lashed out with her power as she dropped towards the ground. Twin golden orbs shot towards the Devil. The first smacked into his left hand, knocking the spear from his grasp and sending it spinning through the air, and the second slammed into his chest, sending him flying into the towering doors of his fortress. He hit them hard, the boom from his impact echoing around the courtyard.

She ran to Veiron and pulled him up off the ground, struggling with his weight and finding it hard to keep a grip on his slippery bloodied shoulders. He groaned and relief washed over her, replacing the chill in her blood with heat that even her power couldn't contend with.

A droning thumping noise filled her ears and Erin froze with her hands against Veiron's shoulders. That didn't sound good. Veiron moved at last, pressing his palms into the cracked black slabs beneath him and pushing himself up.

"Time we were leaving," he growled and swayed as he stood.

"What? No. We're so close, Veiron. We can't leave now." She pointed towards the Devil where he was slowly pulling himself up onto his feet. "We can take him."

Veiron caught her shoulders and turned her in the opposite direction. "But we can't take them."

Black shapes filled the dark distance.

Hell's angels.

The Devil had called for reinforcements.

There had to be hundreds of them. Veiron was right, there was no way they could defeat the Devil and a large part of his army at the same time, but she refused to give up. They had injured him. They could finish him off before his angels reached them and swooped in to protect him.

Erin looked back over her shoulder at the Devil. He waved a hand over himself and the blood and dirt disappeared, his suit fixing itself and leaving him perfect again. A black patch appeared on his red shirt. He frowned, touched it, and grimaced. His eyes glowed and the black blood disappeared. It didn't reappear this time. A pleased expression crossed his darkly handsome face.

"We have to leave, Erin... I hate it as much as you do but I won't risk you or our baby." Veiron grabbed her around the waist and went to toss her gently over his shoulder, but stopped and held her pressed to his front instead.

She growled in frustration. She hadn't missed this part of Veiron. She wrapped her legs around him and kicked his backside, and rained her fists down on his shoulders, but he didn't put her down. He tightened his grip on her and began walking away from the Devil.

"No!" Erin threw another fireball at the Devil and he didn't even raise a hand to deflect it this time. It shot upwards before it reached him. He smiled at her. Erin glared at him. "This isn't over... I swear to you... I will kill you."

CHAPTER 39

A bright white light chased the darkness back and Hell disappeared. The scent of saltwater filled Erin's lungs and she caught a glimpse of a tropical island before it too disappeared, replaced by a jungle, and then a mountain, and then another island.

Veiron set her down and she threw up again. On his boots.

He growled, stepped back and shook his feet one by one.

"Why did you do that?" Erin straightened and frowned up at him.

"We couldn't take them all on, Erin, and you know it. Now is not the time for our revenge." He lifted his hand and cupped her cheek, his palm warm against her face and comforting. "Can you teleport us back to the island we left from?"

Erin wanted to teleport them back to Hell but the worry in Veiron's dark eyes stopped her from going through with it. She wanted to end this but Veiron was right. They weren't strong enough to take on a legion of Hell's angels and the Devil at the same time, not without risking their baby, but one day they would be and she would come good on her threat. She would kill the Devil and help end this game.

Erin looked down at her stomach and touched it. It was hard to believe that she was pregnant.

Veiron settled his hand over hers and she looked up into his eyes.

"What if he comes out looking different?" she whispered, ashamed to voice her fears but needing Veiron to reassure her.

"So what if he does." He smiled softly and stroked her cheek with his other hand. "Nothing will change our love for him."

She frowned. "But can we really raise a child together when we're constantly in danger? Do you really want to do this with me?"

Veiron sighed and cupped her cheek. "Of course I want to do this with you, Sweetheart. We'll take it one day at a time and I won't let anything bad happen to either of you. I love you, no matter what the future has in store for us. I will always love you and our child."

Tears filled Erin's eyes and she sniffed them back. Her warrior with the heart of a poet. He always knew the right thing to say to melt her. She leaned into his touch and closed her eyes. Nothing would stop them from loving their child. They would protect him from anything, from everything. The world. Heaven. Hell. They would raise him surrounded by love and compassion, and devotion, and he would know good things, positive things, and not just darkness.

"I'll do my best to be a good father... I just don't have a clue what that entails." He chuckled and she looked at him again, smiling along with him.

"I don't have a clue about being a parent either, but I know a great man who can teach you about being a great father, and I'm sure he would like to meet you." She placed her hand over his and held it against her cheek, her heart warming as she thought about the couple who had raised her with Amelia. They were her real family. Her father would love Veiron for his protective streak. Her mother would have loved him too. "We can learn together... and hopefully we can give him a good life."

"We will give him a good life, Erin. He will have a life full of love and he will never come to harm, because I will protect you both."

Erin smiled. "I'll protect you both too."

"Why do I get the feeling you're going to try to wear the trousers in this relationship?" He grinned, dipped his head, and pressed a brief, hard kiss to her lips, leaving her breathless and unable to tell him that she was going to do just that. "Now... it's time we were getting out of here, don't you think, Mrs Veiron?"

"You're going to have to make that official, Mister." She giggled, stepped up to him, tiptoed and wrapped her arms around his neck. The darkness swept over them and receded to reveal the small makeshift shelters of the island.

Apollyon sat on the white sand near the circle of rocks that acted as the fireplace.

Erin tensed, waiting for him to explode at her for what she had done.

"I am glad to see you both well." He eased onto his feet with only a few grimaces. A deep cut on his thigh pulled and split open again, spilling blood down his dirty leg.

"I'm sorry I sent you away," she said and he shook his head and smiled. "How did you know the Devil had visited me in my cell?"

"My doppelganger... Asmodeus... told me." Apollyon prodded the cut on his thigh and frowned.

"Why would he do such a thing?" She couldn't believe that Apollyon's evil twin would want to help her, but then he had tried to convince her to leave her cell with him. Maybe he hadn't intended to take her to the Devil after all.

"He is complicated." Apollyon shrugged. "There is some good in him."

Veiron released her and crossed the sand to Apollyon. He crouched and held his hand out over the wound and the blood slowed to a trickle as it healed.

"How can you still heal?" Erin said and Veiron looked up at her, his expression blank.

"I don't know. I just can." He healed another of the deeper cuts on Apollyon's stomach and then moved to one on his arm. He paused and looked back at her again. "Can you heal?"

Erin shrugged.

"Try." He pointed to a cut on his own bloodied arm. "Maybe it's an ability I picked up off you when we exchanged vows rather than one Heaven gave me."

She didn't need to try. She already knew that was what had happened.

"He healed himself." Erin cursed her father. "That was why he looked so smug. He bloody healed himself while we were distracted by his men flying towards us."

She held her hand out over Veiron's arm and focused. The wound instantly closed. Erin healed a deeper cut on his side, and her head felt light. She pressed her hand to it and Veiron took hold of her arm.

"You need to rest," he said and she nodded. He was right again.

Veiron helped her sit on the sand but she felt worse and stood again, pacing a short distance towards the water and then back again.

"Are you unwell?" Concern laced Apollyon's deep voice and he held out his hand to her. A dewy bottle of water appeared in his grasp.

Erin took it, twisted the cap off and swallowed a mouthful. The icy liquid instantly cooled her insides but she held her sigh inside when she caught Veiron's black look. He had once wondered if he could produce water for her if he concentrated enough and hadn't been sure it would taste good even if he managed it. Apollyon hadn't seemed to concentrate at all. One moment his hand had been empty, and the next perfectly tasty water had been in it, leaving Veiron looking as though he might kill the dark angel for being able to provide for her when he couldn't.

"Thank you," Erin said to Apollyon and offered the water to Veiron. He snatched it, gulped it down and then crushed the bottle in his fist.

Apollyon raised a single dark eyebrow at his behaviour and then returned his attention to Erin. "Are you feeling better?"

She shrugged. "I'm peachy... a day in the life of being pregnant, I guess. I have months of this to look forward to. I'm not even sure how many. God, do you think demonic pregnancies have the same span as a mortal one?"

Apollyon frowned at her. "Pregnant?"

Veiron slung his arm around her shoulders and pulled her against his side. She glanced up at his face to find all trace of darkness gone. He positively glowed with pride. Erin bit back the temptation to bring up that he hadn't looked so sure it was his in Hell, or looked so comfortable with the prospect of becoming the father of a boy who had the potential to be more powerful than both of them combined.

Apollyon's blue eyes flicked between her and Veiron, he opened his mouth and then just shifted his broad shoulders.

"Stranger things have happened." He paused and cocked his head to one side, and his eyes turned unfocused and glassy.

Erin raised an eyebrow and whispered out of the corner of her mouth to Veiron, "What's wrong with him?"

"He's on a call," Veiron said and lowered his head, pressing a kiss to her brow.

"A call?"

"Telepathic communication," Apollyon said. "Sorry about that. Marcus and Amelia are safe and on their way back here. They ended up somewhere in the Sahara."

"I can do that." Erin leaned into Veiron's side, remembering the conversation she'd had with her father and how surprised she had been. "When we were on the beach just before the Hell's angels came and took me, I spoke to the Devil in my head. Do you think I could do the same with you now that you're my servant?"

Veiron frowned. "Less of the servant talk, Missy... but I imagine we will be able to speak telepathically now that we're bonded."

Erin liked the sound of that, but not as much as she liked the thought of winding Veiron up about their new master and servant status.

"Besides, you are my servant. That means you have to obey me now because I'm your master." She grinned at him, meeting his scowl and not backing down.

"You're a little too comfortable ordering me around already... if you're not careful, I'll show you who's boss."

Erin's grin turned sassy. "Oh yeah?"

"Uh yeah." Veiron snaked his hands around her hips and drew her up against the hard planes of his body, causing her stomach to quiver. His gaze flickered down to her mouth and she tipped her head back, luring him in for a kiss.

Apollyon cleared his throat. "And on that note... since it seems that the two of you will be alright here until they arrive, I must leave. I have been away from Serenity for too long and I desire to see her again."

Erin nodded and drew back from Veiron. She understood that need and she wished she had the strength left in her to teleport him back to his home in Paris and the woman waiting for him there.

"Thank you for helping us." She held her hand out to him and he just smiled.

"I will see you again soon enough. I am sure my little witch will want to meet you once she learns you are with child, and it will be safer now if we remain together." Apollyon unleashed his black wings and ran his hands down them, preening his feathers. "Until then."

He beat his wings, blowing sand against her legs, and lifted into the air.

Erin waved.

Apollyon turned, flapped his wings again and disappeared beyond the palm trees.

Veiron squeezed Erin's shoulders.

She waited.

"So... alone at last," he said, as casual as anything, and she smiled, turned and wrapped her arms around his waist.

"Indeed." She stared up into his eyes. Red and gold ringed his dilated pupils, a corona around them that she had always liked because it told her that she was bringing out his wicked side. "We probably have a little time before Amelia and Marcus arrive."

She bit her lip and swirled her fingers in circles over his back.

"You're all filthy. I think you need to wash." She moved her hands lower, over the metal strips that protected his bottom.

Veiron pursed his lips and then cracked a smile. "No amount of washing could stop me from being filthy."

She laughed, happiness bubbling up and bringing her smile out. "I missed you."

Veiron grabbed her backside and raised her up him, so her eyes were level with his. "I missed you too. Thank you for not listening to Amelia and not giving up on me."

Erin wrapped her arms around his neck. "I will never give up on you, and I will never listen to Amelia. Never have. It drives her crazy."

"You drive me crazy too." Veiron turned and started carrying her towards the water.

"But it's a good sort of crazy." She wrapped her legs around his waist and stared into his eyes. He flashed a smile but it faded a second later.

"The Devil lost both of his pawns today. He will seek to gain us back or destroy us, just as Heaven and Hell seek to destroy Amelia and Marcus."

"You think he'll come after us soon?" Erin didn't like that thought.

The Devil had come close to killing Veiron and she couldn't lose him again. She had wanted to end their fight but now she just wanted to rest and regain her strength, and train hard with her powers so when they next faced danger, they would be victorious.

Veiron shook his head. "Amelia and Marcus will be here, and Apollyon will come back, as will the others. Together we are too powerful for him. He may have healed himself but he's still weakened and he's trapped in Hell. He will bide his time, waiting for his chance."

Waiting for their son to be born. She knew in her heart that was what Veiron wasn't saying. The Devil wanted their child as his vessel.

She would never let that happen.

Joined with Marcus and Amelia, Apollyon and the others, they had the power to take on Heaven and Hell, and end this vicious game forever. She would take her father's place on the throne in Hell, the balance would be maintained, and she could use the power of her realm to protect everyone she loved. Heaven would never get its hands on Amelia. Everyone would be safe.

Veiron set her down and the warm water lapped at her shins.

She stared up into his striking eyes, skimmed her hands down his arms and covered his.

"We will have our revenge, Erin," Veiron whispered, the gold in his eyes brightening and chasing the darkness away. "But right now there is something more important that needs our attention."

He settled his hands over her stomach and smiled down at her with so much love and affection in his eyes that she couldn't help smiling back at him.

Erin held his hands to her stomach and then shifted them around to her hips. His pupils dilated and his gaze dropped to her mouth.

"I can think of something more urgent that requires your attention," she said and his lips quirked into a smile.

"Do tell," he husked and slowly lowered his head towards her, his gaze fixed on her lips.

"Me." Erin tiptoed and captured his lips with hers. He pulled her against him and she sighed into his mouth, loving the feel of his hard body against hers. He slanted his head and softly brushed his lips over hers, until her insides lightened and began to heat and she felt as though she would float away if he let go of her. His grip tightened as though he had sensed it, or perhaps had felt the same, and she smiled against his mouth, savouring his kiss and how it felt to be reunited with him, memories and all. She had never needed anything as much as she needed Veiron, and now they would always be together. His hands shifted to her backside and she giggled and pressed her forehead against his. "You're insatiable. I only have so long before I blow up like a balloon. Will you still love me then?"

He laughed. "You're mine... now and for all eternity... and I will love you forever, Erin... both of you."

"And you're mine." She pressed a soft kiss to his lips and then looked down between them, and back up into his eyes. "And we'll love you forever too."

Erin smiled and kissed him again, her tongue brushing the seam of his mouth. He opened to her and groaned as she swept her tongue along his, and she moaned with him and leaned into the kiss, relishing it and the fact that nothing could come between them now.

They would hone their powers.

They would fight the Devil.

They would win.

And they would have their forever.

The Devil's daughter and her demonic angel.

And their son.

The End

ABOUT THE AUTHOR

Felicity Heaton writes passionate paranormal romance books as Felicity Heaton and F E Heaton. In her books she creates detailed worlds, twisting plots, mind-blowing action, intense emotion and heart-stopping romances with leading men that vary from dark deadly vampires to sexy shape-shifters and wicked werewolves, to sinful angels and hot demons!

If you're a fan of paranormal romance authors Lara Adrian, J R Ward, Sherrilyn Kenyon, Gena Showalter and Christine Feehan then you will enjoy her books too.

If you love your angels a little dark and wicked, Felicity Heaton's best selling Her Angel series is for you. If you like strong, powerful, and dark vampires then try the Vampires Realm series she writes as F E Heaton or any of her stand alone vampire romance books she writes as Felicity Heaton. Or if you're looking for vampire romances that are sinful, passionate and erotic then try Felicity Heaton's new Vampire Erotic Theatre series.

In 2011, four of her six paranormal romance books received Top Pick awards from Night Owl Reviews, Forbidden Blood was nominated as Best PNR Vampire Romance 2011 at The Romance Reviews, and many of her releases received five star reviews from numerous websites.

To see her other novels, visit: **http://www.felicityheaton.co.uk**

If you have enjoyed this story, please take a moment to contact the author at **author@felicityheaton.co.uk** or to post a review of the book online

Follow the author on:
Her blog – http://www.felicityheaton.co.uk/blog/
Twitter – http://twitter.com/felicityheaton
Facebook – http://www.facebook.com/felicityheaton

FIND OUT MORE ABOUT THE HER ANGEL SERIES AT:
http://www.felicityheaton.co.uk